Tokh leaned forward and rested the tip of his sword between the general's shoulder blades.

"A warning can leave a dagger in your back."

The general turned with an incredulous look. Tokh pulled his blade back to carry position. "Boy? You better return that blade or I'll sheath it so far up your ass you won't be able to blink. Are your *khatas* too big for that uniform? Do they block your vision? Do you see my rank, boy? You dare threaten a general? A *dahneg* general?"

Cadet Tokh replaced his saber so fast it seemed to jump into place on its own. "Never, General! No threat was ever intended. Repeating the lesson you just taught me, Great Lord, to assure you I won't forget."

General Trahseg eyed him with a strange glare. "You're playing a deadly game, boy. Your ambition exceeds you. You think you can play with the big boys? Fine. I want you in my regiment for training tomorrow morning. I need men with *khatas*."

Regiment? Without graduation?

Honor to the Emperor

It is impossible to give an in-depth account of Tokh's life without crossing over the life-changing events that occurred in *Prisoner of the Mind* and *Conflicts of Interest*. Although now seen from Tokh's point of view, and with information only he knew, some passages have been reprinted verbatim from both stories.

Also by Susan Olesen

Prisoner of the Mind
Conflicts of Interest

Best Intentions
Best Efforts
Broken Trusts
Best of Everything
Ancient History

Brain Splatter

Kerasi Caste System under Emperor Nághtas

Caste is everything; who you touch, where you live, how you dress, who you marry, your employment, how high a position you can achieve, who can do what to you,

Thósikh: The Emperor, his wives, and eldest son. If the son dies or dies without heir, the next eldest son becomes *Thósikh*.

Bhísroti: The dumping ground for relatives of the Emperors for the last thousand years. They do much of the actual running of the government.

Fáhganid: Sheriffs of Nottingham, they control much of the military and the police forces, and can punish anyone on the spot, save for *Bhísroti*.

Dáhneg: Lowest of the upper castes, they have strong power but remain the lackeys for those above them.

Díhnarwharl: "Honorable *Nhasarwharl*" One of the smallest castes, sometimes considered upper caste; sometimes middle-caste.

Nhásarwharl: The bullies of the middle castes.

Whátaral: The lowest acceptable caste for *aghát*. It remains the largest, the caste of the common man.

Rhibáni: Lowest of the middle-castes. Lowest level of commissioned military officers, highest of the non-coms.

Tághinet: "The casteless caste," service caste equally sought after by all other castes: artists, librarians, musicians, entertainers, writers, undertakers.

Tápahtin: Originally educated slaves, they are limited to low-level trade jobs.

Soláhrin: The original slave caste, now freed. They're in high demand because they don't have to be paid much.

Ghinadín: a destitute caste historically made up of unambitious slaves, used and abused by all other castes.

** 1 **

Tokh dar-Giláhn, a senior cadet at the Nar Rhede Military Academy, found seats in the crowded lunchtime cafeteria with Pakihl, one of his three roommates. Tokh had no close friendship with his roommate, but Pakihl was bordering on suicidal and Tokh wasn't going to allow that.

Pakihl picked at a little marrow pie, then pushed it away. "I can't go back to his class. I'll have to drop Optimization and take a fail, and that means I won't graduate with the class."

Tokh devoured a roasted *hyrak* squab with a side of reds. "You can, and you will, to prove to him and everyone else that you won't be intimidated. What if he were the enemy? Would you give in that quickly? We train for such situations. Treat it no differently."

Pakihl stared at the table with the look of someone trapped and about to die. "He's not supposed to be the enemy. He's an instructor. How can I report I was assaulted by an instructor? They'll tell me it's not true and put a mark against my name."

"I'll work on that. Talk about something else. Tell me about your graduation project. You were researching something about heat, last you mentioned it."

Pakihl took a steadying breath. "Yes. We were having trouble with the exothermic output of the leaf-coupler array – about eight different wires feed into it – and were trying to find light-weight solutions for heat dispersal that wouldn't require additional energy requirements, which would only increase the problem."

Pakihl was training as a computer and technology specialist; Tokh was training for a career in intelligence. There were scores of things Tokh would rather hear about than issues in miniature power supplies.

Tokh had just thrown down the last little wingbone and wiped his mouth and chin hank to ensure no dishonorable crumbs remained when a trio of students stopped at the end of the table. A large cadet with senior insignia and communications division badges led the pack, the ID stripe on his uniform reading Ambeslogt.

He gave a snigger. "Hey, Pakihl! Heard you had to stay after class for Falvek. Better get that grade up or he'll make you stay after every week."

Pakihl's copper skin faded to a weak tan, and his wispy chin hank gave a quiver. His hand clenched his glass and couldn't let go.

Ambeslogt was of a more hirsute race from the southern regions; already he had a monstrously thick adult-sized chin hank, the hairs curling until it was more of a fat handle than a properly groomed and fashionable tassel. The disdain in his face would have befit a *dahneg*, let alone the seventh-caste *nhásarwharl* he was.

Tokh met the taunting gaze. "How do you know what goes on in electronics?"

"Ghojorek's in that class. Instructors get punished if too many students fall below a grade of 80. Too many low grades and Falvek provides a little, uh, *tutorial incentive* over his desk that sort of *drives home* the idea of not failing again." Ambeslogt laughed, and so did his cronies. "So, Paki-Paki, how's class sitting with you?"

Pakihl managed to set his cup down and release it. "I sit rather well, thank you."

One of Ambeslogt's cronies snorted. "On a cushion?"

Anger prickled up the back of Tokh's neck. "So if I understand you correctly, you're saying that you're aware that an instructor is assaulting students as routine practice, and you have not reported it?"

"Who are you, Little Director?"

Tokh tapped a badge on his shirt. "Student judicial council. It's our business to know."

Ambeslogt didn't flinch. "So? Are you two lovers? Is that the problem? Don't like sharing your territory with instructors? Or is Pakihl drilling you?"

Six years Tokh had trained to ignore insults, ignore inflammatory statements, the first thing an enemy would do to provoke a reaction. He knew that flat out drunk on a training maneuver, but his brain seemed to blank it all out. In a millisecond he was on his feet and his honorary saber was in his hand and the point rested in the hollow at the base of Ambeslogt's throat, right where the collar of his uniform dipped.

Tokh's voice fell cold and soft, the same silky noise his sword made when drawn. "Do you threaten my honor?"

Ambeslogt didn't blink. "Tsk, tsk! Demerits and a day's detention for drawing a weapon on an unarmed student. That isn't honor."

"And if I cut out your tongue, it's my word against – well, not yours, then."

"DESIST! ORDER ARMS!" The command boomed across the cafeteria. The noise of the room faded, then three hundred cadets took to their feet in a flurry of banging and boot heels to stand at attention. Tokh lowered his sword and saluted.

"We're all dead," Pakihl whispered.

The Educational Director entered the cafeteria, accompanied by a well-decorated level-three *dahneg* general and an entourage of six lesser officials. An impromptu student swordfight was not the way to make a strong impression about the discipline and order of your school.

Aaka on a trixahg!

The general strode toward Tokh, the Director scurrying after like a delayed shadow. He stopped at the end of the table, arrogance raining downward in a waterfall whose churning spray chilled everyone in a ten-*parr* radius. Tokh's insides shriveled and he saw his career go up in flames of expulsion. The rule about drawing weapons buffeted the back of his head like a flag in a windstorm.

"This is what you call discipline, Dothnar?" the general drawled. "Children allowed to play unsupervised with deadly weapons?"

"It is most rare," Director Dothnar apologized. "I assure you, I will personally see he never carries one again."

The general eyed Tokh's shirt. The thick *dahneg* finger reached out and flicked the merit badges for swordsmanship. "You like your weapons, eh, boy? Let's see how you handle them, then. Back where you were."

"Great Lord?"

The general moved Tokh back into position, took his sword arm, and replaced the tip at Ambeslogt's throat. "You were threatening him, Cadet. You only draw a weapon if your intention is to harm. You had him at point. Now do it."

Khatas between an anvil and a hammer! Tokh had no intention of harming Ambeslogt, no matter how he might deserve it. It was a

3

threat of passion, the kind warned about every week in sword practice, and he had failed to conduct himself properly. He couldn't back down before a general, and he would no doubt pay for it when Ambeslogt sought revenge later. Ambeslogt was a hulk of a beast, Tokh a full head shorter and not yet as beefy as he wished. Tokh steeled himself, glared Ambeslogt in the eye, and with a deft flick nicked Ambeslogt in the chin, right in the middle of that dreadful fat handle of hair, parting it. A thin line of blood appeared through the hair.

Tokh lowered his sword. "I meant only a warning."

The general, Trahseg by his ID tag, gave a harsh scowl. "Mean it, or don't do it. A warning can leave a dagger in your back when you sleep." He seized Tokh's sword hand by the wrist and drove the sword straight through Ambeslogt's heart. Students as far as three tables away gasped, while the rest broke out into an unsoldierly buzz of fright. Director Dothnar gasped as well. Ambeslogt fell to the floor, clutching his chest and shrieking as blood poured down his uniform and onto the floor. No one dared break rank to help him.

"That is called discipline," Trahseg said. "Would you have done that on your own, boy?"

Tokh was no less shocked than the others, perhaps more. His hand didn't actually do the slaughter, but the general left no prints on the hilt. Tokh would be given the blame. He swallowed his terror and met the general's mocking gaze. "Yes, your Lordship. If the insult had been greater, I would not hesitate."

Trahseg raised an eyebrow. "You've got *khatas*, boy. You think you're good with that toy?"

"Yes, Great Lordship. The best in the Academy." It wasn't the entire truth; he ranked number three.

Trahseg drew his own sword and swung upward toward Tokh's belly in one fast motion. It was a powerful swing meant to flay him open. Tokh jumped back, tripping on students behind him, but deflected the blow just in time. Students scattered in a wave. Ambeslogt's friends dragged him out of the way to die with honor.

Tokh's blood ran cold. There was no doubt in his mind the general meant to kill him. He couldn't kill a general, especially a *dahneg* general. Just wounding him was an offense. But if he didn't kill the general, the general would kill him. And if he somehow did manage to kill a seasoned general, then he would most likely be put to death.

4

Tokh didn't have time to dwell on it. The general came after him, fast and nimble for his age and size, blow after blow after blow; the crowd flowed out of their way. Tokh scrambled backwards, spinning sideways, shoving chairs, rolling over tables to stay out of range. His breath came in hard gasps, not just from the exertion. Each time he managed to parry and deflect, but the power behind the attacks required every ounce of his strength to control them. Never once did he manage to make an offensive thrust.

After ten or twelve attacks, Trahseg sheathed his sword and laughed as if he'd just finished a ballroom dance. "Quick, with courage. You spoke truth. You have strong promise." He turned to the Director and asked several questions about the training programs.

Tokh never knew where the nerve came from. Maybe because he'd just seen a fellow student skewered to death for no reason but whim of power. Maybe because he'd just fought a terrifying fight for his own life. Maybe he was just angry over a *dahneg* toying with students as a form of amusement. He leaned forward and rested the tip of his sword between the general's shoulder blades.

"A warning can leave a dagger in your back." It was suicide. If not death from the general, than from the Director.

The general turned with an incredulous look. Tokh pulled his blade back to carry position. "Boy? You better return that blade or I'll sheath it so far up your ass you won't be able to blink. Are your *khatas* too big for that uniform? Do they block your vision? Do you see my rank, boy? You dare threaten a general? A *dahneg* general?"

Tokh replaced his saber so fast it seemed to jump into place on its own. "Never, General! No threat was ever intended. Repeating the lesson you just taught me, Great Lord, to assure you I won't forget."

General Trahseg eyed him with a strange glare. "You're playing a deadly game, boy. Your ambition exceeds you. You think you can play with the big boys? Fine. I want you in my regiment for training tomorrow morning. I need men with *khatas*."

Regiment? Without graduation? How the... Tokh dropped to a knee and bowed his head. "You honor me most highly, Lordship. I will serve with my life."

"I expect nothing less. Report to my caravan in two hours."

Tokh bowed to the general. "With deepest thanks, General." When the general turned his back, Tokh shrugged at Pakihl and ran for his dormitory as if the general still chased him.

5

* * 2 * *

Twelve castes separated the people of Kerasím, a hierarchy formed over thousands of years. Caste could not change no matter how successful one was; every caste had its wealthy and its poor. Children were born to the caste of their father, though additional privileges could be granted. Females could marry up or down, taking the caste of their husband. Caste controlled every aspect of Kerasi life: jobs, education, housing, clothing, even restaurants and shops. *Thósikh*, the top caste, pertained only to the Emperor, his wives, and his eldest son; they made the laws and answered to no one. Any other relatives were considered *bhísroti*, the caste of nobility. At the opposite end, *ghinadín*, once the slaves of slaves, lived like vermin among the slums. Just touching another caste carried a death sentence.

Tokh and his father Talekh, his two mothers, his three brothers and his sister, were *dihnarwharl*, eighth-caste and only four below the Emperor. Wealthier *dihnarwharl* who lived among the upper castes due to employment or status were referred to as high *dihnarwharl*; most were considered middle-caste and known as low *dihnarwharl*. *Dihnarwharl* was a privilege in itself, a small caste considered by tradition to be honorable above all others. Honor bought respect and privilege, and privilege meant power.

Caste also set how many wives a male could have: below *whátaral* could have one, up to the Emperor, who could claim as many as he desired – the current Emperor, Nághtas, was already up to seven. Tokh's mother, Filuhr, was his father's second-wife, short, dark, and so assertive she often frightened people, the opposite of taller, paler, gracious first-wife Galisse. Galisse ran the household, but Filuhr was the rare married Kerasi female with a career: she was a trained midwife, and helped deliver hundreds of babies.

Soldiers not involved in combat were given two weeks leave twice a year, to return home and get family matters squared away. An eldest son was expected to care for a widowed mother and any unmarried sisters. There might be property to look after, a business, or any other number of legal tasks that needed attention. As the third son of a living father, Tokh had no family responsibilities, not as long as his father was alive. His older brothers, sons of first-wife Galisse, would handle those, but he went home on his first leave anyway, eager to brag of all he'd seen and done.

No sooner had he greeted everyone than his mother tried to corner him in the lavatory.

"Let me see you," Filuhr said, grabbing for his pants. "Best to stop diseases before they get embedded too deeply." Filuhr wasn't shy about asking family or strangers the most intimate of questions.

Tokh spun out of her way. "I'm a soldier in His Majesty the Emperor's Army. I promise, I've made every required inspection at the base. I'm clean. I take my birth control; I've left no offspring behind."

"Base medics are too busy to pay attention. They'll miss things I don't. Let me see." She waved her fingers as if she could summon his parts from his pants.

Tokh shouldered her out of the way and escaped. "It's not happening, *Ama!*"

If he thought giving in to his mother would have saved him from his father, Tokh would have dropped his pants and slapped his *khatas* on the table in the middle of dinner. Talekh was a reputable physicist who taught at the local branch of the Emperor's Foundation for Sciences. His chin hank bore only a few pale hairs and he wore it longer than most, pinched into a rope by four yellow bands. He was deep-thinking and even-tempered, and thus Tokh never anticipated the blade at his back.

"You're a man now, Tokh. An officer," Talekh said. "You're eighteen, with a career ahead of you. It's time you married. There's a colonel I know who has a daughter of good age. You'll meet her while you're home."

Tokh's breath stopped. His eyes blinked instead, and he gave a nervous snort. No. Oh no. "*Bo*, I'm eighteen. This is my first leave. I don't even have full rank yet. Most soldiers wait until their careers are established, until they've gained some rank and real pay. I can't deal with wives when I'm focused on my career."

"Nonsense. There are sons that are betrothed at fourteen, before they enter the academy. It keeps them grounded, knowing what they are working for. Your older brothers are married, your sister has perhaps another year, and Hamiran has two years until manhood. I told Colonel Hagh you would be a good match."

"*Bo*, have you met those guys? They're the saddest cadets in the school! They work harder because they're trying to forget what happens when they graduate. They never get a shot at life. I'm too busy right now."

"She's a nice girl, sixteen, so she's old enough to handle childbirth," his mother added. "She's healthy, and will bear you strong sons."

"I don't want sons right now. Right now I just want to make my commanding officer happy. Do you know how important that is? I can't blow this sponsorship," Tokh insisted, but Talekh wouldn't budge.

Tokh's heart sank. He gave serious thought to packing up and heading back to base, finishing his leave in his own cot, where he was Emperor of his own destiny. Wife was the last thing he wanted. If he did, he would ask General Trahseg to find him one, creating an alliance of families and officers that might benefit him at a future date, the way all good marriages were made. It would please Trahseg and strengthen the ties between them. Any colonel who hadn't married his daughter off to his own officers by the age of sixteen meant there was something seriously wrong with the girl, ugly as a *muuht* or mentally or physically damaged. Tokh's stomach clenched with dread. Each time he thought about her she grew a new deformity – bald, twisted teeth, one eye, a clawed hand, crossed eyes, maybe even a horn on her head. Perhaps she had a humped back, or pocked skin, or maybe she couldn't walk without sticks. He never suspected himself of having a strong imagination, until now.

A dinner meeting was agreed, and Tokh ran out of excuses. He trimmed his chin hank under his father's watchful eye, but decorated it with an intimidating clasp in the shape of a leering skull. He wore his brown uniform and applied fragrance to his neck to appease his father. The mirror pleased him, at least. His skin was a desirable shade of copper, his jaw firm, his hair black and thick, even if it was cut to regs. His chin hank was no spindly teen wisp but announced his masculinity. He slicked his eyebrow, thick but not overgrown like some, the bulge of his brow-bone not so heavy as to hide his dark eyes. After six years of military training he was in top form, lean and muscular, with strong shoulders, a straight back, and he exuded the arrogance and power of one who knew he was in charge. He was young, but he was already a *dihnarwharl* officer. Granted, an officer of cadet rank, but he had plans.

They dined in a private room at the back of a middle-caste restaurant. There was a formal introduction, but Tokh said nothing to the girl the rest of the night. Their heads remained bent, eyes darting to glance at the other, hoping the opposite party never noticed. She was tall and skinny – Majesty's sakes, she was almost as tall as he was, and weighed about as much as his leg. Jet-black hair fell just below her shoulders in manufactured curls. Her skin was the rich copper of a sunset and her eyes dark and sparkling and surrounded by a pleasant amount of cosmetics, her eyebrow well-cared for and shaped like a female's, not the bushy fringe of an old officer. Her mouth had a pretty shape, frozen in a nervous smile, accented by lovely high cheeks. Tokh's mother spoke to her often, and the girl answered in a pleasant, intelligent voice. Her nose, though – There was the problem. It wasn't an ordinary nose, but thin and arching in the middle, with narrow nostrils, a trait that came from her colonel father. It was fine enough now, but given fifty years, Tokh could see it starting to bend and hang, like the beak of a carnivorous bird or an impotent old man.

Tokh's summation of the evening: she was better than he'd hoped, but he didn't want to spend the rest of his life tied to her. He tried thinking about her with his hand in his pants, but even that wasn't helping. He wanted to run, fast and immediately, to any one of the half-dozen cities he'd been to on duty. Anywhere but where he was. Checking his comm every hour for an emergency recall didn't save him; all was quiet at the moment.

The second visit would take place at the colonel's home. Tokh slammed doors and refused to speak to his parents. This time the parents withdrew to another room, leaving Tokh and the girl – *Zheníhda*, he finally remembered – alone at the dining table. They sat across from each other without speaking for perhaps ten *fasím* before she got up the courage to ask him if he would like refreshments. Tokh agreed with a shrug. She made him a cup of cold *raffin* with fruit and cream garnish, and presented a plate of tiny cakes. If she had truly made them herself, Tokh was impressed. They tasted like they should, not superior but not bad, and they were expertly decorated with colorful swirls of sugared cream. Having a wife who could make decent food was a bonus.

"What is it exactly that you do in your unit?" she dared.

"I'm a swiftly climbing officer in His Majesty's grand army," Tokh said with a touch of disdain. Zheníhda was only *nhásarwharl* to his *dihnarwharl*, a caste below him, and he could be as uppity and arrogant as he wished. "I was so good they didn't graduate me but put me straight to work. I work in intelligence, and one day I plan to be a general. I'm currently with General Trahseg's regiment. We're all over the planet, running drills and learning things. I'm almost never on base."

"Oh." The news didn't seem to impress Zheníhda as much as he'd hoped. "That sounds very interesting, at least. You must be very smart and ambitious, to be assigned to work before you graduate. I'm sure you'll be promoted very quickly."

Tokh gave a snort and took another confection. "I know I will. I'll make sure of it. That's the purpose of intelligence: to know what's going on at all times and how to take advantage of the situation. Only a fool would fail to get promoted. I've already killed a man to get where I am. Does that scare you?"

Zheníhda gave a tip of her head, not giving away an emotion either way. A calm wife was a good find. "It means you're a brave warrior already, and you'll be a great protector of your wife and property."

"With luck, my name alone will be a deterrent. When I'm of higher rank I'll have to entertain my men. They'll need food and drink, of quality such that they'll feel honored, and honor my name in response. Would you be capable of that?" Tokh's voice was condescending and brusque; even he would admit he'd been too rude.

"If I didn't feel capable of preparing a proper feast for my husband's affairs, I would order sufficient quantities from a reputable caterer to please his guests."

That made sense. Tokh liked someone who already had contingencies in place. It made for a capable officer, and no doubt a capable wife. Grilling her on how she'd manage his estate, once he had one, was all he could think of to talk about. A fraction of a percent of females had careers; they simply became wives.

10

The second visit still didn't trigger any interest. She could cook. She smelled nice. She had put more effort into herself, her hair and cosmetics worthy of a videomodel, her clothing well-tailored and sophisticated for *nhasarwharl*, and she seemed to be trying very hard to be pleasant to him, but the bottom line was Tokh just didn't want to be married. Maybe if he'd met her on his own, instead of having her forced on him. He was eighteen years old; he wanted to live before he settled down. Maybe once he was a general, then he might look for a wife.

At the end of the week, the families forced them together a third time. "Think hard about this," Tokh's father counseled him. "This is a good pairing. Being married to a colonel's daughter will give you leverage in your career. His contacts will now be your contacts, blood-kind. It's good for the colonel, because his daughter is marrying upward to *dihnarwharl*. That increases his leverage. She's a good solid female of excellent heritage, with no faults to be hidden away. A little more experience, she'll make you a wife to be proud of. It's an excellent opportunity."

"I'd do better having General Trahseg find me a wife. When he thinks I'm ready!" Tokh snarled.

"Save your breath, Tokh," his sister Nihren told him. "You can't win this. Colonel Hagh's son is in *bo*'s class, and Colonel Hagh has his finger on a funding source for science research that he would rather see go to a family member. If *dihnarwharl* were allowed three wives, *bo* would have married her himself. Since he can't, that duty falls to you. Be kind; she has no choice, either."

Doom wrapped its cold fingers around Tokh's *khatas* and squeezed.

Dread sucked inches from his spine. Tokh shuffled around the apartment bent over like an old man, just as sick to his stomach. He drank through eight bottles of *muhr* before his mother cut him off and made him get ready.

This time, the couple was given freedom to walk around the gardens of the colonel's apartment building. If the dar-Giláhn's son was of the type to molest a female the minute witnesses were out of sight, it could seal the deal. Tokh, however, hated the idea of marriage so much he didn't even try.

The strain made him blunt. "Do you even want to marry me?"

11

"I want to marry *someone*," Zheníhda said, walking along side but one pace behind. "I think you're handsome, strong, intelligent, and that you will make a fearsome general some day. I look forward to hearing stories about your battles and deeds. If I don't marry you, they'll marry me to an old man who will bore me and leave me a widow. I think you'll make beautiful strong sons, and I would be happy to raise them for you."

"I don't want to marry right now," Tokh admitted. He swung his head about as if he could shake off the words. "I'm being sent somewhere new every week; I don't want to be burdened with a wife and home. There is so much to see and do in the world! But they're going to make us marry anyway, whether we want to or not. Do you at least *like* to *push*?"

It was a terribly rude thing for him to say. *Pushing* was the common crude term for sex. It wasn't a requirement that females be virginal at marriage; assault was so common that only a quarter of females made it to marriage untouched, but it was foul and ill-mannered to accuse a female of promiscuity. Some females were raised to fear males, however, and he didn't want a wife who wouldn't please him.

Zheníhda gasped. Her eyes went wide and she stopped walking. Anger loosened her tongue, and she bit back.

"How should I know! I assume that with a proper husband who knew what he was doing, I would expect to enjoy it every bit as much as he did. If he was kind and pleasant to me, I'm sure I would be more than happy to please him."

A tiny spark of respect began in the back of Tokh's head. He stopped and turned to look at her. "You aren't the cloud-fluff I feared. It's good to have a little fire. I can't fight battles on two fronts; I can pay more attention to my work if I know that my wife can raise her voice without coming to me for every little issue. I can't promise you anything right now. I have plans, but it will take me time to make them happen, and you'll have to be patient. I'll need a son, of course; maybe more if he turns out well. I believe in military discipline: a good commander does not beat his crew unless he can't avoid it; it's bad for morale, instills fear instead of discipline and undermines loyalty, which can be fatal to a commander. Therefore, as long as I feel you're trying your best and not undermining my authority, I promise never to beat you if I can avoid it."

Zheníhda gave a snort. When let to run, her tongue could flay with the finest of cuts. "I suppose I should thank you for that. I won't forget that promise. What you're looking for, then, is a fellow officer that you can bed at will and will manage your household so you're free to go off and enjoy the world with minimal responsibility while I sit at home, lonely for your company."

Tokh thought a moment. "Well, yes, I guess."

"What about love, and kindness? Do they fit into your plan? I won't have an unkind husband, even if he has the estate and respect of a *bhísroti*."

"I'm always kind! A good officer balances discipline with kindness, instilling loyalty and improving the morale of his troops. Did I not just say I promised not beat you unless you were unruly to me? I can be a very kind person, if a person is kind to me in return."

"You don't sound convinced of that. Must you phrase everything in military terms? I'm not a soldier." She began walking again, and he followed.

Tokh shrugged. "It's all I know. Is this what you want?" They approached a patch of blooming flowers in a raised bed. He plucked a purple flower the same color as her skirt and waved a dramatic hand toward the blossom. "You are like this flower, blooming under the caress of the sun. Whenever I see a flower bloom, I'll think of you." He tucked it into her hair, the first time he had made any physical contact with her at all. The black curls were soft as nightfall.

Zheníhda didn't smile. If anything, she looked morose. "If only you meant it."

Tokh spun her around by her shoulder, startling her. "I say what I mean, and I mean what I say. My word is my oath. Whether I marry you or not, when I see a flower, I'll think of you."

Zheníhda nodded, and a coy little smile broke across her lips. "Okay. I thank you, then."

He gazed into her eyes – it wasn't hard; Tokh didn't even have to tip his head. He lifted her chin with a finger and gave her a tentative kiss on her warm throat. "Did you like that?"

Zheníhda blushed a deep bronze. She bit down shyly on her lower lip and nodded. "Yes."

"Then take that as my pledge, I guess. I'll have you as my wife, but it will have to wait until my next leave. I have four days left, and it will take more time than that for the paperwork. I'll have to get

13

dispensation for married officers, allowing you housing while I'm on duty, but you may tell your father I said yes."

As the families parted, Zheníhda approached her husband-to-be and handed him a small paper flower she had cut from an advertisement. "Carry it with you until we meet again. I'll hold you to your words. I will think only good thoughts of you. Please think only good thoughts of me. Stay safe in your duties."

"I will do that," Tokh said. He didn't kiss her, just bent his head in polite reply. "Until next time."

Rings were decoration on Kerasím but a necklace was the traditional gift of a husband to his bride to be, a token of promise. A glamorous necklace said the female was spoken for, off limits, created jealousy among other females, and was a sign of her husband-to-be's status. Tokh wanted no part of it, but Talekh dragged him to a jeweler the next morning.

"Whatever's good," Tokh said, hands in his pockets, eyes on the walls, anything to get out of there faster.

"No, you must put some thought into this," Talekh insisted. "Even if it means nothing to you, it will to her. What did I tell you about keeping wives pleased? What do you think she'll like?"

"I have no idea! I've spoken to her three times, *Bo*, and we never once mentioned clothing or jewelry. What pleases them? Gold like the Emperor? Then choose gold. *Orak* stones like the blackness of my heart? Then choose that." He turned his back to the displays and leaned on the glass.

Talekh slapped his arm to make him stand. "Stop your dramatics. What color does she like?"

"I don't know! She wore purple each time. Something purple to match her clothing, then."

"Now you're thinking like a man," Talekh said in triumph. They settled on a single strand of semi-precious purple *gallah* stones, interspersed with small gold beads and a single sparkling clear *nemsihl* gem in the center. It was simple and relatively inexpensive and got Tokh off the hook. He had it sent to Zheníhda, rather than giving it to her in person, the thought of which set his guts to roiling.

Tokh didn't know about Zheníhda, but her mother spouted joy to his mother for more than twenty *fasím*. Both agreed, the wedding would have to wait until Tokh's next leave.

Tokh didn't see the end of his leave so much as returning to duty but escaping home while he still had his *khatas* attached. In the army, he had his own destiny.

"She's not so bad," his crewmates said, eyeing the photo Tokh had been given. He had to admit, it was a rather flattering portrait, and after a few weeks it felt good to have a female's photo posted in his duty locker like so many of his fellow officers. The more he looked at it, the more attractive she sort of became.

"Just that nose," said another. "Did someone shut it in a door when she was a baby?"

"Easy enough to fix," said an officer who had worked medevac for a year. "Surgery can knock that thing flat in an hour. She'd be pretty fine after that. You want to kiss her feet? Check out the *ullajak* that Rengand over in M unit got stuck with."

"Mmph." The group grunted sadly in chorus. Tokh had seen the photo, a pale yellow girl with stringy brown hair and a face like a balloon. Her nose was small and pert and turned upward, pulling her lip with it so she looked as if she were forever pressed against glass, and her red-brown eyes were small and too close together. Rengand was saving every coin he could beg so he could divorce her on their third anniversary. He swore he had only bedded her on their wedding night and not once since, terrified she'd give birth and seal his fate forever.

Maybe Zheníhda wasn't so bad after all.

"That's a bit young, isn't it, Tokh?" Colonel Bandret, General Trahseg's lead commander said. His face had a permanent scowl, so it was impossible to tell if he was angry or not. "You can't find enough females to *push*, you need a wife on top of it? You weren't chosen for this command just to run off and fail it at the first opportunity."

"It wasn't my decision, Colonel. Neither of us wish to marry, but our parents arranged it."

Bandret sighed. "Why do they do that to officers? You have a career with an excellent future. You can't be a success if you're running to a crying wife every other week."

Tokh was all too aware of that reality. Each day that brought him closer to his wedding was another day closer to a dead-end job as a high-level errand boy for a ranking officer who would have the career Tokh longed for. "I understand, Colonel. I am an officer first and foremost. I will do my very best."

General Trahseg, however, was not about to lose a promising officer. A month before his leave, Tokh found himself on a four-month mission to one of the colonies. It meant, of course, that he would miss his scheduled leave and wouldn't be there for his wedding. All the plans had to be shifted.

He sent a direct call to Zheníhda to apologize. "I said I would marry you, and I will. I don't back out on my word. This is the life of a soldier; I don't control where I'm sent or for how long. I'm in intelligence; we follow trails and hunt down information. I'll send you a photo of where I am, if I'm allowed. There are mountains in the distance with faces of pure silica; when the rising sun hits them, they reflect every color of the rainbow. It's stunning."

Disappointment rang heavy in Zheníhda's voice, but she put none of it into words. "I'll wait for you, as long as it takes."

As his second wedding date loomed, Tokh was anxious to get it over with. It had been a full year, and he was tired of everyone being upset with him – his parents, her parents, his commanders, and Zheníhda's unspoken disappointment whenever he videoed her. He was nineteen years old, and being crushed by everyone he knew. Tokh just wanted to get on with his life. The idea of marriage no longer bothered him. Someone was waiting for him to come home, someone who would welcome him with open legs.

Not long after, he made an unscheduled call. "I have only three *fasim*," he said rapidly. "The entire regiment is bugging out. I don't even know where we're going. Tell my father to get in touch with personnel services, and they'll give him any details they're allowed. Can you remember that?" He couldn't ask her to write it down; Zheníhda was barely literate, and reading and writing above the most minimal sentences were difficult.

"Yes! I'll remember that. Personnel services."

"I'll call you if I'm allowed, or at least send you a message your father can read to you. I'm committed to marrying you, I just can't promise right now when that will be. You must be patient."

"I believe you," she said. "Stay safe, Officer Tokh. I would like my husband in one piece."

"That's always my goal. I'll be in touch."

It was four months before anyone received a word from him.

His unit was embroiled in quashing a strike on a mining colony. They'd lost more than a hundred troops to tunnel collapses and decompression, and Tokh was monitoring communications and tracking down subversives. His messages home were infrequent, brief, often limited to text, and Zheníhda had no way to send a message back.

I looked at your paper flower today, so I am thinking of you. It's the only flower here.

I know you don't believe I'll ever marry you, but my word is my word. Eventually this will end and I will marry you, even if we don't have a party for it. I don't want a party, but I'm starting to warm to the idea of marriage.

I was forced to take a man's head today. He killed one of my enlisted while trying to escape from captivity. It was not pleasant. I felt ill the rest of the day.

Today was a very hard day. I wish you were my wife already, because I could use your comforts right now. Please think them for me anyway.

Don't be frightened, but I was injured today. I took a knife in the side and in the thigh. My surgery was brief, and I'll make a full recovery in a week.

A full year passed before Tokh returned, armed with four weeks accumulated leave. He showed up with five citations on his shirt – a campaign ribbon, off-world service, wounded in the line of duty, one for bravery, and one for excellence in duty. And he wore a promotion: he was twenty years old, and a full Grade-One lieutenant with enough points to shave more than a year off his next promotion, if he was careful.

Tokh messaged her after arriving. *My intended Zheníhda – I have arrived home with leave. If you still wish to marry me, it will be this week or never. Please inform me of your choice.*

Zheníhda responded with a voice message just two minutes later. "I can be ready in ten *fasím*, if you wish to skip festivities."

Tokh didn't think their mothers would allow that, but he was very tempted.

* * 3 * *

The wedding plans had been in a holding pattern, waiting for a date. Four days later, in a hotel gathering room rented for the occasion, Tokh stood before Zheníhda's father in his dark brown dress uniform, not nearly as nervous as he expected. He'd spent three years as a man of the world, seen battle, been wounded, seen friends die. He'd gained rank, gained respect, and was on track with his career. He was ready.

Zheníhda's father, Colonel Hagh, in his own dress uniform, gave a short speech and read off the questions that made up the legal marriage contract. "Tokh dar-Giláhn, do you claim Zheníhda Porenthal as your wife?"

Tokh stood at attention, his black hair combed to perfection, his single eyebrow slicked into a gently curved line, his chin hank trimmed to exactness and braided into a tight rope with gold threads and tiny black *orak* beads at the crosses. His chin was high and square, and there wasn't a tremor on him. "Yes, Sir!"

"Do you promise to serve her as a proper husband, share with her all your property, ensure her health and safety, give her children, and treat her with the same respect you would wish to be treated with, until one of you joins his ancestors?"

"In the name of the Emperor, I do promise."

"Choose your bride."

In a popular marriage game, all single females of marrying age stood together, their faces hidden behind lacy veils, and Tokh had to find his bride among them. To choose wrong was bad luck; sometimes an unlucky groom was made to marry the mistake. He had not seen Zheníhda in two years save a few videocalls, but it wasn't difficult: she was almost his height, and he now knew her favorite color was purple, so picking out a tall, thin female in a beaded lavender gown with a *gallah*-stone necklace was not difficult. The smile she gave him when he lifted her veil made him pause.

Tokh blinked, unprepared for the depth of the feeling that hit him. Her cosmetics were flawless, and she looked far more beautiful than he remembered. He couldn't remember anyone ever being that happy to see him. Maybe he really had come to like her. Maybe her nose wasn't really that bad. Maybe his father had been right all along. He led her over to her father for her questions.

"Zheníhda Porenthal, do you accept Tokh dar-Giláhn as your husband?"

"Yes."

"Do you promise to serve your husband as a proper wife, protect his property, care for his offspring, and tend to all his needs, in health and sickness, obeying his every command, until one of you joins his ancestors?"

"I promise."

Colonel Hagh smiled down on them. "By the law of the Emperor, you are now joined."

A raucous howl went up from the crowd. Tokh swept Zheníhda off the ground and planted a kiss on her throat that left a toothmark and made the guests screech with glee. Zheníhda gasped in surprise, blushing and laughing when her feet returned to the ground.

They didn't remember much after that without the prompting of photos. Tokh fed Zheníhda the first bite of her meal and the first sip of *lunahl*, as the provider of the new household. Zheníhda fed Tokh his first bite of his meal and his first sip of *lunahl*, as servant to her husband. Ten courses were served, each fancier than the one before. Halfway through the third course, the footstomping and chanting started on the *nhásarwharl* side of the room.

"Table! Table! Table! Table!"

Zheníhda blushed and hung her head.

Tokh looked about in confusion. He'd only been to one wedding celebration, and it hadn't been formal at all. The word meant nothing to him.

Zheníhda's father stood up and banged on an empty *lunahl* bottle until the chanting stopped. "Calm your calls. This is a *dihnarwharl* wedding. It's a ceremony of honor and reverence, as the very name *dihnarwharl* implies. There will be no tabling of the wife or anyone else. Let us act like civilized people above our caste, at least for one night."

19

Catcalls erupted among the colonel's friends, while the females buzzed. Zeníhda sighed with relief.

Tokh leaned over to his father and whispered, *"What did he mean?"*

Talekh whispered back, *"It's a barbarism of the lower castes, demanding the wife be taken on the wedding table for all to witness. We are* dihnarwharl, *and we have morals to uphold. You'll do no such thing before a crowd or your commanding officer, ever. Obey my word on that."*

Tokh nodded. General Trahseg was a *dahneg*, superior to even *dihnarwharl*. He sat at a separate table with two other invited *dahneg*. To shame his commanding officer was unthinkable. Nor did Tokh have any desire to bed his wife in front of his mother. Oh no.

The evening slid into a haze of drunken revelry. Tokh remembered drinking, remembered the females dancing in a circle until the colors of their dresses spun into a blur. He remembered the males circling him and toasting repeatedly. He was pretty sure he remembered toasting with his troop mates, but not so much that he didn't take his bride aside as the last course was cleared away.

"We need to leave," he whispered to her.

Zeníhda looked about the party, the most fabulous spectacle she'd ever seen. "But… The desserts haven't been served!"

"We need to leave now, when no one is watching, and take care of our business. If we don't, we'll have far more of an audience than either of us desire. Come."

He snuck her through the kitchens of the hotel to the elevators on the far side, to the marriage suite reserved for them on the *dihnarwharl* floor. Fresh flowers filled the room, the floor and bed strewn with loose petals and tiny red *yarum* buds. Several bottles of high-end spirits waited on a table, gifts of the hotel and various guests. A mound of gifts waited on another table. Zeníhda looked about in awe.

Tokh removed his uniform jacket; Zeníhda took it and hung it up. He removed his belt and his sword, then peeled off his liner shirt, damp with sweat. He was beautiful to look at, his shoulders broad and stacked with youthful muscle. A brown scar crossed his waistline from his knife wound. "Have you had enough to drink?"

Zeníhda blushed and looked at the floor. "I don't know. Enough for what?"

20

"Then you haven't." Tokh looked over the bottles, almost chose *varvet*, but settled for *flehdan*. She needed to relax, not fall asleep. He poured her a glass and handed it to her. "Drink, and don't waste too much time with it. Tonight won't be the best for either of us. We will get it done, and then tomorrow we'll learn to please each other better, when we don't have to worry about interruptions."

Zheníhda took a gulp, made a face, and nodded. It took her several minutes to finish the glass. She handed it back to him, flushed and woozy.

He left the glass on a table and began to kiss her, her mouth, her face, her jaw, down to her neck. His hand touched her chest, and she jumped backward.

Tokh growled, just a little. "Don't flinch. If you have too much *flehdan*, your dinner will be on the floor. Relax. I don't plan to hurt you."

Zheníhda kept her eyes on the floor, no less tense. "I'm sorry. I want to please you, I'm just very nervous. I've never been bedded and I've heard many awful stories from other females... Please don't make me do those things. Please."

"*Relax*," Tokh whispered, and resumed kissing her neck. She tried her best to kiss him back. Her hands went to his shoulders but stiffly, as if they didn't want to be there. He unfastened her expensive dress, and it fell to the floor. She shook under his hands as he removed her undergarment. She wasn't just thin, she was downright bony, all ribs and hips and shoulders.

"*Shu*. It's our wedding night. This is the worst. It gets better after this. Once we do it, you'll enjoy it. I promise."

He stepped back to admire her, but Zheníhda turned away and tried to cover her body with her hands. "Please don't laugh at me."

"I don't laugh at beauty." Tokh pulled her hands away from her breasts. They were larger than he expected, and when he tasted them, he felt his desire start to rise at last. He pulled off the rest of her underthings.

She resisted at first, but he rubbed her hand over his *hihvat* until she continued clumsily on her own. It didn't take much for it to finish firming, the sensitive ring of tissue at the end dark brown and ready. He eased her backwards onto the bed, then rolled her over.

"*Shu*. Relax now. Do as I say." He pulled her narrow hips to him, white and yellow flower petals clinging to her bronze back.

21

Tokh's thumbs played with her opening. "Deep breath," he warned, then entered her in a single violent thrust. Zheníhda yelped and clutched at the bedcover, but between the spirits spinning her head and Tokh's cryptic words of guidance, she calmed down and caught on, matching his rhythm.

Kerasi genitalia were similar to many races throughout known space, with some variations. The end of the male *hihvat* and the opening of the female *aminet* both contained a sensitive ring of tissue that swelled up hard. Once the aroused male penetrated the female, her ring would also swell, making separating difficult and painful until one of the party lost their arousal. Torturing couples caught locked in acts was such a widespread problem the Emperors had long ago passed harsh laws against it.

Despite her fear, Zheníhda's own ring swelled at the contact, squeezing Tokh and making them as one. Tokh was panting, driving hard against her, and Zheníhda was starting to understand the pleasure of it when a loud banging made her shriek in panic. She lunged forward, only to be stopped by the searing pain of trying to uncouple. Laughter and howling sounded outside the door.

"What is that!" she cried.

Tokh held her and tried to resume his pace. "What I was trying to avoid. My troop mates. They'll hound us all night. Try and ignore them." The laughter grew louder. A rhythmic pounding began on the door.

"Stroke! Stroke! Stroke!" "Give it to her!" "You can do better than that!" "Are you sure it's in the right place, soldier?" "Ah! Ah! Ah! Ah!" The pounding became faster.

Tokh found his release in a long, low growl, but any pleasure had been stolen. He held her hips to him until he was able to separate. "Go. Hide in the lavatory. I'll rid us of the noise."

Zheníhda flipped the bedcover over her shoulders in a hail of flower petals and disappeared in a matter of seconds, locking the door behind her.

Tokh pulled his sword from its sheath and opened the door, stark naked. Four of his fellow lieutenants giggled drunkenly.

One saluted. "Armed and ready for action, Lieutenant Tokh!"

"You had your chance. It's only fair to share with your fellow officers. Loyalty, duty, and female persuasions," laughed another.

The third gave a sputtering bray and leaned on another to avoid falling. "Look out, he's got two swords at the ready! Be careful which one he swings at you!"

Tokh eyed them with a dark glare. "I've waited two years for my wedding night and you're ruining it. It's my bride and I won't share her with a bunch of drunken fools. Now leave me alone or I'll make sure you'll never have a wedding of your own!"

He swung his sword and hacked it deep into the doorframe. His mates stumbled back in surprise.

"Hey! What the *hih*?"

A heart-stopping war-cry filled the hall. Tokh rushed them with his sword and they fled down the hallway. He chased them, naked, as they stumbled and tripped on each other, hearing their curses and shouts as he slapped the slowest one hard in his flank with the flat of the sword.

"Now leave me alone!" he shouted as they ran down a staircase. Two tripped on each other and fell, rolling bonelessly down the stairs. "I have more important business than you!"

Tokh returned to the room and knocked on the bathroom door. "It's Tokh. They're gone. You can come out now."

Zheníhda opened the door but didn't come out, wrapped in the bedcover and crying.

"Did I hurt you?"

She wiped her face and caught a breath. "No. I – maybe I had too much to drink."

"Are you sick?"

"No. I just – This isn't what I expected. I wanted a nice quiet evening to show you I can serve and please you. I haven't done any of that."

"*Shu, shu.*" He peeled away the coverlet. "You've pleased me well. That's the risk of a wedding party. There's much to be said for just filing the papers and telling everyone afterward, but this was the doing of our mothers." His lips brushed her several times, calming her tears. "The first was for me. The second will be for your joy. Let me change your mind."

Even on drunken R&R in a consort house, Tokh couldn't remember having so much sex at once. Was this what marriage did? His libido wouldn't quit, and it seemed as if his arousal at her presence never went away. After breakfast he had her bathe him,

23

then *pushed* her over the side of the tub. They broke open a bottle of *lunahl*, and he pulled her onto his lap and *pushed* her while he sat in the chair. Feeling lazy after lunch, he lay on his back on the bed and taught her to climb on top of him. He lost his fluid but not his firmness, so he grabbed her and rolled until she was underneath him; a few quick strokes to engorge his ring and he *pushed* her a second time without ever uncoupling. They napped a bit after that. Zheníhda got up to bathe; he waited, entered the bathroom to take a piss, and wound up pulling her from the water and *pushing* her against the wall, his hands under her backside and her long legs wrapped tight around his hips. They managed to dress and leave the hotel for an exquisite dinner, Zheníhda as radiant as a *bhísroti* on his arm, though his pants felt as if they were chafing him every minute. They returned to their room, where he broke open the bottle of *varvet* and poured them each a glass. He sprawled back on a chair, content, while Zheníhda straightened the room.

"Do you know what I need? A lipping," he said. He loosened the front of his trousers. "Come kneel before me."

Zheníhda froze, a pair of his dirty socks in her hands. "Please don't ask me that, Tokh. Take my household money and pay for a consort to do that. I am your wife. You may *push* me all you like, but save the strange habits for consorts."

Tokh paused, unprepared for a refusal. The females he'd known had never refused him anything – not that prisoners or consorts or camp followers could. He stood up and approached her. Zheníhda backed up a step. "Lipping is the Emperor of all pleasures, Nihda. I'll gladly do the same for you. You're my wife, and I asked you for a lipping. You promised to obey me. Don't make me have to discipline you already."

Zheníhda looked about to be sick. "Please, Tokh! I beg you! Please don't make me do that! Not so soon!"

"It's just a lipping, Zheníhda. There is nothing to it. Everyone does it, from the Emperor's wives to the *ghinadín*. I am your husband and you are my wife. I can accept your request, but this once you'll kneel and obey me."

"Please, Tokh! I'll bend in any direction for you but don't …"

He dropped his pants. His hands pressed down on her shoulders. "I won't be denied by a wife. This once, you will obey."

Zheníhda began to cry. "I don't even know what to do! Please, don't!"

24

"I'll show you."

Such a simple thing, but it was the most unsatisfying lipping he'd ever had. She didn't swallow his fluid; it poured out over her chin, thick and yellow, and the sight and feel of it caused her to run and vomit.

Her behavior irritated him. "Fine! You want to just *push*, I can do that," Tokh said when she left the lavatory. He grabbed her, bent her over the bed and *pushed* her roughly, as if punishing her for ruining the evening. When he uncoupled, Tokh shoved her so she rammed face-first into the mattress. Zheníhda retreated into the bed and wrapped herself tight in the covers, weeping, while he sulked in the lavatory.

He came out several minutes later and lay next to her. "I'm sorry. If it's that big an issue, I won't bother you with it again."

"It's okay," Zheníhda said quickly. "May we just sleep now? I'm very tired tonight."

"Once more. I want you to sleep on pleasure, not tears."

"I'm good as I am."

"No. I won't let you sleep on tears." Tokh worked at her for a full hour, kissing, stroking, tugging, and finally *pushing*, until willing or unwilling, Zheníhda reached her joyful place and they slept, Zheníhda nestled on his chest.

A week left until he returned to duty, and Tokh had not yet been granted married housing on the military base, and as a mere lieutenant he was not allowed to live elsewhere. The alternative was to leave her with his parents, something Zheníhda dreaded as much as – maybe even more – than lip work.

"Your father tries to discuss subjects that I have no concept of," she explained. "Your mother demands information on our bedding practices and gives me advice that embarrasses me, and your Galisse-mother treats me like I'm stupid because I'm *nhásarwharl*. Please, Tokh! Find a way to take me with you."

"I've tried everything I know of, short of keeping you in a hotel, which is neither safe nor possible on my salary. I will keep trying," he said.

Tokh didn't believe in the Fortunes, and no magic miracle appeared in time. He returned to base, leaving his wife as servant to

25

his parents after twenty-four days of marriage. It amazed him, how much he missed her after just twenty-four days, and not just the sex.

* * 4 * *

Four months passed before Tokh was granted an apartment. He rescued Zheníhda from his parents' house and flew her back to the base in Khasoohrin, a four-hour flight. There would be no surprise visits from family, Thank the Emperor. It was tiny, just two furnished rooms on the eighth floor of a middle-caste building, but it was theirs alone.

Zheníhda stood in the middle of the sitting room. The furniture was worn and outdated but clean. A kitchen area and small table took up half of the sitting room, and the single window over the sofa illuminated every flaw in the carpeting. The bedroom contained the bathroom and a large closet, and a second window. For something billed as worthy of *dihnarwharl*, it was frightfully depressing.

But his parents weren't there. She turned to Tokh and hugged him. "It's fantastic!"

They spent his one day of leave stocking up on everything she might need while he was on duty. Then he *pushed* her on the sofa. And the bed. And he added a stain to the threadbare spot on the sitting room carpet. Then she made him dinner, all by herself, in her very own home.

Having a base apartment didn't mean Tokh could live there, it simply meant his wife was close by and available if he had time off. Kerasi women didn't walk around in public without a male escort or they risked being assaulted by males who saw them as free for the taking, a practice frowned on, but legal. Husbands, fathers, older sons, and trusted family were always in demand to escort females and their friends to various places, or a bonded escort could be hired. The army base apartments made it easier, having a large fenced area outside where females could walk or sit, or watch their children play without fear. The main doors had guards, and identification had to be swiped to enter. The less an officer worried about his wife, the more focused he was on his duty. The ground floor contained various shops where wives could purchase necessities without leaving the building, though the prices carried a premium for the convenience.

Zheníhda hated living with Tokh's family, but she soon found the apartment lonely and hollow. She'd been married one hundred and twenty-eight days, and she'd spent exactly thirty-two of them with her husband. At times it felt as if she weren't married at all, waiting for an imaginary hero to fill her days with purpose. Perhaps it hurt more because she'd had a hero for a few days, and the Emperor took him away again. He was shipped off, three weeks here, then a month there. His few hours of leave when he returned left little time for anything other than *pushing* each other.

Ghirelle, of the apartment on her right, was the first to befriend Zheníhda and introduce her to the Waiting Wives. Ghirelle was a twenty-four year old *nhásarwharl*, wife of a captain, with a six-year-old son. Ghirelle was sharp, self-sufficient, and seemed to have her ear on every door in the building.

"You'll learn, my little Bleeding Heart. I got married, got pregnant a month later, and they shipped him out on a two year mission. I sure as sunrise wasn't going to just sit around and pine my life away, and neither should you. We're our own family. There's safety in numbers. If twelve of us beat someone to death, no one knows who actually did it, and they can't prosecute us all. Need a hand? Give a yell. Hear a yell? Lend a hand. Once a week we pool our money and hire an escort and go into town, whether it's shopping or to a theater or just out for dinner and drinking. Just because he's away doesn't mean you sit here and grow old. Yan Nor in 6-D knows cosmetology. If you know your husband is coming home, she'll do your nails or hair or skin for a small price. Usmihn's a *dahneg* in 9-A. She hosts game day on the fourthday of every week. Do you follow the serials on the ComNet? Depending on which ones you watch, there's a wife who hosts gatherings every day so we can watch them together. Kalilli in 7-G grew up in a family of doctors; she can tell a fungus from a plant rash. If a husband is in town, we'll take turns watching kids so the parents have time together. We can't help too much if a husband gets out of hand, that's his business, but we'll be there a second later to help you in any way we can. So don't feel like you're all alone here. We're *all* all alone, which makes us family."

Zheníhda smiled. It was like falling through a hole and discovering a secret world. "Thank you, Ghirelle. I would love that."

Zheníhda had gone from pining teen to new wife in just a few short months. She had a husband who treated her well enough, her own apartment, and a support network. There was just one thing she didn't have.

"Are you pregnant yet?" Tokh asked her after every leave. They'd been married eight months. He'd pumped her so full of his fluid she should have drowned. Most families had a child quickly to prove the couple was fertile, then took their time thinking about a second one. A female who had not produced offspring by the third year of marriage could be divorced, a disaster for the female, who could then be married off to an undesirable husband – usually an elderly male looking for a young wife to flash about, sold into a labor situation, be resigned to spinsterhood in the care of her family, or worst of all, sold to a consort house to spend the rest of her days as the sexual property of a wealthy male, for his own use or rented out to his friends. A wife might not have a child in the first year, but she made sure she was visibly pregnant before her third anniversary. Tokh's mother had been relentless in asking about their private life; a pregnancy would get her off their backs.

"It's not my fault, Tokh," Zheníhda reminded him. "You have to be here for me to conceive. I want to give you a son every bit as much as you want one."

"It's not my fault, either," he snapped. "You knew this was my life, never knowing where I'll be day to day. What do you think my commander will do if I request leave because my wife thinks she's fertile at the moment? I'll be the laughingstock of my unit. They'd demote me just for thinking such a thing."

"It's the Emperor's army; maybe I should ask the Emperor to either send you home or fill in for you!" Zheníhda spat back.

The remark met with a backhand to her cheek. Zheníhda didn't hold it against him; she knew full well the remark deserved it. They each retreated to a different room to cool off.

Tokh was granted two days' leave before shipping out for a six month assignment. He *pushed* her nineteen times over the two days, until they both ached.

He called her two months later, ever hopeful. "Any new developments I should know about?"

It was an innocent question, but Zheníhda knew what he meant. Her face twisted up and she tried so hard not to cry on the ComNet

29

screen. Tears were a shame, a weakness of females that males looked upon with scorn. "I'm sorry, Tokh. Not yet. Next time, for certain."

Zheníhda felt her marriage slipping away from her. When Tokh was home on leave, all he did was *push* her. Then he'd be off again, the apartment and her arms empty, and the clock ticking.

She started checking the ID on her incoming messages, and though Zheníhda missed him with every ounce of her being, she let the calls go to message. When she did answer, she would claim to have been in the bath, or at the neighbor's, and didn't get the message. The calls became less frequent, and the cracks in her heart became more painful.

With all his long assignments, Tokh had three weeks' leave coming. Zheníhda cried for days in advance, hoping to get it out of her system before he came home. She visited Yan Nor, a tiny, wrinkled colonel's wife from the far lands, and got her hair and nails done. She bought a new dress, a lacy, low-cut thing of white with red flowers, very daring for her, and met him at the door with his favorite drinks and food already on the table. Zheníhda tried so hard to be the most perfect wife, grateful for everything he did or said to her, eager to rub him down with oils, make him foods, serve him *lunahl*, and after a gut-wrenching third glass of strong *gohr*, so tipsy she could barely speak, she offered to lip him, which he accepted with surprise. But after the first day or so his *pushing* dwindled down to once or twice a day, and although he didn't seem to be avoiding conversation with her, he didn't have a lot to say. He praised her cooking, praised her keeping of the apartment, praised her ability to keep his accounts to the smallest decimal with the housekeeper programs on her personal com despite her poor education. He still let her curl up against him to sleep, his arm around her, and she was grateful for that. He didn't hate her. Not yet. Zheníhda waited until he was asleep, then slipped into the bathroom, closed the door, and cried herself sick.

After three weeks he was gone again, at least four months this time, between an advanced class in behavioral assessment and deeper study in surveillance. Zheníhda knew she was in trouble, and there was nothing the Wives' Club could do to help her. Tokh's mother called with brutal regularity. They were nearing their second anniversary. Tokh was gone far more than he was home. After two years, they were still strangers to each other. In another year, if they remained childless, Tokh could divorce her, and she would have no say in it. And with the pressure on him from his family and the growing distance between them, she truly feared he would.

Religion was a loose term on Kerasím. Small regional cults were tolerated as long as they didn't step on the Emperor's toes or start wars over their beliefs. Emperors didn't take lightly to religious wars, and it was Naghtas's grandfather that put down the last major conflict by sending in troops to execute every last practitioner of the offending cult. The official religion listed ten Spirits of Fortune, one corresponding to each month. On the first of the year, the Emperor would follow a millennia-old tradition of dropping a forecaster into an ancient stone circle marked in ten sections, one for each Fortune. Wherever the forecaster landed, that was the Fortune of the coming year and the Spirit to be honored. It might be fertility, fortune, veneration of mothers, a year for marriage, or a dark year of conservation. Every city had a Temple of the Fortunes, but attendance and offerings were up to individuals, never required. Zheníhda had been to a temple only once or twice in her life, but she began to make pilgrimages with the other wives, and while most of them prayed to Fortune that their husbands would return alive, Zheníhda prayed to the Mother, and to Fertility, and only then to Fortune.

A month after their anniversary – spent apart, Tokh called to tell her he expected to be routed home in another month. Zheníhda always smiled at his calls, but this time her smile seemed brighter.

He noticed. "Did something good happen today?"

"Well, not today, but the last time you were home," she teased. "The answer to the question you haven't asked yet, is yes."

Tokh looked annoyed but didn't reprimand her. He hated the word games females played. "Which question?"

"You always ask if I have news. Yes, I do."

"What news?"

The words burst from her lips at last. "That you'll be a father in just six more months!" Her smile stretched until it seemed to cover her entire face.

The information sank in. Tokh's eyebrow leapt upwards and he nearly dove through the communication screen. "A baby?! You're pregnant?! You're really pregnant?"

31

Zheníhda squealed. "Yes! I haven't told a soul. I wanted you to be the first. I thought I would die, waiting to tell you. I thought you'd want to be the one to tell your mother. They confirmed it last week."

Tokh sat back with a happy sigh. "Finally." He remembered to ask, "And you? You're okay?"

"Yes. A little sick now and then, but I'm fine."

There was such sweetness in his smile Zheníhda couldn't help forgiving him for anything he might ever have done to anger her. "As long as you're well."

A lieutenant's salary wasn't much, even a *dihnarwharl* lieutenant, and Tokh had rent on the apartment, food and clothing for Zheníhda, and the cost of a certified escort every time she had to leave the complex, but several days later a package arrived. Zheníhda used her com unit to scan the label and have it read the words aloud. She opened it, curious. Tokh had never sent her a package before. It was a necklace of alternating *orak* and *nemsihl* gems, shimmering black and sparkling clear, symbols of male and female, since they didn't yet know the sex of the child. Zheníhda sat down hard, speechless. She'd never seen anything so beautiful outside of a store. She fastened the strand around her neck with shaking fingers and stared into the mirror for several minutes. Only then did she pay attention to the card inside the box. She recognized the three letters that made up Tokh's name, and sounded out the rest.

All my love to you, Tokh

Zheníhda broke into tears of joy. She didn't take the necklace off until Tokh's next leave, three weeks later.

* * 5 * *

They lied to his mother.

Filuhr was *furious*. Tokh deliberately told her a due date two weeks later than expected. By the time Zheníhda's labor started and Filuhr caught a flight, the midwife wisemother was denied the chance to deliver her own smallson. She entered the birthing hospital already in a tirade, and her very first action was to slam Zheníhda in the side of the head.

"You dumb, stupid *nhasarwharl* trash! How could you not know you're in labor until the last minute? Did I not explain it to you over and over? I knew I should have come to stay with you last week. Do you know when he is hungry, or will you starve him, too?"

Tokh had three days' leave, to recognize his son and celebrate his naming day. He grabbed his mother by the arm. "If you hit my wife again, I will banish you from the room. She is the mother of my son, and you will respect her."

Filuhr gave an angry grunt. "How, when my own son disrespects me? Five hundred and six babies delivered, but not my very own smallson." She seized the infant from Zheníhda and showed him off to Talekh, who was not one for touching infants. She lay the baby on the foot of the bed and undressed him, confirming the sex and checking for birth injuries. Filuhr bent his little limbs in every direction, pressed on his belly, then pressed on his bladder to watch him pee into the air. She poked him until he gave a shivering scream of insult before wrapping him back up and consoling him.

"He seems strong and healthy, Tokh," she said with approval. "Your brother already named a son after your father, so you should name him after your grandfather, Kokhruhn. It's out of fashion, so it will stand out among his peers."

Tokh paused as if considering it. He was twenty-two, married and had a son, and he felt in charge of his life. "No. Let my sister honor him. My son's name is Zenak. He begins with Zheníhda and ends with me, as he does in life."

Tokh's father shifted feet unhappily, but his mother continued to spout. "Don't be crazy, Tokh. You're *dihnarwharl*, and your son should reflect that honor. If not Kokhruhn, then my father, Rifarensi. It means 'defender of the skies.' What better name can you find? Think of the strength of the image it projects! Defender of the skies!"

"His name is Zenak dar-Giláhn, and so it has been written," Tokh said. "It's bad luck to change a name after it has been given. It will make him indecisive and weak. If Rifarensi was such a great name, you would have given it to me or Hamiran. My son will be called Zenak. That is my word."

Zheníhda lay back and said nothing. This was Tokh's battle. All she wanted was her baby, whom Filuhr finally handed over when his screams of hunger became so loud no one could hear themselves argue.

Tokh returned to duty and Zheníhda returned home clutching Zenak, but there was no peace. Talekh returned home, but Filuhr stayed with Zheníhda, as well as Tokh's betrothed younger sister Nihrin. A few days later Zheníhda's mother joined them, a humble *nhasarwharl* in a household of *dihnarwharl*, four women in a two-room apartment, squabbling over one small newborn. If Zheníhda couldn't have Tokh home, she wanted only one thing: to be alone with her new son.

Filuhr criticized every movement Zheníhda made, demanding to examine the body-shy Zheníhda's underside, massaging her breasts, and demonstrating to Nihrin how things should be done. Anything wrong was chalked up to Zheníhda being from *nhasarwharl* stock and not knowing any better. Once Zheníhda's mother Amikise arrived, a dangerous line formed. Amikise, too, was squashed by the thumb of Filuhr, and being *nhasarwharl*, there wasn't a thing she could say or do about it. The stress tore Zheníhda down her middle; hit by post-partum hormones, she burst into tears.

Filuhr ripped the baby from her breast mid-suck. "Stop! Never feed a male infant while you cry. You'll make him into a miserable and morose child, and upset his stomach. Tears are for the weak-willed. Stiffen up, or you'll ruin him for life."

"My son is crying because he's hungry," Zheníhda said. She tried so hard to be polite. She had been a dutiful servant to Filuhr in the first days of her marriage, having a place to live and a family to

34

care for her while her husband was away. She knew that, should Tokh's brothers be unable to care for his parents in their old age, the task would fall to her. As the wife of their son, she was supposed to show them deepest respect. But Zeníhda also knew she was about at her breaking point. If it wasn't for the thought of the pain it would cause Tokh, she briefly considered grabbing her son and jumping from the window.

The next day, her patience ran out.

Filuhr was arguing with Amikise over how a newborn should be dressed. One had the top half of the baby, the other the bottom, each trying to take it from the other. Zenak began to shriek.

"Let go of him, *nhásarwharl*! My mother knows far more about infants than you!" Nihrin dug her pointed nails into Amikise's wrists until the wisemother gave in.

Zeníhda's temper took over. She was *dihnarwharl* by marriage, and that fact could not be changed. It was her apartment, and her baby.

She ransacked the closet in her bedroom. Tokh wore his favorite sword at all times but he had several older ones, as well as knives and pistols that he'd kept from his school days. Zeníhda grabbed a slender saber, pulled it from its holder, and charged out to the other room.

She pointed the sword at Nihrin. "YOU! Hands off my *ama*! YOU!" She pointed the sword at Filuhr, "Hands off my son! He is MY son! Not yours! You raised yours, and now it's my turn to raise mine! I want you out of here!" She flailed the blade through the air and slapped it on the table with a crack. "NOW! Take your things and go! You have overstayed your welcome."

Filuhr sputtered. "You can't speak to me that way! I am the mother of your husband!"

"And I'm his wife and you're upsetting his son, who I will protect with my life. Now get out!" Zeníhda took her son in her free arm. "Move! Don't make me have to place a call to Tokh!" She had the audacity to tap Filuhr on her backside with the sword, though her heart wanted to make the swing full force.

"This is what happens when *dihnarwharl* marry beneath them," Filuhr said with certainty. She and Nihrin gathered up their bags. "I'm going to report you to the authorities. You're crazy and dangerous and shouldn't be near an infant. Then I'm going to tell my son everything you've done and he'll take it out of your skin."

"Don't you lecture me in my house, you spiteful old tree-lizard!" Zheníhda raged. "Pick on someone who doesn't have a choice. I do. Out! You may charge your escort fare to my account. Consider it my gift to you." She ran them out the door with the end of the sword.

Zheníhda stood panting for a moment. She kissed Zenak's dark-haired head. "There," she said to her mother. "Perhaps now we can all have some peace."

Amikise paled to a washed-out yellow. "My dear daughter, you shouldn't have done that! She meant what she said! She'll have the authorities up here to seize him from you. You can't anger a *dihnarwharl*!"

"I'm a *dihnarwharl* now, *Ama*, and the wife of an officer, fully her equal. Here, take him."

Amikise answered the door with restrained terror a scarce hour later. Zheníhda sat on her sofa in a long bed-gown, nursing her new son without tears. Three armed military officers stood in the doorway.

"We had reports of a female attempting to assault an elderly woman with a sword, and a child in danger," one officer said.

Zheníhda smiled at his words. Filuhr was just forty-six. "That's silly! There are no swords here. My husband has several, but he is part of the honor guard for his division, so he keeps them with him when he's gone. I assure you, my child is not in any danger. He was crying a bit loud, but he's fine now that he is eating. He's a hungry boy with a bit of a temper. I'm sorry if he disturbed someone. I'll try to quiet him faster next time."

The officer bowed his head to her. "May we search your rooms anyway, Lady Tokh?"

"Absolutely! Be my guest, Officer! My husband is currently in Bar Danan Su, with the intelligence division. You can contact him there, if need be. He'll confirm my words."

The officers were thorough, searching drawers, the closet, behind furniture, under the mattress, inside travel bags. They had Zheníhda and her mother stand up and searched the sofa cushions. Zenak had fallen asleep on a full belly; an officer unwrapped him to find a healthy-looking new infant with no marks, content and asleep.

"I'm sorry if your time was wasted," Zheníhda told them. "I had a disagreement with my mother-in-law earlier and made her angry.

36

No doubt my husband will have choice words with me when he returns."

"That's probably a sure bet," the officer said. He handed Zenak over. "I'll mark down no weapons were found, and that the infant seems healthy. You might want to stay away from your husband's family for a while, though."

"I'll do that," Zheníhda assured him.

Zheníhda spoke truth: not so much as a carving knife could be found in the apartment. She had relied on the Waiting Wives club, passing all weapons to Ghirelle, wrapped in a baby blanket, no questions asked.

A video message came in the following morning on the comm system, and she hit play when she saw the sender.

My Little General: Please be careful with my toys; you are untrained. I'm sure the tales of your prowess are exaggerated. I'll fix that when I return. Please continue to keep my son safe. With my love, Tokh.

Tokh returned to base, allowing him frequent visits home. He listened to Zheníhda's side of the story of the fight with his mother. Zheníhda sat on his knee, head down, apologetic, knowing he had every right to beat her for insolence toward his mother. She waited with dread, but he laughed.

"Come," Tokh said, and retrieved his knives and daggers. "Don't touch the swords. You don't know how to use them; they aren't sized for you and you'll get hurt. Use these if you must defend yourself." He showed her how to carry the knives, both in view and hidden on various parts of her body, how to draw them, how to use them. "Only in self-defense," he warned her. "Always aim to kill, never to wound. And don't threaten anyone of higher caste, for any reason, for your life will be forfeit."

"I know," she said. "By the luck of the Emperor, may I never have to use them."

Tokh was promoted to Lieutenant Grade Two with little ceremony, but a small raise in pay. Zenak began to walk, then run, a bounding little boy with a shock of black hair and dark eyes, and skin the color of antique copper. Tokh brought him a play sword, and he went about beating it on everything, including Zheníhda's shins, and she took it away as soon as his father returned to duty.

Zenak was three when Tokh was granted two weeks' leave, months ahead of schedule. He packed up his family and headed for a retreat at a lake in the mountains. For five days they did nothing but lay about, watching Zenak play in the water and chase eels and little rock-lizards. Sometimes they sat and chatted with other *dihnarwharl* on holiday while the children romped together. But at night, while Zenak slept in exhaustion, Tokh *pushed* on Zheníhda for hours, sometimes in a fury, but more often slow and lingering, until Zheníhda became frantic to achieve her joy and more than once cried out from the strength of it.

"What's with you? You're never this slow," she said as they caught their breath.

He gave her a distant smile, gazing down at her in his arms. He kissed the arch of her nose, flicked a thumb over a *raffin*-brown nipple. "When I return, we're moving out on a long mission. Could be a year before they start rotating us home, depending on how fast it resolves. I'm trying to memorize every inch of you, every little thing you do, so I can remember it while we're apart. Sometimes, when the missions get difficult, I think back to moments like this, and it makes the difficulties bearable."

Zheníhda's heart melted. Sometimes she felt so lost and forgotten when he was away, as if he were ignoring her on purpose, losing track of the strict rules and disciplines married officers had to follow. She combed her fingers through his dark hair, stroked his chin hank until the wiry hairs came back together in a neater twist.

"Oh, Tokh! I forget sometimes what you go through. Tell me, what can I do for you to make it better? How can I bring you better memories to hold?"

He kissed her throat before rolling over on top of her. "Just be you."

* * 6 * *

Communication with her husband while he was away was never easy. If the mission was routine, if he was stationed on a distant base and had open access to communications, Tokh might send Zheníhda messages every day, sometimes a video message, sometimes a voice message, and if he was just taking classes or training, he could message her live once a week for ten *fasim* and they could talk face to face. All communications were monitored; little could ever be spoken about where he was or what he was doing, and she wasn't supposed to tell him anything that might upset him and take his mind from his work, only inspirational things to make him work harder. Zheníhda knew he worked in intelligence, but wasn't quite sure what that meant. Surely it meant doing smart, intelligent things, and in her head she always had a silly picture of him standing on a hilltop above a battle, with soldiers running to him to ask questions, and he was always able to supply the correct answers. After all, he could understand other languages besides Emperor's Tongue, so perhaps some of it involved answering information in languages the junior officers didn't know. When he was in the field somewhere, communication was spotty. It could be weeks before she received a line or two of fast text, letting her know he was still alive. Sometimes he couldn't do that much, and she would receive a note from his commanding officer, forwarding his thoughts to her, or a form-response from the commander that he was well and couldn't be in communication at this time.

This mission was one of the tough ones, and Zheníhda cherished every rare word he sent. Tokh had been gone a long, lonely nine months when she received a note from his commander:

Lieutenant Grade Two Specialist Tokh was wounded in action two days ago. He is stable and alert, and will be returning to Khasoohrin Base by the end of the week for recovery. You will be informed when he returns to base. Upon discharge from the base, he may return home to complete his recovery.

Zheníhda's heart stopped. Damn the military and their cryptic messages! The word "recovery" meant they didn't expect him to die, and "complete his recovery" sounded as if they expected him to return to duty, so it couldn't be that bad.

She waited by the comm for four days until the message came. *Lieutenant Grade Two Specialist Tokh is in the medical unit pending recovery from injury. Female visitation is limited to wives, consorts, mothers and sisters.*

Zheníhda left Zenak with a Waiting Wife and was at the door of the medical building in ten minutes. The courtesy to notify his mother somehow slipped her mind.

She entered the hospital determined to be a good wife, to bear her husband's burdens so he would rest easy. One glance at him and the room went black, and she fell to her knees.

Zheníhda pulled herself up a moment later, apologetic. Tokh's leg was shattered, held together by bone grafts and wires. A projectile had gone through the top of his shoulder; he wore it in a sling, waiting for the muscles to heal. A shrapnel grenade had exploded near him; he'd been peppered with razor-sharp pellets. Surgery had removed seventeen of them. It would be at least fifteen weeks before he might return to any form of duty.

He pulled her down onto the bed next to him, kissing her hair, kissing her face. "Nihda! My Nihda! You're my strength. Just – lie next to me," he said, groggy with medications. "Watch over me. Keep guard." Zheníhda lay next to his less-injured side, put her arms around him, and didn't move a muscle for two hours, every ounce of her being overjoyed just to hold him again.

Tokh returned home a week later. He was twenty-five years old and had five new medals to his name, for bravery, injury, heroism, leadership, and campaign. His unit had been involved in a horrific battle: their major had been killed, and Tokh had crawled over the bloody remains to keep giving orders, getting the men out of danger. Of three hundred and fifty men in the company, only his twelve came back. He'd been promoted two grades to full Captain Two. No fewer than three generals had given him written commendations, and made offers to have him join their units.

Tokh wasn't supposed to walk on his healing leg, but using supports was difficult because of his shoulder. He was supposed to use a wheeled chair for transport outside of the apartment, but Tokh wasn't one for sitting. His leg caused him considerable pain, but he insisted on using it beyond orders, face twisted, breath hard, covered in a mist of sweat, balancing with just one of the walking supports. Much of the time he lay on the bed, Zenak playing with his toy vehicles and aircraft on the covers next to him.

Zheníhda cuddled next to him at night. "Is there anything my husband desires? Anything I can do for you? I am at your command."

Tokh raised weary eyes to her. His hand stroked her breast through her nightwear. "It's not for lack of want," he assured her. "It shames me to say I can't summon the energy to do my wife justice. The medications they shove on me leave me weak as a baby."

She smiled back at him. Her hand ran down his belly and teased his *hihvat*. "Your leg needs all your strength right now. If it would please you, I could give you a handshake, or ride you rocket-style if you wish. That would save your strength yet give you pleasure at the same time, my captain."

The thought brought a smile to his face, and he kissed her in the soft little valley where her eyebrow met her nose. "I like your offer, but what I would like most right now is an oil rub, top to bottom. Just go very easy on the healing parts. I don't know if the oil is good for the wounds."

"Of course, my husband." She chose his favorite scented oil and massaged it into him, starting with his scalp. He fell asleep before she got to his waist.

Tokh's avoidance of sex confused her. In six years of marriage, she could probably count on her fingers the number of days he hadn't *pushed* on her – when he was home, at least, and three of those were the days after Zenak's birth. Now, two weeks after his return, she wasn't sure what to think or say or do. He still seemed interested, he just didn't want to *do* anything. His leg was healing well; the heavy cast was off, the metal pins were out; he wore a stiff brace instead, and his pain medication was gone. And still he didn't put himself to her.

On the other hand, he wasn't himself the rest of the day, either. He was idle, watching news programs on the planetary ComNet, or watching Zenak run on the playground outside the apartment building, or staying in constant communication with other injured officers and his commander. And he was drinking his way through

41

their liquor stock. Perhaps it was being away from duty; he hadn't been without orders this long since he was eleven years old.

When Tokh was away, Zenak slept in the bed next to Zheníhda. When Tokh was home, Zenak was allowed to fall asleep in their bed, and when they were ready to use it, Zheníhda would carry him to the backless sofa, where he would sleep the rest of the night. She would leave a breakfast of bread and sweet-nut butter and a glass of *harfa* juice on the table for him, and when he awoke he would be fairly self-sufficient in the morning, watching the ComNet until she rose. That night Zheníhda put him to sleep on the sofa as usual, went back to bed, and once again tried to stir Tokh's interest, but he merely kissed her and fell asleep, fumes of *dhurwah* spirits drifting over her with every heavy breath.

Sometime in the middle of the night Zenak crawled onto their bed. Zheníhda opened an eye, but didn't think twice. Tokh, however, felt the bed move, and sat up with a gasp. From under his pillow he pulled out his service knife, a murderous thing with a thick blade longer than Zheníhda's hand. He pressed the boy into the bed, knife at his throat, and bellowed.

"Where's the head of the tunnel? Answer me! Where does it lead? Who's responsible?! Where is the head of the tunnel?!"

Zheníhda screamed and pulled on Tokh's arm as hard as she could. Zenak began to cry, then gasp. Tokh pressed down on the little throat with his arm, choking off the noise. Zheníhda let go long enough to turn on a light.

"Let him go! He's your son! Tokh! It's Zenak! It's just Zenak! I order you to let him go! Officer! I order you to let him go!" For a split-second she thought about biting him, or if she had the nerve to grab one of the daggers and stab him, as he'd taught her to do.

Tokh gave a shudder, and his eyes realized what his hands were doing. He gave a shriek and dropped the knife, clenched Zenak to his chest, and began to howl. Zheníhda grabbed the knife and ran to the other room, burying it deep in a container of *ohr*-flour. She ran back and managed to get Tokh to release the shrieking boy. A thin red line ran under his chin, a scratch of the blade that would heal in less than a day.

Tokh breathed hard. "I'm sorry, Nihda! I'm sorry! I don't know what happened! I don't know why I would do that! You know I

42

wouldn't hurt my son! I would never hurt my son! He popped up…
out of a hole… "

Zheníhda held Zenak on her shoulder with one arm, and
comforted Tokh with the other. "*Shu, shu,* my husband. I know you
wouldn't. *Shu!* It was just a dream gone bad. You didn't realize it
was him. He's okay. You're okay. Everyone is unharmed. Everyone
will be okay in the morning. Tokh, you must promise me, no more
weapons in the bedroom, ever! Swear it! Until you aren't having bad
dreams, there can't ever be a weapon in the bedroom. Promise me!"

"I promise! I promise. I wouldn't hurt him. You know I
wouldn't. No more weapons by the bed."

Zheníhda released Zenak to her lap and hung onto Tokh with
both hands. In an hour Zenak would be asleep again on the sofa,
belly full of sugar wafers and *muuht*-milk. Tokh stayed wrapped in
her arms until the sun rose, quiet and repentant, only then falling
asleep again.

As the weeks passed, Tokh was more active, putting real
pressure on his leg. The sling was gone from his arm and his
shoulder gained strength. The little cuts from the shrapnel had
healed, leaving a spattering of small brown scars Tokh was rather
proud of.

They lay in bed together, Zheníhda idly fingering his *hihvat,*
hoping to start a spark. Tokh didn't object in the least, rubbing her
breast and kissing her neck lazily, but no matter how long she
played, his *hihvat* remained a fat brown worm in her fingers.

Tokh gave a soft chuckle. "Do you know what it needs? A
lipping. Come kneel before me."

"*Gah,* Tokh. You know I don't do those things. That's the
business of consorts and *trixihn.* I am a *dihnarwharl* wife."

He licked her ear. "No. I want you to do it for me. Go on. Kneel
before me."

She shook him off. "Go. I told you, *push* me all you want, but
save the other pleasures for hired females. I'm your wife. I don't
want to do those things."

Tokh's mouth pulled tight and his eyes blazed with a fire she'd
never seen. He seized her by her shoulders and threw her onto the
floor before he grabbed her by her long hair and pulled her to her
knees before him.

43

Zeníhda squealed in fright. Tokh shoved his face to hers, nose to nose. "You are my wife, I am your husband, and I gave you an order! Now give me a lip job!"

"Please Tokh, don't make me do that." Zeníhda fought his pull. "You know I hate that. Please don't make me. Please, Tokh. I don't want to do that. Rub it on my thighs, my belly, I'll rub it with oil, but please don't make me – "

She gasped as he backhanded her cheek so hard she fell over flat onto the floor. His hand twisted in her hair, yanked her up, and pulled her head backward. With his other hand he grasped his *hihvat* and stuffed it between her lips.

Zeníhda gave a muffled cry. He sat on her tongue like a cold floppy eel, the stench of rancid sweat and oils filling her nostrils like soiled underthings, and she gagged at the thought. The motion of her tongue as her mouth tried to reject the assault was the spark he needed, and she felt his *hihvat* jump to life.

Tokh thrust himself deeper. His ring began to swell, rubbing against the back of her tongue and the roof of her mouth until Zeníhda felt herself choking. He pulled at her harder, while Zeníhda punched his stomach, beat against his thighs, raked him with her nails, desperate for air. She felt his *khatas* crawl upward, readying, and after several more ramming blows he gave a loud groan and his musky fluid spilled over her lips.

Zeníhda pulled away, turning her head just in time. She vomited into the carpet four times, screaming between each wave, before scrambling up and running for the bathroom.

It was several minutes before the door opened. Zeníhda was scrubbing the inside of her mouth with a cloth and a bottle of tooth rinse, crying so hard she couldn't see. She gave a shriek and flattened herself against the wall. "Get away from me!"

"I need to piss." He leaned over the shining metal toilet, hands braced against the wall, and let loose. Halfway through he started shaking. "I'm sorry," he said softly. "I-I don't know why I did that. I'm sorry."

Zeníhda wanted to say something, but she couldn't get any words to form. Saying "It's all right," just wasn't going to work. Neither was "Apology accepted."

He finished and turned to her, hands pressed against his head. "I just – Sometimes – The flies –."

44

Tokh gave a strange gasp, and Zheníhda realized he was – *his spirit was leaking*. Her invincible husband, the mighty warrior of almost a dozen medals in seven years, a lieutenant so brave he was skipped an entire rank, was leaking tears. Kerasi men did not cry. To lose their *hihvat* to a *trixahg*'s teeth was a far lesser shame. Leaking one's spirit was a dishonorable discharge. Leaking spirit could get you shunned from town and family. Her eyes cut to the side, saving him embarrassment.

He pleaded to her, "I can't make them go away! And it makes me want to do terrible things."

Zheníhda found her tongue. "Like what?" They warned the wives things like this could happen. Was he going to kill her? Should she grab Zenak and run to a neighbor?

He sat down on the bathroom floor, naked as his birth, and spoke to his knees. "The battle. Nihda, you can't imagine. Three hundred of us meaning only to keep the peace, form a barrier until things could be worked out. But we were too late. Everyone had been massacred. They'd made great X's from beams and sunk them into the ground to make a fence, then tied people to them and cut them open so their insides hung out, and all the insects and animals were upon them. Huge clouds of flies, this great mass of yellow crawling on everything. A pregnant female… The buzzing was so loud we couldn't hear each other speak. One thousand? Two thousand? We couldn't count them. And the flies. Everything was covered in flies. Pamekh cracked and shot himself in the head."

Zheníhda's heart froze. She grabbed her dressing robe, sank down next to him, and wrapped it around both of them.

"A few were still alive, begging for help. We shot them. There was nothing else we could do. Then the weaponfire started. We were caught on the street between buildings. They picked us off like eels in a trap. Major Lintran sent eight of us to take out the snipers. We located them and took five prisoners. We took their heads, right there. One of them was female. Gandrihn wanted everyone to have a *push* on her, but there wasn't time so we just took her head. Then he sets the head on the ground and gives himself a handshake until he splattered onto it. The flies were on us before we even left.

"We were half a *nali* from rescue when the final battle came. They had assault weapons beyond what we carried. They just kept pouring out of the buildings, picking us off if we moved from cover. We shot. We shot anything that moved. They threw a child out a

45

window, no bigger than Zenak; we shot him. We used every last projectile, every last power pack, we used swords on those that came close enough. Major Lintran had us pull ammo off the dead. The noise ceased for a moment and he stood up to take recon, and they shot a *ghinadin*-loving rocket at him. A rocket! I was kneeling just an armslength from him. It cut him in *pushing* half, Nihda! One second he's standing there, the next second there's a terrible whistle and he's in two bloody pieces, still trying to give the next order. I crawled over him to get the comm unit and started screaming orders. Any of us that could move, did. We were in sight of the rescue when I was hit in the shoulder. As I fell, a shooter came up from a sewer and threw the grenade that took my leg. Two of my men ran back to get me, and we made it aboard. Twelve of us. And then the destroyers arrived. I've never seen anything like it. Five of them, side by side, blocking the sky with their size, and they laid everything waste. There is no more rebellion in Kanok Nevas. Kanok Nevas doesn't exist."

Zheníhda's blood had turned to ice, making it difficult to move. This was Kerasím. They were a peaceful world. They were a civilized people, with colonies among the stars. If there was a war like that, surely it would be on the news, wouldn't it? Why wouldn't anyone have heard of it?

Zheníhda patted his shoulders. "Tokh, I'm going to get you some *gohr*. *Gohr* will help calm the thoughts. Can you sit here for half a *fasim*? Just half a *fasim*." He nodded and she sprinted from the room. She didn't bother with a glass. He accepted the bottle gratefully and took a long swallow.

She hugged him, head on his shoulder, until he seemed calmer. "Tokh, you have combat sickness. You know it. You know we must report it. It will look much better if you report it yourself. Come, my husband. You can't do it naked. Let's dress you."

She got him into his off-duties and sat him before the comm, but she tapped the numbers for emergency herself.

Tokh spoke in a fog. "This is Captain Two Specialist Tokh dar-Giláhn, and I think I have combat sickness. There are flies in my head and I can't get them out. Please... send someone."

Four heavily armed soldiers knocked on their door in less than five *fasim*. Zheníhda opened it. One poked his head in, took note of the bruises blossoming on the side of her face, saw Zenak sleeping on the sofa, saw Tokh immobile before the ComNet. "Wife, are all weapons secure? Does he have a weapon on him?"

"No. I dressed him myself. His weapons are in the other room."

The officers entered, stun sticks at the ready. "Captain, you've been ordered to accompany us for medical evaluation. Will you accompany us?"

Tokh nodded, and rose slowly to his feet. Zheníhda kissed his cheek. "Courage, my husband. I'll see you very soon."

When the door shut, she fell to the floor and cried until morning.

Tokh was gone two weeks. He returned home his old self, happy, talkative, and active. Zheníhda was leery at first, watching for signs of trouble, but she couldn't find any. He lay on the floor and played with Zenak for an hour.

"I don't know what they did," he told her. "They sent me out on a flight to a facility somewhere. Some experimental machine they have now. They strap you down, put a machine over your head, give you medication, and make you tell everything you can remember about your battle. They record the memories, and then they take you through it again the next day and fade the memories a little bit. Then they do it again the next day, and the next, until it doesn't bother you anymore. I needed six days of treatment. At the end, they show you back the recordings of your memories, but now it's like watching a ComNet program. I see it, I remember it, but I don't feel it in my neck like I used to. It's just another memory, like my first wounding. It's like being given your life back."

Zheníhda listened with rapt attention. "That's amazing, the technology they have today. To watch your own memories on a screen! They should try that with Major Vol Nag's wife, Arettis. She still can't bear to leave her apartment – you know, after that awful assault she had the other month."

"I don't know where they treated me," Tokh said, "but maybe some day it will be for everyone."

Things changed at night, too. Tokh was on her before she even climbed into bed, kissing her neck, pulling at her nightwear. "I missed you," he breathed in her ear. "It's been far, far too long."

"I missed you too," Zheníhda said, returning the affection with every bit as much energy. "Tokh, I want another baby. Zenak will be in school soon and I'll be alone. Please, let's have another."

He picked her up and dropped her on the bed. "Then lay back and let me plant him in there."

Tokh reported back to active duty the following week. He'd been promoted, but had no assignment. He returned to the apartment a few hours later, paperwork in hand.

He kissed Zheníhda's hair. "Start packing. We're out of here in one week."

Zheníhda gasped, unsure which direction to turn first. "What do you mean? Where are we going? Where will we live?"

"Captain Two Tokh dar-Giláhn will report for duty to General Poruhnet at Dahn Bohr Training Base as of next week. We are promised an apartment. It won't be on base, but it's guaranteed to have four rooms."

"Four rooms? Tokh, how can we afford that!"

He lifted her under her arms and swung her in a circle. "Because I'm a Captain Two now, not a Lieutenant Two! And Dahn Bohr is not Khasoorihn."

"Where is Dahn Bohr? How long will you be there?"

"Medical would prefer I stay on light duty for a year, to give my leg proper rest, so I'll be instructing officers in techniques and procedures. Poruhnet is rated highly as a commander. I had three generals requesting me, but Poruhnet is the one who had a desk job available. I don't know what will happen after a year, but we're set until then. I can train upward while I'm there, too. Dahn Bohr's 800 *nalis* from here, the center of the region. Hot summers, cold winters, but lots of trees and public forests. You will like it." He lifted her off the ground and squeezed her again, the pommel of his sword digging into her thigh. "You'll see."

* * 7 * *

Tokh was right; Zheníhda loved Dahn Bohr. Their apartment building was just outside the base, walking distance if she had an escort, and it held just *dihnarwharl* and *dahneg* families. Some were Waiting Wives, others – like Zheníhda now did – had husbands who returned home every night. The apartment seemed huge after the tiny rooms they'd just left – Zenak had his own bedroom, and two small baths just for them.

Living among *dahneg* made Zheníhda nervous. *Dihnarwharl* were the dividing line, sometimes middle caste and sometimes upper, a huge difference in expectations and power. If their family didn't meet the upper-caste criteria, they would be ostracized and treated as servants. Zheníhda reined in her mannerisms, clamped down on Zenak showing proper respect, made sure her clothing and Zenak's were up to standards, and proceeded to make over the apartment as best she could on Tokh's limited budget. What a wife did reflected directly on her husband, and Zheníhda refused to do anything that could hurt Tokh's standing. Having strong *dahneg* contacts could boost a career. It paid off: in one afternoon of socializing, the wives accepted her as high-*dihnarwharl*, and Tokh's family became upper-caste.

And, despite the difficulties she had conceiving Zenak, they hit paydirt on the first try: Zheníhda hadn't fully decided on where the furniture fit best when she realized she was pregnant. Tokh, home every night for the first time since childhood, was there to witness it. He didn't watch the delivery – fathers weren't welcome in birthing rooms – but waited outside to see his newest son, just minutes old. Tokh chose the name himself: Kitras, the one who prospers.

Tokh made peace with his mother this time: she could be present, but the doctor wouldn't allow her to deliver the baby. He flew Filuhr out one week before Zheníhda was due, on the stipulation she wasn't allowed to criticize Zheníhda. Not a word. Her duty would be to keep Zenak out of the way so Zheníhda could care for her new son. Filuhr came, but her mouth stayed pinched up the

49

entire time, as if she'd actually sewn a button over it, and her eyebrow, middle-aged heavy, stayed sunk over her eyes in a permanent scowl.

Most Kerasi males had little patience for infants and never touched them; Tokh, too, was not a baby-handler, but several times Zheníhda caught him adjusting a blanket, or petting Kitras on his fuzzy black-haired head, and her heart hurt from happiness.

Tokh's year came and went at Dahn Bohr, but General Poruhnet didn't want him to leave.

"You've done excellent work here, Tokh. Keep it up and you'll have a very successful career. I've been in contact with your superiors, and they have agreed to let you remain under my command. I want you to make every use of the training programs available here. If you want to advance in intelligence, the language you need to be most proficient in is Union Standard."

Tokh frowned. "Union? The language of our enemy? I have a level-one certificate in it."

Poruhnet's face remained dead serious. "Not good enough. Nothing will open the doors of advancement faster. Anyone can squeeze a confession out of a *tápatihn*. Learn to decipher Union, tap into their communications, interrogate Union prisoners, and you'll always be in high demand by the elite, on a galactic scale. A new class starts next week; I want you in it."

It wasn't something Tokh had ever considered, but Poruhnet seemed to have a plan for him that included advancement. He gave a bow. "May my studies bring you honor, General."

Tokh took as many classes as he was allowed, as well as further studies in building rapport for interrogation. Poruhnet kept his duties light, instructing new students on basics. Tokh no longer worried about being called to Poruhnet's office.

"Tokh, you're one of my top men in Intelligence. There's some interesting research coming down to us from medical, research in the field of memory recall, a boon for interrogation if they can get the procedure to work consistently. It has a high complication rate, but it has great potential. I want you to observe it. It's top-secret research. I can't tell you where it's happening, but I've seen it myself, and it's a wonder. Learn everything you can, and report back to me alone."

"As you will, General."

Tokh waited. A day passed, three days, but no orders came down. Finally, on the sixth day, Poruhnet called him back.

"I'm sorry, Tokh. I've tried to pull strings, but they are firm. They'll allow no one below major to observe a test. If I could grant you the rank I would, but you're nowhere near due to move up. I'm keeping you at the front of the list anyway, and the minute I can sneak you a place in there, I will. Have you had advanced training in interrogation techniques?"

"I should be ready to test for Level Three."

Poruhnet nodded. "I want you to take two classes when they open next month: advanced behavior conditioning, and medically-enhanced interrogation. In the meantime, I want you to shadow one of my top interrogators, learn what you can while you wait for formal instruction."

"I'll begin as soon as you give the word, General," Tokh said.

"Report tomorrow and I'll introduce you. Of course, it would be very advantageous to a captain in intelligence gathering if he read up on everything non-classified he could on memory investigational engineering. Memory investigational engineering is certain to play a large role in the future of interrogation, and someone who is already familiar with the concept would be placed ahead of other candidates." Poruhnet sighed. "Memory investigational engineering. I wish there'd been something like that around when I was your age."

Tokh smiled and bowed his head. "That's rather amusing, General. Memory investigational engineering is an interesting new hobby of mine. I'd be most happy to share my knowledge with you."

"I look forward to it, Captain. Dismissed."

Tokh gained several security clearances and couldn't speak of what he did anymore. Sometimes he was sent away for days or weeks, sometimes he slept home for just as long. They made friends with other officers and wives. Zenak did well at school. Kitras learned to walk, and by two was playing battle games with his brother.

For not having much say in her marriage, this was the life Zeníhda had dreamed about as a young girl. A caring young husband with prestige, even if he wasn't home enough; two beautiful sons, a desirable apartment, a beautiful wardrobe, bits of enviable jewelry, and the privileges of the upper castes. This was a fairy tale, and she felt as blessed as the Emperor's daughter, a far cry from her *nhásarwharl* childhood.

But fairy tales had a dark side. Most females went through life in relative safety, but Kerasi society was stacked against them. Females lived in a state of semi-confinement. Young girls were sequestered from the age of twelve or so, until they married, so no one mistook their age. Some husbands were controlling, and kept their wives tied to the home. A female loose on the street without a male escort was often seen as free bait by any outranking caste, and by the age of forty, ninety percent of Kerasi females could report some sort of non-consensual contact.

Perhaps seventy percent of Kerasi males didn't prey on females – most often those of the majority middle-castes, who had wives and mothers and daughters at home and hoped that if there were a crisis, another male would treat his wife or mother or daughter with the same respect he would show theirs. Upper castes preyed on females because they could; a lower caste female or male couldn't deny someone of a higher caste any request. Lower castes preyed on the next lower caste because that was the only power in their lives. *Sohlahrin* were picked on by everyone but *ghinadin*, therefore they took out their frustrations and injustices on them. *Ghinadin* were the bottom of the food chain, save for outcasts, and therefore fed on themselves with a vengeance because no one cared that they did. The exception was a servant in uniform, displaying the proper identification. Those were considered the property of the person they worked for, and to dishonor them was to dishonor the owner, and some of them were of high caste and unforgiving demeanor.

Hundreds of laws surrounded caste and etiquette. No child under the age of fourteen of any caste, male or female, was supposed to have sexual contact of any sort. That was Emperor's law, irrefutable and harshly punished. Veils helped; the sheer cloth blurred the face beneath it, be it an off-limits twelve year old or a crone, a beautiful new bride or a female with the face of a *jappa*. It removed some of the temptation and cut down on stalking, but it was personal choice, not law. Consorts were property; it was up to the owner to share them with a guest or not, but sharing was expected courtesy.

Everyone knew males *pushed* any female they could. It didn't mean anything; it was what males did. Males bore the brunt of birth control; if they didn't want to pay to raise a child, then they needed to make sure they didn't make one. Male birth control was extremely effective, but the side effect was an increased libido, a frequent ache in the *khatas* that could be relieved through sex. Zheníhda didn't think at all about Tokh *pushing* other women when he was away from her; she assumed he did and that was that. A wife worried more about her husband's comfort than petty jealousy. What was important was who bore his children, who managed his property, who kept his money. That was where a wife's power lay. And woe to the male who fathered a child out of wedlock, or worse, with another man's wife. That was a legal mess no one wanted, with consequences ranging from expensive fines to forced marriage to prison time to castration or death. That was the lure of sterile consorts – free *lihx*, no risk.

Wives were a different matter. Wives were not property like consorts; they had select legal rights. Kerasi males were touchy about their wives. A wife was the mother of their sons; they didn't like having to question if a child was theirs or not because someone took a liberty. A good husband never volunteered a wife, and a good friend guarded his friend's wife as he would his own, not ask for privileges. But a guest of equal or higher caste could ask to borrow someone's wife, and even though it was rude to ask, it was also rude to deny a guest. Even then, the rule was one and done, in and out, very nice of you, sorry to take up your time. Wives were always aware of the possibility, and learned young how to blend into the walls and not call attention to themselves. It was just a part of life.

Zheníhda had made it safely through twenty-seven years of her life. She wasn't a shy person, but she appeared so because she'd always been self-conscious. Too tall for a female – five inches taller than most, built like a stem of grass, and every time she felt half-way pleased with herself, girly and pretty in a new outfit or piece of jewelry, that nose, that *nose*, that horrible thin nose with the bump at the top, poking of out the mirror and laughing at her. Some days she felt like taking a spoon and beating it flat. It had taken her years to feel comfortable around Tokh when undressed, so embarrassed by her bony body that she stiffened up until Tokh had trouble bending her. She gained confidence around him, but with strangers she went right back to rounding her shoulders, bending her head to shorten herself and hide her nose, and trying to be unnoticed. When Tokh entertained, especially now with a separate kitchen to stay in,

Zheníhda was a perfect invisible wife, making sure the food and drink never ran out, clearing dirty plates without a sound, then retreating back to the kitchen to ready the next round. Tokh had nothing but praise for her hostessing skills, and Zheníhda allowed herself pride that her husband was pleased with her. Living in a building of just *dahneg* and *dihnarwharl*, Zheníhda kept the slight caste difference in the back of her head, but among the wives, no one paid much attention to the difference.

She would never make that mistake again.

* * 8 * *

Tokh had never been in once place this long since his commission. He'd had friends in the barracks and friends in the trenches, but they shifted positions so often that even though the friendships might be very strong, they were just passing ones. Here at Dahn Bohr, a huge regional center with both a student academy and a training facility, friendships weren't as strong but people stayed in place long enough that social groups formed. Tokh made his way into several circles, including one or two with the males in their building. Several of the officers played a game called Tabs, a table game played with little white tablets marked with various symbols. Adults played with cash bets, which wasn't illegal as long as the cash wasn't above a certain amount, or run as an unauthorized business. Sometimes several games were happening on a single night, and players might move from one game to the next. The players weren't always the same, depending on duty, and thus the apartment wasn't always the same. When it came Tokh's turn to host the game. Zheníhda was ready with a proper array of spirits, juices, small sandwiches, *vortag* legs cooked in a fiery sauce, *rhee*, a common flat fungus dipped in batter and fried to a crispy snack, and *mohro*, a whole clove of spice wrapped in soft cheese and oiled pastry, then baked. Those were Tokh's favorite, but he sweated out the spice for two days afterward. Along with a tray of *raffin*-flavored crème-filled dessert puffs, it was a nice little buffet. She put the boys to bed a little early so they wouldn't disturb the game and she could pay attention to the table.

Most of the players were familiar. There was Ramek, the *dihnarwharl* major across the hall, who was in charge of the computer maintenance team. Dilvar was also familiar, his chin hank wrapped tight in four inches of mustard ribbon so that it thumped against his chest like a finger when he spoke. He was another Captain Two who worked Intelligence. Kahfengar and Ahn Jor both worked base security. Ahn Jor was a *nhasarwharl* from Gha Robbek, his skin a dark red-brown and his bald head tattooed with a single blue dot to identify him to his home clan. He stayed quiet and humble in the house of a *dihnarwharl*, well-mannered and gracious. Behretan was a *dahneg* colonel, the Director of Weaponry and Ammunition for the base, and he'd played against Tokh in at least three other games. He was perhaps fifty, a sly player, but the longer they played and the more he drank, the worse his playing became.

The game was winding down when Behretan tipped his head back to peer into the kitchen. He stretched and sighed. "Well, Tokh. You've just about cleaned me out of my money. Do you mind if I borrow your wife before I leave? I've been watching her walk all evening. She has a most desirable little posterior that has caught the attention of my soldier. I would like to caress it in person."

The table laughed. Not ten *fasim* had gone by the entire night without some sort of sexual innuendo. Tokh smiled, taking it as a compliment. Kahfengar anted, but the play stopped at Behretan.

"I'm serious, Tokh. I wish to borrow your wife. Call her out here to me."

The table went silent. Tokh lifted his head. He couldn't deny a *dahneg*. "She is the mother of my sons. I'm not in the habit of sharing her."

"I didn't say I wanted to keep her," Behretan said. "Just borrow her for a few minutes. Come, come, Tokh! You've been a gracious host tonight. Don't make me pull caste on you. Call her out here."

Tokh didn't blink, desperate to think of a way out, any way. He couldn't fight him; not only could he not hit a colonel, but he couldn't touch a *dahneg*. To do so could cost him his hand, or worse. He knew in his heart Zheníhda would rather die.

Anything, anything.

The room waited. Tokh stared unfocused into space, but no technicality jumped out to save him. "Zheníhda, come here."

Zheníhda poked her head around the doorway. "Tokh, you can't be serious."

"Behretan wishes to borrow you. Please accompany him to the other room. He may service you once and only once."

"Tokh!" Zheníhda's fingers dug into the doorway. "What are you saying?"

Tokh stared at the table, feeling his stomach rise in dread. He raised his voice. "*Zheníhda!* He is *dahneg*! You will accompany him to the other room and please him as our guest. Don't make me repeat it again." He wasn't sure he'd be able. Not one of the other men so much as smiled.

Behretan stood up and hooked an arm around her waist, pulling her from the kitchen. "Come, *fallah*. I'll bet you've never had a *dahneg* horn. I like feisty, but not too much." He polished her backside through her skirt. "Oh, that is lovely." He pulled Zheníhda, fighting, into the bedroom, and shut the door.

Tokh have a shudder and downed the rest of his drink in one long swallow.

"It happens, Tokh," Dilvar said quietly. "She understands."

"It doesn't happen to me," Tokh snapped, and slammed the glass down. "That filthy son of a *trixahg*. If I'd known he sampled, I would never have invited him."

"That's the risk of inviting *dahneg*," Kahfengar said. His fingers played with his stack of tabs, clinking them over and over until the noise got under Tokh's skin.

Zheníhda's cry of protest leaked into the room. Tokh felt his insides quiver. "Play!" he barked at the table. "Just play the damned game!" He tossed his tabs onto the table so hard they bounced off the other side and Ahn Jor had to retrieve them.

One round, two rounds. Ramek played the third round. Zheníhda's raised voice came through the door, but Tokh couldn't make out the words. Tokh seized his snack plate and threw it with an angry growl. The *vortag* sauce left a streak where the bones hit the wall.

The first scream sent Tokh to his feet.

"Let it go, Tokh," Kahfengar said. "There's nothing you can do."

Tokh knew the sound of Zheníhda in distress. His honor sword hung on holders high on the wall behind him; on the second scream he seized and drew it. The table jumped to block him, but the screaming continued.

Dilvar's hands held his shoulders. "No! Tokh, no! You can't go in there."

"Tokh, you can't touch a *dahneg*. He'll have your head."

"Calm! You must stay calm."

Ahn Jor hung back; as *nhasarwharl*, he couldn't touch any of them.

Tokh snarled, "What good is an officer who can't protect so much as his wife? Maybe I can't touch him, but it's well within my right to bear witness!"

"Without the sword!" Ramek said. "Put the sword away. Don't tempt yourself."

Tokh stabbed the sword into its scabbard and they released him. He burst into the bedroom.

A shriek of rage escaped him, and the sword sprang free. "What did you do! What did you do to my wife?"

Behretan collapsed his incentive rod and replaced it on his belt, adjusted his pants, and spat on Zheníhda. "You need to teach your wife courtesy, Tokh. When I order a *dihnarwharl* to warm me with her mouth, I expect it done. She won't forget her place again."

Tokh trained the sword on him. "Get out! Get out of my home now!"

"Don't point that at me, Tokh. I can end your career in one call."

Dihnarwharl Captain Tokh stepped nose to nose with the *dahneg* colonel. "Whether I strike you with my hand or cut you into pieces with my sword, my penalty will be the same. The choice is whether you walk out my door on your own, or they put your pieces in a bag and carry you out. Tell me which."

Behretan patted Tokh on the cheek. "Don't make me write you up for insubordination. What a shame for such a pleasant evening to end so poorly. I think I'll play with only *dahneg* from now on. The females are much sweeter. Carry on, men." He left the apartment without a glance.

Tokh dropped to the floor and lifted Zheníhda in his arms. She was half-dressed, sobbing and shivering, and a bloody wreck. Behretan had beaten her face, split her lip, and knocked out a tooth. The backside Behretan had professed to adore had been hit with an incentive rod so harshly Tokh couldn't see the skin for the blood.

"I don't care," she managed to sob. "He took his turn; he wasn't getting another thing out of me. You said once."

"*Shu, shu.* My brave little general. You were in your right." Tokh stroked her hair.

"Do you want me to call for medical?" Kahfengar said, and Tokh gave a faint nod.

"I'll get my wife," Ramek said, backing toward the door. "She'll stay with your boys."

Tokh held Zheníhda tight, seething anger rolling off him in palpable waves. "You will have justice. I promise you; he'll pay for this."

* * 9 * *

Tokh's word was his honor. After too few hours of sleep, they arrived at the Office of Military Justice before the doors opened. Tokh explained the situation to the legal minister. Behretan was sent for, and they were shown together into the office of *fáhganid* General One Dahsuhlar, Justice for the Dahn Bohr military base. He wore a bold red uniform, with a short red cape falling from his shoulders just in case someone missed the color and caste-badge.

Behretan tread lightly. *Fáhganid* controlled too much. Four armed officers stood at the back of the room, ready to tackle plaintiffs if things got out of hand. Tokh sat when given permission, but Zheníhda, her face bruised, her eye blackened, her lip scabbed and swollen, preferred to stand beside him, far away from Behretan. She wore a sheer pink veil to hide behind, but Tokh made her lift it in the office.

The Justice listened to Tokh's story. He looked over the medical report. He looked over the three witness reports that had come in.

"I will see the wounds," said the *fáhganid*. Zheníhda approached the desk, while Tokh pointed out her injuries. The Justice had him lift Zheníhda's skirt and show the bruises on her thighs and the hideous marks on her backside.

"She can't bear to sit because of the pain," Tokh explained. "By medical order, I'm not to *push* on her for five days, until she heals. Should they leave scars, I'll be reminded of his intrusion and suffer humiliation every time I bed my wife."

"Do you deny this?" the Justice asked Behretan.

"I did *push* her, yes," Behretan admitted. He was in daily uniform, not nearly as intimidating as he could have been. "I disciplined her when she tried to refuse me, but that is my privilege and right. Then this little worm thought he would pull a sword on me for doing it."

"What is it you want?" the Justice asked Tokh.

"I want an apology, for taking too much liberty with my wife. I want him to pay any fees involved with getting her tooth replaced. I want him to pay the fee for five days' consort service, as it's directly his fault I can't bed my wife. And I request justice so that no other man may have to take time to defend his wife from a predator."

"I am not a predator," Behretan said with disgust. "I was a guest, and you were ungracious hosts."

The *fáhganid* whacked his control stick on his desk, an *arghol-wood* baton half as thick as a wrist, drilled out for a lead core, the tip wrapped in strong metal. Swung right, it could break a thighbone or crush a skull in one blow, and it was almost impossible to snap it. "You were not given permission to speak!"

Dahsuhlar folded his hands around his chin hank and rested his head on them with a sigh. "Wife: speak. Did your husband order you to please your guest?"

Zheníhda's voice was soft and trembling. She kept her head bent. "Yes, Your Reverence."

"And did you let him?"

"Yes, Your Reverence. I allowed his attentions until he was content."

"Then why would he beat you?"

Zheníhda's face twisted up, but she didn't cry. "My husband told me to service him once and only once. The colonel asked for favors beyond his allowance. My husband's word is law in my home; I could not disobey him. It was then that the colonel became angry with me."

The Justice pursed his lips but gave away nothing. He sat quietly for several minutes, thinking.

"Borrowing another man's wife with permission is legal," he said at last. "It's poor manners, but it is legal. *Dihnarwharl* are supposed to show noble behavior, which Captain Tokh displayed through willingness to share his wife with a guest. *Dahneg* are supposed to be superior to them, but what I see before me is a serious lack of control and respect from a member of that caste. Yes, it is illegal for a *dihnarwharl* to refuse a *dahneg*, but a husband's word is law over that of his wife. It is agreed that the offer was set at one favor; the wife was right to hold to her husband's order, and the guest was wrong to supersede his privilege.

"Second, it is illegal to beat another man's wife, regardless of caste difference. If there was an issue, the husband should have been consulted and then the husband would discipline the wife as he saw fit. This is law, irrevocable. Colonel, you broke that law the moment

61

you left a mark on this man's wife. You owe Captain Tokh an apology for superseding your rights, harming his wife, and infringing on his ability to perform his rightful duties with her. You will incur the costs of any medical treatment needed to restore her health and her appearance to its previous form. It is not unreasonable to ask that you pay for a consort until Captain Tokh can resume activity with his wife, as you're the direct reason he cannot bed her. You will pay him that fee."

"Very well," Behretan said. He sighed as if hopelessly bored. "I'll pay him five days' consort fees and cover the medical costs. I apologize for overstepping my bounds with your wife. She pleased me so well I couldn't stop myself. There. May I return to duty now?"

"There remains the matter of justice," *fáhganid* Dahsuhlar said. "Lady Tokh, your injuries are above and beyond appropriate discipline, whether from your husband or a guest. Personally, I find it reprehensible, coming from a *dahneg* guest. I believe punishment is called for, to remind Colonel Behretan there are laws and rules of civility and that they do pertain to him, and he should think twice before borrowing and battering another man's wife. Colonel Behretan, I give you a choice: ten public lashes and the loss of one inch of your *hihvat*, or ten public lashes and the loss of one *khata* to remind you to control yourself. Please state your preference."

Behretan uncrossed his legs so fast he nearly fell forward onto the desk. "What? I'll have no such thing! No one is going to dissect me on account of an uncooperative female."

The *fáhganid* slashed a finger in the air, and two of the room guards stepped forward in a forceful clattering of boots. Zheníhda jumped between Tokh and the desk.

"Choose your punishment."

"That's not fair! I did nothing to warrant the loss of my *khatas*!"

"*Khata* it will be, then." Dahsuhlar banged his control stick on the desk to seal his word. "Guards, take him outside to the disciplinary courtyard." He signed an order, stamped it, and handed it to a guard. "Tell the discipline master ten lashes, and here is the written order. When they are done, he is to be taken to medical."

The guards seized Behretan by his shoulders while a third guard locked his hands in restraints. They guided him from the room.

"You go too far, Tokh!" he yelled over his shoulder. "I demand an appeal! No female supersedes my rights!"

"Does that satisfy you?" the Justice asked Tokh.

"Absolutely, Your Reverence," Tokh said with a bow. "You are most considerate. I have an excellent wife who in no way deserved such abuse. I fear I may have destroyed her trust, allowing her to be abused in such a way."

The *fáhganid* bowed his head. "Lady Tokh, in the eyes of the law, neither you nor your husband is at fault. My apologies for your insult. May you heal quickly and without incident. Dismissed."

The outpouring of support stunned Zheníhda. Hundreds of little caring messages filled her personal comm from friends and other wives in the building as well as dozens of women she didn't know, friends of friends of friends both *dihnarwharl* and *dahneg. Dahneg* males Tokh had never spoken to stopped him to apologize for the behavior of one of their own. Neighbor wives swooped in to take care of Kitras and make sure Zenak made it to school and back, while others made sure her apartment was spotless. Wives sent their best dinner creations, freeing Zheníhda from having to cook not just for a day or two, but a week's buffet. Zheníhda had nothing to do but lie on her stomach and rest.

Tokh didn't hire a consort but banked the money paid to him by Behretan, promising Zheníhda that when she felt better, he would take her out and she could spend half of it on herself, whatever her heart desired. The night after their meeting with the Justice, a *bhántanok* officer appeared at their door and handed Tokh a small package. It was a plain white box, closed with seal-strips, Tokh's name and address written on it by hand.

"What is it?" Zheníhda asked.

"I have no idea." Tokh slit the strips. Inside was a thick plastic bag containing a pale roundish thing half the size of Tokh's fist. A small amount of brown and yellow liquid squished inside the bag.

"What is that?" Zheníhda repeated.

Tokh poked it with a finger. "It's – No! I think – It's a *khata*! Behretan's *khata* the Justice threatened to remove. They sent it to us as part of the reparation."

Zheníhda squealed in horror. "What are we supposed to do with a *dahneg*'s *khata*?!"

"I don't know. But I'm happy that son of a *trixahg* is missing it."

Tokh stared at it the rest of the evening. He carried the bag room to room with him, and it sat on his shirt drawers while he readied for bed.

"We can't keep it, Tokh. It's going to smell."

"I know, I know. What's the biggest insult we can do to it?"

"Cook it and send it back to him, hoping he'll eat it? Smash it with a stick and wish it was still attached?"

Tokh started to shake his head, then a light went on. He gave a hoot and a cackle. "I know exactly what to do to it. We'll do it together. Take me in your mouth."

Zheníhda jumped away from him. "Tokh! How could you ask me that! My lip is – "

"*Shu!* Trust me! Ten seconds, that's all I ask. Use as much spit as you can make."

"Tokh!"

He chucked her under her chin. "*Trust me.* You will approve, I promise."

Zheníhda knelt as if he planned to behead her but she complied, even though it hurt to open her jaw. She held him as motionless on her tongue as if he'd placed his knife there instead, and jerked away the very second he allowed.

He unsealed the bag. "Now spit on it." Zheníhda eyed him as if he were crazy. "Spit!"

She couldn't bear to look in the bag, but scrunched her eyes and spit as much as she could.

Tokh smiled at her. "What's the one thing he wanted? Why did he hurt you?"

"A lip job?"

He chucked her chin again. "Precisely. And that is what we'll give him. Your coveted spit from the end of my *hihvat*, my fluid, and his *khata*. We'll mix them in the bag and I'll take it outside to the gardens and bury it in the dirt. It will fester for all eternity, bathed in *my* lip job. All you need is to give me a handshake, so we can add my fluid to the bag."

Zheníhda broke into a huge grin, showing off the new gap in her teeth, even though it pulled sharply on her split lip and squeezed the swelling by her eye. "You're brilliant, my husband! With pleasure! That will truly be justice."

64

The medical staff warned Tokh that females could get jittery after a sharing or an assault, especially the first one, and he should treat her gently for the first month and not be excessive in his demands. He remembered Zheníhda in her early days, jumping every time he so much as touched her shoulder. The details were foggy in time, but he seemed to remember it taking years to stop. He didn't have patience for that anymore, and he didn't look forward to it. It surprised him, then, when they lay in bed and her hand slid down to caress his rump.

"*Push* me, Tokh. Please," she whispered.

"I'm supposed to let you rest for five days. It's only been three."

She nuzzled his throat with her healing lips. "I don't care if it hurts. I want you to *push* me. From the front. I want to see your face. I want to know it's you inside me."

Tokh kissed her in return. "If that's what you wish." He poured them both a glass of *flehdan*, hoping it would dull some of her pain, and rubbed an extra layer of anesthetic onto her aching buttocks. He made sure she was well on her way to her joy before climbing onto her, but he could see the discomfort in her eyes. Grabbing her tight, he gave a mighty roll and switched places, without ever uncoupling. Zheníhda didn't care for sitting on him, she claimed she felt like a *trixahg* on display, but it took the pressure off her wounds. A shy little smile broke her face, and she moved to please him on her own.

He didn't stop until she writhed with joy.

Most officers didn't make Major until they were close to forty. Just shy of his thirtieth naming-day, *dihnarwharl* Captain Two Tokh was promoted to *dihnarwharl* Major One Tokh. Tokh was the youngest major on the base, commanding men who were older and had waited longer for promotion and bore him instant resentment. If he were careful, Tokh could make colonel by forty or so, perhaps even general before he retired.

He took the thought back. If battle didn't do him in, he wouldn't retire *until* he made general. It was his own pact with himself, and one he was determined to keep. A general! The idea amused him the rest of the day.

General Pohrunet kept his promise, too. At the first opportunity he sent Tokh on the top-secret mission to a top-secret place to observe the top-secret method of memory investigational engineering. Tokh had read every non-classified article on the subject and a handful of low-clearance ones he'd been allowed to access. Everything he read implied it was the same procedure used to treat his combat sickness years ago, and indeed the early applications and development had been for medical purposes. The military, however, had seized on the technology and twisted it for their own use.

An unmarked aircraft picked up three officers from the base, flew elsewhere to pick up four more officers, then flew into the night to land somewhere under the cover of darkness in an unmarked hangar, next to a second anonymous aircraft. A military transport took them to a building, where they were searched, processed, their security clearances double-checked, and then sworn to secrecy. Tokh had the lowest rank of anyone in the group.

A *dihnarwharl* colonel looked down his nose at Tokh as they waited for admittance to a lift. "Aren't you a little young to be a major?"

Tokh tipped his head and returned the condescending stare. "Aren't you a little young to be questioning General Pohrunet? Colonel One Ghandon sor Tran of Bixighar Space Academy. Age forty-four. You failed in your bid to become director of the school by a vote of thirteen to six and had to settle for Director of Education. You teach exopsychology but your second wife's brother is a liaison with Special Services, so I presume that's why you're here." Tokh gave the colonel an oily smile. "I like to know who I'm working with." It didn't matter he'd just done the research on the flight in. He was prepared when needed. That's what intelligence was about.

The colonel's face went tan, and the group became very quiet. At last the colonel lifted his chin high. "Common knowledge. You do your research, Major. I'll grant you that. My compliments to General Pohrunet." The lift arrived and they were ushered in. No one spoke to Tokh again, but they all looked at his ID tag and remembered his name.

He couldn't discuss it with Zheníhda – the only one he could discuss it with was Pohrunet – but he wanted to. "I can honestly say I have no idea where we were, but it was a two hour flight."

"But you work intelligence," she said. "Surely you can find out."

"Possibly, but the security level is so high they could probably trace me if I so much as entered a word about it. Don't think they won't be watching my communications for a while. And I'm not sure I want to know. Some things are best left alone, Nihda."

The light went out from his face, and his eyes were lost in memory. "I can't tell you what I saw, but let's just agree it was unsettling. Thank the Emperor there's allegedly only one experimental military facility in existence. When it works, it's wondrous, amazing. They tried it on one of us as volunteer, and it was simple and painless and easy. Then they brought in an actual enemy prisoner who didn't want to be there and didn't want to give up correct information. What he seemed to go through – it wasn't pleasant to watch, even though it didn't leave a mark. It has serious potential, but it needs much refinement."

Zheníhda's eyes were wide. "What happened to the prisoner? Did they free him when they were done, or did they execute him?"

"He burst an artery inside his head, which they didn't know until he began to bleed from his nose and ears. Then he began to seize and they couldn't stop it, and he died. I know it wasn't planned, but it still felt as if they'd executed a man for our benefit. It wasn't pleasant."

Zheníhda hugged him from behind as he sat at the table. "Then come and focus your thoughts on something more pleasant."

Tokh sighed and sipped at his drink. "I will, Nihda. When I'm ready."

Tokh shipped out for a training class at another facility, returning home for two days every two weeks, leaving Zheníhda home with two growing boys. His next assignment put him on the road following a special project. He was in one region one day, a different continent the next. Zheníhda had no idea what he did, only that it pleased his superiors. He might have been ferrying documents, he might have been assassinating people. He couldn't tell her, so she didn't ask.

"I'm instructed to learn things," he explained with a shrug. "I go where I'm sent, learn what I'm told to learn, and then report the information back to the proper person. That's my job, in truth. Sometimes it's not easy to get the information and I must track many things and speak to many people to uncover it. Sometimes it's not in Emperor's Tongue and I must either translate it myself or find someone reliable who can. Sometimes I must research the information, word by word. I might listen in to communications, hoping for leads. Other times I command officers who do the work for me. Sometimes it's interesting, but much of the time it means waiting for the right person or the right opportunity, and sometimes that takes days. I don't like sitting still."

When Zenak turned twelve, Tokh enrolled him at Nar Rhede Military Academy. Yes, they were stationed at Dahn Bohr, which had its own well-respected academy, but Nar Rhede was where Tokh went. It was the school he knew and loved, and thus his sons would learn to love it, too. It was in his home town, and they would spend three days visiting with his parents.

It had been fourteen years since Zheníhda had spent her first married months living with her in-laws. She didn't like them then, and nothing had changed during their infrequent visits. The air crackled when Filuhr and Zheníhda were in the same room. Galisse, Tokh's other-mother, was pleasant and welcoming, forgetting any past issues with Zheníhda. Talekh usurped his smallsons' time, letting them play with his instruments and grilling them on their knowledge of physics.

Kitras came with them on the first tour of the school, planting seeds of the future in his head. Nar Rhede ranked high as an under-academy, even higher as a full military academy. The grounds were breathtaking, the academics rigorous, the training superb. The quality of the food depended on one's caste: *rhibani* would find it superb and remember it fondly; *dahneg* would find it bearable but never cease grumbling. Nar Rhede produced only *bhántim* officers of command rank; no one lower than the most exemplary *rhibani* was allowed.

"Father, what if I don't want to be a soldier?" Zenak said. He wasn't crying, but his face had a trapped look to it.

Tokh's eye was cold, but he didn't bark back. "There are those who graduate and choose to go on to a civilian career. Not many, but some. Even if you were to choose that path, graduating from a military school will boost you higher on the employment list, higher on the housing list. It will never hurt you, and always help. You'll still call upon your classmates as brothers, should you ever need favors. They'll teach you everything you need to know in life, any career you want to choose. It's my choice to put you here; what you do with yourself is your choice, six years from now."

Zenak kept his eyes downward. "Yes, sir."

On the third day Zheníhda left her first-born son in the hands of the military, his back straight, his still-bare chin high as he had been taught. His eyes held a look of terror, but he didn't make a scene as he bid them goodbye, not to return home for five full months. Zheníhda wore a veil in public, fastened to the back of her head. Unless she felt uncomfortable in a situation, she left it hanging down her back. On their flight home, she flipped it over her face, so Tokh and Kitras wouldn't see her cry.

Not a month passed before Tokh was called into General Poruhnet's office late in the afternoon.

"Congratulations," Poruhnet told him. "I just received the paperwork. Your name is on the list. Tomorrow you're being promoted to Major Two at ceremonies. The Emperor has a strange notion that wives should watch their husbands receive honor, so they are making a reviewing area for the wives. You may bring yours if you wish."

Tokh's eyebrow rose. He was six months short of thirty-five; he didn't expect even the possibility of promotion for another year at the earliest. He bowed low and held it for a count of three. "I'm most honored, General. This is a complete surprise."

"I knew your name was being considered," Poruhnet admitted, "but I didn't expect to see it until next round." He clapped a hand on Tokh's shoulder. "I told you your skills would attract attention. Slow down, now. I don't want to lose you."

"Thank you, General."

Tokh received his new rank with two dozen officers all receiving honors. Zheníhda watched the ceremony from a fenced off area with a handful of wives – it resembled a cage more than anything else, Tokh's name pinned to her dress on a small card so he could "find" her and "claim" her afterwards, as if he couldn't recognize her and she weren't capable of speech. He took her to the officer's commissary for lunch, returned her home wearing his shining new rank insignia, and went back to the base.

Immediately he was called into a meeting with General Poruhnet; General Marmot, a level-four general; and two officials. Tokh was used to being at meetings with high-level staff, but the way General Marmot ordered him to sit made him nervous, as if something had been decided before he entered the room and he was merely being informed.

Of course he was right.

To ease the news, Tokh came home with an armload of purple flowers. "I'm shipping out two hours before sunrise," he informed her. "I've been traded. I'll now be part of General Marmot's team, out of Rhagadan."

"Rhagadan? Where is that?" Zheníhda asked. "Is that closer to Zenak, or farther away?"

"Across the ocean, in Holboth. That doesn't matter. If he needs family, my parents are there in town. He'd fly home to us anyway for his breaks. Now he'll fly in another direction. I'll be gone three days, maybe four, and I'll find us housing while I'm there. We'll leave in six days."

Zheníhda's hands moved in a hundred directions, flustered and helpless. "Can't they ever promote you without moving you about? What about schools for Kitras? We won't speak the local dialects. What if nothing is in Emperor's Tongue? What if the schools are bad?"

Tokh played with numbers in his head. "Major Two is one below colonel. If it's not too much, maybe we can afford a private academy. I'll research that while I'm there. There must be other officers with sons. They'll know the best schools."

Zheníhda nodded, resigned to yet another upheaval. "Maybe we'll get lucky."

* * 11 * *

The apartment in Rhagadan was in an upscale but urban area, with towering buildings, businesses, and street and air traffic noise. It was modern and multi-lingual; with a high military presence, residents came from all over Kerasím, and to Zheníhda's relief everything was in the universal Emperor's Tongue. Their building was surrounded by a high brick wall, enclosing a garden area with flowers, trees, and tables for the wives to gather at and watch their children play. There was no army flight field in the middle of the city, just a large office tower with air traffic access from the roof; half the aircraft flying by their apartment landed there. Tokh found them a four-room corner apartment, filled with afternoon light. Little brown balconies overlooked the gardens, and Zheníhda learned fast what time the wives gathered on them to exchange gossip. In afternoons children's shouts could be heard calling each other to games. Tokh found a private academy for Kitras, now seven. Only time would tell about the weather; it rained seventeen days of their first thirty there.

General Marmot didn't hesitate, dropping Tokh headfirst into a new project, then shipping him out after just six weeks' training.

Zheníhda kept a brave face while she packed his uniforms, but she couldn't keep the waver out of her voice. "How long will you be gone this time?"

"At minimum, a number of months. I'll probably be silent during that time. I would hope General Marmot will keep you updated. I'll try to remember to ask."

Zheníhda's head snapped around. "You're not going into another war zone, are you? Tokh! You almost lost your leg last time!"

"No, no war zone. I can't give you details." He stopped her packing and hugged her. He whispered faintly into her ear, *I'm crossing the treaty border. No long-range communications allowed.* He worked in Intelligence; he knew that sometimes living quarters were bugged, to make sure officers could be trusted. He didn't have sniffing equipment to check, but he was the new man on crew. He had yet to prove himself to General Marmot.

"No! Tokh, no! I don't want you far away. Please! You just got here. There's nothing else they can assign you?" *Union?* she mouthed silently, and he nodded. Her eyes grew large as moons.

"I was traded because they thought I was best for this job. I'm commander now; it's not as risky."

"Oh no!" Zheníhda sneered. "Last time your major was cut in half by weaponry, if I recall. Silly me."

"That was a war; this isn't. I'm not going into a combat area, and if I did, I know not to stand up from a safety hole, so no worries, yes?"

"You have sons that need a whole father! What are they supposed to do if you don't return? No, Tokh! It's not all right with me!" She stalked out outside onto the balcony, slamming the door behind her.

Tokh counted to five, then followed her. He had to admit, she may not have been educated, but Zheníhda wasn't a stupid wife. She remembered things he told her. A female snit and sulk would never be questioned, real or pretend.

She grabbed him on the balcony and hung on. Yes, there were ears everywhere, but traffic noise would cover whispers. "Union territory? They're the worst enemy! Tokh, you know what will happen if they catch you!"

He kissed her ear. "I speak the Union tongue, Nihda. I'm certified to level three. That means I need to be out there. It will be safe. I'll message you as often as I'm allowed, but don't expect it. Don't worry."

Zheníhda wouldn't let go. "I never used to, but I'm not young anymore, Tokh. What will happen to me if you're captured or killed? Zenak isn't old enough to speak for me. I don't want to wind up in an auction house."

"I've never thought about it before." Tokh had never considered asking a friend to take Zheníhda as a second-wife should he die in battle. It would be difficult for her, sleeping with a stranger, but she would adjust. Zenak could be the legal Lord of the house, with custody of his mother, but he had to be fourteen first. At worst case, Zenak would be left with Nar Rhede as his home, Kitras would go his parents, or if they refused, one of Tokh's brothers, and possibly be admitted to Nar Rhede at ten. Zheníhda, without other arrangements, with no male to take responsibility, could wind up at a consort auction, without the looks or youth to put her in demand. She might luck out as servant to a *dahneg* or *fáhganid* woman, or her parents might take her back as a servant to them in their old age, but Nihda would never survive the direct sex trade. She wouldn't survive the first day.

"I'll make some sort of arrangement before I go," he promised. "I'll name a brother as regent of my estate until Zenak's ready. I'll inquire with the Widow's Society as well. They might be able to take you for the interim. Have no fear. I'll start by simply not being killed."

* * *

Tokh had done a number of dangerous missions over the years. When he was young, life was an adventure, and he and his troop mates believed they were invincible. The battle of Kanok Nevas changed that, scarring him both physically and mentally. His missions since had dealt with covert assignments, seeking out people and information. The people he sought were often lower in caste, yes, but neither did they respect caste, hard-core criminals wanted by several factions of His Majesty's government. Had they realized Tokh was there to gather information and bring them to justice, they would have killed him on the spot and not thought twice.

General Marmot brought the danger up several levels. Two week's spaceflight from Keranihn, Tokh found himself and a small crew darting about some of the border worlds, star systems whose worlds gave allegiance to neither the Union nor the Coalition. They were neutral territory; both Union and Coalition were welcome, but enough bad blood flowed both ways that visiting such places was risky. No one cared who died.

Skadi was a wet town; the ground swampy, the people dirty and mostly lawless, and buildings were raised up on pylons and pillars to keep the floors from rotting. Buildings were connected by swinging sidewalks of chain and wood. Days that didn't rain left the city shrouded in mist and weak sunlight, and fast-growing vines covered anything that stood still – including the unfortunate drinker who collapsed in the mud.

Tokh sat with Binma, who had set up the deal. Binma was from Gha Robbek; with his shaved head tattoed with three red lines and a curved piercing sticking out from under the skin of his forehead like silver horns – a deadly weapon when used to smash people in a fight – he didn't look like a common Kerasi. Tokh wore civilian clothing, worn and dirty as a *soláhrin*'s. His hair hung to his shoulders, thick and oily, and he had shaved off his precious chin-hank for the glory of the Emperor.

"Just transportation," Binma said to the Pyridian pilot before them. He wasn't whispering, but his voice was soft enough that even Tokh had to pay attention to hear all his words. Binma spoke Union as well as Tokh, with so little accent he could have been from twenty different worlds. "Have you heard of Lillut Maar, on Kye? Rumor has it that blasting has uncovered a deposit of *rali tu* stones. They're lying around in the slag, and anyone can hunt for them. One good day and you can make enough money to last ten years of luxury. We need a lift to Kye."

The pilot was an ugly brute, easily the same weight as Tokh and Binma together, a great green boil visible under the folds of his neck every time he lifted his head. "Kye's a Union world. Hire a Union ship."

Binma rolled his eyes. "Union wants cash. If we had cash, we wouldn't need to get to Lillut Maar. We need someone willing to work on trade."

The pilot glared at them with a stone face. "You haven't got anything worth my time."

"I'll bet we do," Binma said. He gestured to Tokh with his chin.

Tokh wore baggy cargo pants. He pulled a cloth-wrapped object from a leg pocket and handed it over. "We can offer three bottles now, and three when we reach ground on Kye."

The pilot unwrapped the flat bottle, looked at the label, then dropped it below the level of the table before anyone else could see it. "Is this what I think it is?"

Tokh nodded. "Kerasi pepper rum. One full case. Six measures will kill a human. You can get ten thousand for each bottle, easy. That should pay our fare ten times over."

The cold eye returned. "If you have this, why are you going to Kye?"

Binma stared back with annoyance. "Because we can clear that much in a day just sifting rocks! I know someone who was there; he told me all about it. He found one stone – just one – and a company bought it off him for thirty thousand. One stone! I saw his cash! And he didn't have to kill anyone to get it. After a month, we'll never have to work again."

"No one has six bottles of this stuff, not even Kerasi," the pilot said, though he kept the bottle clamped between his rubbery thighs. "Even they can't afford that. If you killed a Kerasi to get it, prove it. Throw something Kerasi in to sweeten the deal. The shit's illegal inside the Union. I sell it, I might get pinched. I don't sell it, I'm out money. I sell it all, I got nothing but cash. I want a Kerasi memento to prove it."

Tokh and Binma exchanged glances, Binma looking encouraging and Tokh looking increasingly irate, a well-rehearsed act.

"Go on," Binma said. "Give it to him."

"You said it was mine! That was the deal," Tokh argued. "You can't take it back now."

"You want to get to Kye or not? *Money*," Binma emphasized. "Tons of it, just lying there. You can buy a new one. You can buy three and eat with them."

"It's not the same! I got this one hard and fair!"

Binma continued to stare until Tokh gave a petulant glare and reached into another pocket. He placed a Kerasi Army knife, standard issue, on the table.

The pilot whistled, turning it over in his hands. He studied the markings, recognizing them even if he couldn't read them. The nicks in the blade said it was real, not just a cheap copy bought in a shop. The dried blood on the handle made it better.

"It belonged to the owner of the case," Binma said.

The pilot eyed the knife longingly. "Okay," he said. "The case and the blade for transport to Kye. Deal."

"Excellent," Binma said, and shook the pilot's hand. "When will we leave?"

Tokh grabbed the knife. "This is still mine until we arrive."

Six, seven, eight planets. Tokh and his crew slunk in and out of Union territory to find sympathizers, contacts, and shadowmen willing to trade favors and information for a touch of illegal spirits and "war" souvenirs. Information and names were turned over to deeper contacts to make sure promises were kept. Tokh didn't question; it wasn't his job to question. He spoke Union, he knew how to make people talk and bend to his will, and this was his mission. All he cared was that he hadn't been outed as a Kerasi behind enemy lines, and that his success pleased his superiors.

* * *

Zheníhda received exactly three messages from Tokh:
I'm alive and well and wish you could be here.
So far I am successful and well and missing you very much.
I hope it won't be much longer. I haven't seen a female in so long, I hope you'll forgive me when I get home.
Zheníhda received four identical voice messages from General Marmot, the most formal and least informative of any general she'd received information from:
Major Tokh continues to perform his duties in good health, and will be routed home at the first possible opportunity.
Each one brought her a moment's relief: he was alive and well, but still out there, somewhere, doing something, but not coming home yet.
Then, eleven agonizing months in, came the one she'd been waiting for:
Major Two Tokh dar-Giláhn has completed his mission and will return to Rhagadan base for four weeks' leave one week from today.
How a single week could cause more anxiety and last longer than eleven months Zheníhda would never understand.

She waited for him in a room with a handful of other Waiting Wives. He walked in as if he knew exactly in which spot she'd be standing, lifted her off the ground, and held her to him without saying a word. Zheníhda had resolved days before that she would be the perfect wife and not make a female scene when she saw him. The smell of him, the pressure of his touch, to hold him after so long was too much, and she cried on his shoulder. He held her for several minutes, never speaking, and carried her out of the room without putting her down until they reached the street.
They grabbed a public transportation *eel* bus for the eight blocks home, the conversation light as they readjusted to each other. As they entered their apartment, Tokh shut the door, dropped his bags where he stood, and attacked Zheníhda, dragging her to the other

room, his mouth on her throat, as she hung from his neck with her arms. He *pushed* her over the side of the bed twice without stopping, both of them still fully clothed.

He dropped next to her on the bed, his *hihvat* framed by the open flaps of his trousers; she squirmed into his arms. "*Khatas* to the Emperor, Zheníhda! I missed you."

She wiggled her nose up under his chin to kiss him. His chin hank was short, just an inch or so long, too short to pinch together let alone decorate, and she teased the bristly ends with her fingers. "I missed you, too." They lost half their clothes to the next two rounds.

He calmed down after that, taking in all the little details of the children he'd missed, of weather and the city and his family while she made him lunch. He told her the generic bits he was allowed to speak of.

"It wasn't combat, but because of the risk I'm paid the same rate as combat. That's like an extra half-year's pay I tucked away. And I earn promotion credits at an accelerated rate, too. One more assignment like that and I'll make colonel in three years."

"Don't rush it, Tokh," she said. "They'll just send you off somewhere else."

He pulled her over until she sat on his lap. "Possibly. But the higher up, the more removed from combat I am, so there's less risk."

"Maybe, but I liked it better when you came home at night."

"I'll make you a deal," Tokh said. Her hair was still down, and he ran his fingers through it. "I have three levels to go, and I'm already well on my way to colonel. If I keep this pace, keep taking the tough assignments, I can make general in under ten years. General, Zheníhda! Do you realize the prestige general buys? Do you realize the pay scale of even a level-one general? I can arrange my own schedules, move us anywhere you want, sleep home every night if you wish. And I'll make you a promise: when I make general, I will buy you a house."

Zheníhda gave him a disbelieving frown. "A house? How will we ever afford a house? Houses are for the upper castes, Tokh. I'd be thrilled with a new-construction apartment, maybe one with five or even six rooms. One of the *dahneg* wives has a room just to eat in, nothing but the table and chairs and a separate cabinet to keep the glassware and spirits and extra dishes in. It makes the other rooms so spacious."

78

"No, I mean a free-standing house. We are *dihnarwharl*, and high *dihnarwharl* are upper caste. Combine that with general and I will have a house so that everyone will know we belong to the upper castes, even if it takes every last *dakra* I have."

A sparkle lit Zheníhda's eyes. "Oh, Tokh! I've never even been inside a free-standing house. It's too much to think of. Like living inside that mystery story on the ComNet, *Inside Connections*. It's about a *fáhganid* family that's always undercutting each other with schemes and conspiracies. The house they live in is breathtaking. Like the hotels we've stayed at, but just for them. And the servants! Oh Tokh! If we get a house, can we hire a *ghinadín* servant as well? It wouldn't look right if another wife came to visit and I was scrubbing a floor."

Tokh bowed his head and waved a hand toward her. "If I have enough prestige to own a house, I will not allow my wife to wash the floors. You may have a servant for that. But it's still ten years off, so don't go hiring her yet."

Zheníhda laughed and hugged him again. It was nice to play such cloud-games. Tokh wasn't prone to fantasies like that. The chances of it happening were zero, but she would be quite happy with a large, sunny five-room apartment in a good upper-caste neighborhood. "Not yet. But I'll practice it in my head."

* * 12 * *

Tokh was thirty-eight when he made Colonel One, young enough to make quite a few officers jealous. On average, no one expected colonel until fifty. Colonel was a huge step, a frightening step. As a major, he was a high-level soldier, overseeing captains and lieutenants and making sure things ran smoothly, but he reported back to colonels for every decision he made. Now, as Colonel, he had to plan with care. He didn't send men into danger because he was told to, he sent them to die because he himself needed them to take that risk. If they died it was his fault, not someone else's, and he would answer for it. Now it was his responsibility to discipline his men as he saw fit, not just carry out someone else's orders. As Colonel he was still at the beck and call of the generals above him, but more in the way of a business leader answering to an investor.

Here are my men: make them a success, and don't make me look bad while I sit back here and play Tabs with the other generals.

As Colonel, Tokh was allowed to choose his own commanders, his own permanent team of men that he saw promise in, advisors who would make strong decisions, men Tokh could rely on to keep troops trained and in order, men who would succeed far more often than fail. Colonel also meant he was allowed deeper into the politics that ran Kerasím, deeper into the levels of classified information that hung like fog among the intelligence officers. Half his time was spent in meetings and half among the men in his command wherever they were located, making frequent but short trips around the globe. He remained under General Marmot's command, but other generals came sniffing at him after meetings.

"I'll be watching the promotion lists," said several of them. "The day you make Colonel Two, I'll be calling you."

Having generals fighting over you was a good sign that you were well-respected, but it came with a cost Tokh was aware of but didn't yet understand. Generals commanded colonels, but upper generals commanded lesser generals. There were six levels to general: sixes were appointed by the Emperor and oversaw the branches of forces, and fives were so rare and usually so old it was a rank of respect; they were usually unfit to command anything more than their dinner. Four was about as high as any general hoped for. Emperor Nághtas himself was considered the head of the army, Grand Leader of the Armies of Kerasím, one of his many titles.

Once someone hit the level of general, he sometimes wound up not with another general giving him commands, but a *bhísroti* sponsor, someone from somewhere high in the government, someone from the Emperor's many cabinets exerting influence. Whether the commands or suggestions came from a *fáhganid* general who was fed orders from a *bhísroti*, or the orders came direct, playing the game at the level of general meant touching on palace politics. Tokh knew he was being observed and tested for the upper levels of Kerasi politics, maybe even as an assistant to the imperial cabinet, but whose politics and whose vision he would follow he had no idea. He'd sworn loyalty to the Emperor at every promotion; how was he supposed to know which of the cronies was the most loyal?

Tokh's schedule let him sleep at home more frequently, allowing him to be an active father to Kitras. Tokh knew it was a deliberate move, whether on Marmot's part or those above, to slow him down. Too many important missions and he would move up too fast. He'd already skipped one rank and sped his way through two others. No one wanted a forty-year old general in their midst. They were working him, training him, but he really wanted to be out there practicing what he was learning. Colonel One was a weeding position; officers were tried in various places, with various difficulties of tasks. Those that failed stayed in low positions, taking years, if not decades, to accumulate enough points to gain rank. Those that cleaned up the messes moved up faster. Tokh knew he was a contender for something, but he didn't know what. He couldn't see the puppeteers in the shadows, and that annoyed him.

He'd been a colonel all of four months when he was ordered to Keranihn, the capital city of all Kerasím, where the Emperor's palace sat, and all the top-caste officials who made the government run. Keranihn was the heart of Kerasím, a true world capital, nine million people spread out like a pockmark at the end of a 300-mile long ocean sound, a city to be proud of. The Emperor had declared cities should reflect the best of everything Kerasi, the most modern developments, the most artistic endeavors; artwork and colors and beautification were highly encouraged, and annual contests were held for most decorative buildings, most improved neighborhoods, most beautiful gardens. Modern towers of bright white stone, glass, and metal made the skyline look like an outdoor art museum, while smaller buildings relied heavily on bright colors and rich folk-art details. Kerasím dealt with several other planetary systems – none of them Union – and Nághtas insisted his planet should mesmerize foreign dignitaries with its beauty.

Or else.

Tokh was given almost no information – standard procedure, just where he was staying and who to report to when. Gone were the days when housing was a cot in a barrack with other low-rank officers who were traveling place to place. Now he warranted a tiny but private cell of a room, with toilet and shower facilities down the hall. The only difference between the guest quarters and a detention cell was a bar across the outside of the door, but he found no traces of old hardware nor evidence of wiring for electronic locks, and he rested with confidence.

Until he reported to the office.

"This way, Colonel," said a *nhásarwharl* captain, a high rank and caste for a mere secretary. He escorted Tokh to an unmarked door. The captain knocked once, then opened the door without looking into the room. "You may enter."

Tokh was glad he'd used the lavatory beforehand; his innards froze solid, and his *khatas* squeezed tight in panic. Three *bhísroti* in capes, two *fáhganid* generals in ornate red uniforms, and a *dahneg* general sat at a long table. It wasn't so much a meeting as an execution squad. A seventh figure sat to the side of the room, with no military identification at all. The clothing said *bhísroti*, but the figure wore a sheer black veil like a female, clouding his identity. The figure was too trim to be the Emperor, the hands too young, the well-groomed fingers indented from removed rings that might have given identity, so who the glory was he?

Tokh bowed low and held it for a count of five. "Colonel One Tokh, reporting as requested."

The *dahneg* general in the center pointed to the empty chair before the table. "Please be seated, Colonel." He introduced himself but not the others, least of all the mystery figure under the veil. Tokh would swear that the eldest *bhísroti* was a brother to the Emperor, and on the inner council. He would try to match the face on the computer if he left the room alive. Tokh sat as bid.

"Colonel Tokh dar-Giláhn, you have come to our attention as being an officer of strong capability and exemplary record. You have a high security clearance and carried out numerous classified duties. What is your current expectation of your term of duty?"

Tokh tipped his head. The statement made no sense. "Please clarify."

"What are your goals for service five, ten, twenty years from now."

"To serve the Emperor to the best of my ability, as I have sworn. I go where I'm sent and I do what I'm commanded. In time, it is my goal to achieve the rank of general before I retire."

"You have no specific placements, assignments, or locations in mind? No long-range political goals?"

"Not at this time. I go where I'm sent."

"What is your opinion on females, Colonel?" drawled a *fáhganid*. He wasn't as sniffy as some *fáhganid* tended to be, but his words were brittle and accusatory.

"That would depend on what I'm required to do with them." Perhaps humor was too much for the situation, but it cut his anxiety a notch. Most of the table laughed lightly.

"When was the last time you disciplined your wife?"

"Define 'discipline.'"

"Beat, struck, hit, punished, humiliated, or used other forms of corporal punishment to control her."

Tokh shook his head. "I have never disciplined my wife in such a manner. I don't recall ever striking her. If I did, it was not more than once, and many years ago."

"Do you value your wife's advice? Do you seek out her opinions, listen to them, allow her to make choices of her own free will without your approval first?"

Tokh had to think a moment. "Yes. There's little I can ask her opinion on, as I can't discuss my duties due to the sensitive nature of my work. But as for personal decisions, situations regarding my sons, our home, or such, I do consider her opinion before making my choices. When I'm gone, she must make those choices on her own."

"Would you ever take orders from your wife? If she told you to go to a store and purchase a tart for dessert, would you do it?"

Tokh raised his hands, not understanding the question. Was this because of something he said? Was his apartment truly spy-bugged? Was something misinterpreted? Which side was he supposed to be on?

"Possibly? I wouldn't consider that an order, but a request. A wife does not order a husband, but a wife can make a request. If I felt like a walk, I might do it."

"What about from another female? If a female ordered you to call for assistance, or ordered you to discipline your child for a minor crime, would you follow their order?"

"Again, it would depend on the situation. I don't consider a call for assistance an order, nor a request to discipline my son if he has committed a crime. I would do that with or without a request."

"Colonel, do you feel females are capable of higher functioning within society? That they are capable of performing tasks alongside males, in a similar manner? That they can be educated to a useful capability? Do you feel they are capable of commanding others?"

"I know they're capable of commanding each other. And should I ever have a house servant, I know my wife is quite capable of ordering that servant around. I know for fact that females in some of the agrarian regions perform harvesting labors alongside male counterparts, to the point of navigating machinery and vehicles. In my own case, my wife is able to keep my accounts with reasonable accuracy with the aid of her helper program, despite a very low level of academic education. If she'd received more than two years' learning, I'm certain she'd be even better at it."

"What is your opinion on predatory males?" said the *dahneg* general. "Do you feel yourself capable of controlling yourself around females, or do you feel that every female should bend for you? When was the last time you pulled a female from the street for your pleasure? Do you share your wife among your friends, or make demands on the wives of friends?"

"No, General, I do not. I was forced by caste to share my wife once, a situation in which my trust was betrayed. I then pursued legal action in the name of my wife and justice was served. I find males who cannot control themselves near females to be poor officers whose greater loyalty lies with their loins, not their oaths of service. I have never stopped a female on the street for favors nor borrowed another's wife."

"Have you disciplined your men for unwanted acts against females?"

"I have not been colonel long enough for that situation to occur."

"Your service record states you spent more than a year within Union territory."

"I spent more than a year on the border, with some of that time behind enemy lines, yes."

"And you speak the Union tongue?"

"I'm certified at level three."

The second *fáhganid* scanned down the lap pad before him. His chin hank was thick and twice as long as regulation allowed. It was braided and speckled with tiny gold beads, making it sparkle when the light caught it as he spoke. "Colonel, by your training record, you have some familiarity with the concept of memory investigation technologies. If the result was admission into a new, extremely classified program being designed by His Royal Majesty Emperor Nághtas and meant working directly under his orders, would you be willing to undergo an investigation on yourself to prove the truth of your words here today?"

Tokh's heart missed three beats in a row, and he had to force his lungs to inflate to make it start again. His lips twitched in a submissive grin, and he bowed his head to the panel. "You place me in a most difficult position, General. My words are truth and won't change, nor can my loyalty be shifted no matter what prize is offered. But in my experience, memory investigation led to a very torturous, gruesome death of a prisoner whose crime I was not even informed of. If the Emperor wishes my life I will gladly comply, but ask that you take my head cleanly and properly instead."

The panel erupted in a flutter of uneasy shifting and shuffling, save the veiled observer in the corner, who remained motionless as a mannequin. A *bhísroti* spoke. "No one wishes your head, Colonel, nor your death. Low-level investigations have proven remarkably safe and effective in cooperative subjects. We are dealing with an ultra-high-security project of the Emperor's, one that will take many years to put in place and may have galactic reach, and we need to be absolutely certain we choose the proper candidates for His Majesty to depend on. You may leave now with no repercussions to your name or service, return to your duties, or you can proceed further here. The choice is yours."

Tokh hesitated only a second. The bait was too strong. It couldn't have been personal guards; the Emperor's guards were always *fáhganid*. Supervisor of palace security? Personal interpreters from the Emperor to the Union? Zheníhda's feet would never touch the ground, living in Keranihn among the ruling castes. "May I request special dispensations for my wife and son if something was to go wrong during the scan?"

The panel glanced at each other. A *bhísroti* said, "Yes, I think that would be acceptable."

Tokh spread his hands before him. "Then let us continue."

Tokh couldn't remember the last time he was ever so nervous. He'd seen horrific battles, men tortured, mangled bodies, been through the disorienting black of deep space, been behind enemy lines where one wrong move could have resulted in death, parachuted from aircraft, been caught alone once as a cadet and made to bend, but this time he knew what evil he faced, and even the glory of the Emperor couldn't put speed into his movements. Because it was voluntary, Tokh knew the risk was low. He'd seen that before, too, but everything depended on the hands of the technician at the controls.

A *bhísroti* accompanied him to a sub-basement. He, a *dihnarwharl*, with a *bhísroti* guard! The technician explained the procedure with each step, calm and professional, but it didn't stem the feeling of panic as Tokh was strapped down into the machinery before the *bhísroti*. A dose of tranquilizer eased the terror, but made him feel as if he were floating. Hair-thin pins were placed into his scalp, and a strange humming noise seemed to throb inside his skull, just beyond his hearing. If anything, it made the inside of his ears itch, but he couldn't scratch. After a half-hour of set-up, the *bhísroti* began to question him again, with more questions and in greater depth, not just about his opinions of females but his political ties and his loyalty to the Emperor and what he'd done inside the Union. Some of the questions were asked three times; the intensity of the machinery must have been increased, for more and more Tokh felt as if something were squeezing his head and his hair was standing on end, but his answers didn't change. Truth was truth.

And then it was over. The hum of the machinery died; the lights came back up. The technician removed the equipment in far less time than it took to attach it. Tokh sat up, blinking, the remnants of tranquilizer making him feel intoxicated.

The *bhisroti* nodded. "Excellent. You are indeed a man of integrity, Colonel Tokh, and very much the type of officer we're looking for. Your results will be brought before the board of inquiry for final vote, but I can tell you that you're in good standing. We're seeking perhaps fifteen to twenty men for various functions; you're only the fourth to pass our preliminaries. Please don't leave the city until you've been contacted further."

"May I ask one question, Grand Revered Lord?"

"Speak."

The question wouldn't stop nagging the back of Tokh's head. "Who is the man under the veil?"

"If you're chosen, you'll know his face well. Dismissed."

Tokh returned to his room and slept off the tranquilizer for a few hours. He called Zheníhda to tell her he was well and heading to dinner. He walked about the city for a bit, admiring its stunning beauty. Keranihn was the cultural center of the planet; nowhere else was there such a concentration of money itching to be spent on the latest must-have. No street vendors were in sight, no tradesmen shouting for attention as there were in the lesser cities; everything was orderly and controlled in private shops. A window draped in luxurious satins and pillows like opulent bedclothes caught his eye. The window was full of jewelry, and the poster in the window read, *She'll feel like a million* dakra *adorning your pillow, and thank you a million times*. The dangling ear fobs in the window were purple and pink opalescent *habivend* stones surrounded by a ring of glittering *nemsihl*, gorgeous to behold, and no doubt something Zheníhda would love to show off to the *dahneg* wives. Tokh entered the shop to enquire about them, but the prices were meant for *bhisroti*, not *dihnarwharl* out window-shopping. He settled on a smaller, more reasonable pair that sparkled just as brightly but had two less digits in the price.

His personal comm chirped too early in the morning. *Report to location at two past the quarter for further instructions.* Tokh rushed there as fast as possible, but stopped on the street before the building, letting his racing heart calm as much as it could before he strode in, looking confident and in charge.

This time he reported to a different office. One of the younger *bhísroti* sat behind a desk. "Congratulations, Colonel Tokh. You have passed screening and been approved by the board of inquiry. Do you still wish to be involved in this project?"

"Yes, I do," Tokh said without hesitation, though he had no idea at all what he was agreeing to. For all he knew, he'd just signed on as a political assassin.

"Then please read and sign these documents here," and they were slid across the desk to him. They were standard security clearances, promising pain, death, and dishonor at highest levels should he break secrecy. Tokh signed them with pride.

The *bhísroti* snatched them back. "The Emissary Project is a long-term assignment that won't begin until all personnel have been chosen. It's expected to take up to another year to complete the selection process. Until that time, you may continue with your regular duties under General Marmot, although you may be given additional orders on top of those. General Marmot will be informed that any additional duties will take precedence over his. You'll discuss none of this with General Marmot. The only person you may speak freely with will be your contact, who is *fáhganid* general Four Trannor Shill. Not one word can be mentioned outside of your contact. You'll receive a small stipend as retainer until the project officially starts. When it does, you will be informed where to go for further training, and to choose the men who will serve under you."

He handed Tokh a small folder of papers. The folder was blank on the outside, but the packet on the inside was stamped *Emissary Project, Authorized Access Only*, and the few pages were sealed. "You will be contacted when necessary. All information you will need is contained herein. You're free to return home and to your regular duties. The Emperor thanks you for your loyalty and service, Colonel."

Tokh bowed. "Yesterday I was informed that should I be chosen, I would learn the identity of the observer in the veil. I'm interested to know who else passed judgment on me."

The *bhísroti* didn't look pleased. "Veils exist for a reason, Colonel Tokh. It's because the person does not wish their identity known. As someone who has risen this high in intelligence, I would think you understood that."

"With due respect, Grand Revered Lord, as someone who has risen this high in intelligence, it's because I know exactly who I am dealing with at all times, who is my ally and who is my enemy, and more so, who are the enemies of my ally, and the allies of my enemy. I'm already sworn to secrecy."

The *bhísroti* nodded. "Very well. You'll learn it eventually. Learn his enemies, learn the allies of his enemies, for you'll know some of them well. His Royal Highness, Heir Apparent to his Majesty Emperor Nághtas, First Son Nadigh. Dismissed."

Tokh returned to his room to reclaim his belongings, then went to the airhangar to catch the next flight home. His heart floated inside his chest. What was going on? What would the mission be? Emissary program? Was Nághtas sending people into the Union officially? Was that why he was chosen, because he'd been behind the lines? Something that would take years to begin, and years to end, probably see him right into a general's rank. Something so important that Nághtas's son himself was screening people. Was it Nadigh's project, or his father's and Nadigh was acting on the Emperor's behalf?

It was a four-hour flight home. Tokh opened the folder and broke the seal on the pages. Inside was a code, then a list of computer encryptions, nothing else. He scanned them with his comm unit and hit decrypt. It contained the contact information for General Trannor and a list of file codes. He chose the first one, entered it into his hand unit, typed in his identification number and his security clearance, then his authorization code from the front page. The file opened, and he began to read the purpose of his new endeavor.

Tokh was a seasoned intelligence officer, able to change the mood on his face or eliminate it entirely at will. He couldn't stop his eyes from widening in surprise as he read. After just a few sentences, his head whipped up to survey the craft, making sure no one was paying attention to him. What he read was treason. Revolutionary. Unimaginable. And approved by the Heir himself. *Did the Emperor really order this?* Tokh had never been afraid of a printed word before, but he was frightened just to be seen holding the coded file, a file outlining a program to crown a female as Emperor of Kerasím. *A female.* It could not be done. The craft was sparsely populated; at least three rows of seats separated him from the next flier, and he returned cautiously to reading.

Zheníhda was floored by the earrings, and didn't remove them for an entire week. Tokh thought about the ad in the store window. Zheníhda didn't look like a million *dakra* – she never had, not even in her youth – but the joy of the unexpected gift gave a special glow to her face, even without the fancy pillows. She was waiting for him on the bed when he exited the lavatory, wanting his attention, or at least pretending it to thank him. It was a nice surprise.

"Was it something good?" she asked, knowing he could never give specifics.

He held her close, his cheek on her head, breathing in the scent of her perfumed hair. She'd learned that from the *dahneg* wives; upper-caste women always smelled of expensive scents, the more exotic the better, a practice he enjoyed. The more upper-caste she acted, the more successful he would seem to his peers. "I'm hoping it will be. It's very strange. Strange things are happening, Nihda."

She picked her head up to look him in the eye. "Not a war?"

"No, no. Nothing like that. Just, strange. At my level, I get to see some of the politics involved at the upper levels, see who directs the action of the army. I don't understand it. I probably don't want to understand it. I just carry out the orders. Sometimes I think they just come up with ideas because they're bored and want to see what would happen. Anyway, I'm set where I am for a year or more, so rest easy."

Zheníhda stroked his chinhank, then kissed his lower lip. "You can't go anywhere until Kitras goes to academy next year. You have to see him off. Then you can go."

"I can't promise, but I'll try."

* * 13 * *

Tokh checked in once a month with his new contact, learned new updates, but the project was in its infancy. Zheníhda no longer worried about his long trips; Zenak was seventeen, and if something happened to Tokh, she would have a place to live and someone to look after her. Her safety was ensured.

Tokh took a week's leave, packed up Zheníhda and Kitras, and flew off to Nar Rhede to settle Kitras into the underacademy. Kitras was far more enthusiastic about the idea than his brother had been. Tokh had been home for Kitras more than he had been for Zenak, filling his head with stories of glory, training him for hand combat and marksmanship, teaching him little ways to succeed over the other students. Kitras was ready.

Zenak was in his last year of academy, and would keep an eye on his brother. He walked the grounds with his parents, tall and slender like his mother, his dark chin hank tied with bands per regulation, handsome and sharp in his cadet uniform, the air filled with the scent of blossoming trees, and it was there he dropped a surprise on his stunned parents.

"I've decided against the military as a career," he said. "When I graduate next term, I'm getting married, and I plan to teach, like *Dihnarbo* Talekh."

"No," Tokh said immediately. His voice was neutral, as if someone had asked him a choice for dinner.

"*Bobo*, you said coming here was your choice, but what I did after that was mine. I've remembered it every day I've been here. It's not that I don't like it here, it's that I don't want to leave. I want to teach here. I'm an excellent student assistant. I can be certified in two years, and then I can teach."

"No," Tokh insisted. He stepped in front of Zenak, demanding his attention. "You want to teach, that's fine. I won't object. Your *dihnarbo* can guide you. But you'll do a two-year tour of active duty first. How do you expect your students to respect you if you haven't been out there? They'll ask questions and you'll say, *Well, I think it's this way...* and they'll ask, *Don't you know? You're teaching us about duty, but you haven't done any of this?* You'll lose every young mind you set out to train. You'll never be hired here but be stuck teaching the dregs of *rhibáni* public education. You need at least a small amount of experience to relate to your students and earn their respect. Discuss it with your advisors if you don't believe me."

Zheníhda changed the subject before a fight could bloom. "Do you have your eye on a girl, or is it just a plan?"

Zenak's face lit up, and his cheeks blushed brown. "I do, but her father says I can't marry her until I graduate. Avalihn. She's the third daughter of Major Rinveld. You'd like her, *Ama*."

"What's her caste? How old is she?"

"*Dihnarwharl*. She's sixteen, just a few months younger than me."

"That's too young to be marrying," Tokh cautioned.

"You said *Ama* was sixteen when you were promised."

"The difference was I didn't marry her until she was eighteen, because my duty kept me away. I had time to think on things. I was ready at twenty. I wasn't ready at eighteen."

"But I am. I'm an adult, and this is what I want, *Bo*."

"I would at least like to meet her," Zheníhda said.

Zenak smiled with relief. "I want you to, *Ama*. We want everyone to have dinner together tonight."

Zheníhda had brought good clothes with her but not her very best. Marriage had not been on her radar. Was the family high *dihnarwharl* or low *dihnarwharl*?

"You! You have it easy!" she raged at Tokh. "You stick your pretty ribbons on your uniform, shine your sword, and you impress everyone you meet. It's so much harder on females, always guessing." In the end she chose her lilac blouse, her white skirt with the sheer overlay embroidered with shiny pink meadowflies, the precious *habivend* earrings, and a four-strand choker of pink beads. She rolled her hair up fit for a *dahneg* and anchored her purple veil to her hair with a tall silver veil-clasp. She layered her cosmetics carefully, rounding out her cheeks and nose.

Tokh nodded with approval. "If you're trying to intimidate, you've succeeded. You would make any male proud to be seen with you. You honor me with your presentation."

Zeníhda tipped her head down and blushed. "Thank you, my husband. I think I do mean to intimidate. You only make a first impression once. I don't want to be the one underdressed."

"I don't think you will be." Tokh took her hand and led her out.

Restaurants were a neutral territory for parents to meet. Tokh outranked Major Rinveld by two grades and at least a dozen ribbons but only three years of age; there was no contest as to who was the superior male. Walking into the private dining room, her back tall, a *dahneg* air billowing around her, Zeníhda was secretly pleased to see Lady Major Rinveld – Avia – pale at the sight of her. Avia was dressed in popular style, but her informal familiar welcoming couldn't compete with Zeníhda's years among *dahneg* women.

Low dihnarwharl.

Zenak couldn't have been prouder, introducing Avalihn to his parents. She was a charming young thing, with the slender willowiness of a young girl. For a Kerasi, she was unusually fair, her eyes a striking pale brown and her hair a bright red-brown, the color of *tabbat*-tree bark wet with rain. Her skin was brass more than copper; combined with the light brown tones of her cosmetics, she looked as if lit up from the inside, a painted female shade over a glowing ball of light. She bowed until her forehead almost touched the ground.

"You do me great honor, Lord Tokh. You do me great honor, Lady Zeníhda. Thank you for dining with me."

Zeníhda couldn't help but thrill at the look of panic in her eyes.

Males sat on one side of the round table for the meal and females on the other. Zeníhda ratcheted herself back down to *dihnarwharl* and found much to discuss with Avia. Three military men didn't need any help in finding common conversation. Avalihn seemed sweet and intelligent, no matter what questions Zeníhda threw at her.

"Well, what do you think?" Zenak said as dessert arrived, his gloved hand tight in Avalihn's. Proper manners forbade skin contact between unmarried people.

Tokh made stern eye contact with Major Rinveld. "Your daughter is a beautiful young girl and most pleasant company, but as I told Zenak, I think they are too young. Seventeen is too young for a male."

Avalihn couldn't hold back her voice. "I'll be seventeen in two more months! I don't want to be an old maid."

"I was fifteen," Avia said.

"I told you, *Bo*, it won't be until after graduation," Zenak insisted. "We don't need a big party. A dinner like this would be fine."

"I want Zenak to put in a tour of duty before he settles down," Tokh said. "It will help him in his career."

"That's reasonable," Major Rinveld agreed. "But what guarantee will you then give my daughter, should the unthinkable happen?"

"Fine!" Zenak snapped from across the table. "Fine. You want me to see the other side of duty, I'll do it, but I'm marrying her first. I'll marry her after graduation, then do my tour of duty. I won't wait that long to marry her. We are in love and we're going to get married, with or without your approval. I can sign my own papers today if need be."

"Love!" Tokh snorted. "Love has nothing to do with marriage. Your firstwife should be someone who will build your strength, support your goals, help you build your fortune, someone to keep your estate and make you look better in the eyes of your peers, raise your children so they may bring you honor. As you grow, you find your love for each other through respect. If you still need someone to worship the steps you take, wait ten years and take a second wife.

"Don't go having children right at the start," Zheníhda warned. "If you aren't choosing a military career, you can't count on a steady income until you're permanently employed. You can't afford a child until then."

"She speaks truth," Avia told her daughter. "Your sister didn't have a child until she was twenty-one."

Tokh sighed with resignation. "Very well. We'll set a date after the class graduates, but Zenak will do a two-year tour of duty after the marriage. If that is agreed, I'll support their marriage on one condition."

Zenak hesitated, afraid to speak. "Okay. What is it?"

Tokh pointed his finger at him. "If you value your wife to be, you're forbidden from telling my parents about it until the day before."

"I can promise that." Zenak smiled with relief. He had a pleasing combination of his mother's eyes and his father's jaw, a thinner nose than his father but without the horrid bump, making him quite charming when he smiled. Avalihn never stood a chance. After the dinner, after Avalihn and her family had left, he hit his father up for enough money to buy her a necklace.

Kitras completed his first year of Nar Rhede second in his class, with a medal for being first in marksmanship, to Tokh's great pride. Zenak graduated with low honors, but honors none the less, Tokh, his *dihnarbo* Talekh, and Major Rinveld watching from up close, and Zheníhda, Avia, Filuhr, Galisse, and Avalihn watching from a fenced-off female section. They weren't going to let him out of his promise. Finally, twenty-two years late, Tokh wandered the streets of Nar Rhede with a graduating class, walking with his parents, wearing a uniform and sword, and celebrating in the restaurants. It was everything he'd long imagined.

Kitras had a break between sessions, and three days later his brother Zenak married his love Avalihn, Zenak's necklace at her throat. Despite the distance involved, Tokh asked General Marmot to officiate. Having an authority – any military officer with a rank of captain or higher, or any male *dahneg* or above, or the Keeper at any Temple of the Fortunes – impart wisdom and read the questions was a personal choice, a tradition with some but not required. Having a boss do it was a nice piece of *khata*-kissing that set a child up with immediate upper-level contacts.

The small wedding dinner numbered thirty-five, by the time Tokh unavoidably invited his parents, Zheníhda's parents, his siblings, Rinveld's daughters and sons in law and his relatives, and General Marmot. Tokh made sure he rented the wedding suite in his name, and wouldn't give Zenak the key or tell him where it was until he and his bride were leaving the wedding, so as to avoid uninvited guests.

Zenak and Avalihn had a week alone in each other's company, then they spent four days with Avalihn's family. Zenak had one more week until he needed to report for duty. As the bride was now part of Zenak's family, they returned to his family's home in Rhagadan, where Avalihn would stay until Zenak returned to her, just as Zheníhda had stayed with Tokh's family when she first married.

Zheníhda sat on her bed, listening to the squeals and giggles and voices leaking through the wall between the bedrooms. There was a distinct look of terror on her face.

"What's wrong?" Tokh said when he entered the room.

Zheníhda waved a hand to the wall. "You don't hear that? How are we supposed to sleep with that going on all night?"

"You've never heard two people *pushing* before? They're newlyweds. That's all they do, if you'll recall." He leaned his head against the wall and bellowed out the groaning noises of a male about to spend his fluid. There was a louder squeal behind the wall and a commotion of people moving, then just a faint giggle.

"There. What's the matter? You look ill."

"I just…" Zheníhda *did* feel ill. "I'm not ready to think of my son as married and *pushing* on females."

Tokh undressed for bed. "What do you think he's been doing since his manhood celebration? I was there, remember? He's been an adult now for four years. Don't think he hasn't been *pushing* on anything that held still long enough for his hands to catch her."

"I know, I just – Maybe I'm just old fashioned."

"No, you've always been tense when it comes to *pushing*. You've never been relaxed about it."

Zheníhda turned to him with offense. "I'm relaxed about it! Have I failed to please you? Have I ever denied you?"

"No," he admitted, "but you don't enjoy it."

Her eyebrow puckered into a frown. "I do so enjoy it! I enjoy it very much, thank you! I'm just… private about it." Tokh sat on the bed next to her, and she leaned her head against his arm. "I feel so old. I feel like my life is over and I'm undesirable as an old servant no one looks at, sagging and drooping like stretched-out clothing."

Tokh glared at her. "You're thirty-eight years old, Nihda. That's nowhere near qualifying for old, and there's nothing about you that droops yet. You're still the mother of a child. Is that what you want? Another child? Something to prove you're still young and fertile?"

"Gah! No. We don't need that. I've got that Silly Little Wisp to look after now, remember? That should be a joy, listening to her pine for Zenak. I don't know if I ever once mentioned you when I lived with your parents. He hasn't even left yet and she's moaning for him."

"That's not why she's moaning," Tokh said as another noise leaked through the wall. Zheníhda tried, but her repressed smile burst forth and they both laughed.

She ran her hand along his arm. "Tokh? *Push* me? *Push* me as if you really want to, as if I still make your heart race."

"You do make my heart race, especially in that nightdress." She wore a short, sleeveless little thing of conservative copper lace, almost matching her skin tone; at fast glance, it looked as if she wore nothing at all. His hands pressed her shoulders until she lay back on the bed. "I can do that, but you must give one loud shout and scare them in return."

Zheníhda's face held panic. "No! No, Tokh. Don't call attention to us."

Her pleas fell on deaf ears. Tokh took his time, making certain she found joy in their coupling, and then he pinched her, hard, at the exact right moment. Zheníhda gave a shriek of surprise, which Tokh followed with howling grand moans as his found his own release.

The noises in the other room stopped cold.

"And again!" Tokh bellowed. Zheníhda slapped at his chest and they lay there in the dark, laughing.

Despite Zheníhda's dread of the "Silly Little Wisp," Avalihn was a delight. Perhaps it was because Avalihn began her first day without her husband by making breakfast for her new mother in law. Perhaps it was because Avalihn was desperately anxious to please her new family, and jumped in to help with cleaning without having to be asked. Zheníhda soon had her watching all the same dramatic programs on the ComNet, and together they gasped in horror or wept in relief at the storylines. One of the few belongings Avalihn brought with her was a machine to make and repair clothing. She showed Zheníhda how she made her own skirts and fancy veils and pretty things for her hair, some of which she sold to the other wives and daughters in the building. She used half of the money for more supplies, and put the other half away as a gift to her husband when he returned.

Zheníhda was impressed. Avalihn may have been low *dihnarwharl*, but her son had been right not to let a good wife get away, no matter what her age. She taught Avalihn how to be high *dihnarwharl*, how to cook a decent meal, and how to avoid her husband's nosy wisemother.

Kitras turned fourteen, and Tokh threw him a randy manhood celebration, away from the apartment. Zenak's tour of duty ended, and as Tokh knew, he returned a much wiser, much more mature husband with three ribbons to his chest. With the savings from his small salary and the money Avalihn had earned doing alterations and selling small handicrafts, he found them a one-room apartment in Nar Rhede, where he took a position as an assistant until he finished his teaching credentials. Zheníhda, mother of two sons, missed the constant female companionship she'd had, and the apartment seemed lonelier than ever.

Tokh struggled with his new assignments. He now knew the scope of his secret assignment, a high-risk, clandestine mission that in the end could pay off immeasurably for the Emperor if it succeeded, a major step toward peace with their greatest enemy, whether or not a female ever took the throne. He met with some of the other chosen officers on his four-times-a-year special meetings in Keranihn. They learned each other's names, but mostly they said nothing to each other, afraid of saying too much. The project was moving, but with the speed of a *dinkorhat* out of water. Buildings were being built, paths laid, logistics worked out, and more information was coming in from covert sources than ever before.

Out of nowhere, General Marmot called him to his office. "I don't know what's going on, Tokh, but someone somewhere likes you a little too much. I have been instructed not to make a display of this." He tossed a set of rank insignia onto his desk. "You're being promoted to Colonel Two, and you'll be moving out of my jurisdiction. You should have had at least three years before any chance of promotion, but someone wants you railroaded up to general as fast as possible. I hope you're ready for it when it hits. It's been an honor, Colonel. A strange one, but an honor. I do hope someday I'll be able to learn what you're involved in."

Colonel Two Tokh stepped back and saluted the general, a fist to the chest, then an open palm out. *The heart and the hand of the Emperor are always open.* "There are days, General, when I ask myself the exact same thing."

* * 14 * *

Pestrahn Surveillance Base, Gimsith, Iérot Thorán. Tokh knew this would be their last move for a while, so he tried to fulfill a promise a little bit early. While scouting out a place to live, he humbly asked his contact, General Trannor, if it was possible to get a small grant for housing, as he would be gone much of the time and he wanted his wife to feel comfortable with the living arrangement. Trannor didn't send a word of reply, just a dispensation for 30,000 *dakra*. Tokh choked. He'd hoped to ask for ten. Zhenihda wouldn't be getting jewelry this time.

The move ate at her. Tokh told her nothing, just that he'd found a place in an upscale *dihnarwharl* neighborhood. Zhenihda fretted the entire five-hour flight. "What kind of light does it get? What direction do the windows face? What color is the furniture?"

Tokh adjusted himself in the seat and tried to nap. "I didn't have a compass with me. Light enough to look around. It had furniture, that's all I remember."

"Your handcom has a compass function, you *dinkhorat*. The least you could have done was taken photos for me, or seen if there was a picture on the networks. You're intelligence; don't tell me you couldn't have requested a satellite photo."

Zhenihda huffed and sighed herself into a frenzy by the time the aircraft landed at the base. He requested a fleet vehicle and drove them off the base a *nali* or so. It was a busy main street dense with tired single homes that ended at the base itself, the cross streets bearing markets and cafes for the immediate needs of the local citizens. Tokh stopped the vehicle and got out. Zhenihda waited.

Tokh opened the cargo hatch of the vehicle and began removing bags. "Are you going to sleep there, or are you getting out?"

Zhenihda climbed out in confusion. "I thought you were meeting someone. I didn't know I was coming along."

"If you want to live indoors, you'll come. I promised you a house, and this is it. It's not the best, but it is a house."

Zheníhda's eyes grew until they seemed to be the reason her nose was pinched. She leaned against the vehicle, hands over her mouth in shock. "Tokh! No! For real? This is ours? You managed a house? *How?* A free-standing house? Tokh!" A large army transport rumbled past them on the street, rocking their vehicle with its draft.

Tokh smiled and carried several boxes toward the front door. "Unless you prefer me *pushing* you in the barracks."

Zheníhda had never been inside a free-standing house. She followed Tokh on tiptoe, not sure what to expect, afraid to be treading on territory outside of her caste. Houses were for the wealthy elite; she was just a *nhásarwharl* who'd married up. It was a small house, white plaster with green corners and trim, a bright green roof and fancy colored tiles around the door. It had four rooms on the main floor: a kitchen, a sitting room, and Zheníhda's long-envied room for dining; a bath, and a small room for a hired woman to live in. At the end of the house was a staircase, and upstairs were five small bedrooms – five! More bedrooms alone than rooms she'd ever had to herself. Two tiny baths finished it. It was shabby and outdated and the furniture and colors were just plain awful. Zheníhda sat in a bedroom and cried with joy.

From a window – most rooms had two – Zheníhda could see a little walled yard outside, enough space for some chairs and a table so one could enjoy a pleasant day while a child frolicked in grass. Orange and white flowers covered one side of the boundary wall, and a hedge of *theringa* berries lined another, its thick pink blossoms promising a bounty of fruit. Traffic could be heard through the windowglass, and the big transports going by made the panes rattle hourly. It was miraculous.

Tokh found her upstairs, still speechless. "Do you like it? I know – five bedrooms for just two of us. I'll take that room at the top of the stairs for an office, set up all my business so I don't have to be disturbed. Kitras still needs a room for when he comes home, and that leaves rooms for Zenak or your mother if they come to visit. The question is, do you wish a room of your own? We have space for it now. I'll visit you or you can visit me each night."

"That seems silly, Tokh. I've slept by you for more than twenty years. I'm used to it, unless you wish to rid yourself of me. You're not here half the time, anyway. But I might make a room into a sitting room for me, a nice little place where I can escape if you have people over."

He kissed her throat. "Take your pick."

For a week Zheníhda wandered around the house, opening cabinets, peering inside, and wandering again. No voices leaked through the walls, ceilings, or floors from other apartments; the house, beyond the traffic noises, was silent as a crypt. There were no balconies or elevators or lower-level *raffin*-bars to socialize at, no fellow wives to depend on in an emergency.

Zheníhda had never felt so alone in her life.

It didn't last long. Ohla in the yard behind her was a *dahneg* with three children who slipped through a gate in the wall to say hello, her husband on a long assignment. She introduced Zheníhda to the six houses running on each side, and the back street. Twelve houses in a row, back to back between two streets, counted as a cluster, twenty-four women, give or take secondwives. Cross a street and it was a new cluster. Clusters looked out for each other. Most of the neighborhood was highest-*dihnarwharl* scratching at the ankles of the upper castes, and the rest were low *dahneg*. The nicest house on the back block contained an elderly *fáhganid* couple who had lived there for sixty years and refused to move, even as the neighborhood slid down into *dihnarwharl*. Clusters had friendly competitions; whether decorating for holidays or gardens in summer, there was almost always something to keep Zheníhda busy.

As promised, Tokh found a house woman, an aged *tapatihn* of perhaps sixty-five, small and wrinkled as a dried fruit but eager to avoid being sent to a facility for elderly females. She said little, made no noise, cooked well, and kept the house spotless. Zheníhda, former *nhásarwharl*, now high-*dihnarwharl* house-dweller, had joined the upper castes.

In twenty years, Zheníhda had never placed a call to Tokh while he was away to an off-base site. She couldn't; the best she could do was use an emergency contact number to call his supervising general, who would then be able to relay the message if he thought it warranted it and wouldn't distract Tokh from his work. Otherwise, he wouldn't get the message until he was back in a position where he could call her. He'd been gone five weeks into a new task when Zheníhda decided the news wouldn't wait. Sometimes Tokh could come home earlier but volunteered a few extra weeks to extend his pay and earn more points. And Tokh liked to be informed.

General Sobak, Tokh's new local supervisor, agreed to put the call through. Tokh must have been off-planet, because there was an annoying pause between transmission and reception, and there was static on the line. Tokh's face carried a touch of alarm, something he almost never showed at work or at home.

"Nihda! What's wrong? What's happened?"

"I'm sorry to disturb you, my husband. The news couldn't wait too long, and you would want to know. Congratulations. If you don't return home in time, you'll be a wisefather when you do."

The words sank in. "What? Zenak?"

Zheníhda exploded into a beaming smile. "Yes! They are expecting a baby, five months from now. I wanted to let you know before it was born."

Tokh let loose a braying laugh that carried across the parsecs. "*Ahkh!* I knew he wouldn't wait long. Thank you, Nihda. That is indeed news I wished to know. All is well?"

"Absolutely," she insisted with a smile. "Everything is delightful. Your work is going well?"

"Very involved," he admitted. "I sleep only a few hours a night, but I'm learning managing skills. I'll make sure I'm home before the date."

"I'll be waiting."

Tokh was home in time to fly with Nihda back to Nar Rhede to be there for the birth of Zenak's son. He and Avalihn named the baby Khourbas, after the Emperor's father. Zenak wouldn't let her have the baby at home, so they chose a birthing hospital that would allow Filuhr to deliver the baby. Filuhr hadn't forgotten Zheníhda's embarrassed snubbing of her twenty-one years before, and her barbed comments made Zheníhda seethe until she left Zenak's apartment to hide her tears. Tokh seized his mother by the shoulders and escorted her back to her home, dressing her down like a raw recruit the entire way, and left Zheníhda to visit with the new family in peace.

Most Kerasi families were small, as desirable housing was expensive and the wait list for a certain neighborhood or school could be lengthy. Couples often had one child right away, to prove they were fertile. Two children was common, unless both were female, in which case a third might be tried. If that was also female, less-wealthy couples stopped, while those with means sought help from clinics who would use advanced procedures to guarantee a boy. Those that could afford such things didn't wait until the fourth try.

Zenak and Avalihn knew full well how to avoid pregnancy – Filuhr made sure to remind them every time she visited. Thus it was a shock when Zenak announced they were expecting again when Khourbas hadn't yet begun to crawl. Zivas followed his brother by just sixteen months. Avalihn had trouble managing a toddler while trying to feed a newborn, so just before Tokh's next campaign from home, he brought Zeníhda out to stay with them for three months while he was gone.

How strange it was, not to have to worry about losing an apartment because it was vacant! Nor did she have to worry about the house, because the housekeeper remained behind to maintain it. No wonder the upper castes always seemed so worry-free. In some ways it annoyed Zeníhda – a *tapatihn* living in a free-standing house all by herself for three months. It was unacceptable privilege for a greedy little *tapatihn* – not that the housekeeper, Hada, had ever been anything but polite and grateful – but it was the *possibility* of the maid feeling privileged that bothered Zeníhda.

The convenience, however, soon eased Zeníhda's jealousy. Not long after, she stood with Tokh to watch Kitras graduate, second in his class, and the only one to graduate as a sharp-shooter. The gatherings were growing larger: Tokh and Zeníhda, Zenak and his family, Wisefather Talekh and both wives, two of Tokh's brothers, and Zeníhda's parents.

Tokh was certain it was to have a free celebration meal at his expense. Two babies present meant wisemother and wisermother could each fill their arms without fighting, but not a single word passed between Zeníhda and Filuhr the entire day.

General Marmot was right.

Nothing was so frustrating as the army's incessant secretive need-to-know nonsense that left most officers walking around in a semi-informed haze. Tokh had been run ragged with duty, much of it considered high-level, and off-world counted at a higher point rate, but he wasn't ready to be sent into an office to find a roomful of generals having a cocktail party with drinks and small food, including General Trannor of the Emissary Project, a *fáhganid* who rarely ever showed his face. In six years Tokh had met him in person just three times. Tokh had not yet turned forty-six, his double workload was crushing him, and he had failed to remember an end-of-shift check on personnel the previous week, for which General Trannor had cursed him so well that Tokh's ego still smarted. No doubt this gathering was to throw him off the project in disgrace.

Tokh bowed before the room and held it for a count of three. "Colonel Tokh, as requested."

Trannor held a small pink-encrusted glass high. "Honored Officers, may I present the newest addition to our ranks, General One Tokh. General Tokh, welcome to our circle." The room raised their glasses and gave a deafening *Yaaaah* in response.

General Sobak removed Tokh's Colonel Two rank and replaced it with General One pins. General Gho Nan handed him a glass of pepper rum, its pink vapor film still crystalizing up the sides.

Tokh's heart had stopped beating. He bowed three times before the room to give himself time to recover. "I truly have no words," he said when his tongue moved again. "I am weak with honor. May I never fail to uphold your welcome."

Trannor, with all his level-Fourness, General of the Razor Tongue, clapped a *fáhganid* hand on Tokh's shoulder. "You're ready, General. We've pressured you hard and fast, and you rose to the challenge stronger than the rest. That says much for your character and ability. Time grows short. We have perhaps five years left to get this off the ground and we need everyone in position, trained and ready, before that can occur. You're the first to make it this far. I apologize if my harshness last week was too strong. Please understand, my job is to find your limits, so we know when we may expect you to break. By the time you take your place, I promise you, you'll be ready for anything."

Tokh sipped at his pepper rum, an elite, unaffordable privilege. It burned through his stomach and made his head spin even faster. He still didn't know the specifics on the new project. He hadn't been told that yet, despite six years' service. Whatever the final plan was, he was going to be in charge of something big, and his performance had pleased the upper ranks. He took another sip of the rum to calm his nerves. Something big indeed.

* * 15 * *

It was General Sobak who started the trouble. Sobak, Tokh's immediate local supervisor, a level-Three general who wasn't directly involved in The Big Project but was part of a distant circle of it. They both attended an out-of-region meeting; he held Tokh back after the meeting dismissed.

"Tokh, I've been meaning to speak with you for a few weeks now. You're married, I know that. Do you consider your marriage happy? Do you have pleasant discourse with your wife?"

In the face of his Big Project, Tokh often fielded questions on his opinions of females, and didn't think twice. "Twenty-five years now. Yes, I would say we have a pleasant marriage. She wishes me home more than I am, and I wish I was with her more than I am, but she is used to it. We don't argue much."

Sobak nodded. "I'm glad to hear it. You're *dihnarwharl*, with one wife. Have you ever considered taking a second? I ask, because my brother's daughter has recently been widowed. He was lost in a skirmish attack out in Pahdrot Na Gho four months ago; an explosion took out the vehicle he was riding in. She's a beautiful girl, loved her husband very much, and she is utterly heartbroken. My brother and his wife don't want to support her, and have given her two months to find a husband or be put to a consort house. She doesn't deserve that. I would ask if you would meet her, see what you think of her. Now that you're general, your salary is high enough to support two wives. He left her with no children, so that burden wouldn't be on you. If you don't want her, I'll try to find someone else, but if you would please dine with us, at least let me know what you think of her, or if you know of someone else to recommend. She's twenty-five, Tokh. She's far from undesirable. She just needs some care right now and I know you're a caring husband. Will you dine with me and meet her?"

Tokh's tongue stuck in his mouth. A second wife? He didn't see enough of the one he had. Yes, perhaps half of the upper-caste generals had a second wife, often a good deal younger than the first.

Zheníhda was forty-three, old enough to be this new female's mother, a truth that wouldn't be lost on her. Zheníhda wouldn't react well; he knew that for a fact. On the other hand, if a boss was trying to set you up with a family member, how were you supposed to decline? A union with Sobak's contacts could be very beneficial to a fast-climbing general, and Tokh was climbing so fast he couldn't catch his breath. Sobak had left him an out: marry her or find someone else to marry her. Perhaps she was as ugly as an eyeless rock-fish, and he would have no trouble finding a reason to decline. Perhaps she would be a good match for his son Kitras. Tokh had *pushed* so many females on his campaigns he couldn't begin to count a fraction of them; he'd never had a desire to keep one of them. On the other hand, Zheníhda had never been adventurous when it came to *pushing*, and having a second wife to *push* on would ease demands on her.

"I can commit to dinner," he said.

Tokh hadn't been forced to meet a female in decades. He wore his regular uniform with all his medals and citations in perfect position; the line was embarrassingly long. He combed his hair, still black as his youth, trimmed his chin hank and clipped a gold clasp around it, bands of red enamel circling the top and bottom. The mirror displeased him; he was starting to form a gut over his belt, a far too common occurrence among Kerasi men of certain rank and caste, as too much good food and too little footsoldiering took their toll. He sucked in his stomach and tightened his belt. It would have to do.

General Sobak appeared at the restaurant with his brother, his brother's wife, and niece. His sister in law was an elegant woman, her hair piled high and dangling down again in ringlets. That was a good sign; Zheníhda wouldn't tolerate anyone who couldn't live up to caste standards.

"General Tokh, I would like to present my niece, Umara. General Tokh is stationed in Gimsith, out in Iérot Thorán, but he is here on business. He's a highly respected member of my team."

Umara bowed in his direction but kept her eyes downward. "It's an honor to meet you, General."

Tokh bowed in return. "Likewise." His eyes dissected her quickly. Yes, she was no more than twenty-five; that was no lie. She was short to average in height for a female, not thin like Zheníhda but pleasantly rounded in the areas Zheníhda wasn't, especially the back end. Her face was agreeable; more gold than copper, her hair cut to shoulder length and rounded out, a light brown underneath with a golden wash above making it seem to glow like the sun. Her cheeks were round and golden as *patigha*-fruit when she smiled; her lips full and dark and soft as a kiss waiting to be given. She wore a youthful red dress with yellow and orange embroidery and a little matching jacket; a sequined red veil hung down her back from a gold veil-clip. She was eye-catching, for certain.

The conversation flowed, greased by a plentiful supply of *lunahl*. Umara laughed easily. "And the birds of the wind/ and the eels of the waves/ shall hear my words /and spread the news from shore to shore."

Tokh bowed his head to acknowledge her. "You like poetry."

Umara tipped her head back and smiled at the ceiling. "It makes my heart soar! I have thousands on my reader. I love Grand *Bhísroti* Transindal best. She wrote love poems that make me weep for their beauty."

Tokh swirled the *lunahl* in his glass. "...I lay my hand upon his breast /and felt not life in clarity, /so in response my own lay down /and stopped in solidarity."

Umara almost crawled across the table. "You know her!"

Tokh gave a soft snort. He hadn't read a poem in thirty years; he had no idea the author was the same. "I'm well studied in many arts."

"She has the most beautiful imagery. In many of the books they pair her work with famous paintings, so I have learned much about art as well. My husband – I have been to an art museum once, and I have never been so overwhelmed by beauty as that day."

"You read?"

"I do read and write," Umara admitted, "but I find it tiresome after a while, so I listen to more than I read. Sometimes the readers find the spirit of the poem better than I do."

"What did you think?" Sobak said as they rode back to the barracks.

"She's better than I expected," Tokh admitted.

Sobak sweetened the deal. "She has a dowry, her husband's estate. It's not huge, he was only twenty-six, but it's a nice little package."

Tokh had a free-standing house and a general's rank. He had no other financial goals, so the money did little to sway him. "I give no promises, but I will dine with her again tomorrow."

The dinner was at Sobak's brother's home, where Umara was living. She cooked the dinner herself, a complicated but tasty meal of *hyrak* in a spiced cream sauce, bread rounds, handmade grain ribbons, and three different vegetables, as well as a molded pudding dessert. Tokh took seconds on everything, and not from politeness. He had researched a short stanza praising food in advance, and recited it at the end of the meal. Umara smiled shyly, her cheeks bronzing dark with pleasure. She responded with the next stanza of the poem; Tokh wasn't sure how much education she had – obviously more than Zheníhda – but she certainly had a phenomenal memory.

On the third day he took her to lunch. Sobak remained as chaperone, sitting with a colleague several tables away but still in sight, giving Tokh and Umara a chance to speak privately for the first time. Alone, Umara was quite shy but conversed without effort. He questioned her on her husband, not to cause her pain but to give her a topic to speak extensively on, watching how she spoke of him, listening to what she said. He was a seasoned interrogator and she was an ignorant young wife; pulling information from her was as easy as pouring water from a glass. Her face lit from within when she spoke of her husband, and Tokh ignored her when tears welled up.

"And children?" he asked. "Do you like them? I have two young smallsons who frequent my house. They're quite active."

"I love children," she said wistfully. "We planned on having them, but Bujan wanted to wait until he made captain first. They made him captain posthumously, but it didn't help." She blinked her eyes before the tears could fall.

On the fourth day Tokh found an art museum in the next city, Sobak's brother and his wife following them at a distance. No tears clouded Umara's face. She radiated joy at the paintings, even the ones of brutality and violence. Songs fell from her lips several times in a clear, sweet, voice. When Tokh thought about it, it was no surprise. Songs were poetry put to music, and poetry made her heart sing. Umara wasn't Zheníhda. She was dreamy and imaginative, her mind wandering and wondering, the opposite of Zheníhda's logical, calculating, analytical head. Her manner around him was one of shyness, but it was most likely because she knew why he was there. Yes, Tokh could feasibly marry her to Kitras, just six years her junior, but he was starting to find her charming. Maybe it was because he hadn't spent this much time with a female outside of Zheníhda in twenty-five years. Conquests and consorts didn't spend much time in conversation.

On the fifth day, Tokh called upon her at her parents' home, and they were allowed to walk together without escort. He took her to a little café around the corner.

"It's not an easy life with me," he said. "I'm not home much of the time. I'm married to a very good wife, Zheníhda, the mother of my sons. I have no complaints about her whatsoever, but Sobak has asked me to consider having you also as my wife. I find you to be delightful; I'm willing to accept you as a second-wife. To do that, however, will put you in a difficult position. Zheníhda's an opinionated female who has spent much time among *dahneg*. She won't be happy at your presence, but as with all things, in time she'll adjust. I have a free-standing house; I would give you a separate bedroom away from hers. I make no lies: Zheníhda is my firstwife and controls the house. This won't change. I'll do my best not to favor one over the other, but I won't upset Zheníhda's life more than necessary. She has her friends, she has her sons, she has her smallsons, and you won't disrupt that. You'll find friends; if they are the same, that's fine, but don't disrupt her status with them. If you want a child, I'll give you one, but it will be your child; don't expect her to raise it. I have a housemaid, so your tasks will be minimal. Do you have questions of me?"

Umara gave an anxious smile and gazed at the table between them. "You've been most kind to me, General. You're most pleasant company. I'm grateful that you would consider me as a second-wife. I would ask you, How do you discipline your wife, and what things would you find offensive that you would discipline her over?"

Tokh sat back to think. "I've never had to discipline Zheníhda in the formal sense. She's always been most attentive to my needs. I would consider repeated disobedience to be a case for discipline, shameful behavior before guests, theft, willful adultery, or any other behavior that dishonors me to be grounds for punishment. I'm used to discipline in my ranks and would follow a similar guideline at home if necessary, from reprimands through strokes with an incentive stick if needed. I've never gone beyond reprimands with Zheníhda. Stick to your duties as wife, and we'll never have issues."

Umara smiled with relief. "You're truly kind, General." Tokh watched her struggle, wanting to say something but afraid to say it.

"Speak freely. We are in public; I won't shout."

Umara looked down at her hands. "I'm sorry, Lord, but as female and as wife one hears many terrible stories. I wish to know in advance if you have any... unusual *night* behaviors, ones that could make me uncomfortable in marriage."

Tokh frowned. "Such as?"

Umara blushed darkly and fought to get words out. "I have heard stories involving... unnatural acts, or humiliation, or other such abominations. Not of you, of course, but others. Do you share your wife, Lord?"

"Not unless forced to by caste. I've had to share Zheníhda exactly once, against my will. I have no unnatural habits; as far as I know, my tastes are quite average. You do like to *push*, yes?" The last thing he wanted was another Zheníhda, tense and jittery around the subject. Some sweet and spontaneous affection would be nice.

"Yes! Yes, *pushing* is fine with me," Umara said. "Bujan enjoyed all of my attentions. Thank you, Lord. I just wanted to know what to expect. I understand the difficulties I will face, but I would be honored to be your second-wife."

Of course you would, Tokh thought to himself. *Anything to avoid a consort house and unnatural acts.* He pulled a slim box from the pocket of his uniform and presented it to her. "Then take this gift as a promise from me. I'll retrieve you from your home tomorrow, sign the papers at the marriage office, and we'll spend a week together alone. Then I'll bring you to my home, for I must return to duty." He reached across the table and squeezed her hand, the first personal contact they'd made.

Umara's pretty lips spread in a joyful smile as she opened the box. It was a necklace of matched blue beads from the Vendrihgon region; a sizeable gift but not nearly the cost of something he would have bought for Zheníhda, like the one tucked inside his luggage to give her when he returned. "It's most lovely, General Tokh, and I'll be most honored to wear it for all to see. Thank you!" He fastened it around her throat for her.

He had a week of joy to look forward to, before the coming storm.

110

* * 16 * *

Tokh signed off on his marriage, Umara wrote her name on the paper with far more ease than Zheníhda had, and he took her for a private celebration dinner at a restaurant. She was nervous her first time bedding him, but not jumpy and frightened like Zheníhda. She knew what would please him, lipping him voluntarily in play, to his utter delight. He made sure to please her, and after that she relaxed with him, happy, chattering, eager for attention. She didn't hide herself, comfortable to walk about the room without a shred of clothing to fetch him a glass of spirits while he watched the round curves of her backside wiggle, curves that overflowed his hands when he squeezed them, eager hot curves that pressed against his *hihvat* with every stroke of his *pushing*. Her hands reached out to caress him without having to be placed there. She most definitely could read – Tokh realized he could no longer leave papers about in the open, something he never worried about with Zheníhda. She had read of far-off places and wonders and he let her choose where she would like to visit, what her heart had always wished to see, and he took her there: the museum-home of her favorite poet, the ancient ruins of a fortress romanticized in a great epic. At night she *pushed* him with her wiggly rounded backside as hard as he *pushed* her, and she carved herself a space in his heart.

Tokh waited until the day before to inform Zheníhda. He kept his face neutral, so as not to make her feel bad. "I'll be home tomorrow. I need you to make up the larger guest room, the one to the right of the stairs. I'll be bringing home a permanent guest."

"Permanent?" Zheníhda said. "How can a guest be permanent? Tokh, you're not bringing your mother here, are you? I need more warning than that."

He dropped the bomb with nothing to soften it. "I've been induced to take a second wife. Umara will need a room of her own."

"You what?" The words slipped out before the idea took hold. Her face in the viewscreen looked as if she'd just taken weaponfire

111

to her chest. "What! *Tokh!* Why? What did you do! What have I done to displease you?"

"Nothing at all. I'll explain the whole story to you when I get back. I promise, everything will work out. Don't worry."

* * *

The moment he ended the call, Zheníhda sank to the floor and screamed. She screamed again, a shriek of agony so long and loud and profound her comm unit began lighting up with calls from the neighbors. She ran outside, past the concerned housemaid, and collapsed in the yard. One by one the neighbor females crept into the yard, Vardani from the house behind and one over with two of her small children in tow.

"Zheníhda! What's wrong? Is it your husband? Were you attacked? Are you hurt? Do you need someone to call Tokh?"

Zheníhda let out another wail before gasping, "He's coming home… with a second wife!" The outpouring of sympathy made her cry harder.

No less than six neighbors took turns holding her hands or lending a shoulder to cry on at all times. They drank through three bottles of *lunahl* and an entire bottle of *flehdan*. Dishes arrived from across the cluster, food to feed those already in the house and fancier things for the next day, to relieve Zheníhda of the duty.

A wife slipped her a strip of three tablets. "Here. Use these. They'll make you not care about anything. Take one and let him do whatever he wants, maybe something he's never thought about before. He'll pay attention to you."

Zheníhda was so crushed she could barely breathe. "It's too late for that. He's not seeing another female, he's already married her. What am I to do? I don't know what I did wrong. Twenty-five years. Twenty-five years. I gave him sons he is proud of. He has smallsons. His line will continue. What did I do wrong?"

"Nothing at all!" said one of the older wives. "Males are males. They care for nothing but their *hihvats*. Trust me. Enjoy some sleep for a change. If he's looking for a *push*, send him to her. Dig your feet in."

"Maybe she's very nice," Vardani said. The baby on her knee began to wail, and she jiggled her leg to quiet it. "Maybe she'll be a good friend to everyone. Maybe it will be a good thing. You have to welcome her, even if it hurts. You don't want her to become an enemy, whispering bad things about you to your husband."

Erahl, eldest of the cluster, cuffed Vardani in the head hard enough to make her cry out. "*Shu!* Don't make things worse! Everyone, take a deep breath. We all know how it works, becoming a wife. There is nothing to say this female had anything to do with her marriage. She may not have had any choice in the matter, and is coming here in absolute terror of Zheníhda. Did he say how old she was?"

Zheníhda wiped her eyes and shook her head.

"See? She could be fourteen and saved from a consort house, or she could be thirty with a huge dowry to entice a husband. He could have been caught dipping and forced to marry her. We won't know until tomorrow. Everyone, calm down. You too, Nihda. Some of us are first wives and some of us are second wives; Alawhin is a third-wife. Imagine how she felt. We all know what you're going through, but speculation won't help. Tomorrow you can find out the truth. Make the house welcoming, as if you were the one coming to a new home in the shadow of an established wife. You know everyone here will have your back. I'll stay with you tonight, if it helps. Tomorrow, ladies. A new wife named Umara is coming to the cluster and you will make her feel welcome, because that's only fair. Tomorrow."

Zheníhda spent a miserable night, though the company of her neighbor helped. Hada the maid made sure the house was spotless – without Tokh and without children home, it was never anything less. The spare room was aired and fluffed and Zheníhda put a bowl of fresh flowers in the room, purple and white, since she didn't know what color the new wife preferred. She dressed in some of her best clothing and made sure she draped herself in her best jewelry, intimidating as a *dahneg*. The necklace she wore was the one Tokh gave her for their wedding; a not so subtle dig at him. Her best veil hung down her back from an expensive jeweled clip, adding inches to her perceived height. Her neighbor left midmorning, and she had nothing to do but sit and wait until Tokh returned, and try hard not to cry.

"Does Lady need anything?" Hada asked kindly.

Zheníhda fought the trembling of her chin. Her stomach wouldn't let her eat a single bite of food, crawling into her chest until her heart crushed against her ribs. "A new husband." It was then they heard a vehicle stop in front of the house.

Zeníhda went out as expected, though she took her time. She knew there were eyes in every window that could see even a sliver of her yard. She bowed to Tokh, but kept affection out of it.

"My husband."

Tokh kissed her under her chin, ran his hands over her shoulders. "This wasn't my idea. I'll explain it all to you inside. May I present Umara, my new second-wife. Umara, meet Zeníhda, she who is in charge of my home."

Umara came forward and knelt on the walk. "Zeníhda-firstwife, I'm most honored to meet you. Tokh has been unending in his praise of you. I hope I'll be able to please him half as much as you have."

Zeníhda gave a shudder. "I would guess you've already surpassed me." Louder, she said, "If you'll come this way, I'll show you to your room."

She led Umara inside and up the stairs. "This will be yours. You have a closet, but there's no private bath except in Tokh's room, which is conveniently across the hall from yours. I hope it's to your liking."

"It's lovely!" Umara exclaimed. She sniffed at the flowers. "These are so pretty! Thank you!"

"You're free to redecorate it as you please. Hada cleans the upstairs on Thirddays and Sixthdays. Next to Tokh's room is his office; no one but Tokh is allowed in there, so do not enter. My room is at the end of the hall. If you go downstairs, Hada will show you everything in the kitchen. I'll leave you to unpack."

Zeníhda turned, but Umara's voice stopped her at the door. The waver in it matched the waver in Zeníhda's stomach. "Zeníhda, I'm sorry! I'm sorry for invading your home. I had little choice. I promise to do everything I can to make this work between us. Please, give me a chance."

Zeníhda's shoulders heaved with a monstrous sob that threatened to bring her stomach up with it. "I don't think there's anything you can do." She walked down the hall to her sitting room and shut the door.

Perhaps twenty *fasím* passed before her door opened without a knock. Zeníhda lay on her reclining sofa, choking on tears. Her head lifted.

"How could you!" she screeched. "How could you do this to me? Twenty five years I warm your bed, give you sons, raise them to think you're the rising and setting of the sun when you're never here, and this is what you do to me? What have I done, Tokh! What have I done to deserve this? At least tell me what I have done!"

"You've done nothing wrong, Nihda. I can't praise you enough…"

"Twenty-five years I sit and wait for you all alone, crying for your comfort, and you go and bring home some under-age consort to take my place? Why? Because I won't act like a consort in your bed? You couldn't have warned me? Given me a chance to please you? Why would you do this to me! Am I so worn and broken you just throw me away?"

Tokh allowed her to rant. When she seemed to run out of words – no small feat – he took his turn.

"You've done nothing to upset me, Nihda. It was General Sobak. What am I supposed to say when an L-3 general who happens to be my immediate superior directly asks me to take his niece as a second-wife? She's a widow with no children; her parents threatened to send her to a consort house because she is twenty-five years old and they didn't think she would be married again." It didn't seem right that Umara's age matched the length of his marriage. They were both old enough and married enough to be her parents. Acceptable or not, it seemed wrong.

"What was I supposed to do, Nihda? Tell my superior no? Do you know what that would do to my career? Do you want to tell her I should send her to be a consort? I have three years in which to do it. Is that what you would want someone to do to you?"

"I have sons!" Zheníhda spat. "Stay away from me, Tokh! Just stay away! You have your new little plaything, go play with her. This is my room, and I will now stay here."

Tokh's face darkened. "I've just returned from a lengthy trip and I expect my wife in my bed tonight, where she belongs."

"You brought a wife! Go to her! Maybe you should find a third! Or a fourth or fifth! One for every day of the week to keep you happy. Maybe your empty old heart will give out from that much *pushing*!"

He stepped up to her, slow and threatening, but Zheníhda didn't back down, meeting his cold glare with one of her own. "If I chose to have ten wives, that would be my business, not yours, and you would have no say in it. Umara is now also my wife, and you will be polite. You don't need to be her friend, but you will be polite to her, or face discipline. You will be in my bed tonight if I have to drag you there by your hair. Is that understood?"

"Get away from me!" Zheníhda dropped to the floor and screamed her frustration to the carpet.

"You will present yourself at dinner." Tokh spun on his heel and left the room, slamming the door behind him.

Zheníhda came down when Hada repeated Tokh's request for dinner. She'd stopped crying, but she looked awful. Tokh sat at the long side of the table; his wives sat at the ends, far apart.

Umara nibbled each bite as if she expected it to bite back. "Your food is wonderful, Firstwife Zheníhda."

Zheníhda picked at her plate, unable to eat more than a mouthful. Her trembling hand held her third glass of *lunahl*. "Thank you, Secondwife."

Tokh ignored the tension crushing the table. "I have it worked out. If I'm to have extended time home, I'll alternate weeks with each of you. One week one of you will share my bed, the next week the other. If I have only a few days, we'll alternate days. If I have only one night, then we'll split the night. The wife who's turn it is will be hostess. If I have more than two or three guests, both of you will hostess. And that's the way it's going to be. If I'm not here, you'll work out your own schedules, but I will tolerate no discord. If you can't work out differences, I'll be forced to resort to discipline, which I do not want to do. Is that understood? IS IT?" he boomed when no words came forth.

"Yes, Tokh," Zheníhda mumbled.

"Yes, my husband," Umara said softly.

Zheníhda didn't back down. Tokh didn't drag her by her hair, but he did pick her up around her middle and carry her kicking and yelling to his bed, where the arguing continued. Umara cowered in her new bed, waiting to hear blows.

"This! Is this what you want?" Zheníhda raged, and tore off her nightclothes. "Is this because I won't act like a consort for you? Then here! Come get what you want." She dropped to her knees and held her breasts out to him.

Tokh watched her with disgust. "You're drunk."

116

"What if I am? I have every right to be. Is your baby asleep, or am I supposed to sing to her first?"

"I told you, this has nothing to do with you, or what you are or do. Nothing! I brought you gifts, but I won't give them to you if you're going to behave like this. I haven't seen you in two and a half weeks. I looked forward to coming home, until you started tantruming like a child."

Despite Umara's fears, he never hit Zheníhda. He did have to pin her down on the bed, arms crossed over her head, where he *pushed* her three times in a row while she cried. She fought to leave when he released her; he took his belt, buckled it around her and slid his arm through it. With his other arm around her, and his leg over her, she had no choice but to stay put. After some time she fell asleep, torn between wanting to claim him for herself in no uncertain terms and stabbing him to death.

Tokh left for work as if nothing unusual had happened at all. Zheníhda stood in the kitchen, drinking a cup of hot *raffin* that was doing nothing to fill the emptiness in her heart. She watched out the door, listening to a variety of whistles and chirps and calls.

Umara tiptoed in behind her and bowed. "Pleasant day, Firstwife. You have a lovely home and garden. I'm most honored to be here in it." She got herself a cup of *raffin* and made a breakfast out of a flatbread, a *doga* fruit, and some sweetnut butter. She sat quietly at the table, listening.

"What are the noises? Are they animals or insects?"

"That's the Cluster. They're calling me. They wish to meet you."

Umara sat very still. She swallowed her bite of breakfast. "The Cluster?"

"The other wives. They expect me to introduce you. Come."

Zheníhda went outside to the yard and gave a soft whistle. From the gates in the walls, every last wife came pouring forth. Most went immediately to Zheníhda, hugging her.

"Nihda! Are you okay? He didn't hurt you, did he? We could hear the shouting from our house. You're so lucky; Rhanna would have blackened my eyes if I yelled at him like that. So, how did it go? Who did he sleep with last night? He didn't make you both... ?" All the eyes kept glancing at Umara.

Zheníhda took a deep breath. She'd cried herself dead inside. The tears would return, but not now. "This is Umara, Tokh's new wife. Please welcome her."

The attention turned to Umara, embraces and welcomes and introductions. Vardani from the house behind and over one was still younger than Umara by six years. Her clothes said *dahneg*, but her appearance said exhausted mother.

"Do you like children?" she said, baby on one hip and toddler on the other.

Umara smiled. "I love children. I didn't have a chance to have my own before my first husband died."

Vardani smiled back. "Here, then. You can hold him. My arms get so tired." Umara took the baby, Vardani let her toddler down to run, and she stood up straight for the first time that day.

General Sobak put Tokh on local duty for a few weeks, allowing him time to straighten out his home life. And it did help; Zheníhda's heart remained broken, but with Tokh around, it couldn't fester. Umara brightened up her room and inquired if Zheníhda minded if she added some things to the rest of the rooms. Umara played everything as correct as she could, asking Zheníhda's permission over the smallest of courtesies. The Cluster accepted Umara as one of them, but Umara did what few of them could: she read well, and instead of socializing she would crawl away to read or listen to poetry. She was friendly and polite, but she didn't crave interaction.

Zheníhda was ice cold in Tokh's bed, until it became Umara's week. The noises drifting down the hall were faint, but so happy Zheníhda cried all over again. She cornered Tokh in his forbidden office.

Her face said she'd been crying for some time. She threw herself against his chest and held on. "Tokh? You keep saying this wasn't about me, that I still please you. I'm not terribly old, Tokh. I'm still fertile. Please give me another child? It would keep me busy. There are other young children in our cluster, so it would have friends. And if Umara had one, too, we could raise them together. They would be almost twins. Please, Tokh? I beg you."

He lifted her chin so she had to look him in the eye, but his gaze was warm and kind. "Would that make you happy again?"

An honest smile lit her face. "Yes! It really would."

118

He gave her the gifts he'd brought back with him, a dark yellow *keransel* stone pendant and matching earrings. Zheníhda was floored by it, and her attitude improved.

And four weeks later, forty-four year old Zheníhda's hopes came true. Her babies were nineteen and twenty four, and she was expecting another. This time, her tears were for joy.

"Congratulations, Firstwife," Umara said, her own womb hollow and aching. "A child in the house will be a joy for everyone." The Cluster wives were just as thrilled.

Zheníhda strutted when she walked, queen of her world. She, Nihda the Firstwife, was pregnant, but that baby her husband had brought home was not. Perhaps she was barren, and Tokh would divorce her in her third year. After all, she bore her first husband no children, either. But Old Zheníhda – she still had it! Weeks passed, and still Umara had nothing to share. Now Umara was the one who looked uncomfortable and desperate.

By her fifth month, Zheníhda had begun to show. She wore waistless, snug-fitting dresses that showed off her bump. "I can feel it moving. Can you feel it, Tokh? Right here. Very faint." Tokh pressed his hand to her belly and agreed. Umara, too, was allowed to feel. Her smile was joyous, but her eyes held a silent pain.

"I'm on the road again," Tokh informed them. "I leave next week for a training session. I'm not leaving Kerasím, as far as I know, so if it looks like it's getting close, I'll arrange to be home for the birth. Umara will be here if you need help, as well as Hada."

Zheníhda wrestled herself out from under his hands. "Why do you always seem to be away for births?"

Tokh frowned. "Only Zenak. I was home for all of your pregnancy with Kitras. I go where I'm sent; that's my job." He kissed her neck. "I promise, I'll be here in plenty of time."

Two days had passed when Zheníhda watched Tokh get dressed from their bed. She gave a grimace and rubbed her belly. "Gah. I don't feel well, Tokh."

"You're pregnant. You vomit your breakfast and dinner and live on fruit juice. Why should today be different than yesterday?"

"No. Not that kind of sick. I feel really sick. My head, my back, even my legs hurt."

Tokh squinted at her. "You do look sick."

Zheníhda rose from the bed and grabbed her middle. "Ow. The baby doesn't like it either." She took two steps toward his bathroom and fainted onto the floor.

Zheníhda miscarried her third son several hours later. Tokh was able to take her home that night, strung out on tranquilizing tablets to ease her pain. He carried her into the house and up the stairs and put her in his bed, even though it was now Umara's week. Umara overstepped her bounds, hugging Zheníhda and crying. Whether it was from needing the comfort or the tranquilizing tablets, Zheníhda didn't object.

"I'm so, so sorry, Zheníhda! Whatever you need, please tell me and I'll get it or do it for you. I'm here to help. Do you want me to tell the Cluster for you?"

Zheníhda nodded, and Umara sent a voice message to Vardani, who spread it down the street. Flowers and token gifts and consolations began arriving before Tokh left in the morning. It took Zheníhda three days to leave her bed, and then it was only to see Tokh off on his assignment. After that, she did nothing but sit in a chair and stare into space.

* * 17 * *

Tokh wasn't under communication blackout, so he called his wives once a week to check in. Zheníhda spoke to him, but she was a ghost of herself, a blank hearth with no fire at all. Umara took his latest call behind locked doors.

"I'm scared, Tokh. I feel so bad for her, but I'm frightened. I can't bear to tell her."

"Tell her what?"

Umara's face looked so sad on the small screen, for something Tokh knew she wanted more than anything. "I'm pregnant; ten weeks. She was still pregnant when we tried. I didn't know she would lose her baby. I don't want her thinking I did this to spite her. You know I didn't! I don't want to be cruel, but eventually I'm going to show, and she'll realize it."

Tokh gave a hard, heavy sigh. "How long until you think she'll notice?"

"I don't know. Maybe another six weeks. I'll start wearing looser clothing now, so she won't think about it."

"Okay. I'll make some calls today and come up with a plan. Stay calm."

Five weeks later, Tokh stopped home briefly to escort Zheníhda out to visit Zenak and his family. He left her there an entire month. Zheníhda's mood improved, and she was full of affectionate smiles when he retrieved her.

"I have good news or bad news, depending on how you look at it," he told her during the flight home. "Umara is expecting. We know it to be a boy. I know it's not good timing for you, but I had intended to give you your wish, both of you having children at once. I never thought it would turn out this way. She's very ashamed to be pregnant around you. Please don't add to her stress."

Zheníhda groaned with anguish. "How much do you expect me to take, Tokh? How many insults?"

He patted her hand. "It wasn't my intention, Nihda. We'll adjust."

Umara greeted her as an old friend. "Welcome back, Firstwife. I tried to keep your house as perfectly as you do. I hope you find it to your liking."

Zheníhda's gaze ripped Umara from head to toe. She wore a layered skirt and a ruffled shirt, and a long open jacket that covered her to her heels. Umara kept her shoulders hunched forward a little, as if she were sucking her stomach in. She might have been pregnant, she might have just gained weight.

"Thank you," she said, and went upstairs to sulk in her room.

"Kept the house clean?" the wives whispered with her. "How could it be dirty? She sat outside reading to herself most of the days. That's all she does. She was polite, yes, but she didn't seek us out once. Really, who teaches a female to read that well? Why? What good does it do? She walks around the gardens singing to the flowers, then goes and sits all by herself with her nose in her comm unit, doesn't invite us over for *ráffin* once. *Gah!*"

"Sometimes I don't think I can take anymore," Zheníhda admitted.

Erahl slapped her palm on the table and made everyone jump. "Get over it, Nihda. Time to move on. You've done your mourning. Imagine just for a moment what it's like to be her. You had your husband's youth. You had him when he looked good and could throw a *push* into an aircraft and make it hum. In five years he'll be how old? More than fifty, I'll bet. She'll only know him as an old man. You're sad because you're older? She's young and couldn't land a *hihvat* under forty. How does that make her feel? She's not a bad looker. She's going to be in the mood for a good bedding and no matter how much she entertains him he's going to wilt under her fingers. Imagine if you'd been wed to an old man at that age, like poor Salunah in the Mahleks Cluster, sixteen to fifty-three. Tragedy. Your smallsons are older than her children; hers will never know him as anything but an old man they'll have to care for. They'll be trying to find a wife while their *bo* wanders off and talks to trees. You're not the sorriest wife in the world, Nihda. You have memories she'll never have."

Zheníhda scowled. "True, but it doesn't make me any happier."

Umara was pleasant and social if the wives were visiting with Zheníhda, but she never sought them out. "I don't think it's fair," she explained to Vardani. "If I come out with the group, everyone will want to touch my belly and ask me questions, and I think that would be very rude in front of Zheníhda, after all she's been through. I won't do that to her."

"You're robbing us of a joy in our lives," Vardani fired back, "but you're kind to think like that. I'll explain to the others."

Tokh took a week's leave when Umara gave birth. Zheníhda wouldn't go with him to confirm the baby, but she sent Umara a congratulatory voice message and left the expected gift for both Umara and the baby on her bed.

Umara came home two days later, hiding the baby under a blanket like a ball of laundry.

"Stop it!" Zheníhda growled. "You hid a pregnancy, but you can't hide a baby. Do you think I'll never know he's in the house? He is what he is. May I at least hold him? He is a brother to my sons."

"Of course, Firstwife." Umara handed him over, praying Zheníhda wouldn't dash him against the wall in retribution.

Zheníhda smiled at the tiny balled fists curled against fat little golden cheeks. She blinked away the tears that rose. "Tokh has beautiful sons. What's his name?"

"Joralan," Umara beamed with pride. "After my father, Joral."

Zheníhda kept the sneer to a minimum. "Perhaps my memory is faulty, but why would you name a child after someone who threatened to send you to a consort house?"

Umara forgot to breathe. "I-I – It's just the way it's done. Maybe he'll feel better about me now."

Zheníhda snorted. "It's your baby. You can name him whatever you want. That was just my thought."

She spent the weeks in Tokh's bed while Umara recovered; a small pleasure, perhaps, but one Zheníhda neither looked forward to nor resisted. Something was just not there anymore.

* * 18 * *

Zheníhda's sniping began. It wasn't a planned thing, it just happened. She didn't say it to be mean – she truly didn't. It just leaked out without thought.

"You look tired today, Firstwife," Umara said at breakfast. She always chose the honorific over Zheníhda's name. Tokh and the wives called her Nihda, and sometimes Umara would use Firstwife Zheníhda, but no one would ever accuse her of disrespect or not minding her place.

"Perhaps if there were less noise at night, I could sleep better," Zheníhda mumbled to her breakfast.

Umara looked wounded. "I'm sorry, Firstwife. I'm doing the best I can. You've raised two sons; perhaps you could show me a better way to quiet him."

"I could, but he's your son. You know him best."

In some ways, Zheníhda treated her no differently than she had Avalihn when Khourbas was born, reminding a new young mother of the thousands of things they had to remember with a child, but Umara wasn't Avalihn; Zheníhda wasn't her mother in law and no respect was required, nor was she barely twenty. Umara could stand only so many reminders.

She sang to Joralan as she bathed him, making happy faces as he gazed back at her.

"Did you test the water before you put him in there?"

"Yes, Firstwife."

"Did you feed him first?"

"Yes, Firstwife. That's why he's quiet and content."

"Did you make sure he had time to pee? Otherwise you're just soaking him in dirty water."

"He peed the second I went to take his wrap off. Yes."

"Did you check him for rashes?"

Umara turned her head. "I'm not witless, Zheníhda. I have cared for infants before."

"Hmph. How am I supposed to know that? I'm just making sure."

Umara returned to rinsing Joralan. "Perhaps I should write you a list, then."

Zheníhda left the room in a rustle of skirt.

Kitras caused a cease fire before the needling could get out of control. He called Zheníhda on her personal com. "*Amama*! Is *Bo* home, or is he away on assignment?"

Zheníhda missed him, her baby, now all of twenty and a Lieutenant One. He was all grown up and manly, not as tall as Zenak but much like his father, with Tokh's sharp eyes, thick hank, and shoulders. He was rakish in his brown uniform, and Zheníhda burst with pride every time she saw him. "He's at base for a few weeks, so he's been home at night. Did you wish to speak with him? I can bring him the com."

"No, don't bother. I've got some free time, so I was going to catch a transport flight to the base and stop in for a few days. Is that okay? I've got some things to talk to you and *Bobo* about."

Zheníhda's heart raced. "Of course, Kitras! The guest room is yours. Stay as long as you like."

"How's that new baby brother of mine?"

It surprised Zheníhda to hear him say the words; when he said it, it didn't hurt. Her son had a baby brother. It might not have been hers, but it was his father's. It seemed very natural, and it made her happy.

"Very well. Three months now, and growing like a weed. Umara is a very loving mother to him."

"Can't wait to see him. I'll be there sometime after lunch, so see if *Bo* can stick around."

"I'll tell him. I can't wait to see you, my son! Until later."

Zheníhda forced herself not to rush outside the moment she heard a vehicle stop in front of the house. Tokh beat her to the door, Zheníhda all but jumping in place behind him. Umara was in the middle of feeding Joralan. She broke him off and tucked her breast back into her shirt.

Kitras and his father banged shoulders and grunted loudly in greeting. He hugged Zheníhda and kissed her on her hair. It was only then they realized someone else had entered behind him. Kitras

125

backed up and pulled the girl forward, announcing proudly, "*Ama, Bo,* I'm most pleased to introduce you to my wife, Dalo."

"Wife?" Zheníhda gasped.

Tokh blinked. "Wife?"

Kitras smiled so hard it was possible to hear the strain of his cheek muscles. He gazed at the girl in a trance of joy. "Three days ago. We talked for days, then we finally just said, 'Let's do it!'."

Zheníhda forced her mouth to close. Her son's arm rested around a slender girl with... with hair the shocking pink color of a candy-flower, short and sticking up as if it hadn't been combed in weeks, the same as the hair-like tufts of a candy-flower. She wore a low-cut black shirt that stopped two inches above her – Zheníhda wasn't sure what to call it. It wore like pants, but the waist was so low as to show her navel. The bright fabric hugged her hips tightly all the way down to her legs, where it ballooned out into acceptable female trousers that hid her knees under loose fabric, then pulled together again at the ankles. She wore no proper shoes, just soft thongs that left her feet bare despite the cold Iérot Thorán rain. Her narrow curved toenails were painted pink to match her hair. Under the layers of cosmetics – from the thick black and white eyeliners to the glittering gold shadow and cheek powder – she might have had a pretty face, but it was impossible to tell. The necklace around her throat appeared to be made of rough natural stones plucked from the ground on an evening walk, no style, no shine, no status, no... dignity.

She did bow forward with manners. "Lord Tokh, Lady Zheníhda, I am honored to meet you."

"Dalo?" Zheníhda still stared at her hair. "Welcome to our home. We are... honored."

Umara had moved to greet Kitras, but stepped into the background. Zheníhda had enough to deal with.

Kitras couldn't see beyond the sparkles in his eyes. He lifted his bride off the ground and for a moment seemed as if he were going to rip her throat out with his teeth. Dalo leaned back and laughed, slapping his shoulders in play until he let go. "Isn't she fantastic!"

"Come, sit, let us stare at you," Zheníhda said in a sticky-sweet voice. She led them to the dining room.

"What would prompt you to get married?" Tokh said. He wasn't yelling – not yet – but his brusque words gave away his displeasure. "I had some very nice prospective females for you to meet when you came home next month, daughters and smalldaughters of high-ranking officers. They would have set you up well for promotions."

Kitras and Dalo eyed each other, and both of them giggled. "I dunno. Her father runs a clothing store in Kanok Moht, all that high-caste trendy stuff, you know? So I went in there to inquire about someone we were looking for, and she was behind the counter. We started talking, and then I just kept coming back, and finally I asked her father if she was spoken for, and he said no, so I asked for her. And here she is!" He grabbed her hand and they rocked together, bumping shoulders.

Zheníhda's smile bore a polar wind. "Perhaps you could tell us about yourself, Dalo? Your family, how old you are, your caste, are you pregnant."

"Oh no!" Dalo said. She still gripped Kitras's hand. "My parents wouldn't have gone for that. Unless it just happened in the last three days. I don't have much to tell. I went to school until I was eight; I've helped out in the store ever since. I turned seventeen last month. My parents are *dahneg*, which is why they get all the high-caste business."

"And they let you walk around in public like that?"

Dalo rolled her eyes. "That's what all you old people say. This is how we dress in the city. Kitras said things were more conservative out here, but I didn't think it was this bad."

Umara slipped through the dining room on her way to the kitchen.

"Hey! Is that my little brother?" Kitras took the baby. He swung him up over his head, making him laugh. "Hey, little guy! You have to start walking soon. I can't buy you your first scope and rifle until you can walk." Dalo pawed Joralan and chucked him under his chin.

"Do you like babies, Dalo?" Umara said.

"Of course! I can't wait to have one!"

Umara smiled and tipped her head to Tokh. She took the baby from Kitras. "Why don't you come upstairs with me, then? I can show you the adorable little outfits he has. You can change him if you want; he's got a tiny uniform we can dress him in and show Kitras. I'll show you the guest room while we're up there."

"That'd be the cream!" Dalo followed her out of the room.

Tokh waited until he heard the footsteps on the stairs, then backhanded Kitras in the side of his head with a resounding crack.

127

"What the bloody *lihx* were you thinking?!" he snarled. "A damned Lieutenant One with no sponsor yet – how the *aaka*-hole do you think you're going to get anywhere? I had connections lined up that would have set you for life! Shaved years off your promotions just for the names you were connected with! Gotten you the choicest commands, the best assignments. A clothing store? What is that supposed to get you? Half a uniform that lets your gut hang out?"

"She will not come down those stairs again until she puts real clothing on!" Zheníhda hissed. "Your father is an honorable man, but you can't expect him to control himself with a young thing like that prancing around half-naked! Have you no decency, Kitras? That is your wife! She is supposed to reflect and amplify your grace and standing. Are you trying to signify you came from a carnival? You are *dihnarwharl*! High *dihnarwharl*!"

Kitras glared. "I knew you people would react this way. You're so medieval! I love her, okay? I die a little every time she leaves the room and I fall in love with her every time she walks back in. I don't care if her hair is pink or green or black. It's part of her, and part of what I love about her."

"Kaaaaah!" Zheníhda growled. "Love! Love has nothing to do with marriage! Marriage is a plan to survive the future. A good marriage matches two people with the same goals who can work together successfully so they can lead comfortable, prosperous lives. You complement each other so the world looks upon each of you with respect. 'He's able to achieve because his wife can handle everything at home and he does not need to worry.' 'Look at her! There's a wife with a husband who appreciates her.' What do you plan on getting out of her, Kitras? Party cakes?"

"Ama! Look, she's my wife and that's all there's to it. We didn't want some big thing. I'm a damned good soldier! I graduated a sharp-shooter! The only one in my class! I've got my sniper badge and fourteen kills to my name already. I've got four – four! citations, and I'm only twenty. Your connections would have been nice, *Bo*, but I can work my way up on merit. I thought you'd be happy, me marrying a *dahneg*. They were really impressed that you have a house. They don't even have that, just a seven-room apartment over their store. You haven't even given her a chance! Have you been to the cities? Have you even seen how real people dress? Not everyone grows up in uniform. Most of the people we defend are not army."

Tokh paced the small dining room. "Truth. I can still pull connections for you, but it won't be as wide a net. But you will make her dress appropriately while she is here. You invite unwanted attentions, allowing that behavior. If she does it on purpose, she's a *trixahg* who should be divorced as soon as possible. If she isn't, it reflects poorly on you, not protecting your wife from stray eyes. Would she enjoy being shared among your friends?"

Kitras sighed, eyes downward. "No."

"Then you keep her covered," Tokh growled. "That is the job of a husband. We won't discuss her hair."

It was Zheníhda's week in Tokh's bed. His hand was between her thighs, teasing her while she stroked him into the same state. Sometimes it was difficult to connect if both partners were already swollen, but a touch of slippery stuff and some harder thrusting gave both partners an extra spark when things finally popped into place, and Zheníhda needed every spark. Kitras was quieter than Zenak; no noises leaked down the hall through the closed doors.

"Love," Zheníhda snorted. "Both sons ignored us for 'love.' Did we miss something, Tokh? Did we do it wrong?"

His lips moved across her throat. "I don't think so. I wouldn't have chosen as wisely at that age. My father made an excellent choice, even if I was too young and stubborn to know it at the time. If I could go back and do it again, knowing what I know now, I wouldn't choose any differently. If I could, I would use stronger discipline on my sons, so they wouldn't dare disrespect us."

"Truly? You wouldn't choose someone better than me?"

He withdrew his hand. She rolled over onto her knees while he took his time ramming the swollen rings of tissue past each other, each contact exciting them further and making it more difficult. Zheníhda gave a moan that was half pain and half pleasure when he made it inside. He sat back on his heels and pulled her onto his lap, facing away from him. His hands ran up her long sides and squeezed her breasts, pulling her back against his chest.

"I've seen many generals' wives, shorter, fatter, thinner, paler, darker, maybe even prettier, but I have yet to see one better than you. No. Like me or not, I won't trade you." He clamped down with his teeth where her neck met her shoulder, grinding himself against her.

Zheníhda groaned with pleasure and exposed more of her neck to him. "Tell me again."

Dalo wasn't pregnant at her marriage, but all it took was a honeymoon. Kitras's son Lanag was born just eleven months after his Uncle Joralan. Zheníhda didn't know whether to cry or be happy for them.

* * 19 * *

Joralan blossomed under his mother's care. Umara read poems to him, sang him to sleep, sang song-games to him when he was awake. She could tell what he wanted by the look on his happy face. She put great thought into purchasing his toys, and he delighted in each and every one. In his world crawling was too slow; he wanted to run. And in Zheníhda's world, Joralan was Umara's son, not hers, and thus she kept her nose out of raising him.

Some of the time.

"Umara!" Zheníhda yelled. She dashed across the room, but not fast enough to prevent the crash. "He's knocking down my lamps!"

Umara pulled her nose out of a poem and scrambled to her feet. "Sorry, Zheníhda." She picked Joralan up. "He was playing with the toys just a second ago."

"You can't keep your nose in a personal unit all the time when you have an infant," Zheníhda said without patience. "You have to watch him!"

"I am watching him!" Umara protested. "He's just very fast."

"Then you need to be faster. What would happen if the lamp had broken? He could have been cut by glass, or worse yet, eaten a piece! How would you explain that to Tokh? That his son was injured because you couldn't watch him fast enough? We both know he wouldn't be pleased."

Umara's face pinched with regret. "I'm sorry, Zheníhda. I won't let it happen again." She hugged Joralan and kissed him. "Come, Jora. We'll go outside where you can't hurt anything."

"And pick up these toys!" Zheníhda kicked one across the room. "This is my sitting room, not an infant center! If I fall I will throw away every one I see."

Umara gathered the toys, then went outside.

Zheníhda was watching her favorite program on the Kerasi Global ComNet, the *fáhganid* drama *Inside Connections*, when the thumping sounded down the stairs, followed by the screams of a

131

small child. She took her time, but did pick him up and make sure he was okay.

"Umara! Where are you, you lazy *jappa*! He just fell down the stairs!"

Umara came running and took him from her, cuddling and comforting him. "I was getting his lunch – He was with me just a second ago! Not two seconds ago! If you saw him on the stairs, why didn't you stop him?"

Zheníhda looked down her nose. "He's not my child to watch. I didn't know he couldn't manage stairs yet. What are you going to do when he can open doors?"

Umara's anger started to surface, but she backed it down. "Does Tokh know how cruel you are to his son?"

The threat hit its mark. Zheníhda shut off the ComNet and went to Erahl's house.

Zheníhda seemed to have forgotten all the times Zenak smashed his fingers in doors and drawers, or how many times she caught Kitras throwing things off the balcony in Dahn Bohr, or the time Zenak managed to run out of the apartment and down the entire hall stark naked while she was drawing his bath, or when Kitras was two and found his father's knife and stabbed holes in a chair. She caught Joralan upstairs, playing with hot water in the sink, his hands, face, and shirt covered in hand cleaner.

"Water!" he told her, splashing another wave onto the floor. "Water!"

For a moment Zheníhda considered letting him continue, but the risk of burns was real, and it was more than she was willing to allow in good conscience. She carried him downstairs.

"Umara! You good for nothing, unfit waste of motherhood! You're lucky I came across him playing with the sink. He had the water all the way on hot. He could have scalded himself. Don't you ever watch him at all?"

Umara scrambled off the sofa and put her poetry down to take her son. "He was napping! He was asleep in his bed not ten *fasím* ago! I wouldn't have left him if he wasn't. I swear you're doing this to me on purpose!"

"I wouldn't waste my time."

"Hmph! Same way you won't waste your time at Kitras's with their son, because Dalo told you off!"

132

"That's not true!" Zheníhda spat.

"Tokh knows the truth. *Dihnama.*" The grandmother comment hit home. Umara carried Joralan upstairs to change his shirt. When she returned, her poetry book had been torn in half.

"She's awful," Zheníhda said to Tokh when they were alone. "Always trying to read instead of watching him, like she's some wise scholar who must study all the time. She's lucky he's never been seriously hurt. Poems! *Gah!* Filling her head with useless airy trash. Maybe she should read a poem on how to watch a child. I'd go spend time with Dalo, but I'm afraid to leave the house for fear something terrible will happen."

Tokh stumbled on Umara by accident. Joralan was asleep for the night, but he followed the sound. Umara was hidden behind the door of the guest room, crying to herself.

His hand slid over her shoulder. "What's happened?"

Umara wiped her eyes and laughed it off. "I'm being a silly little female, that's all. Really, Tokh. I'm fine. I'm sorry. It's just one of my moods. You know how I get."

Tokh wasn't impressed. Umara's moods made her mopey, not weepy. His foot shut the door and his eyes bored into hers. "I asked you a question. What's wrong?"

Her smile radiated love. "I wouldn't burden you with petty things, my husband. My sillinesses are mine to work out. I apologize for making you notice me."

"Umara!" he barked, and she cowered, trapped between him and the wall. "I gave you a directive and I expect an answer. Do not anger me over it."

His hand rubbed her shoulder, until Umara broke down in more serious tears. "I can't take it anymore, Tokh! The way she needles me! Day after day after day, for the littlest things! If I put a spoon in the tray and it doesn't line up right, she points it out to me. She's always done it, but since Joralan was born, she's so much worse. I don't like being in the house with her. If he coughs, I've let him get sick. If he scrapes a knee, it's because I'm careless. If he spills his cup, it's my fault. He's two years old, Tokh! There hasn't been a single time when he's been hurt or sick because of me! I'm a good mother! I am! I'm sorry her baby died, but that wasn't my fault, either. She has no right to take her unhappiness out on me! I've tried

133

being nice. I've tried ignoring her. I've tried telling her to stop, but nothing has worked."

Tokh softened. He pulled her into his arms and didn't yell at her about the tears. "*Shu, shu.* I know you're a good mother. I see it in my son's face. I see it when you're with him. *Shu.* Give me a few days. I investigate things in my duties, remember? Let me work on it, and when I think I've uncovered the issue, I'll know what to do about it. Can you last a few more days?"

Umara wiped her eyes and nodded. "Yes, my husband."

Tokh investigated high-level issues for His Majesty The Emperor's army. Bickering females required no effort at all. He sat back and watched, noting who did what and when, who said what, what the reactions were. Zhenihda kept to her schedule, eating breakfast with or without Umara and Joralan, then going off to meet at a house with the other wives. Umara waited until she left, then sat and played with Jora. Zhenihda returned for lunch. Umara made Joralan lunch, put him down for a nap, and sat down to listen to music and read her poetry while Zhenihda watched programs on the ComNet, then called the other wives on her com unit to discuss them. Joralan woke up and Umara took him outside to play. Zhenihda decided what to have for dinner, and helped the housemaid begin.

Zhenihda rapped on the windowglass. "Umara! He's tearing up my flowers! Watch him!"

Umara called him over to her. "He's just playing in the dirt. He's a boy. Let him be! 'And from the dirt and dust and rains/The seeds of creation hath sprung.'"

"Don't let him bring dirt into this house."

Tokh let it run two days, but he'd figured things out by the first. There was little he didn't already know; Umara and Zhenihda were two very different people, two city transports running on parallel lines, each resenting the other for moving in an opposite direction and getting angry in each other's wake. Zhenihda did go out of her way with comments, but not as much as Umara thought, and some of them were truth. Umara was too sensitive; *any* word from Zhenihda made her startle in dread. She retreated deeper into her poetry to escape the stress, and in the process didn't always pay enough attention to her very busy toddler, which made Zhenihda more furious. It was an endless spiral into a black hole, and it needed to be stopped. He wasn't giving each wife her own house, nor dividing his down the center. They would learn to work together just like his officers did.

If they didn't kill each other first.

He waited until Jora was asleep for the night and called them both upstairs.

"It's never been a secret that you're both very different people. Different ages, different cities, different education, different attitudes, originally different castes. You don't work together but try to do the same tasks separately, and it's creating friction. Zheníhda, you need a better sense of humility. Umara, you need to grow a spine and stop avoiding the conflict. I've dealt with this among my officers before, with great success. Part of it is education, part of it is making them remember that their personal feelings are irrelevant. There's a job to be done and personal feelings have no business in the execution of the tasks. I've cleared my schedule and taken a week's leave. Hada will assist me. From this moment on, for the next week, you will both serve me. You will attend me at all times, day and night. You won't speak unless I speak to you first. You won't make a single move without my permission and you will carry out my orders without fail, no matter what I ask.

"Your one and only task in this house, every day, whether or not I'm present, is to serve *me*. Whether it's washing the floors, trimming my hair, caring for my offspring or pleasing me in bed, you are both tasked with serving me. Nothing else. That is your job as my wife, a title you both carry equally. Firstwife, secondwife, thirdwife – they are titles of respect, nothing else. Both will serve me equally. Any failure to obey will be met with discipline." He seized his incentive rod from the top of his clothing chest. It whistled through the air and smacked the bed with a resounding thump. Zheníhda and Umara danced backward and clung to each other.

"See? It's working already. Is that understood?"

The wives let go. "Yes, Tokh." "Yes, my Lord husband."

"Good. You can start by giving me an oil massage. Umara, take the top half because you're very good with shoulders. Zheníhda, do the bottom half. You're very good with my feet." He took his utility belt off and put his arms out, waiting for them to undress him. Both females glanced at the other in bewilderment. Tokh had always

135

treated them as separate wives, never together for anything but meals, but they stepped forward.

Half an hour later, when they were sweaty and oily and tired from the exertion, he lay back and sighed. "Much better. Now I'm feeling aroused. You will strip."

"Which one of us, my Lord?" Umara said.

"Both. You'll both attend me for the next week."

"*Kaaah!*" Zheníhda threw her hands in the air and walked away from the bed. "You carry your folly too far, Tokh. There are some things you know I won't do. You want me, fine, but it will not be with an audience."

"I said to strip!"

"And I said no!"

Tokh swung his legs over the bed and crossed the room in three steps. Zheníhda backed up against the door. His hand grabbed her blouse by the collar and with one violent yank tore it straight down the front. Zheníhda cried out, raised her arms, and cringed to ease a potential blow. "I ordered you to strip!"

Umara hung on his arm. "Lord husband! Please don't! Please don't hurt her! Look, I will strip for you! Please, let me please you tonight. Oiling you has set me on fire. I need your pleasure. Let me serve you, Lord." Umara slipped her shirt over her head and worked at her skirt fastener so fast all she did was fumble it. She slipped out of her clothing and stood behind him, pawing his shoulders to distract him.

Tokh's eyes stared into Zheníhda's, cold and hard. Zheníhda turned her back and removed the remains of her blouse, then her skirt and underthings.

"At least turn off the lights!" she hissed, trying to cover all of herself at once.

"On the bed."

"What is with you! You're not even drunk!"

Zheníhda was thin and had always taken care of herself, but her forty-six year old wisemother's body couldn't compete with Umara's twenty-eight year old fleshy voluptuousness, and she withdrew inside herself with unnecessary shame. Tokh took them one at a time, making one sit on the end of the bed while he went at the other. The second time he made them kneel side by side, finishing with one and moving directly to the next, so they each felt every movement he gave them. Zheníhda buried her face in the bed

136

and wept. The third time he was tiring – six in a row was a lot of *pushing* for someone his age, so he settled for nursing Umara's breasts while Zhenihda reached around and gave him a handshake. He collapsed exhausted on the bed.

"No no," Tokh said to Zhenihda as she stood up. He patted the bed next to him. "Right here."

"Unless you plan to sleep in a puddle of my piss, you'll let me use the toilet," she snapped.

"Three *fasím*," he allowed. "Umara, you may go when she returns. Then I want you right back here."

Umara wasn't crying – yet – but she kept her chin glued to her chest. Tokh slept with one on each side of him, but he did allow them to pull up the sheets.

When not actively engaged in bathing him, dressing him, massaging him, feeding him, bedding him, or any other task he could think of, Tokh made them stand at attention, awaiting his next command. Hada did nothing but nanny Joralan; Zhenihda and Umara were given her tasks. Whatever he asked, he made sure they had to do it together, be it cooking or setting the table or scrubbing the floors. Tokh wanted them working together, in each other's way, bumping each other as much as possible. Neither was supposed to speak unless necessary. Twice Zhenihda received warning slaps to her backside for ripe comebacks. When he ran out of tasks, Tokh made them move every piece of furniture from the first floor into the yard, scrub the floors and carpeting, and then move it all back. When Umara tried to complain, Tokh made them disassemble the guest room and scrub it ceiling to floor. Sore muscles were no excuse in Tokh's book; he *pushed* them just as hard those nights. They were allowed a short break for bathing and dressing, each in a different bathroom at the same time, and a five-*fasím* toilet break every hour. Every other minute of the day, Tokh directed their activities. Either female was allowed to address Joralan if he approached them first but couldn't waste more than three *fasím* with him; Hada made sure of that. Those were the times Umara cried the hardest.

For four days the wives endured: tired, worn out, ashamed, embarrassed, frustrated, hopeless. That night he gave them permission to sit at the table with him.

"This ends here and now. Your purpose is to serve me, and nothing else. Not better than the other; just serve me. I'll tolerate no more bickering. You do the tasks, you honor me, and that is that, no more, no less. You're interchangeable. Joralan is my son; as my wives you are equally responsible for his safety. You will both check to make sure all tasks are done; if you find one undone, then you're the one that will complete it. I took each of you as wife; when a wife insults the other wife, you insult me. If you wouldn't give the insult to my face, it shouldn't be said to my wife, for that is the same thing. Two wives, one task: serve me. If you can't remember that, I will deliver reminders with my incentive stick. I'll have longer missions away coming soon, and there will be no relapses or there will be severe consequences. Is that understood?"

Both wives sat with heads bent. "Yes my Lord Tokh. Yes my Lord husband."

"You're free to sleep in your own beds tonight. Dismissed."

Both females flew to their rooms, wrapped themselves in layers of nightwear, and dove into their own private beds. Both cried themselves to sleep, but from misery or relief neither was ever sure.

* * 20 * *

Tokh's Emissary Project was getting close and he was starting to put together his team, observing and testing candidates from all over. Umara waited until dinner on a day he was home.

"I saw a doctor this week, Tokh. I'm pregnant again."

Tokh sat back. It wasn't his intent, but sometimes things happened. "Well. That is news. Good news, no?"

Umara gave a faint smile. "Yes, I think so. Jora will be three by then."

Zheníhda rephrased her snort. "He's such an active little boy. It will be difficult to chase him and feed an infant at the same time."

"I take it you'll be helping her, then," Tokh said. "You've had two. I'm sure you would have appreciated an extra eye."

Zheníhda bent her head to keep from biting her tongue. "Of course, Tokh."

"Do they know what it is?" Tokh asked.

Umara nodded. "I'm sorry, Tokh. This one is female."

"Female?" Zheníhda said.

"Female?" Tokh hadn't expected that. That changed all the rules. He'd have to ask among his peers how one raised a female. "I've fathered three living sons, with three smallsons. I never thought about having a female. That'll be another long-range plan, I guess. I'll keep an eye out for other officers with young children, see who her potential prospects will be for marriage."

Umara blinked. "You can't marry her off at birth, Tokh."

"No, but fifteen or twenty years is a long time. A good name and prospect now can go bad by the age of twelve. A second choice can blossom in military school and become a first choice. An officer today may have great influence and control in ten years, and marrying his son can set my daughter up well. My first sons didn't consult me in their marriages, an insult that has never healed. I won't allow that with my second children. I'll make sure they are married well, in positions that will help them in their lives, not hold them back."

"Zenak does well," Zhenihda said in his defense.

"He's a teacher at a military school. He might rise in the administration, but he doesn't have the caste or rank to be director. Unless there's an interstellar war and all men of training are activated, he'll never rise from where he is. Kitras..." Tokh sighed. "Such potential, but now he's held back by his partybird wife and family. Fool! Enjoy the female all you want, but *pushing* a female doesn't mean you must marry her."

Umara's voice was small and timid. "Is that what you wish for your daughter?"

The words hit Tokh like cold water. His unborn daughter was a noble chaste maid, waiting for her father to choose her a kind husband of wealth and power who would give her a happy life. The kind of females seized for personal pleasures were just nameless, pedigree-less females who might as well have been orphans, for the amount of thought given them. How could both exist? What if his daughter was someone like Dalo, attracting attention by showing off her body and bending open for the first soldier who stopped to speak to her?

He would chain her to the wall before he let that happen.

"Of course not!" he snapped. "She is *dihnarwharl.* She'll be raised properly. Like her two mothers," he added.

Zhenihda's tongue loosened in the kitchen. "Congratulations, I guess. It's not like him to be so sloppy."

"It must have been during *that* week," Umara said. She stacked the dirty plates to be put into the washer. "I don't think it was on his mind at the time. Little boys are easy. How in the Emperor's name do I raise a female?"

Zhenihda's words were sharp and stabbing as she loaded the washer. "Teach her young to lie still and let a male humiliate her to his heart's content."

"That's what I mean," Umara said. "I want to avoid that for her. I want her to have happiness in her life, to never worry about things like that. How do I make sure she has a husband who will treat her well? How do I think ahead to teach her all the things she will need to know, from running a house to caring for a child to avoiding males except her husband? Her young heart will be full of lovely thoughts and then her life will take them away. Oh Zhenihda! I'm a terrible mother!" Umara covered her mouth with her hand as if

140

physically holding in her tears. "If Tokh had been angry, I would have gladly stopped the pregnancy. I can't bear the thought of her unhappiness all her days."

"You aren't a bad mother," Zheníhda relented. "You're just afraid for her in advance, before she knows what to fear. That's the risk of being born female. They say that is why we are always on the edge of war with the Union. They won't trade with us because of the limits on our females. Union females have no restrictions. They marry or divorce at will, study like males, even take public work, and no one is allowed to assault them. We blame the frustration from that for their aggression."

"Where did you hear that?"

"Sometimes they discuss it on news programs, but Tokh speaks Union. He was stationed behind their lines for several months and I know he still monitors their transmissions. He has told me many things. I think that's part of the program he's working for. He can't say, but my guess is they're tied together."

Umara snorted. "I can't imagine such a place."

Tokh managed to juggle his schedule so he had two days home to acknowledge the birth and name the baby, even though it was most definitely female.

"Kesseh," Tokh said.

"Kesseh," Umara agreed with delight.

Zheníhda made a face. "Kesseh?"

"Kesseh daras-Giláhn," Tokh said. "You expect me to name her Dalo?"

Umara explained, "Kesseh was the beautiful heroine of the epic poem *Ballad of Water's Run*. She was kidnapped by a rival prince, and when the great warrior Elskhid Rho rescued her, he was caught by the evil prince and about to be beheaded when Kesseh picked up a sword as tall as she was and ran the evil prince through with it. Elskhid saved her and Kesseh saved him, and they lived happily ever after."

"Hmph," Zheníhda snorted. "I supposed I should be glad it wasn't a boy for you to name Elskhid.

* * 21 * *

Tokh came in the door in a flurry, one of his officers in tow behind him. Umara was feeding the baby, and flipped up a corner of the blanket to cover more skin.

Joralan ran up to him. "*Bobo*!" Tokh swung him up once and wrestled him with affection, then set him free.

"Joralan! Come sit with *Ama*. *Bobo*'s busy," Umara said, and patted the sofa next to her.

Zheníhda glided into the sitting area in hostess mode. "Welcome home, husband. Pleasant day, Major," she said, noting the guest's rank. "Will you be needing lunch?"

"Ask me in a little while," Tokh said. "I'm not sure how long we'll be here. Major Mátokhan, my wives, Zheníhda and Umara."

The major and wives all bowed to each other. The major was distracting in appearance; his face seemed distorted: his skin so pale it was nearly colorless, his forehead smooth where he should have had a heavier ridge above his eyes, and his single eyebrow had been pared into two distinct ones. His chin hank, symbol of male virility, had been shaved back into a very short point, a goatee of sorts. Tokh wore a *bhántim* officer's uniform, a dirt-brown color for every day, occasionally a brown camouflage if he was on field duty, or his dark brown dress uniform if on a more important call. Low-caste enlisted *bhántanok* officers wore green uniforms. Zheníhda had never seen the major's dark blue before. It wasn't even a military cut; he wore a white blouse with a jacket of *bhísroti* design, and dark blue trousers.

"That's a most interesting uniform, Major," she said. "Where are you stationed?"

"At the moment I'm working out of Keranihn, Lady Tokh." His heels clicked together as he gave another crisp bow.

"These are the new uniforms for the *aghát* diplomatic corps," Tokh said. "It's what my men will wear. Mátokhan is the first officer I have chosen. I'm in a rush to choose the other five. I'll be in and out and all over for the next few weeks, maybe months, until I find them." He held his arms out with a smile. "The project is a go! We're live!"

Zheníhda's mouth fell open. "Finally?! After ten years! Tokh, that's wonderful! You've worked so hard!"

"Congratulations, my husband," Umara said from the sofa.

"The hard part is just beginning."

For the next eight weeks Tokh wasn't home more than a day at a time, in and out with the chiming of a clock. His first stop was Keranihn, to choose a technician. On all of Kerasím, there were only sixteen medically qualified memory investigation engineers; twelve were being pulled for the project. By the time he got to Keranihn, three of Tokh's top choices had already been picked by other generals.

"Gah." He tossed the booklet of prospectives and their résumés on the table. "Everyone left is second-rate. Harwanan has a mortality rate of twelve percent. *Twelve percent!* How can anyone run a successful campaign when the technician has a twelve percent fatality rate at the task he is supposed to be expert at?"

Mátokhan scanned down a table of names and statistics. "This one has a complication rate of four percent, and a fatality rate of one point six. Have you interviewed him?"

Tokh puffed his cheeks and blew the air out slowly. "He's a loser's prize. No one will touch him. Serious discipline problems and many of his practices are downright disturbing. Our purpose is to make subjects relaxed and compliant and gather information, not torture reluctant prisoners."

"Not to be insubordinate, General, but I put my name in for your consideration because of your record of success. What you're saying is that even though he is far more successful than any other candidate, and by his résumé has more experience, you would shun him because you feel incapable of maintaining discipline with him. Is it not better to take a risk and succeed than play it safe and fail the mission? You'll never know unless you interview him."

Tokh swelled with anger, but didn't let it explode. Mátokhan came from a privileged background, had been given choice assignments with high connections, and even though he was quite skilled Tokh had already seen the superiority rise several times. It only added to the fact the major was correct on all counts, and it stung. He raised a warning finger. "Right or wrong, you will never address me in that manner again. You will never speculate on what I am or am not capable of. You are a Major One and I am General Two. If you wish, you may complete your service to me as Captain Two. Is that clear?"

Mátokhan bent his head. "Clear, General. My apologies for overstepping my bounds."

Tokh sighed around the sourness building in his stomach. "This isn't a game, Major. The stakes are unbearably high, not just for us, but for the Emperor. But an interview isn't an acceptance, is it. Let's see how I can break him down."

Arrogance! Tokh had met General Fives, and impossible *fáhganid*s, and even some hoity toity narcissistic *bhísroti*. Only a handful of *Thósikh* existed: the Emperor, his heir, and the Emperor's twelve wives; Tokh had been in the presence of Heir Apparent Nadigh perhaps a half dozen times, and even the Heir to All Kerasím wasn't this arrogant.

Kassán kai-Imahr sat across the interview table from him, cold and impossibly smug. Tokh was a well-seasoned interrogator, excellent at breaking men down and extracting information with or without violence; Kassán was old-school interrogation with ten years more experience. For every question Tokh gave him, for every piece of information he tried to extract, Kassán had long seen it coming and directed the conversation elsewhere. Tokh would admit to anyone but Kassán that he was outmaneuvered, and Kassán knew it. Tokh wasn't so much the interviewer as the interviewee. After an hour of useless probing, Tokh threw down his file.

"What is it you want? If you don't want the job, why did you put your name in for the mission?"

Kassán cackled with delight. He was a scary figure, even to Tokh. He appeared short due to the fact he sat hunched over much of the time. His skin was bronze and wrinkled, his head bald but for wisps of white hair clinging to the sides, his face scarred from unknown battles with his subjects. A larger one cut through an eyelid, another puckered the skin near his mouth. He wore thick lenses balanced on his nose and still he seemed to squint when he looked at things. His wrinkled brown uniform bore a Colonel One rank with a variety of ribbons and medals on it, few of which Tokh was familiar with, probably from medical service. By age and years of service he should have been at least a General One; Tokh suspected his rank had been revoked at least once. His résumé read like a one-man university: a medical degree, a surgical license, advanced neuroanatomy, pharmacology, memory engineering, interrogation, level three qualification on Union Standard language plus two others, six campaigns, a security clearance that was higher than Tokh's, a written statement in his file warning of alarming personal tendencies, and at least fourteen reprimands.

"Now we're getting somewhere," he said with the most chilling smile Tokh had ever seen. "As you can tell by my paperwork, not one other candidate can come close to matching my success. I am, simply, the best. You need a memory technician. I need research. I can coax a bedbug to give up its secrets, but I want time to pursue my research in exchange."

Tokh didn't blink. He didn't say a word, chewing on his lip, waiting. "Your file attests to your brilliance. You were the first technician to adapt the machinery for military use. You have more experience than any other candidate. That's the only thing that has stood between you and your disciplinary record or you would be incarcerated right now for repeated insubordination. This mission is outside the jurisdiction of Kerasím. Where we go, I am the law; justice, jury, and executioner. Why would I choose someone who will cause me grief? What guarantee can you give me that you'll follow my word to the letter, unquestioned, and gain my trust?"

Kassán tipped his head, still in control. "Because Tokh dar-Giláhn likes to win. You think I don't know who I deal with? Who the players are in this game? I'm already a step ahead of this, General. I've worked on the project longer than you, but you couldn't know that because it was classified. This is a unique scientific opportunity. I wish to be part of it. Because you are out of jurisdiction, there are things I can do there that I can't here. I respect you, you respect me. You'll find that I'm a formidable ally, if given a chance. Put me on your team, grant me my research, and I'll give you my loyalty and service without issue."

Tokh remained motionless. "Because it's impossible to know a situation that does not yet exist, I would be a fool to promise such things at this time. What I can promise is that I would be willing to give consideration to such a transaction. However, it's my command and I will know at all times what 'research' you plan to conduct, how, why, and what you hope to achieve from it, and the results you do attain; your files will be open to me. I'm not unfamiliar with scientific studies. Because you have alluded to the fact the research you wish to conduct is not approved by any scientific board, I'll assume it has been deemed illegal for whatever reason. Where do you plan on obtaining subjects?"

Kassán shrugged. "Prisoners, if they are taken. Leeway with any subject sent to me. *Ghinadín* taken from the streets."

"There will be no *ghinadín* where we are going."

"*Gah!* There are always *ghinadín*," he said irritably. "Unwanteds. Street dwellers. *Trixahgs. Thanak tohr.* Every society has them and no one misses them if they disappear."

"I'll need to see your work in action. I've observed the procedures before, undergone it myself. You won't catch me a fool. I warn you now, disobedience and insubordination will be dealt with most harshly. I am the law. I am not above execution and requesting a new technician. A check of my record will confirm that. I'll leave that up to you, as your security clearance allows you access to my file. I have nothing to hide; I expect the same in return. You are honest and loyal to me, I will support what work you wish to do, as much as I'm willing in good conscience. That is my offer."

Kassán scratched the inside of a nostril with the point of his curved nail. "Very well. Make a request for time at the scanner in the Investigations building, and I'll show you tricks you don't know."

One by one, Tokh assembled his unit. He took the word seriously. A team consisted of individual members who could move and think as one, and they would need to do that for him. He started them early; he narrowed his choices down, and as each member joined the team, the growing team would sit in on the interviews for the next member. Tokh would keep his pick to himself, then ask the opinions of his men, asking them to rank the candidates as to who they would pick, why, and if there was anyone they would refuse to work with. It created a deeper responsibility among the men, a deeper sense of investment, trust, and participation. His respect for Kassán grew rapidly; with his extensive background, Kassán could spot personality flaws in officers Tokh missed. In the end his six diplomatic *aghát* specialists ranged from age forty to twenty-two, from uniquely experienced to fresh out of training, but each one was exceptional in their specialties and all were excellent speakers of Union. All had been training for this mission at least six years; one of them had been groomed for the job longer than Tokh. He worked them together, from physical training to tactical to communications to procedures to hiring consorts to break their tension, until they were so aware of each other they didn't need to think; they *knew*. After three months, he was confident in his choices.

He went home to bid goodbye to his household. "I go to base with my men for two weeks, then we're off world," Tokh told the wives. "If I'm allowed, I'll be in touch as often as I can. If you must contact me, you know how to submit through General Trannor."

"It's not a war zone, is it?" Zheníhda said.

Tokh sat in his favorite chair, Joralan on his lap playing with the clasp to his chin hank. "No! In fact, the opposite. A very peaceful place. I've been there before, on scouting missions. A beautiful new building, a strong cover business, a peaceful community to hide in – it should be very safe."

Tokh had never been on a long mission while married to Umara, nothing more than two months. Her chin trembled. "How long will you be gone?"

"At least six months. Probably a year, but the best case is six months. I can accumulate days off, but I can't use them until I get back."

"I'll miss you every day you're gone." Umara's voice carried a depth of sadness Tokh wasn't used to hearing.

He reached up to pat her cheek. "I'll be missing you as much."

He had but one night at home. He bedded Zheníhda first, the first for his benefit and the second for hers. She was more responsive to him than usual, no doubt because he was going away. She clung to him in the bed as if frightened.

"I worry, Tokh. Please tell me it's not dangerous. I know you can't say much, but please tell me that."

"Gah. It's one of the safest missions I've ever run, really. Yes, I'm going behind enemy lines – and if you leak that to the wives I will send word to General Trannor to come here and personally give you ten stripes, don't doubt my word – but outside of that fact, all I have to do is oversee a diplomatic mission. It will consume every ounce of energy I have, cause me insufferable headaches, I'm sure, but it's no more dangerous than running an office in the city." He kissed her on her hair. She unrolled it for him at night and it hung down to her waist, thick and black like the space between stars. It wrapped around her shoulders, tangled in his fingers, and he let it pour over him like perfumed midnight. He would miss her comforts, as steady and sure as the rising of the sun.

He sent her off and called Umara to him. Yes, the bed was damp, but that was the disadvantage of being second in line. It would be far wetter. Umara was weaning Kesseh, now a year old, but she still lactated, a feat that drove him crazy with lust. Her breasts were a glorious bronze and as globular as the sun and he loved everything about them: the smell, the taste, the weight, the squish under his hands, the way the studs of brown nipple squirmed under his thumbs. She held them out to him and he nursed his share while she lay back at the mercy of his fingers. Tokh clamped a nipple between the points of his teeth while she thrashed and wailed in her joy, pulling at it until his cheeks hurt. She was still firm when he withdrew his hand; he wasted no time separating her legs and shoving his ring past hers on her own fluids, making her jump with pleasure again. It was less than a minute before he finished in a stentorous grunt. He lay on her and licked the lost milk from her belly before rolling off next to her.

His hands pulled her against him, and she squirmed in tight. "Must you go?" she said in a timid little voice.

"I've been waiting ten years for this day. You know I must."

"I promise, I'll lose the baby weight before you return. I've been so slow about it, I know, but it's hard when I have two to chase all day…"

Tokh placed a finger over her lips. "*Shu.* I love you as you are. Just don't gain more. You are perfect." He meant it. Umara had shape, like an overstuffed pillow. Her buxom chest was meant for playing with. It swooped in to a narrow waist, then curved out again like the rising of a song to hips that swung side to side when she walked, just enough wiggle to draw admiration. She wasn't what Tokh would call fat, just… meaty in all the right places, in all the right proportions. Yes, her belly was still loose from pregnancy, but not so much that it bothered him. She was just delicious, head to toe.

"Do you love me, Tokh?" She sat up on an elbow. "Do you love me, so that it feels as if the stars go out when we are apart? As if my smile commands the sun to rise? Would you 'crawl across the universe on my hands knees/just to hear you speak my name/like a whisper through the trees'?"

Tokh chuckled to himself. "You and your poetry. I'm a soldier of calculation and action, not a *bhísroti* of fancy words and flights of thought, but yes, I do feel like the sun rises in your smile. It shines on your face and makes my heart glad to see it. I love watching you with your children." He bent his head and nipped at her throat. "I love the face you make just before you find your joy, as if you never felt it before and didn't know it was coming. I can never decide if it's pleasure or panic."

Umara blushed. "Sometimes it feels like I'm in free-fall, and I want to grab something." She nipped him on his earlobe. "You're too kind. Thank you, Tokh. Thank you for marrying me."

He *pushed* her twice more, taking his time, making it last, once from the back and once from the front so he could watch her face. Umara wrapped herself in the sheets to sleep, but he rolled over and tapped his com unit on the table by the bed. Moments later Zheníhda opened the bedroom door, half asleep. The pungent musk of male fluid hung thickly in the air, and she waved a hand before her nose in annoyance. Tokh patted the bed next to him. "Come."

"No. I don't care if you beat me until I bleed. I won't be put through that again."

"It's my last night here for many months and I want both my wives next to me. I'm done. I need sleep. Now come sleep with me."

Zheníhda sighed. "If that's all you desire, then move over. You take up too much of the bed." Umara slid over, Tokh moved over, and Zheníhda climbed in next to him. He lay on his back, one arm around each of them, and they slept.

Zheníhda wasn't given to great displays of emotion. If she made a scene, it was from true terror, pain, or fury. Tokh had left her before for long missions, stiff-lipped, straight-spined, the epitome of the perfect wife, making sure her husband never had to worry about a thing while he was gone. Umara wasn't as adept. Tears oozed as she cleared the breakfast. She wiped them as fast they formed, but she couldn't always keep up. The army sent a vehicle for him. He picked up Kesseh and kissed her forehead. He swung Joralan up, tossed him in the air a little and caught him, making him giggle.

"Remember, you're the Lord of the house while I'm gone. Behave for your mothers and protect your sister. I don't want to have to stripe you when I get back."

149

"No sir!" Joralan replied, and saluted his father. "Honor to the Emperor!"

Tokh returned the salute. "Honor to the Emperor." He kissed Zheníhda once on the throat. Umara clung to him, weeping.

"You will stop now," he ordered in her ear.

"Don't go!" she wept. "I sent my husband away once, and when he came back it was as pieces in a box. Please, Tokh! I can't bear that again! I can't!"

He lifted her chin and looked her in the eye. "I will return, and it will be on my own two feet." Tokh kissed the top of her nose. Zheníhda pulled her away. He entered the vehicle, and was gone without a look back.

* * 22 * *

The next two weeks were spent on base at Khumroh Interstellar Spaceport outside of Keranihn, rehearsing the last pieces before departure. His men were anxious, both at the tasks they faced and to get underway, and Tokh tried to give them as much recreation time as possible before they left. It was in the second week that Tokh's life took a complicated turn, one that would change his life for better and for worse.

Dahneg General Three Engmar stopped him after the last meeting let out. "Tokh, you play Tabs, don't you? A couple of officers and I are having a game at my son's house tonight. Why don't you join us? We could use a sixth player; full table."

"Thank you, General. I would enjoy that very much." A *dihnarwharl* didn't say no to a *dahneg* invitation, not when an upper-echelon tie could be made. Tokh had a full pocket at the moment, so he didn't mind in the least. He liked General Engmar, a man of respect and good standing.

He did not, however, like his son, another upper-caste brat who rode his father's name to get where he was and thought far too highly of himself. He was jittery and high-strung: tapping the table, jiggling his legs, or compulsively pounding back glasses of spirits. His humor was tactless and his laughter too loud and grating on the ear. Engmar's son had two wives, sullen, soulless beauties with empty eyes who served refreshments and kept the spirit glasses full, silent and lifeless as corpses when they weren't flinching at noises. The son also owned a consort, a young girl of perhaps sixteen or seventeen, beautifully attired but blinded as some consorts were. She was breathtaking to behold, with skin the color of golden oak, wavy black hair that tumbled down her back, and a pert little mouth that burst into smiles as she listened to the conversations, the only ray of sunshine in the dour house. The son kept her close at hand. She responded to his wins with cheers and touches and backrubs, and when he lost a hand, or grew annoyed, or he caught her smiling or laughing at something someone said, he'd slap her, or pinch her, or punch her brutally in the arm or leg, none of which she could see coming. It was no business of Tokh's how someone kept their consort; property was property and Tokh had no right to tell another male what to do with his toys, so he didn't. But he had no tolerance for bullies. He'd never put up with one among his men and over the evening he lost all patience for this one, but a *dihnarwharl* could never correct a *dahneg*.

Tokh made his living out of reading people and directing them to do his bidding without them realizing it. He couldn't touch a *dahneg* or so much as argue with him. But he could coax the *dahneg* to cut his own throat. He watched the son play, learned his pride, learned his weaknesses, and when the time was right, when he knew without a doubt he had a hand that couldn't be beat, he goaded the son to bet higher and higher, until all others had dropped out, and the son was short of money.

"You're bluffing," the son insisted.

Nothing ventured, nothing gained. Tokh knew many officers with arrogance issues, and he knew precisely how to manipulate them. The knife was sharp and raised; he just had to make the son release it. "Then I'll double the amount on the table, against your consort."

"If you want to sample her, just ask," the son said. "*Gah*, take her here on the table – everyone can have a turn if they'd like."

"No," Tokh said quietly. "Not a sample. The consort herself."

The son laughed. "That's a foolish bet that will cost you your money, General. You can't beat me."

"In life, no, a *dihnarwharl* will never best a *dahneg*. But Fortune is caste-blind, so I'll always have a small chance at games of skill. If you know you can win, you'll take my money, knowing you're the superior caste," Tokh said. "Otherwise you may fold, and remember that you were cleaned out by a mere *dihnarwharl*." The room waited in a hush.

The consort gasped as the son seized her by her hair and shook her. "This? You wouldn't want this anyway, General. She's one step above a *trixahg*. She doesn't care what you do to her." To prove his point he shoved her to the floor, then ordered her back to the chair with a curse. The consort complied with a pleasant face.

"The bet is to you, Son," General Engmar repeated. "You going to let a *dihnarwharl* take your money? Where's your *khatas*? Call or throw in."

The son gave a look of disgust. "Fine. Throw her in. It's my hand anyway, so it doesn't matter. Sorry, General, but *dahneg* wins, as should be." He flipped over the last of his tabs, making a high combination beatable by only three or four possible hands. He reached for the outrageous stash on the table – a hundred times the legal limit for a private game.

Tokh flipped his tabs, one of the few hands that could beat the son's. The table gave a crow of surprise, and Engmar reached out to stop his son. The son's eyes narrowed under his heavy brow.

"You *trixohr*! You cheated! You cheated me in my own home! I'll have your *dihnarwharl* hide stretched on my wall!"

"He didn't cheat you, boy," his father said. "You cheated yourself by not paying attention. You lost her fair and honest. A *dahneg* is true to his word and always pays his debts. Now man up." Engmar slid the pile of *dakra* to Tokh. With a growl of rage, the son began to beat on the consort, punching her with considerable force before grabbing her around her throat and choking her.

No one heard the sword draw. Tokh seemed to materialize behind the son, the edge of his sword pressed up against the son's throat; not enough to mark, but any sudden move might result in a lethal wound. "She's my property now," Tokh said in a steady voice. "You're damaging my property, and if you don't release her I will remove the offending hand, as is my right. Make your choice." It was a fine line, legally: to threaten a *dahneg* was a serious offense, but allowed if in defense of property. The property was caught in a gray area at the moment.

The son released his hands. He spat on the coughing girl before leaving the room. He ordered a wife, "You've got three *fasim* to pack her things and get her out of my house, and don't you dare give her a single item more than she arrived with or I'll beat you for every extra thing." The wife dashed from the room; the son stalked off in the opposite direction.

Tokh helped the girl to her feet.

"I'm sorry, Tokh," General Engmar said. "That one's always been trouble. It shames me to say he was booted from the military in his second year for hitting an officer, did a year in prison for it. I'll see to it he signs her papers for you. She's really a sweet little thing; personally, I'm happy to see her go with you. I know you'll appreciate her. Maybe losing her will teach him some humility."

"I don't understand," said the consort. "What's happened?"

153

"You've been traded to a general." Engmar smoothed her hair and rubbed a thumb over her cheek. "I think you'll be happy with the trade."

"I have? Who? What's happening?"

"Grab your things, while you still can."

The wife handed her two travel bags, containing several valuable items her husband never knew existed in the first place. "Thank him well." She kissed the consort's forehead. "He probably saved your life."

General Engmar handed Tokh the consort's ownership papers, signed off on in an angry scrawl, and placed her slender hand in his. Tokh paused outside.

"I assume you realize you're no longer his property, but mine. I am General Two Tokh dar-Giláhn, of Gimsith, Iérot Thorán. You have a name you prefer?"

"My name is Mímihn, Lord."

"How old are you, Mímihn?"

"Eighteen last nameday, Lord. I might be nineteen; no one has told me the date in some time. My com assistant was confiscated a while ago."

"I'll get you a new one. We're returning to my room at the base. For now, I wish you to relax. I've been married for thirty-two years to my first wife and six years to the second; I have never beaten my wives in all that time. I've threatened when they couldn't cease their bickering but I've never done it, so be assured, I mean you no harm."

Mímihn bowed to him. "I trust your word, Lord," she said, but her trembling said otherwise.

They didn't speak on the ride back to the base; the other officers sat front while he and his new consort sat rear. It was hard to remember she was blind and needed to be led during movement, especially in and out of vehicles, but she was patient with his ignorance. Tokh carried her belongings while she held to his elbow until they reached the privacy of his room. It was a small room for a general, two chairs, a bed, a table, and a locker-closet, but it had a private bath. "My room is temporary. We'll be here for another four days, perhaps, while I attend to duties. How long have you been blind?"

"Perhaps eight months? My Great Lord didn't like the way I looked at his guests."

154

"Don't refer to him as Lord. He doesn't deserve it."

"Yes, my Lord. Lord, may I enquire as to your caste?"

"*Dihnarwharl*. A step down for you, but not far. What was your original caste?"

"I was born *rhibani*, Lord, then married to *nhasarwharl* General Maghentor at fourteen. He divorced me because I didn't bear him a son. Then I was bought by the *dahneg*."

Tokh snorted. "Maghentor? He couldn't have sired a cold sore. You know he died last year?"

"No, Lord, I didn't."

"Dropped dead while leaving a restaurant. The owner had them drag him to the next storefront, so it wouldn't reflect on his business." Tokh gave a faint laugh.

"I never wished him ill, Lord."

"Of course you did. They wed a child to a senile, impotent old fool. No doubt you tried your best to please him, hoped things would change, but they only worsened. He had no business taking such a young wife at his age. And before you ask, I'm fifty-two and as healthy as they come, as are my wives. The second has some nervous issues, but nothing unusual for a female."

"Lord, may I make a request?"

"Speak."

"I can't see what you look like. May I touch his Lordship, so I may learn to identify you, if necessary? I mean no disrespect by it."

The idea made sense to Tokh. He held still while she ran her hands over him, from his hair to his face, stroked his chin hank, felt his shoulders, his arms, his sides. He wore his daily uniform; the fingers counted the number of citations on his chest, his belt, his weapons; she didn't hesitate to size up his rump or his privates, right down to his boots. She stepped back. "Thank you, Lord. Now, should something happen, I have a chance of identifying you."

Despite the hour, Tokh sent for meals to be brought to them, and they dined together at the small table in his room. Mímihn insisted on serving him, which she managed with some skill even without seeing. Before he would allow her to clear his dish, he took her hand and pulled her onto his knee with a sigh.

He played with her hair, rubbed a knuckle gently over her cheek, chucked her under her chin. "You've brought great complication to my life. I'm not sure what to do with you. You're

155

brave for smiling in the house of that *aakit takhin*, but are you brave enough for where we're going?"

"You're a wise and well-decorated general of great strength," Mímihn said. "You're not afraid to use your weapons. With you to protect me, I will be very brave."

Tokh's laughter exploded in a braying burst. Mímihn gave a soft twitter in reply. "You know that already?"

Mímihn's sweet smile was wondrous to behold. "Of course, Lord. Your uniform has many decorations, which you wouldn't have gotten if you weren't brave and wise with your decisions. The clasps on your holsters are worn, which means you remove the weapons frequently. Your arms and legs are quite muscular, meaning you're used to strong activity. Your right forearm is slightly more developed than your left, meaning it's used to swinging that sword, which, by the pull of the scabbard on your belt, is no light weapon."

She couldn't see Tokh's dumbfounded stare. He patted her cheek. "Half my officers couldn't have told me as much. I'm about to embark on an extended mission off-world in enemy territory, perhaps a year, and you'll have to accompany me. I'll have little free time and you'll be limited to my quarters; the last place I dare leave you is home with my wives. You'll be the only female in the building. I'll keep you under guard as well as I can. I suppose I'll have to hire a castrate as your servant, as I'll trust no one with you. I don't plan to share you, but be aware there may be times when I'm forced by overrank or caste, or as honor to another officer. I'll do my best to keep it to a minimum, and I'll give you warning if at all possible. If anyone, at any time, makes solicitations to you or touches so much as your finger without my permission, you're to inform me immediately. Is that understood? No one is to approach you without my express permission, and if I haven't forewarned you or I'm not beside you, no permission is to be implied or believed. Anyone, of any rank or caste whatsoever. Do you understand?"

Mímihn bowed her head. "Absolutely, Lord. I'm off limits to all persons, unless I have received your direct permission beforehand, or you're beside me to grant permission. I must inform you immediately of any indiscretions, no matter what the caste or rank of the offender."

Tokh chucked her under her chin. "You're smart, for a female. I'm liking you already. Now." He sat back, watching her squirm on his knee in uncertainty. It was impossible to tell if her nervousness

156

was from herself, her consort training, or from the horrific treatment he had seen her receive.

He flipped her soft black curls off her shoulder and down her back. Her sightless eyes sparkled like *dhanwar ashaar*, a smoky-caramel gemstone, gazing almost but not quite at his. "I see you struggling with anxiety. It's late, I'm tired, but I know the worry that's in your mind, *what will he do to me*, so let's get it over with and we'll both sleep better for it tonight. Let's see what I've won."

He pulled her between his knees and began to untuck her shirt. She grabbed it. "Let me please you, My Lord," she said, but he moved her hands away.

"*Shu.* You're my gift to myself to unwrap. Please me another time. Now is my time." He drew her shirt from her.

Exquisite. She wasn't bony like Zheníhda, but there wasn't an extra ounce of fat on her; five pounds or so gained and she would be irresistible in shape. There were still marks on her throat from her previous owner's fingers, several fading bruises of various sizes on her arms and shoulders, and a new one blooming on her arm from the night's losses. "I see this wasn't his first bad game. If I ever leave a mark on you like this, you're ordered to remind me of tonight. Understood?"

"Yes, Lord."

He released her undergarment, a flimsy thing of blue lace, revealing flawless young breasts a little large for someone of her size, more than Zheníhda but less than Umara. He unfastened her skirt and let it fall to the floor as she stood patiently, waiting for him to say a word of pleasure or displeasure. Her waist was slender, spreading out into perfect feminine hips; the sculpted dream of artist. She flinched when he touched the angry black-brown fist-sized bruise on her thigh. Tokh growled. "I have pain relievers in my kit. You may have some. A bruise like that impedes walking."

"Thank you, my Lord. You're most kind to offer them."

He noted the fading brown lines across the curves of her back and the soft arcs of her golden buttocks; she'd been beaten with something thin, probably an incentive stick. Tokh caressed the skin as if he could rub them away. "Are your stripes for disobedience, or his personal pleasures?"

Mímihn bowed nervously, making her breasts wobble. "If it was for disobedience, my Lord, I was unaware of it at the time."

157

"As I thought." He freed her of her lacy coverunders and admired her nakedness for several moments, young, beautiful, and all his. He pulled her forward and kissed her under her ear.

He took his time, more gentle than usual, watching her responses, seeing what pleased her, letting his tongue and fingers explore her from throat to ankles. When he thought she had found her joy, he kept her on her back and pulled her legs apart, bending her feet to his shoulders to watch her further as he *pushed* her slow and steady until he felt her contract around him, and lost his fluid hardly a moment later.

He uncoupled and dropped onto the bed in exhaustion, pulling her against him in a warm embrace. He caressed her bare bottom. "Now you have no need for nerves around me. Sleep, and we can speak in the morning."

Her arms linked around his neck and she kissed him in return. "Thank you, my new Lord. You're too kind to me. Thank you." The room was now dark as space, but he could hear the tears of relief in her voice, felt her tension leave as she snuggled up tight against his chest and went to sleep.

Never had Tokh realized how much of a day required sight. His new consort shuffled around the room, one hand out to keep from bumping into things. A young girl whose beauty made him want to cry out in delight, and she couldn't see his face, read his intentions, tell an officer or caste by the badges they wore, identify friend from foe. Eyes were nerves, and he had a neurospecialist on his team. He brought her to Kassán the next day.

"Can her sight be restored?" was his only question.

Kassán's important equipment was already shipped, but he had a wide enough array available at the base's sickbay. He performed several scans, poked her eyes, asked her questions, but she knew almost nothing.

Mímihn held tight to Tokh's hand. "I'm sorry, I don't know. He told me I needed an exam. They gave me medicine and I fell asleep. When I woke up, I thought I was in a dark room, but I wasn't. They told me I'd be like this forever."

"*Gah!*" Kassán spat. "Useless. Damaging good property out of jealousy is the sign of an unbalanced mind. 'My new aircraft is gorgeous! Let me punch a hole in the side so no one will want to steal it.' Those are the ones who should be castrated, so they can't

158

spawn more of their kind upon the world. You want someone to remain dependent, you cut the ankles. They don't run from you after that, and they remain useful."

Horror made the skin on Tokh's back crawl. "That will not happen on my command," he warned. "Can it be reversed?"

"If it was done haphazardly, the tissue is probably too damaged," Kassán said. He put the scanners and magnifiers back. "If it was done with a laser and the severance was clean, then with patience there's a good chance of reattaching enough nerves to restore a useful amount of sight. I can't tell unless I'm looking directly at the tissue. It may take several tries, but it should work."

Tokh rubbed Mímihn's shoulder. "I can't promise anything until after this mission is over, but I'll see what can be done for you."

* * 23 * *

Tokh wasn't prone to fear, but the pressure of the coming project stole his breath. Failure was not an option. The cargo manifests had been signed and logged; Major Khaním had attested to the boarding of the hundred or so men who would provide support, and Tokh himself stood by the entrance of the transport ship at landing pad 26D, supervising the final moments. The dozen men that made up his command staff stood with him: the six *aghát* diplomats, Colonel Kassán, along with the leaders of his tech crew, communications, personnel, security, and building maintenance. Behind them waited his new consort, under a long veil that hid her to her hips, one gloved hand on the elbow of her new servant, a wiry sixty-ish castrated *ghinadín* named Thrit. Tokh didn't think Kerasi life was bad at all, but when he needed to hire a servant for his servant, he had to admit, Kerasi life could be crazy at times.

He turned to the Zyranian captain of the transport as the last item checked off the list on his handcom. "That's everything."

"Then get aboard and strap down. We'll lift off as soon as I have clearance."

Eight days later they received permission to orbit a Union world called Kye, near enough to the Kerasi border for emergencies, yet a full member of the Planetary Union. This was Tokh's third time on Kye; once on the original contact mission – he didn't know the purpose at the time, and once last year to see how the complex was coming together. Kye was as modern as Keranihn, in some ways even more, with a population that functioned as one great caste, so that current technology was as prevalent among the poor as among the wealthy. Male and female didn't differentiate their tasks; a female was just as likely to be a janitor, or a security officer, or construction worker as a male. That would take much getting used to.

Tokh and his command crew flew directly to a landing area at the complex. The single yellow sun looked larger in the sky than

Kerasím's, whose orange light blotted out the pale light of its white dwarf partner, but the air was just as fresh. The building itself rose five stories, its façade done in a stunning array of brick artistry, carved wooden doors, and sharp white trims. Rolling lawns stretched for five of the thirty private acres, with formal gardens bursting with local flora and a tall pole flying the Union and Kyan flags, and the flag of Silera, the country division they were in.

Tokh felt bad for Mímihn, locked in her forced darkness; females loved flowers, and the blooms before the building were a spectacular show of color and styles. Zheníhda would have spent hours learning every name, and Umara would have made up poems to reflect their beauty. The best Mímihn could do was feel the shape of the blooms while Thrit gave her unimaginative answers to their color.

Keeping a consort sequestered during a highly-sensitive, illegal mission in enemy territory was only the beginning of Tokh's problems. He had an impressive suite of rooms on the top floor of the building, more lavish in decoration than his own home. An ornate sitting room dominated the space, with a small cooking area against the wall for private meals, and four bedrooms. Tokh could house and entertain dignitaries, both local and from the homeworld, without anyone suspecting a thing. The one drawback was a single step that raised the bedroom areas from the living space; nine times out of ten Mímihn forgot it, and tripped going up or down for the first several weeks. Tokh gave her a room of her own for privacy if needed, but she spent almost all of her time in Tokh's room. Thrit slept on a small cot in the corner of her room.

His mission was simple on the outside: locate a high-ranking Union official, seize him, treat him with respect, educate him on Kerasi lifestyle, make him understand Emperor Nághtas's plans for societal reform regarding female power and why he sought the Union's assistance in making it happen, and then release the official without harm back to the Union where he could explain the Emperor's goals and begin a meaningful dialogue that would result in a greater understanding and an opening for further alliance. Once a dialog formed, the Emperor would blame the Union for the reforms he planned, and slowly bring about reforms for females – including putting his smalldaughter in the line of succession. The timeframe was six months from capture to release. Of eleven secret cells

161

carrying out the same orders on different worlds, Tokh's mission was nearly the first to fail.

Everything had gone like clockwork. His building, under the guise of a diplomatic retreat in the countryside, came together like the opening of a gift. His Number One *aghát* officer, Mátokhan, took his place in the community, the local liaison who had open access to Union personnel. He fronted a shadow business of import trading; unquestioned people traipsed through his office, both Union and Kerasi sympathizers, without ever raising a warning flag. He had open access to the Union Common Network and could acquire any Union information Tokh needed without raising suspicion.

His Number Two *aghát* officer was an intimidating *whátaral* captain named Sóghar ahn Wahl. His credentials were impeccable save one or two minor disciplinary measures. His ambition was so strong it seemed a separate entity moving like a shadow behind him. Sóghar ranked quite high on testing and he impressed Tokh at every turn, but there was something in his personality that Tokh just didn't trust, some tone, some extraneous movement, something in his laugh – nothing Tokh could pick out, but he still placed him as his Number Two, supervisor of the other four *aghát*, their scheduling, their duties, and manager of their prisoner. His ambition wouldn't let him fail.

Acquisition of the prisoner was Sóghar's first job, and he botched it. The only way he could have bungled it more was if his team had been taken prisoner. Instead of the highly ranked Union male he was stalking, Sóghar brought Tokh a human child, a *female* human child, absolutely useless to the mission and a danger to have in custody. The child had stumbled upon the scouting party and it was capture or be captured. Tokh understood that, which was the only thing that kept him from strangling Sóghar. He had Kassán keep the girl in a light sleep while he requested instruction from superiors.

Sóghar botched his second chance just a few hours later. With such a grievous error, Tokh had no idea what mission control would request, so he decided to distract Sóghar for the moment. He offered him a chance to visit his Mímihn, a one-time, one-*push* offer. Tokh received a page from Mimihn's servant just an hour later, and he raced upstairs.

Mímihn sat on her bed, shaking and in tears, an arm raised to protect against blows she couldn't see. Blood surrounded her on the bedcover. "I'm sorry, my Lord! I'm sorry! Don't be angry! I'm sorry to call you from your duty, but Thrit says the liquid is blood, and I hurt, and I need eyes to tell me what's wrong and no one else is allowed."

Tokh paged downstairs. "Tell Kassán to bring his medical kit to my quarters immediately." He sat next to Mímihn, pulled her arm down and petted her hair. "*Shu,* my pet. Tell me what happened, start to finish, and leave out no detail."

Mímihn calmed herself. "You called to inform me you were sending me an officer who had your permission for my attention for one hour. He came into the room, I acknowledged him, he asked me to change my clothes, I did. He said he was going to drug me for a few *fasím,* and when I woke my instructions were to fight him and scream. That was all. When I awoke, he was kissing me, and I felt a small pain. I did as he asked, twisted and cried to please him, but when he entered me, that's when the pain became much worse. He finished, praised me, then held me to the bed and took his turn again, and I still hurt. When he finished that time, he thanked me for my cooperation and left. Thrit came in to help me, and saw blood. Now I'm frightened because I don't know what happened."

Tokh's eyes darkened under his brow. He seized her arms and searched them until he found the puncture wound. *Background in chemistry and pharmacology.* Mimihn's hair was combed straight down her back, and the blouse she wore was the same color as his child prisoner downstairs. Tokh didn't need a mathematics degree to add two simple numbers.

Kassán examined Mímihn while Tokh observed. "Looks like a small laceration, an inch perhaps. Clean edges. An object, possibly a knife blade. Just missed the outer ring, so nothing should be damaged. I'll pack it with some medicated gauze; take it out at bedtime. She's your property, your choice, but ideally she should be left to heal for three days or so, or it could tear and infect. Your habits, or a guest of yours?"

"Someone has overestimated my hospitality, and underestimated my wrath," Tokh said. The cold in his voice chilled the room.

Kassán packed up his instruments. "Let me know if I should expect broken bones or a head in a bag."

"I will know soon."

163

Tokh left Mímihn with a promise it would never happen again. Mission Control got back to him with orders that defied everything Tokh had spent years training for: use the girl as his Emissary. The Union was extremely protective of their young females, and having one as hostage, properly controlled, could prove a huge bargaining chip for the Emperor. Tokh was to educate her the same way, providing she proved capable of it. Above all else she had to be kept safe, for if the slightest harm came to her the Emperor would lose all credibility. If the Emperor's goal was to raise the bar for Kerasi females, perhaps the best way to prove their good intent was to educate a Union female. In a strange way it made sense to Tokh, but he had just three hours or so to make alternative plans, housing arrangements, and inform his team.

And rearrange his command. Tokh sighed against his simmering anger. No longer could Sóghar be his Number Two. Predators were common enough and all the pre-screenings were supposed to weed them out of his men, but in present circumstances Tokh could leave no leeway. If Sóghar was using Tokh's consort to act out fantasies with the prisoner within hours of first seeing her, then he couldn't be trusted with overseeing her care. The risk was too great. That left his Number Three, Masákh gha Lil.

Tokh wasn't sure Masákh was right for the position. He was so good that Tokh had trouble reading him. He was chosen for the program almost at its inception, so young he had trained for this almost his entire life. Not a single reprimand marked his record, not a demerit, not a questionable behavior, not a single failed test. He was decorated more than a dozen times, from academics to marksmanship. He wasn't a certified teacher, but had experience as an instructor. His loyalty and dedication were unwavering. His personality profile portrayed someone slow to anger and attentive to detail. Officers that good either snapped when stressed or self-destructed through their blindness to loyalty and inability to think creatively when needed, but his Number Four, Haghíde Kitáhl, didn't have enough supervisory experience to be given control of the entire team. He would have to trust Masákh and work with him to ensure success, while training Haghíde as backup. But first he had a score to settle with his former Number Two. Two of his guards accompanied him.

164

The *aghát* quarters consisted of a common area and three impeccably neat bedrooms, with a private locker-room bath. At least two *aghát* were on rotating duty at any given hour, meaning on average there were never more than three in the rooms at once. By the time Tokh had made his way down a floor, his anger was at full steam. He didn't stop to open the door but kicked it with his boot so the door shattered at the latch. He stormed in at full speed followed by the guards, two *nhásarwharl* officers. His target sat on a sofa in his pants and a liner shirt, cleaning and filing his nails. The guards strode across the room to stand before the other *aghát* present, Haghíde and Ghírandar, the junior number six *aghát*. The guards drew their swords and crossed them, forming a deadly barrier to the rest of the room.

Tokh seized Soghar by the shoulders and hauled him to his feet. He smashed him against the wall, smashed him again, shook him and rammed him a third time. *Whátaral* Soghar put his arms flat against the wall, unable to defend himself against a *dihnarwharl* general. To raise even a hand in protection could mean Sóghar's head. Tokh's thick hands moved to surround his throat, the curved nails digging in to leave pinpoint wounds.

"*Trivarid*! *Ghinadín* bastard! What did you do to her? I accept your reason for failure, find a way to make it work to our advantage, give you my consort as a matter of trust, and I find her bleeding and crying? *What did you do to her!*" Tokh bellowed. "Answer with truth or I'll haul you down to Kassán and he can take a blowtorch to your *khatas* until they char to dust!"

Sweat glittered in a sheen on Soghar's bleached-tan *aghát* skin. He crossed his hands and tried to slide them a little at a time under the general's, anything to give him more air. "I – I was just – I didn't mean to upset her – I just – She reminded me of the prisoner, and I-I-I – just wanted to pretend – pretend to owe a blood price – Just – a-a-a small nick with my knife – I never meant harm."

Tokh leaned in under Soghar's nose, his glare collapsing the heavy brow downward until it seemed he would have to tip his head back to stare. "You couldn't simply enjoy a privilege. You deliberately damaged my property for your own indulgence without my permission, and that is unforgivable."

He released Soghar's throat and threw him face down over the table in the small dining area. Tokh pulled his sword and rested the razor tip between Soghar's shoulders. One thick leg swung over

165

Soghar's, resting between them, and Tokh laid the weight of his pelvis along Soghar's hip. Soghar gasped at the implication. Males could be used in the same manner as females, a tactic for punishment, humiliation, or intimidation. Almost every male knew someone who had been a victim, even if they themselves wouldn't admit to being one. Some commanders of especially vicious reputation controlled their men that way. Sóghar's buttocks tightened in fear.

"Do you have any idea how it hurt me to ask Kassán to examine her?" Tokh growled in his ear. "It will take her a week to heal. I should have you castrated for that. Or perhaps I should take payment in kind."

The tip of the sword arced around and slid between Soghar's legs, under his crotch, and lodged in the edge of the tabletop; Soghar flailed and tried to raise his hips out of the way, but Tokh's weight and elbow held him down. A second nervous gasp slipped out. A little more pressure and Tokh was certain he could make Sóghar soil himself.

"Tell me! Should I use you like you used her? Make you bleed, then pleasure myself on the wound? How do you think that would feel? Will you scream and beg as she did for you?" The sword slid from the table and with a twist of Tokh's wrist the pommel jammed itself firmly against Soghar's rectum, making him jerk and grunt. "What would you prefer – the hilt of my sword, or myself? Make your choice."

Soghar gasped again, fighting for breath under Tokh's weight and the edge of the table digging into his diaphragm. "Lord General, if you – feel you must, I would – humbly ask for yourself only."

Tokh's voice drawled low in his ear. "You aren't worthy of my fluid." He stood, yanked Soghar from the table by his shirt collar and threw him to the floor. Soghar cringed awkwardly against the table leg.

Tokh bent to one knee, and the point of the sword poked Soghar under the chin until he tipped his head up. "If I see you so much as look at my consort ever again, I will personally cut off your *khatas* and see that they are fed to you while I watch. Is that understood?"

Soghar couldn't nod without the sword piercing his chin. "Quite clearly, Lord General. My sincerest apologies to you and your consort for overstepping my bounds."

166

"You are hereby relieved of your command and step down to Number Three. You are no longer in charge of the *aghát*. You won't have contact with the prisoner until you learn to control yourself. One slip-up and I will remove the offending part, be it *khatas* or head. Is that understood?"

"Without fail, Lord General," Sóghar panted from the floor. "Loyalty, Duty, Honor to the Emperor."

Tokh stood and sheathed his sword. Without a glance, he trod hard on Soghar's privates as he strode toward the shattered door. This time Soghar did give a yell. The guards broke formation, eased their swords and followed Tokh out.

Kerasi males didn't cry, but Tokh would have. The day his mission should have begun in earnest and his men had screwed up, his orders had changed drastically, they were now scrambling to rearrange preparations, his consort had been wounded, and he'd busted a lead officer and put him on probation with a written reprimand. He lay on his bed, stuffed a pillow in his mouth, and let loose a yell that would have sent both of his wives running for the door in terror. Mímihn hurried in with an iced glass of *dhurwah*, straight up. He drank half of it at once. His tongue and throat went numb, his stomach burned, and a moment later his head started to follow.

"Is there anything I can do for you, my good Lord?" Mímihn said. "I can prepare you food to your liking. I can draw you a bath to relax in. I'm not supposed to have relations with you, but I can pleasure you with my hands or lips if you would like."

Tokh waved her back. He shook his head in futility when she didn't notice, and patted her shoulder instead. "No. I don't have heart for even that. It's been a most difficult day. Are you good at massage? I would love a massage of my shoulders and back."

"Of course, Lord. Let me grab some oil." She returned from the next room in less than a *fasím*, despite the lack of sight.

"Ohhh." Tokh sighed with pleasure and leaned forward to give Mímihn better access. "Oh, that's good. My wife Umara is very good with massage. She's the best thing after a bad day. She makes me sleep better." He reached behind to pat her arm. "I'm glad you accompanied me, Mímihn. You may be exactly what I need here."

167

Tokh set the new plans into motion. His subject was now a half-grown juvenile human female with the strange name of Aila Perrin, full of hiss and spit but not a lot of fight. By the grace of the Fortunes she was of upper-caste birth, even if the Union didn't acknowledge such things. She was more educated than expected, and knew a surprising amount of information when fed through their scanners. Tokh was pleased with the way Masákh was handling her, and the progress being made. As day followed day without any more snags, he regained his confidence. Sóghar took his demotion without a sound.

"Female?" Mímihn said. She felt her way around the sofa and approached him, her face radiating excitement. "Oh Tokh! May I meet her? Please, Lord? Perhaps I could be a friend to her. It gets so lonely here. I can't understand the local programming, and Thrit is awful at conversation. Perhaps there's something I can teach her for you, or she could teach me."

Tokh chucked her under her chin. "My eager little fledgling! There's only one problem: you don't speak Union, and she speaks hardly ten words of Emperor's Tongue. How would you converse? She can't motion to you because you can't see her. She can't key it into your com unit and have it speak."

"Then teach me Union Tongue," she said, determined not to accept no. "If she can't learn, then I will! I'm smart. *Sukh, ka, koormaht, jihtar saar om seh...* How would I greet her? She comes to the door and I open it, and I say... What?"

"Hello."

Mímihn made a face. "Hay-lo?"

"Hello."

"Ah-lo," Mímihn decided. *"Ah-lo,* friend. *Ah-lo,* General. *Ah-lo,* Tokh. Good. Teach me another."

Tokh put a finger over her lips. "It's a worthy idea. I will see what I can do."

Tokh did try. With two of his *aghát* officers as translators, he allowed Mímihn an entire afternoon in the girl's company. He taught Mímihn five Union words – *yes, no, come, please,* and *hello.* Combined with the girl's pitiful new Kerasi vocabulary, they managed a few tiny independent exchanges, but the rest required his men to translate and explain. Although both females seemed to spark a friendship, the difficulties were too much for frequent contact.

Tokh's men were excellent translators, but Tokh wouldn't trust any officer alone with Mímihn after Sóghar's incident. Interaction between his men and her would be in his presence or not at all, and he didn't have time to waste on females making friends. He allowed notes to be sent, which he could read to Mímihn and have notes transcribed back, but it wasn't the same. Mímihn now lived a pleasant, safe, sheltered life, but it was lonely. She understood the girl's isolation in a way no one else could.

* * 24 * *

Tokh sat at the massive desk in his office when his second brush with disaster announced itself.

"General, an incoming message for you on tachyon beam," said the voice from the communications room.

Tokh frowned. Mission Control used tachyon beams, but that would come direct on his com. He hit the connect switch with confusion. A heavyset, sagging face framed in the trappings of *fáhganid* office appeared on videomessage, its gray chin hank woven with so much ribbon it looked fake.

"General Tokh, this is Áftnahn, Deputy General of the Interstellar Fleet. I've heard rumor that you're attempting to educate a young human female for a project. I wish to see this anomaly for myself. I'll be in orbit by midday. Please have your men ready to receive me."

Tokh's blood froze in his veins, and his eyes wouldn't blink for almost a full half-minute. A *fáhganid* general who outranked him, and whose caste couldn't be denied a single request. Cutting off his own head would be a better alternative. A Kerasi ship found in Union space would destroy the entire program.

He placed an emergency call to mission control.

General Trannor almost crawled through his pick-up screen. "Who? What's he doing in Union space? He has no authorization! He can't! I'll have ships at the border and recall him immediately."

Tokh's words raced from his lips. "He'll be in orbit in less than three hours. What protocol do I use? He can override any of my orders. He can take the emissary from me if he chooses and I can't stop him. Trannor, she's now over the age of consent."

"No, she's not," Trannor corrected him. "Freeze all files, encrypt them under your name only. Allow him no access. He won't know otherwise. This is my immediate direct order, *fáhganid* General Four Trannor, by Order of the Emperor: No male below the caste of Thósikh may bed the female Union Emissary Aila Perrin, or face immediate beheading by any available commanding officer. She is not to be removed from the custody of General Two Tokh. I will have a written copy of the order signed by His Majesty Nághtas sent to you within an hour. If he tries anything, you have your orders, and a direct order from the Emperor supersedes anything a *fáhganid* desires. If you must, refer him back to me. If he's caught by the Union no one will intervene on his behalf, and when he returns to Kerasi space I will personally make sure he never sets foot off-world again."

Tokh bowed to the camera. "With my humble thanks, Revered General."

Tokh sent a high alert throughout the building, informed his commanders of the chaos about to erupt, and got preparations underway. Aftnahn was not only *fáhganid*, but Deputy General of the Interstellar Fleet, a political position which meant his reach extended into the Kerasi senate. He was Palace, and that meant dangerous power. Tokh didn't know Trannor's reach; what public files there were of him didn't mention half of what Tokh knew to be true. Trannor was simply in charge of a secret mission, with no grandiose titles to wave about, but he knew Heir Apparent Nadigh well, and that meant he had a direct ear of the Emperor, no doubt much closer than Aftnahn. Having the protection of a direct order *tansohr Keralihn*, by order of the Emperor, would give Tokh a little legal leeway, but it wouldn't stop Aftnahn from taking his head.

In person, Aftnahn was worse than the *bhísroti* Tokh had met. A parade of lackeys preceded him, ensuring Tokh's living quarters were adequate. A portable dais was placed in the sitting area, since *fáhganid* wouldn't sit equal with lesser castes. Two *whátaral* servants laid red carpet runners down the fifth-floor hall and into Tokh's apartment, so common carpet couldn't stain Aftnahn's shoes. Tokh had met the Heir Apparent himself, and even not-yet-Emperor Nadigh didn't ooze the entitlement that dripped in slimy trails from Aftnahn's pores.

Tokh warned Mímihn of what would unfold. Mímihn would have to play her part. Tokh needed attention drawn away from the female emissary, and he couldn't keep the *fáhganid* from a consort anyway. His words didn't convey half the sickness he felt at the thought of leaving her vulnerable to a *fáhganid*'s desires. Given the choice, he'd rather lend her to Sóghar again.

Mímihn's hand held his cheek, so her kiss could land squarely on his nose. "I understand, my sweet Lord. I can handle a *fáhganid*. They like their ego stroked even more than their *hihvat*. Tell me what you want to know from him, and I will tell you all his secrets. I'll make you proud."

Tokh couldn't decide if Mímihn was truly that brave, that ignorant, or just insane.

Tokh and his command team endured three hours of painful pomp and circumstance, inspections of his men and the building, and roundabout chitchat that avoided dispensing classified information and didn't break protocol before Áftnahn finally got around to demanding to see the emissary. Tokh called below, and his *aghát* brought the detained girl to his quarters. They had dressed her in Mímihn's clothing and briefed her on the situation: *Do and do well, for if Tokh dies, we're all dead, including you.*

Masákh and Sóghar dropped to their knees, heads bowed; the emissary followed. "The girl, as ordered, Lord Tokh."

Tokh smiled at her and held out his hand. Sóghar nudged her, and she placed her hand in it. "Ah! Aila. Come join us. This is the Most Revered General Aftnahn. You may greet him. He does not speak Union." Tokh caught her eye and gave a slow nod toward the Revered. His smile remained friendly, but his eye gave a subtle warning.

The girl dropped to her knees again and touched her head to the floor. *"Hacht doh wih, mantih plakhton."* I am amazed at your presence. It was a blame-free *khata*-kissing of a greeting, suitable for addressing anyone of higher caste, whether one level or ten. Score one for his *aghát*.

"You've taught her to speak! She must be clever, indeed," Aftnahn said with delight. He gave a deep belch, then waved the fumes away with his hand.

"Sit, all of you," Tokh granted. Sóghar shoved a small footstool by Tokh's knee for the girl. "A few phrases. I don't know if they're capable of true bilingual fluency. Time will tell." He replied to the Revered One in Kerasi; Masákh whispered Tokh's words to the girl in Union.

Tokh reached down and petted her brown hair and the spangled veil hanging down her back. "She's been fascinating to observe. Much different than what we expected. Quick. Malleable. Strong, for such youth. After so many months, she's become a sort of pet. Perhaps... even like a daughter."

At the sound of his words, Tokh realized it to be true. Like his little Kesseh, he wasn't drawn to her in a predatory fashion but took great delight in speaking with her, watching her learn, watching her grow. After so long he did indeed feel protective of her, despite her alien nature and distrust.

His Emissary was more clever than Tokh realized. On hearing the translation, she tipped her head back and smiled sweetly at him. He gave her a fixed smile and caressed her cheek with his hand. She leaned her head on his knee, then wrapped her arms around his leg and hugged it, staking her loyalty in no uncertain terms, even if the touch was inappropriate for her gender and age.

"And you've managed to keep her from your men? You put that much trust in them?"

"I trust my *aghát* with my life. I trust them more than the colonels who outrank them."

"You have fed them through that machine of yours, no doubt," the Revered One sniffed. "I saw one used on a prisoner on Tanorgelt; he shook unendingly for five days before dying. I don't see how such a thing can be effective for anything but slow execution. It's cruel, in a way. Sword or pistol is much more civilized."

"I chose Kassán because he is the best memory engineer on all of Kerasím. He rarely needs such force. Resistance is key; prisoners fight in fear, with bad results. My men know to tell only the truth, to release it freely and willingly, and no damage is done."

"Perhaps I'll also observe that while I'm here," Aftnahn mused, but whether due to natural condescension or as a sly warning, the words seemed to carry a threat. "Female, come here." He motioned with his hand. Masákh tapped the girl's backside.

"Go to him."

She approached, but not too close, not only her eyes but her whole head tipped down in feigned respect. Aftnahn pulled her onto the dais, between his knees. He grasped the sides of her head and forced her to look at him, examining her eyes. "Hmph. I don't know, Tokh. I don't see much intelligence there." He squeezed the sides of her jaw with one hand, forcing her mouth open. With his other hand he explored her teeth and gums, then stuck a foul fat clawed finger

173

so far into her throat she nearly vomited on him before he let her go. "She seems undersized. Does she eat well?"

"We feed her special meals balanced for human nutrition. They are tailored to her preferences."

Fáhganid hands sized her shoulders, her arms, her ribs, the width of her hips; one caressed her backside, then the other hand lifted her skirt and grabbed for places forbidden. She gave a shriek and tried to step back; the hand on her backside held her as she twisted and fought the offending one. She glanced back, face begging for help, but Tokh didn't dare intervene yet.

Aftnahn released her to sniff his fingers, taste a claw. "I've never met a human female before. I would like her in my quarters tonight after dinner, perhaps with a bottle of *varvet*. I trust you have some in stock."

"Of course, your Revered Majesty," Tokh said with a greasy pressed smile. "I'll make sure it's available in as great a quantity as you desire. However, I can't comply about the girl."

Aftnahn lifted his head high with a disbelieving frown. The Emissary ran back to Tokh; not just to him, but threw herself into his lap, wrapped her arms around his neck, and buried her face against the sharp corners of his medals, forbidden contact. Masákh and Sóghar pulled her back to her footstool.

"You question the order of a *fáhganid*?"

Tokh bowed in his seat and spread his hands helplessly. "Forgive me, Revered Majesty, but she's below the age set by our Wondrous Emperor."

Aftnahn scowled deeper. "I'm sorry, I couldn't tell her age without clothing, and she didn't understand my words. It was an honest mistake. Since you feel she's like a daughter to you, I'll pay you the fine."

Tokh's apologetic, groveling smile hid the terror choking his innards. Here was the battle he feared. He would either successfully steer Aftnahn away, or he would lose his head for the Emperor, and the mission would fail.

"I cannot, even with misunderstanding. My orders come directly from Our Beloved Royal Emperor Nághtas himself, signed by his own hand. This is a most delicate bargaining situation with the Union. My direct orders are that no one may bed her; no one, not even *bhísroti*. I'm afraid I can offer you only my sweet Mímihn." He took Mímihn's hand and held it high, and she giggled as if she'd won a contest. "Mimi is extremely adept at providing whatever service you desire. I'm sure you'll find her as delightful as I."

Aftnahn's face slid into a cold, unhappy mask. "I would have expected that as normal courtesy, Tokh. If I was in less of a pleasant mood, I would ask you to take her place. I may yet. And I will examine your orders."

Tokh bowed his head. "Absolutely, Most Revered General." To his *aghát* he hissed, "Dismissed!" and they hurried the girl back into hiding.

Aftnahn left after two and a half miserable days, testier than a feverish colonel with a bad case of venereal boils being weaned off *dhurwah*. Aftnahn wasn't used to being thwarted, but Tokh's written orders were firm; he wouldn't back down, and every call to override Tokh was not only denied but demanded Aftnahn return to Kerasi space. By a miracle of Fortune, Tokh's men, to the lowliest enlisted *ghinadín*, performed beyond perfection, and not one officer received a reprimand, let alone lost a head. Tokh had not shit in two days, terrified something would go wrong while he was occupied. He received word that Aftnahn had left orbit while in his quarters, and allowed himself to sink down into the carpeting and become limp with relief.

"My Lord? Lord? Are you ill?" Mímihn's voice held panic, hearing him slump. She felt her way around the furniture until she found him, then knelt down, hand on his back.

He reached out and held her hand. "I'm weak with relief that this is over." His hand squeezed hers. "And you? Are you well? He didn't injure you?"

Mímihn smiled as if she could see him. Her hand clenched his in return, giving him strength, not taking it from him. "I'm untroubled, Lord. Nothing I haven't done before. I told you, their egos are far more sensitive than their *khatas*." She lay down next to him on the carpeting, nose to nose. "Now, how many of his secrets would you like to know?"

Tokh stared at her, snorting soft breaths of disbelief. His pretty little consort had more courage than he did, cool and calm in the face of supreme danger she couldn't even see. He grabbed her in a fierce hug there on the floor and kissed her under her jaw so hard it left a mark. "Blessed Emperor, I love you!"

175

* * 25 * *

Six of the eleven teams failed outright, their emissaries dead or disabled by too rough a handling by the technicians. Tokh was still on target and looking hopeful. Masákh had done an unparalleled job of educating his subject, far beyond anything Tokh could have hoped. Masákh could control her using words alone. She'd formed a dependency on him, willing to obey as long as it pleased him. She'd come to truce with Tokh, too. For a female she had a fiery spirit, argumentative despite her fear of his authority, but she settled in to her captivity after a month or two and caused little difficulty. Tokh spoke with her directly at least twice a week, quizzing her like a school director to ensure she was learning the prescribed lessons. He was impressed. He liked her, more than he expected, which was probably why her treachery hurt him so much. After months of good behavior, neither Tokh nor any of his *aghát* saw it coming.

Slowly, so slowly she played them, biding her time, earning their trust. While they worked at her, it was now apparent she was working at them, requesting innocent amusements, playing with them right under their noses so they would never suspect her intent. Tokh hadn't probed her memory in months, didn't see a need for the risk when her cooperation became routine and he'd learned everything he needed from her. In one swift move, she rappelled out a window and escaped his compound unseen in the back of a service vehicle.

Never had Tokh been so frightened. War wasn't frightening; conflict happened too fast to worry. This was a dream-terror, his feet cemented into place and the world moving past him in twisted slow-motion. If she escaped back to her people, it would cost him his head and start an interstellar war that would destroy his world.

"Find her!" he screamed at Masákh. He could feel everything crashing around him. This was his fault. He was in charge. They wouldn't just behead him; for something this major, they would also come after his family. Perhaps not his older sons; they might escape by their own merits, but certainly his younger children would be sacrificed to eradicate the shame. Never had Tokh been so choked by desperation.

His team saved him, working together as he'd trained them. His emissary was located and retrieved in less than sixty *fasim*. It did nothing to calm Tokh's anger. Anger at his prisoner, anger at his team, anger at himself for being lulled into false security, and he let his anger rule. He struck Masákh in fury, so hard he almost broke his jaw, but there was little he could do beyond suspend him for a day and put a note in his file. He needed Masákh. Masákh controlled the girl, and Tokh wasn't sure she'd cooperate without him. Sóghar terrified her, and Tokh didn't trust him. He couldn't pull Mátokhan back from his duties, and although Haghíde had a good rapport with the girl, he wasn't strict enough to be effective long-term.

He couldn't ignore the act. Tokh had promised the girl she wouldn't be harmed if she cooperated. He also warned her numerous times that disobedience would be punished. He'd been very easy on the punishments. This time, he couldn't be. It would be swift, and it would break her. He'd guided many difficult interrogations when negative reinforcement had been used, his nerves as strong as ever, but he didn't look forward to this one. Her spirit was what he enjoyed most about her; it was a shame to destroy it. Kassán enjoyed punishments too much; he didn't trust Kassán alone, and he couldn't afford another mistake. He would stand witness.

Perhaps he'd eaten something wrong. Perhaps it was the unbearable stress of the day. Perhaps he was losing his nerve, but after they carried the girl back to her cell, Tokh hid in the lavatory and vomited until his chest hurt.

It was later that he learned she'd exposed them, contacting the Union and giving her location. Tokh sent a crisis signal, and ordered his men to break down operations and be ready to move on his command, while he waited for orders from mission control. He couldn't spare a thought for Mímihn, but he found a lone second to fly upstairs and tell her she had one hour to be ready to run.

"I can be ready in half that. Tell me what you need me to do."

He stared at her, half crazed with anger and crushing responsibility, and there she stood, achingly beautiful, blind as in an underground tunnel, helpless and endangered in the current situation, and she was ready to cover his back without a single thought to herself. She was property; if he wanted, he could abandon her with the building and ease his burden. "I have no one left to guard you."

"I can manage." Mímihn shuffled to a table against the wall, opened one of its small drawers, and pulled out a needle-like dagger often carried by *fáhganid* and *bhísroti* women. She strapped it to her arm and flexed it to show Tokh she knew how it worked. "Don't worry. Just tell me where you need me."

It went against all logic – if they'd been on Kerasím, it would have been against the law – but Tokh reached into his holster and pulled out his plasma gun, and he handed it to the *ghinadín* Thrit. "I'm trusting you beyond reason. Anyone tries to touch her, no matter the rank or caste, you are to ordered to shoot to kill. Protect her until I can claim her and I will reward you well. Harm her, and I will see you're burned alive before your family. Is that understood?"

Thrit bowed in half and accepted the weapon. "T'rit's life in your word, Lord General."

Tokh paced before his desk, rubbing the bony prominences over his eyes. "We need a place to store the emissary where she can't escape, and we're forbidden by command from entering Kerasi space. From here we're two weeks' travel from the closest Coalition ally. We'd be intercepted before we made it that far. You can't just cruise around enemy territory and look for a spot to set up an illegal camp. Not with these ships and this much crew. What do they expect from me?"

Major Khaním, one of Tokh's top officers and perhaps his closest friend, leaned close to keep his words private. "If we're looking for a place to forget something, perhaps we should look to the past."

Tokh scowled. "The only thing shorter than our time, Khaním, is my patience. What are you talking about?"

"The Ghilsoohr Experiments," Khaním said in a whisper. "Exploring the time stream. I have contacts on one of the ships who keep me well-informed. Place her even a year out of position and the Union will never find her if they mass every last life raft to the task. I know for fact there's a timeshifter ship at the near reaches of our territory; if we were to meet it part way, we could rendezvous in as little as a day, at most, less than two."

Tokh paused. The eyebrow rose, and a glimmer lit up his eye. "What are you saying?"

"Time travel. Take her back in time and hold her there until we're ready. Go back to a date before we made contact with the Union, and they won't know we're their enemy. It's foolproof."

Tokh's spine crinkled. "That's impossible."

"It's not," Khaním insisted. "It's a project of the Cabinet of Science. It's been going on for six years now. They keep the ships at the edges of our space; if they meet us between zones, we can rendezvous in as little as a day. Then it's just a matter of plotting the numbers and building up the space warp, perhaps an hour after that. Even if we're pursued, we'll simply disappear off their screens."

Tokh remembered to breathe. "And then? We can come back to our regular time when needed?"

Khaním nodded with a smile. "Yes. It's been done many times, without issue. I follow the space developments as a hobby. We go, we come back. No trace."

Tokh patted the major's shoulder. "You may have saved us, Khaním. Get in touch with your contacts immediately. I'll inform command and see what they say. I need access to every study you've read."

Tokh grabbed Mímihn at the last minute, ushering her and Thrit to his transport that took them to a shuttle, which took them to an orbiting ship, which took them to a rendezvous with a specially designed ship that could slip through time itself. He, a General Two, hadn't known such a thing existed. With Kassán's help, he temporarily disabled the girl's ability to speak, leaving her even more dependent on Masákh and his men. If she escaped again, they were safe.

For a time, Tokh thought he could beat the collapse of his mission. They sat for months, hidden in space or on the Union planet Earth in its history, waiting for orders while the diplomats tried to sort things out and reach a deal. Mímihn suffered, most of the time stuck in small rooms, not having any reference point as to where she was or what was going on. The foods were odd and didn't sit well, the language incomprehensible to her, the music hard and pounding. She couldn't sing to it, though she tried, but much of it lent a strong rhythm for him to bed her to. Some days he didn't have the heart for even that; other days that's all he seemed to do, though it didn't help his mood. He was a man of action, and sitting for weeks on end doing nothing but waiting made him want to eat the walls, scrap by

179

scrap. Everything lay in Mátokhan's hands now, bargaining for the return of the girl in exchange for diplomatic treaties.

Fifteen weeks of agony, and the message came through.

By order of Trannor, General Four: Diplomatic relations have failed. Union negotiations closed. Mission deemed concluded. Return all troops to Keranihn base. Retrieve emissary and dispose as desired.

At least the message didn't involve the words *disciplinary action*. Not yet. Tokh messaged his team to grab the girl and be ready for retrieval. Should the mission fail, he had long-ago promised Masákh the girl as his own consort. It was only fair, with the amount of time he had spent with her, pulling her emotions toward him. Tokh knew Masákh's feelings for the girl were anything but virtuous. He was an excellent officer whose discipline was a marvel to behold, but he was Kerasi. It was only a matter of time before his discipline ran out, and Masákh would take liberties with or without permission. Yes, Masákh could have the girl, and Tokh wouldn't ask for first rights as commander. He owed him that much for his loyalty.

Tokh paced on the small bridge of their time-shifter ship, waiting for his *aghát* to make their rendezvous. After jumping time, they would all dock at the science ship waiting for them at the edge of Kerasi space.

"General, we have a ship on sensors." The navigator's voice broke into his self-pity. Tokh and the captain of the ship both jumped forward to observe. "Not one of ours. It just came around the moon, heading for the planet at top speed. Emission trails are modern; it's not of this time period."

"Union?" Tokh said in amazement. "How could they find us? Time slipping is experimental to us; do they know it as well? Are we aware that they know it?"

"I have no knowledge of it. Have they spotted us?" said the captain.

"If they have, they're ignoring us," said the navigator. "Bearing matches our mark. Registration is in Union symbols; matching identification now."

"They're intercepting us! The Union's trying to get her before we do!" Tokh realized. "How could they know!"

"Weapons? Engines?" the captain said.

180

The navigator read down the scans. "Standard Union shielding. No major weapons noted, no cannons, no lasers, no disruptors. Engine output reads similar to an E-Projector 714 drive."

"That's a lot of engine for a ship that size," the captain said. "It's got to be reinforced for that much power, which means extra mass, and therefore extra fuel needed."

"What does that mean?" Tokh said.

"It means we can outgun them, and depending on their fuel situation, we might be able to outrun them," the captain said. He sat back in his command seat. "Get our speeders in there now, retrieve all personnel immediately. Navigator, get us into position by the moon. Plot their most likely course of escape, keep us hidden until they're close on return, then intercept at maximum speed. Disable, but don't destroy. We may want what they have on board. If not, we'll have prisoners for exchange."

"After we know how they managed the time slip," Tokh said. Bringing back top-secret and highly desirable enemy information might just pull him out of this disaster, enough to stop a death sentence. He'd be stripped of rank, shamed, and demoted to grudging desk duty in a forgotten dark hallway, his salary a pittance, his house confiscated, but he would be alive.

"Go to alert status," the captain commanded. "All hands in place."

Tokh sent Mímihn a voice message to secure herself and Thrit, and wait for his next word.

Tokh was not a pilot. He understood the concepts in atmospheric flight, but the details of space flight were beyond him. All he knew was it was deadly on many fronts, from radiation to depressurization to loss of oxygen and extreme cold. Loss of gravity was nausea-inducing, but not deadly. And he faced all of them to get back home.

The Union ship was fast, with minimal weaponry. Tokh's ship surprised it, a minor battle ensued, but during the melee all ships hit the time barrier at imprecise calculation. The barrier was difficult at optimum conditions; in emergency conditions, with several ships hitting it at once, the forces tore the ships apart.

For an unknown time Tokh lay on the decking of the bridge with most of the crew, overcome by the dimensional effects. When he regained consciousness, he wished he hadn't, or at least he wanted a strong drink to calm his head and stomach. Ship's power had failed; everything was on emergency systems, the lights dim and far apart. Pops and sizzles sounded from the control boards, sparks flew now and then to burn the passerby, and the acrid smell of burning solder and insulation filled the air. Crewmen groaned and tried to regain their posts. Gravity tried, tried again, then died out all together, and everyone began to drift around the bridge until they found anchor.

"Report!" Tokh ordered. He clung to a railing on the wall and forced his feet into a more normal position toward the floor, hoping his stomach would stay down in the process.

The captain was plugging at controls as his navigator swam back to his station. "Twenty percent reserve power. Main power at zero. We appear to be back in proper time and space, just outside Kerasi territory. Sending emergency signal now."

"And the other ships? Did they materialize?"

The captain checked a scanner. "No sign yet. Depends on whose stream they got caught in. Khojar, emergency procedures. Move all non-essential personnel to the forward galley. We've got a loss of pressure in compartments six, seven, and eight."

That made sense to Tokh until he realized, "You can't put my consort into an open room of men. She'll be killed."

The captain glared at him. "That's your problem, General, not mine. If I can't get minimum power back, we're all dead."

Tokh wrenched the bridge door open and took off. He wanted to run, but all he could do was pull himself along the dark corridors and try not to smash into anything, especially the men trying to get to the forward sections. The lifts wouldn't work on emergency power, and he was forced to crawl down two sets of access ladders to get to the proper deck.

"Mímihn!"

"Tokh!" she cried out, clinging to the bed in their tiny cabin. "What's happening! I'm about to lose my stomach."

He floated toward her, stopped himself with a foot to the wall, then wedged his knee under the table to stay in place. "We've lost power coming through the barrier. There's no gravity. We've got to move to the front of the ship. Please don't vomit until the gravity returns." He was about to take her arm when he remembered her jewelry. It wasn't as grand as what his wives wore, but they were still worth a good amount. He seized the box where she kept them, emptied the pieces into his pockets, then took extra power cells for his weapon from his luggage and stuck them in the cargo loops of his belt. He swam back to her.

"It's very difficult to move in the corridors. Put your arms around my neck, cling to my back. I'll try not to bump too many things, but I make no promises. Thrit, can you follow?"

"T'rit do his best, Lord."

It took fifteen *fasim* to work his way back. "Get that trash off my bridge!" the captain shouted. "There isn't room enough to swing your *khatas* as it is!"

"I won't put her with general population!" Tokh swore. He'd never attempted combat in zero-G, but he wasn't afraid to try.

"Then put them in my cabin if you must, but get that *trixahg* off my bridge!"

The captain's quarters was two doors down. Tokh dragged Mímihn there and they waited, wedged against the furniture for support.

* * 26 * *

A rescue ship arrived the next day, meeting them as they drifted at less than half-light. Five days later, they reached Kerasím. Two red-uniformed Imperial Guards met Tokh as he exited the shuttle, Mímihn holding his arm.

One of them bowed. "General Tokh. You will accompany us, please. *Fáhganid* General Mirpat requests to see you."

Tokh felt the knife in his stomach already, but he accompanied the guards to the general.

"Leave the pets outside, Tokh," Mirpat sniffed.

"I can't leave my consort unguarded, and her servant would be similarly attacked."

Mirpat spoke to one of the guards. "Keep General Tokh's consort in the hallway with honor. Make sure no liberties are taken with her or her servant.

"Sit," he told Tokh when they were alone. Tokh took the small chair before the *fáhganid*'s desk. Mirpat's attitude dimmed. "Tokh, what the *hihvat* happened out there?"

"From what point? Did the other ship ever appear?"

"Captured by the Union as they emerged from the slip. I need a list of personnel who were aboard. Your emissary made it back alive and is in Union hands."

Tokh felt his stomach sink to his knees. "Five of my *aghát*. I don't know the names of the crew."

"We have much to discuss, Tokh. Until the investigation is complete, you're confined to grounds, understood?"

"I'll require insurance for my consort's safety."

"I'll make specific request to the guards. I'm sorry, Tokh. You needn't have an escort, but you're confined to base. I will also need you to surrender your weapons."

Tokh's heart gave a hard flop. "As you must, General. I assume you'll be requesting a memory scan along with questioning. I will volunteer myself, but I request Colonel Kassán be the interrogator. I trust him at the controls, and it will do much to make me relaxed and conducive to giving information freely."

"As long as he does the job, I won't object. The guards will show you to your quarters. Dismissed."

Tokh eyed the given quarters with a small relief. They were standard-issue rooms for visiting personnel, a little sitting area with private bedroom and bath, not a detention cell. That was a good sign. He and Mímihn would have the bedroom and Thrit could have the sofa, far more luxury than most *ghinadín* were given, but Thrit had earned it. There were guards outside the door but they didn't interfere with him, just kept note on when Tokh entered and left. He took Mímihn on a long walk around the compound. She'd been cooped up inside buildings and ships far too long, and enjoyed walking in open air.

They came for him before the suns rose. The escorts waited while he dressed and Mímihn shoved a bite of breakfast at him. He wasn't sure if having food in his stomach would be good or bad yet, but the day was just a preliminary hearing. He sat before a panel of eight officials, including General Trannor, General Mirpat, and a veiled figure Tokh knew damned well was Heir Apparent Nadigh himself. Every detail of his mission was examined, from taking possession of the building through his return to the base. They broke twice for meals; in all, Tokh spent twelve full hours explaining his actions.

When he returned to Mímihn, he was exhausted and depressed.

Mímihn straddled his lap and unfastened the first two buttons of his uniform. "Let me bring you some cheer, my Lord."

Tokh shook his head and made her stand. "Not now. Perhaps later. I have too much to think about. I'm going to fill out a paper on you, Mímihn. If the worst situation occurs, I'm going to give you to my son Kitras. It might start a fight with his brother, but as oldest Zenak will be responsible for his mother, so I don't wish to burden him with two females."

Mímihn laughed. "That's hardly an even gift: one gets an elderly mother, the other gets a young consort. You obviously have favorites among your sons."

"Both have given me pride and both have angered me. It's Umara and Joralan I fear for; Joralan is nowhere near old enough to

185

take charge of his mother. She won't be pleased, but I'll name Major Khaním as Joralan's regent until he is fourteen. Umara came to me with a dowry; I'll see that it's paid out to Khaním to care for her until then. He'll no doubt take some liberties, but he'll treat her well."

Mímihn rubbed his shoulders, then leaned over to hug him, cheek to cheek. "You talk so morbidly, my Lord. This won't last but a few days. You'll see."

Tokh shook his head. "I've been in the army forty years, Mímihn. I know how things work. This is a politeness on their part, a respect to me because of my record. Depending on the Emperor's call, I could be imprisoned, punished, executed, or simply lose rank and privilege. I don't see a happy way out of this. My mission is a wreck and my top men captured by the enemy; there's no way out."

Mímihn kissed him under his ear. Her tongue poked into the divot between his skull and jaw, teasing him. "I never see anything happy," she said cheerfully. "I carry my own happiness with me instead."

He did *push* Mímihn that night, just once, but it took a long time to work himself up to it, and his feeble release brought him no pleasure.

They gave him a day of rest, but he hadn't taken the last bite of his dinner when they came for him again. This time he was brought to an observation room. He knew them well, having spent years interrogating unfortunate subjects behind their walls. He sat with an interrogator while cameras recorded and unseen people sat behind one-way glass. Specific questions were thrown at him over and over, trying to make him answer any other way than he did the previous time. The hour was chosen so that he would be tired and his thinking muddled. He was kept off balance by random loud noises, flashing lights, shouts and insults from the interrogator, incentive sticks smashed onto the table next to him, or, on several occasions, cracking down across his shoulders as if he were a school boy instead of a Level-Two General. He was released after seven hours. Tokh knew what the procedures were meant to do. His answers didn't change, he said nothing but the truth, but he shook so hard at the conclusion the guards had to help him steady himself before he could walk. He had two glasses of spirits to help him sleep, Mímihn rubbing ointment on his neck and shoulders where he'd been struck, but he did something he hadn't done in years: woke up screaming with a flashback to combat. Mímihn had no idea what was happening, couldn't see the terror on his face, and could do little but cling and cry for him to explain until he calmed down again. Tokh didn't sleep the rest of the night.

Again they gave him a day to recover. Tokh couldn't sit still, and walked Mímihn endlessly around the grounds. He didn't say much, and she didn't pressure him. Thrit opened the bedroom door an hour past midnight at the request of the guards in the sitting room. This time Tokh was taken to the basement level. He knew what awaited him.

Kassán greeted him at the door of the investigation room. There was no leering, no growling, no snide insults. Kassán the Impossible was nothing but professional. "Please relax, General. I know you're well aware of how the procedure works. I've been over the equipment in detail. I assure you it's in prime working condition. You have my word; there will be no errors. If you'll lie down on the chair." Kassán began to thread the dozens of tiny sensor wires into his scalp.

General Mirpat and two others stood witness while Trannor ran the interrogation. Tokh was certain Kassán had used too much tranquilizer; his limbs felt impossibly heavy, and he couldn't have fought back if he'd tried. Trannor was a fearsome interrogator. Tokh could recite the protocols, but if it weren't for the tranquilizers, he knew he would have panicked in terror. He answered many of the same questions for a third time, explained situations and reactions yet again, while his memories were scanned and recorded to be reviewed later.

"Boost the power. Go deeper," Mirpat ordered.

Kassán read his monitors. "I have no evidence of falsehood."

"I said break him down."

Kassán shrugged. He tapped a vein and injected Tokh with yet another drug and adjusted several dials. The lights above the machine glowed brighter, the noise of the scanner increased, and Tokh grimaced, then groaned as pain ate into his muscles and he pulled his feet up against the ankle restraints. Trannor began again.

Tokh needed help to sit up when the equipment was removed. Kassán handed him two large tablets.

187

"Chew these," he said. "It will stop the cramping."

Tokh looked up to thank him, and caught the flicker of a wink in Kassán's unscarred eye. He wasn't in any condition to trust what he saw, but Kassán did it again, deliberately, and Tokh clued in. Kassán had protected him. He hadn't increased the power at all, just induced muscle pain to mimic pain from the procedure. Kassán knew exactly what had transpired on the planet Kye, knew Tokh spoke truth, but to acknowledge it would be to break neutrality and they would send in another technician who might screw things up.

Kassán handed him two smaller tablets on a cellophane strip. "Take these when you get back to your quarters. They'll let you sleep it off."

Tokh patted Kassán's shoulder. "Thank you, friend."

He arrived at his room as the suns broke over the horizon, swallowed Kassán's pills, and put himself to bed, Mímihn pressed up tight against his chest, warm and comforting. Tokh was no believer in the Temple of the Fortunes; they were no more in charge of Fate than a party game, but it was truly Fortune that brought him to that Tabs game and dared him to challenge a *dahneg*. He wouldn't have made it through the last year without Mimihn's comforts, and he certainly wouldn't have made it through this week.

He kissed her sleepily on her forehead. "I love you, my sweet Mímihn."

She kissed him on the soft skin behind his chin hank. "I love you more, my brave Lord."

They eased up on him after that. Days passed without an unexpected visit. His guards let him pass without issue. He walked Mímihn about in the sunshine and dined with her at the general's mess. Trannor called him into conference twice, but it was no more than that, a conference in Trannor's office to update him on the situation. Trannor wasn't friendly but not hostile, and gave no indication whether the investigation was looking in his favor or not. Everything seemed to be one big waiting game. He started *pushing* Mímihn again, just to have something to do.

A second week slipped by before his handcom chirped in his pocket.

"General Trannor requests your presence in his office at extreme speed," the secretary informed him. "There's a call coming in for you, from enemy channels. General Trannor needs you to take it immediately."

"Enemy...?" Tokh ran as if he were being chased.

He burst into the office without so much as a knock. Trannor said nothing, just waved him to the communications screen. The feed was visual, but the coding on the call indicated monitored transmission, respond voice feed only. Tokh tapped in his authorization code as he caught his breath.

For two weeks in enemy hands, his lead officer Masákh looked no worse for wear. He still wore his blue uniform, and his words were in Union Standard, another clue all words were being heard elsewhere. "The Union has restored our Emissary's speech. She has pleaded her case to the Union, and the Union has started to respond. I have met with the Admiral Perrin; he is as powerful as was described. He remains a hostile ally, but believes in the Emissary. He obtained us audience with President Mijono, who is willing to begin a limited trust over the exchange of scientific information, with a likelihood of further diplomatic exchanges as trust is built. Mátokhan is brokering early terms as we speak."

Tokh's heart stopped. "Masákh, if this is a game, your head will be the last thing I cut from you."

"It is scannable truth. I have met with Mijono, the Admiral Perrin, had extensive discussions with the Councilman Wodu in charge of non-Union liaisons, the secondary-president Rill, the investigator Indermeir, an ambassador Kwi-Oc, and a high-level Secretary Hhani. We continue to explore exchanges of non-classified information and protocols. I am also allowed limited contact with the Emissary, by her demand. She has proven to be a ruthless negotiator; you would be most proud of her, General. She has exceeded any and all expectations not just of a female, but of the entire program. Her methods are immature, but effective."

Tokh's breath came in gasps. His head bowed for several seconds. "May her name be praised by all the stars of night! Masákh! Give her my deepest commendations. I will inform the Emperor immediately of our contact. I commend all of you on your most excellent work. Continue, and keep me informed. Tokh out." He sank to a knee, praising the Spirits of Fortune, Masákh, his emissary, and the Emperor himself.

The situation stabilized. Emperor Nághtas accepted President Mijono's request for direct negotiations, the first time Union and Kerasi leaders had spoken to each other in more than thirty years; the goal of the entire mission. After all the mistakes, after all his worries, after so many, many years of preparation, Tokh's men had accomplished the impossible. The mission was labeled a triumph, the only one of the eleven teams that managed even a moderately successful outcome.

"You're free to go, with the deepest thanks of Emperor Nághtas," General Trannor told him with a smile. He clapped Tokh on the shoulder. "Congratulations, Tokh. You're a hero to the future of Kerasím. The Emperor won't forget your dedication and service. You're granted eight weeks leave, and guaranteed six months serve-in-place. Go home and rest."

Tokh felt lighter than air, as if the Spirits of Fortune were blowing upwards under his feet. He could once again put his affairs in order and see to his property, assured at least eight months with no deployments, able to work from home if he wished. And he had hope – still a long shot, but a real chance just the same – that should things continue to improve, a promotion might be on the horizon. General Three was huge prestige, putting him in the running for a seat in the Emperor's senate, or a regional posting in charge of divisions, not just personal teams. General Three could even get him invited to the Emperor's palace, or possibly a special dispensation to allow him three wives instead of two. He had married Zheníhda because it was expected of him, and he had no complaints about her as wife. He had married Umara as a favor to General Sobak; he was quite fond of her, and didn't regret the marriage.

But he realized, in his heart of hearts, he loved Mímihn, the only female he himself had actually chosen, even if he hadn't known it at the time. *Loved* her. With a depth of fondness and affection he admittedly never had for his wives. One saucy glance from her and his heart stopped beating from joy. She never failed to smile, no matter what her pain or anguish. She had an eager excitable boundless energy. For everything she'd suffered, she never said a disagreeable word, no matter what he asked of her, no matter how difficult the situation, with a bravery born of blindness that he could not fathom. She was witty and pleasant and quick to pick up on information; he had no idea how educated she'd been, but she was certainly the brightest of his females. Zheníhda was superb at

190

managing and counting and keeping track of details, a flawless hostess whose motions were so subtle no one was ever aware of her presence; Umara was awful at keeping track of things, fumbling half the things she touched, but she was literate enough to read stories to their children or make sense of a news article, her memory was astounding and she always had a ready song or poem on her lips. Mímihn – was *alive*. She never seemed to have lost her childhood innocence, but in a pinch, perhaps because of her consort training, she could be the most welcoming and gracious of hostesses, putting guests as ease and making Tokh seem as important as the Emperor himself. She dazzled him. He felt an overwhelming need to protect her from the world. And it hurt that he could only keep her as property, not as wife proper. He wasn't of the type to divorce a wife merely for convenience, and after the first three years, divorces were difficult – and extremely expensive – to come by. Tokh faced just one last hurdle to going home:

Going home.

* * 27 * *

The courtesy vehicle pulled up to his house. It hadn't changed, the green trims freshly painted, the stone walkways, the gardens well-cared for in his absence. The yard was covered in victory flags, welcoming him back. Tokh got out, while the driver opened the back to assist Mímihn and her servant and retrieve the luggage. He'd spoken with his wives since being cleared of wrongdoing; they knew he was coming back in glory. They didn't know he was bringing home additions.

Joralan was the first to burst from the door, followed by his sister. "*Bo*! *Bobo*'s home! *Bobo*'s home! *Bobo*!" Tokh swung them up into the air one at a time and hugged them. Umara flew out, followed by Zheníhda, hurrying but not quite running, for running would be undignified and the neighbors were watching. Umara bowed at his feet; he pulled her up, seized her in a hug and kissed her throat hungrily. Zheníhda also dropped to her knees, stood, and received Tokh's greeting. He lifted her off the ground with his embrace and spun her around as if she were still twenty. While he kissed her throat, she caught sight of the people by the vehicle.

"Tokh! You didn't tell me you brought visitors." Another glance, and she realized the beautiful, well-dressed young woman was being led. "Tokh! You! You have a consort? You brought a *consort* to my home? You fatherless *ghinadin*! How could you! How could you shame our home bringing that *trixahg* here! We have children present! Get her out of here!"

Tokh ushered them all into the house, signaled for Thrit to follow with Mímihn.

Zheníhda wouldn't back down. She tried to block him from entering. "Do not bring her in here, Tokh! What were you thinking?! Just where do you think you're going to put her? How much did you bleed our accounts to purchase her? Do you know the taxes on a consort?! How could you ruin us like this!"

Tokh took Mímihn's hand and kissed it. "This is Mímihn, and she will stay here by my decree, like it or not. Mímihn, you have just met my firstwife Zheníhda by her loud mouth. She has many opinions and she shares them more freely than she has a right. This over here is my second wife Umara. Umara, you will greet our newcomer."

Umara bowed her head only. Not that Mímihn could see it. "Welcome to Tokh's home, Mímihn. It will be a pleasure to have someone else to take over the work duties so I may have more time for my children. Please remember they are my children, not yours, and keep away from them. And pay no mind to Nihda: she's always like this."

"That's not much of a welcome," Tokh warned. "Umara, show her to my room for now, and don't let me see anyone making her walk into things or you will know my wrath."

"Come, Mímihn," Umara said, and Thrit led her to the stairs. "It's too bad you can't cook."

"I can make simple things, if I know where everything is kept," Mímihn said. "I can make hot drinks, wash and chop ingredients, stir things, boil foods. I can perform many household tasks."

"Then I guarantee you'll never be bored."

Zheníhda couldn't let it go. Tears of outrage rose up. "How could you do this to me? More than a year! More than a year I keep your house, waiting for you, with almost no words of encouragement from you. It was bad enough when you threw that lazy *jappa* Umara on me! That breaks my limit, Tokh! I won't have that creature in our house!"

"Fifteen months, and this is the greeting I receive?" Tokh countered. "Perhaps I should have taken you with me, left Umara in charge of the house. Then you could have served as bedmate for my men, and sat in a room for months at a time because I had no time to take you for walks, and you could have been on the ships as we tried to outmaneuver the enemy, taking hits and arriving in our territory with crippled engines and only half our air remaining. I'll remember that the next time I'm assigned a mission."

"Then you should have sold her when the mission ended! And bringing a male servant into the house – what are you thinking, with a young daughter? Where will you put him? In case you haven't noticed, we're out of space!"

"He's a castrate, and has proven his trust many times over. I'll create space for him in the basement. He's *ghinadin*; walls and roofs are luxury to them. With freedom to move around the house,

193

Mímihn won't need him as much, so he may attend to yardwork and repairs. He'll be available to escort any of you in public, and save me the fees."

Zheníhda threw her hands in the air. "You ask too much of me, Tokh. I'm your First-Wife, mother of your first sons. I deserve some respect!"

Tokh stared at her with increasing ire. He had missed Zheníhda, missed her prissy way of pretending to be noble when she was only *dihnarwharl*, missed the knowing way she touched him after so many years, missed the way she kept order, a little general of her home. Her tirade evaporated that longing, and he found himself disgusted. "When I receive your respect, we'll discuss what I give to you." He stalked past her to find Mímihn.

His children provided distraction. The wives had gone all-out to welcome him back with banners and buntings hanging from the walls, a plethora of flowers in Emperor's red and gold, the table lavishly decorated and his favorite foods and drink waiting for his dinner. He sat with his children in his lap, Joralan now six and Kesseh now three, Joralan showing him all the glowing reports he'd had from school, and Tokh entertaining them with stories of the planet he'd been stationed on and the space battle he'd survived. Joralan ran to his room and reappeared armed with toy swords and pistols, and he and Kesseh battled through the house. Tokh watched them with a grin. A year ago he would have taken the light-up play pistol from Kesseh and told her weapons were not for *dihnarwharl* ladies, but after observing his emissary for a year, seeing her spirit never cease its fight, seeing her strength and intelligence, he let Kesseh play while he observed. Her delight in the game was no less than Joralan's, even though she could never be a soldier. Mímihn sat on the floor by his feet, listening to the household and learning its dynamics.

The dinner table was crowded with steaming dishes, the smells delectable. Tokh could not have imagined better, and he couldn't wait to eat. Zheníhda's best dishes set the places, with spiced *lunahl* in carafes glowing gold on the ivory linens.

"Don't sit that creature at my table, Tokh," Zheníhda warned. "She's a servant; she can eat with the servants."

Mímihn smiled her eager smile. "I would gladly dine with your servants, Zheníhda. Just point me –"

"Do NOT speak my name! You will address me as First Wife or Lady Tokh and nothing else!"

"She's dined next to me for more than a year. If she doesn't sit at my table, no one will eat," Tokh growled.

Mímihn's hand slid over his hair and down his neck. "Don't be silly, my Lord. Firstwife is absolutely correct. I shouldn't be sitting with you unless it's in private. I should be serving you while you eat. Sit!"

Tokh sat while Mímihn served him, filling his glass without a losing a drop while the housemaid served the children and wives. He took her hand and kissed it, picked a morsel from his plate and placed it in her mouth.

"Well, that's fitting," Zheníhda said, "but you should never feed pets from the table, Tokh. It only encourages them to beg. I'll make sure to place her food on the floor where she can find it."

Tokh's collapsible incentive stick sat in its sleeve on his sword sheath, a convenient place to store something that long and thin. He pulled it out and extended it in one swift movement. It cracked on the table, just missing Zheníhda's cheek. The table jumped. Mímihn skipped backwards at the familiar whistle-*crack!* and put her arms up to protect her face. Umara shrieked and ducked. The children sat wide-eyed, watching.

"Enough!" Tokh stormed. "Not one more word, Nihda, or I will correct you! You should be welcoming me, not draining my patience! I speak of you both to Mímihn in glowing terms, and this is what you show her? My house will not run like this! If this is what happens when I'm not here, then you'll all accompany me on missions, no matter what the danger. I will hear an apology or you will stand by the wall without leave until I do. I don't tolerate such comments from my officers and won't tolerate them from anyone in this house. What is, is, and it will not change. Speak!"

Zheníhda trembled, daring herself to hold it back, but angry tears were in her voice as she said, "My apologies, Lord."

"You're fine, Mímihn," Tokh assured her as he collapsed the incentive stick and placed it by his plate. "Don't worry."

The room fell back into a tense ceasefire. Mímihn resumed her place, silent at Tokh's elbow while the meal continued with idle neutral chatter and stories from the children. After a time she heard his fork clink down onto his plate. "Would my Lord desire more of something, or shall I clear your dish for the next course?"

"See if he wants more of this," Zheníhda spat. She scooped whipped *bhoshu* from her plate and threw it at Mímihn, hitting her square in the face and neck.

Mímihn flinched as it landed. "Oh!"

There was a count of three, and the room exploded. Tokh jumped to his feet with a growl of fury. He started at his end of the table and swept the top all the way down, throwing every last thing to the floor as the diners tried to jump out of his way. He grabbed Zheníhda with both hands as she shrieked and he forced her down over the table.

"I warned you!" he bellowed. "You want humiliation? I'll give it to you. Get everyone in here, servants and all. I want as many witnesses as possible." He tried to wrestle her onto her stomach as she fought him.

"Tokh! No! Don't do that! Beat me if you must," Zheníhda begged.

"Not in front of your children, Tokh!" Umara said sharply, and gathered them to her.

Mímihn realized what he was about to do. She dared to place her hands on his arm as he wrestled Zheníhda. "My Lord, please do not use violence! You'll hurt her. Please, Lord, I beg you, it's not worth it. I'm uninjured. She's just upset. You must give her time. Please!"

Tokh pinned Zheníhda with one hand, reached under her skirts and yanked her underthings down with the other as she screeched and kicked at him. "Mímihn, take the children upstairs and don't come down until you're told. That's an order."

Mímihn looked about to cry, but she bowed her head. "Your word is my law. Come, children. I haven't seen your room. You must show me the games you like to play, so I may learn to play them, too." She took them by the hands and let them lead her up the stairs.

Tokh flipped up Zheníhda's skirt, exposing her bare backside while she tried desperately to free herself. He grabbed her wrist and twisted her arm across her head, pressing her cheek into the table.

"Tokh, don't! Please!" Umara continued to beg. Tears rolled down her cheeks in a steady rain, and she made no attempt to hide them. "You're going to make things worse! Your children are upstairs in the care of a consort! Have some sense!"

196

Tokh unfastened his pants. He snarled at Zheníhda, "I'm missing you for more than a year, and when I return with a guest, you mock her and insult her and humiliate her despite my orders to stop. As if she hasn't had enough humiliation in her life! Now I will humiliate you, so you may feel the same as you made her feel. I won't tolerate disobedience. You seem to have forgotten I am Lord of this house, so I will remind you." He shoved his hand between her thighs as she tried to fight, while Umara and the two servants stood without a sound. When he was aroused enough, he plundered his way inside her without pity as she gave an angry yelp.

"Ow! I hate you, Tokh! I hate you! I won't forgive this! Ow! You soiled my house and now you're soiling me!"

He didn't answer, *pushing* her heartlessly until he spent himself. As he waited to uncouple, she tried twisting out from under him once more, shoving against him and then trying to pull forward over the table.

"*Gah!* Get off me! Get your overweight old bulk off of me, you freight hauler! You fatherless son of a *trixahg!*"

He grasped the base of his *hihvat* and yanked, forcing a premature uncoupling, a painful thing and quite rude for a male to do. A wave of fluid accompanied it, dribbling down her folds. Zheníhda arched backward with a yell, then collapsed down, defeated.

Tokh fastened his pants, then pulled her up by the back of her collar. His hand dove under her skirts and deep into her recesses until two fingers were coated with a gob of yellow fluid. He wiped them down her forehead, over her nose, over her lips, to the end of her sharp chin. He spun her around, underthings still around her knees, and sat her in his chair.

"Do not speak again. Not one word. You'll sit there until I tell you. Is that understood?" Zheníhda stared into space as she tried to bring her tears under control, but she bowed her head once. "Remember this. Because if I need to remind you again what humiliation feels like, I'll repeat it in front of the house, for all our neighbors to see. Do you understand?" Zheníhda bowed deeper.

"Umara, the servants may help you clean up. I'll now rescue my children from the most honorable female in the house."

It was the end of Tokh's marriage.

He didn't seek to divorce Zheníhda, but any fire they might have had went cold and died out. He slept with Umara in her bed that night, alternating days with Mímihn, who had no separate quarters and stayed in Tokh's room. He said nothing to Zheníhda and she said nothing to him or to anyone else. Zheníhda performed all her duties without a sound, and retreated to her room when finished.

Umara didn't want Mímihn near her children but Tokh did, and after a single sharp word from him, Umara slunk back and didn't protest again. Tokh visited Zheníhda one or two nights a month to maintain his status and prevent legal issues. He said nothing, just appeared in her room; she said nothing to him, allowing his motions with as much reciprocation as a corpse.

Zheníhda was easy to read and understand. Mímihn understood her resentment, barging in on her home with no warning at all. Zheníhda was bossy to everyone, not just Mímihn, and Mímihn stopped taking it to heart. It was moody Umara she had trouble understanding. Never in her youth had she realized how much personality, how much communication was caught up in a frown, the raise of an eyebrow, the pucker of a lip. All Mímihn had to recognize people by was the tone of voice in the darkness. The sounds came down toward her from a tall person, like Zheníhda or most males, and sometimes they drifted up to her, such as with the children, and sometimes they came at ear level, like Umara's. Umara, however, didn't always respond with her voice, and it wasn't easy to hear a shrug, impossible to hear a raise of an eyebrow. Mímihn had never touched either of the wives and had no idea what they looked like, beyond Tokh's descriptions. Tokh may have had heart for his wives, but his ideas of what they looked like were as dull as a military briefing.

Mímihn was upstairs to put away Tokh's clean shirts when she heard the sobbing. She placed the shirts on the bed and followed the sound to the bath. The door was open, but Umara sat hidden behind it, crying softly.

"Lady Umara-Secondwife? What's wrong?" Mímihn knelt down, reached out and found a soft shoulder, then reached again and found Umara's hair and began to stroke it. The hair was smooth and came down to Umara's chin in a graceful curve, thought she couldn't see the color. The cheek beneath was round and firm.

198

"Who knows?" Umara said hopelessly. "It doesn't matter. I could have my leg ripped off and Nihda would still yell at me for not getting up and doing her bidding." She cried harder, and Mímihn pulled Umara's head over to her shoulder. Umara leaned against her and allowed herself to be comforted.

"*Shu*, Lady Umara. Zheníhda-Firstwife has learned to be a task-master like Tokh, that's all. She likes everything done precisely. She'll yell at me if the shirts aren't folded perfectly and line up exactly in the drawers, even though she knows I can't see. Or maybe because I can't see."

"No," Umara wept. She wiped her nose on a bathing rag. "She's always hated me. She thinks I'm an awful mother and she says it to Tokh all the time. She doesn't think I hear but I do, and he believes her. Why else would he turn our daughter over to the care of a *trixahg*?"

Mímihn shoved Umara upright. "I am no *trixahg*!" she spat. "I am no different than you! I was married to a general, too, before I was abandoned! Except you were married off again instead of being sent to a consort house! It must be very nice to have someone who cared about you that much!"

Umara gave a wail and bawled into her hands. "I'm sorry! I'm sorry! If it weren't for Tokh, I would've been a consort, too. I can't be half the wife he deserves. I loved Bujan with all my heart. I wanted so much to give him a son, but he wanted to be a captain first. I have nothing to remember him by but photos. Tokh only married me out of pity. He's so kind to me, but I don't love him the same way I loved Bujan. I'm a terrible wife."

"*Shu!* You know he loves you. He had nothing but praise for you when he was away. Stop now. *Shu*. Tokh's different. Of course you don't love him the same way. You mustn't cry about things in the past. You must find the happiness in every day that comes."

Umara had a hard time doing that, Mímihn realized. She moped for days when in her moods. Mímihn did her best to cheer Umara, but nothing seemed to help.

"Why don't you dress up, I'll make your hair fancy, and you can go visit with the Ladies. They have children Kesseh's age. I'm sure she'd love to play with them. I'd offer to watch them, but I'm useless for keeping track of children outside."

Umara gave a hard sigh and found a dreary song on her comm unit. "No. The Ladies are Nihda's friends, not mine. She doesn't like me visiting with them."

Mímihn didn't think Umara tried hard enough, and even if Umara was in one of her angry and ill-mannered moods, Mímihn tried hard to be a friend. Umara didn't seem to have any friends at all.

* * 28 * *

Tokh's break ended and he returned to duty, sometimes at the base and sometimes working from home. Hada was just putting away the lunch dishes on a home-day when he called the house together. He sat at the dining table, pale and gasping as if his chest hurt. He held an official printout in his hand.

"Tokh, what's wrong?" Zheníhda said in an instant. "Are you ill? What's happened? Is it good or bad? You're not leaving again, are you? They promised you six months." Mímihn felt her way by the count of chairs and passed a caring hand across his shoulders.

He slid the paper across the table. Umara gave it her best to read it out loud. After several long sentences of big words she said, "What does it mean?"

Tokh found his tongue. "I just received a call from the Emperor."

Zheníhda looked down her nose at him. "Our Emperor? The Great and Majestic Nághtas, Emperor of all Kerasím? Of all the people on this world, he suddenly decided to call you, a nobody *dihnarwharl*?"

"Yes," Tokh said distantly. "Nághtas himself." He felt lost in a fog, as if the world had misted away from him and only bits and pieces were coming through. Nothing made sense. "The mission I just finished is moving ahead better than expected. My men are making great strides in opening discussions. He was most pleased with my work and wished to thank me personally for my attention to the project. He is promoting me to General Four and we'll be moving to Imahlva, to be closer to the palace."

"We're *what*?" Umara said.

"Four? You're only a Two. What about Three? Imahlva?" Zheníhda said, just as confused. "We can't begin to afford to live in Imahlva. That's a high-caste resort town, isn't it?"

Tokh sighed from deep in his fog. "The Emperor has skipped me to Four at his request, so I may take on duties available only to Fours. There's a seized property on the water that he's giving me in

201

thanks. *Giving.* It was owned by a *fáhganid* and it's now mine, furniture and all. I will also be receiving an aircraft, so I may have quick access to Keranihn when necessary. I have no words."

Zheníhda fell onto a chair with an audible flop. "Keranihn? Tokh, are you serious?"

"Yes. The codes for the house will arrive tomorrow."

Umara pulled herself together for the first time in days. "A *fáhganid* house?"

Mímihn rubbed his shoulder again. "My Lord, that's most wonderful news. The Emperor himself has honored you! You're a most fearsome, powerful general!" She bent down and kissed his cheek. "You worked so very hard for it."

"Congratulations, my husband," Umara said. She came forward and kissed his other cheek. "You deserve every reward."

"A coastal town," Zheníhda mused. "We'll be among *fáhganid*, perhaps even *bhísroti*. We'll be the poorest people there. How will we gain respect? Did they say how big it is? Will it have enough rooms? There are eight of us."

"I'll fly out tomorrow and scout it. Until then, pack up everything we wish to take with us. A transport will be here in two days. We are moving, *tansohr keralihn*, by the Emperor's own command."

Joy crossed Zheníhda's face for the first time since his return. "Oh Tokh! A Blessing of Fortune, indeed! I'll tell the Cluster."

Keranihn, the ancient capital, was situated at the end of a long channel of the sea; Imahlva was situated on the cliffs overlooking the mouth of the channel, an hour's flight south. On a clear day, one could see Lillaret on the opposite shore three *nalis* away. Imahlva was an eight-hour flight from Iérot Thorán, a warmer ocean climate of dry hot summers and humid winters that were cool but not usually freezing. It was a small, upscale hamlet just twenty minutes from the main harbor. The town was built on a steep hillside overlooking the ocean, with hundreds of private properties crammed into the cliffs to provide each with a stunning view. Houses ranged from tiny *dahneg* vacation cabins clinging to the rock to huge sprawling glass-walled *bhísroti* estates at the top with unimpeded views in three directions, many with bright-colored tile roofs; against the white cliffs, they made a vivid tapestry. A variety of red-leafed trees and purple-tipped conifers, no more than twelve feet high, clung to the rocks and tiny garden plots, twisted and bent into fantastic spectery shapes from the constant breezes blowing up the hills from the water. Tokh's gift house was of white and gray stone with a bright red roof, and looked like a fortress from the air. It sat halfway up the hillside, with three smaller estates below it until the sheer drop ended in a narrow ribbon of beach and several docks with bobbing luxury watercraft.

The property ran several hundred feet in a long narrow splinter, with an aircraft landing pad at the roadside end. The craft they flew in touched down with the smallest of bounces and the family emerged, stunned by their new location. Umara held tight to Kesseh, but Joralan ran down the rise from the landing pad and across the front courtyard to the three and a half foot stone wall that ran over the edge of the cliff.

"Look! Look how high up we are! You can hear the water all the way up here!" He leaned farther and his feet dangled above the ground; Tokh called him back with a brusque command.

There was a front courtyard paved in tan stones, and a low wall of pillars that signaled a step-down to the rest of the yard – the narrow band of land that contained a patio off the kitchen, strips of grass and gardens connected by paved walkways, and a small soaking pool in the center, dug into the rock. A pergola of fragrant red *whenir* flowers stood near, a peaceful retreat where one could sit in the shade of the vines on a warm day, perhaps watching your children frolic in the water.

"Thrit!" Tokh called, and the aged little *ghinadín* ran forward.

He bowed low, his knee giving a ratcheting sound in the process. "Your command, Lord."

"You may have two hours to arrange your space. Then I want a rail around that pool so Mímihn can't fall into it if she's walking."

Thrit bowed again. "T'rit do it nicely, General."

Behind the house was a narrow alley with a high retaining wall against the hillside as it climbed vertically to the next property seventy feet above them. The yard alone would have been a piece of paradise anywhere; combined with the house and location, it didn't seem real. A park, a hotel, a seaside resort, but not *their house*. By the roadway, across the gate from the air pad, was a building for ground vehicles, with rooms for servants over it. Thrit would have glass windows to see the world from his own private living space; a *ghinadín* castle.

The smallest of the bedrooms, the one that fell to Kesseh, was still larger than Tokh's master bedroom at the old house. Built and decorated by a *fáhganid*, the opulence was more than Zheníhda herself could have dreamed of – fifteen rooms of it. The main floor opened to a huge great room. To the right was a kitchen and storage pantry, and a back room large enough for one or two kitchen servants to live. Wood beams lined the ceiling, adding architectural interest.

"*Ama! Bo!* Look!" Joralan pointed over the front door where a huge taxidermied *dhastal* head hung, massive antlers and all, flanked by two horned *bagresh* heads, a long-haired *herevelle* head, and a whole stuffed *vortag* perched on the top of a crossbeam, frozen in mid-chatter. Joralan formed his fingers into a pistol shape and pretended to fire off several shots at the *dhastal*. Kesseh would have nightmares about the disembodied head for years to come.

A curved staircase carpeted in red led upward; behind it lay a lavatory, a small guest or servant room, and a comfortable office that made Tokh's heart cartwheel in delight. It was fully wired with the latest in communications and screens, and meant he could work his teams from home. The glorious suite at the top of the stairs, overlooking the great room below, would obviously belong to Tokh. He assigned Zheníhda to the large room at the end of the hall, keeping two guest rooms between them. The room had a balcony from which one could view the ocean in the distance, but mostly it looked out over the gated entrance. He put Umara in a room at the opposite end of the house, overlooking the patio and gardens and the water to the side, similar to Zheníhda's; he wouldn't listen to fighting over rooms. After the children, three rooms were left for visiting guests. Tokh would outfit one with six bunks, in case he housed some of his men. Only one person didn't have a permanent place to sleep.

"Don't you even!" Zheníhda spat in a whisper. "You are no longer a *dihnarwharl* of Gimsith, thrilled to own a single aging residence. This is a home where care must be taken to maintain the appearance of royal connections. This is a house of power, and you do not, under any circumstances, give a consort the same standing as the wives and children of the Lord. Tokh, for love of the Emperor, don't disgrace yourself like that! Put her in the rooms over the vehicle shed, with her servant. She needs to be reminded of her place, not living like a firstwife in her Lord's room."

Tokh sighed. He liked Mímihn in his bed every night, whether or not he slept in it with her. She didn't fall into the jealousy of his wives. Even if he spent half a night *pushing* one and then crept back to his own bed, she would roll over sleepily, kiss him and ask, "Did you leave her happy?" and he would always reply yes, because it was a point with him to make sure a wife reached her joy at least once, and his sweet little Mímihn would always reply, "Then it was good that you visited her." He didn't think of Mímihn as a consort but as a third wife, though he knew it was wrong to let Mímihn think she was anything but property. He could sell her tomorrow and she would have no say, even if he'd rather have sold either of his wives. But Zheníhda was right. Even if there was plenty of space for Mímihn now.

"It's not a problem, Lord," Mímihn said with her sweet smile. "I don't need much space. Anywhere is good." Tokh had Mímihn place her things in the rooms behind the kitchen with the new housemaid, Shanohr, a gray-haired *taghinet* of fifty-eight. Hada had retired rather than make the move. Mimihn's clothes and personal items were kept in the servants' room, but any time Tokh wasn't with his wives, he called her upstairs to sleep by him, or bathe him, or keep him company, which meant that unless he had visitors, Mímihn spent every night in his room.

In Iérot Thorán, Tokh's constant military activities left him little time for making local friends. Any friends he did have were also officers and they all lived either on base or in the military neighborhood just outside the gates. Non-military friends didn't exist. At Imahlva, most of the residents were in charge of businesses or government offices with hirelings to oversee the daily running, so men were often home and non-military hob-nobbing was now necessary. Invitations and visitations had to be reciprocated, if Tokh was to make ties. Tokh soon found himself involved in numerous difficult social situations, none of which he wanted to field. It took only a single inquiry to find out there were only three other *dihnarwharl* families in Imahlva, and two of them were servants. Zheníhda was right; they were the poorest, lowest-caste people on their entire side of the town, and that meant they had to tread with great care. He made pleasant acquaintance with several of the neighbors above and below, humble and submissive.

Gilmaneg, the *dahneg* across the street and two estates up, was one of Tokh's thorns. He had a long balcony wrapping around his house from which he surveyed the entire neighborhood and some of the next. Perhaps forty, Gilmaneg was one who loved to *push*, and he liked to keep tallies and explicit photos of each female he'd *pushed*. Tokh was almost never out of some sort of military clothing, so he never gave off caste signals. Gilmaneg never asked Tokh's caste, but assumed him equal. He caught Tokh outside inspecting the promised aircraft that had just arrived, and invited himself over for conversation.

"I notice you've got a flock of females walking about, Tokh. Do you ever swap them out for a night? I like doing that now and then; something different, reminds you how good you have it, or how you can spice up the ones you've got. Do you have a consort?" He dug out his hand unit and called up a picture of his naked consort on her knees before him, nursing his *hihvat* while her hands were chained behind her and he held her head. She was a huge mound of female, easily twice Tokh's weight if not half again as much, and he was technically over the highest acceptable weight for an officer. An image flashed through Tokh's head of trying to be aroused by the back end of a three-horned grazing *muuht*, the largest of the animals raised for meat, and his *khatas* drooped in horror.

He chuckled. "She's a sizeable female."

The neighbor closed his eyes in ecstasy. "Ohhh, I love'm large! You must try her, Tokh! You can squeeze up gobs and gobs of soft warm flesh; every inch feels like a giant breast. And they retain heat – the hottest piece of *lihx* you'll ever sink your *hihvat* into. Every *push* bounces you back on its own. And if you order her to sit on you, it's like being surrounded by a warm cloud. Nothing can compare. So you're interested?"

Tokh hesitated. Right now, if the neighbor thought they were equal, Tokh had some leeway to refuse. "I'm rather possessive of my consort. She's still quite young and I'm afraid you'd find her too small for your liking. Why don't you come to dinner tonight, you alone, and we can discuss things."

Tokh knew what would happen. It hurt him in his heart, made his stomach twist, but that was a risk of any female. He knew the pain Zhenihda had experienced. He didn't want to go through that again. Not now. Nothing should be ruining his good fortune here. But he didn't know how else to appease *dahneg* Gilmaneg.

He gave his wives a small alert, warning them a *dahneg* was coming to dinner, one with a prowling eye, to dress plainly and blend in to the walls. He ordered Mímihn to remain in her room at all costs with the door locked, and not to be seen by anyone until he told her to come out. The neighbor made a congenial dinner guest, but his eye was on Umara all evening. She'd never been thin or athletic, and after two pregnancies her curves were at their polite limits. She never did regain her shape after Kesseh, and though her curves were starting to overflow, Tokh still didn't consider her fat, just ample. Even in a plain house dress, she made a pretty picture. It was after dinner that Gilmaneg broke the question.

"That's a mighty fine wife you've got there, Tokh," he said. "You're a lucky man, with such variety. Would you mind terribly much if I gave her a try? Spread a little goodwill in the neighborhood?" He jabbed Tokh in the side with his elbow.

Tokh wouldn't look at Umara. He stayed silent for a long pause, sipping at his drink as if it would save him.

Umara stared at him in disbelief. "We have a consort for that," she whispered, loud enough to be heard.

Zheníhda never broke her distant gaze, but she did break her silence, a rude thing for an invisible firstwife to do and something she never did before company. Her voice dripped like an icicle. She didn't whisper when she answered, "Yes, we do."

"I'm a jealous husband and not in the habit, but I think that would be acceptable among friends, just this once." Tokh stood up and poured glasses of his strongest spirits, save for a hidden bottle of prized pepper rum, which he wasn't about to waste on the neighbor. "We'll have a drink, first. To good will between neighbors." He handed a glass to the neighbor, and one to Umara, who continued to stare at him as if he'd ordered her to jump off the cliff.

"You may use the guest room down the hall on the right," Tokh said, and gulped several swallows of his spirits. There was nothing short of a decree from the Emperor that would make him offer his own bed to have his wife defiled in.

"Tokh!" Umara gave a single protest.

Tokh stopped the neighbor as he stood up. "Remember, she is my wife and I'm quite fond of her. Once and only once. Stick to business, don't mark her, and don't stress her more than absolutely necessary. Don't make me have to bear witness."

"I'm always a good guest," the neighbor insisted, and took Umara by the hand.

Tokh shut himself in his office before Zheníhda could say a word. He didn't come out until he heard footsteps on the stairs.

Gilmaneg seemed energized. "A sweet piece of meat, Tokh! A sweet piece of meat. Twitchy, but sweet. You're a lucky man – thin, wide – you have your own variety for whatever your mood! Thanks for sharing. I'll have you over for dinner by the end of the week, and you can sample one of mine."

As he left and Tokh shut the door, he turned to Zheníhda and said, "I'll be out of town by this weekend inspecting my men, if I have to call Khaním and order him to ask me, so don't say a word." It would be illegal for him to impersonate a *dahneg*; leaving for a day or two let him out of the deal without revealing his caste. He ordered her, "Go tell Mímihn she may leave her room now." Then he went straight up the stairs to Umara.

She was already in the tea-cup shaped bath in her room, crying her heart out, an open bottle of spirits nearby as she scrubbed her skin raw. She didn't look up at him. He didn't say a word but undressed and climbed into the water with her, washing her much gentler than she was doing. He found no marks; his neighbor was a slimy eel but his word was good. Tokh pulled her to him and let her cry on his chest while he stroked her hair and held her until the water grew cold.

"*Shu, shu.* I'm sorry. I'm so sorry, my little *falahndi.* There was little I could do; he's *dahneg* and I'm not. I promise you, he won't touch you again. *Shu.* Here. Drink your drink." He held the bottle for her.

"I already… took two of… my calming pills," she gasped, and burst into another wave of tears.

Umara was pretty well drunk by the time Tokh took her back to his room. Traditionally, if a wife had been borrowed by another, the husband then embarked on a mission to rid the wife of the memory by *pushing* her as many times as he could afterward, erasing any signs of trespassing. Tokh was kind, Tokh was caring, but he added to Umara's distress by *pushing* her three times, though by the third time she was so spaced on tranquilizers and alcohol she passed out at the start. After that he threw an arm and leg over her and went to sleep.

* * 29 * *

Tokh had three hundred men under his permanent command: fifty *bhántim* officers and two hundred fifty elite enlisted *bhántanok* whom he leased out for other campaigns, while his team of *aghát* now had permission to work inside Union territory, teaching the Union to understand Kerasi culture and working hard to bring about peace. When they returned, bringing back information for the Emperor, they had no permanent residence, so they stayed as Tokh's guests. Zheníhda had now known most of them for several years and had no problems putting them in their place; Umara took extra pills and drank more when guests came around.

Tokh enrolled Joralan in an elite school for *dihnarwharl* and *dahneg* boys, and Kesseh began her four years of female school. The year passed, and they marveled at the Imahlva tradition of fireworks for the New Year; from their own front courtyard, they could see barges shooting off pyrotechnics every ten *nalis* down the channel, until the sky was filled with colors and noise. The wives here were mostly older, established, wealthy, and non-military; they didn't have as much need to cling to each other, but Zheníhda made several friends and acquaintances up and down the street, and some of them were *fáhganid*. A huge house with extra rooms and outdoor spaces meant Tokh's females didn't have to cross paths for hours, easing tensions. A second year crept by, just as dreamlike. Tokh came up with new excuses to avoid Gilmaneg.

With Kesseh in school, and no close friends, Umara's days were long and empty, and her moody thoughts began to fester. Mímihn tried harder to befriend her, asking Umara to walk her around the yard or read her favorite poems to her, but if Tokh wasn't home, Umara didn't always bother to get out of bed, creating a whole new spate of insults from Zheníhda.

"Oh! It's so terrible living here!" Zheníhda ranted. "A husband like this, a house like this, more than a wife could ever want, and still you aren't happy! Perhaps you should choose the coward's way out."

"I'm sorry if I don't have your *years* of experience to tell me what to think," Umara snapped, foul and nasty. "Perhaps if I'd been married to the same man for fifty years, I wouldn't have a care, either!"

"Thirty-four, you numberless fool!" Zheníhda spat back.

"And that's still three months longer than I've been alive," Umara said with a greasy-sweet smile. "Count again, you word-blind old hag."

Zheníhda gave a squeal of fury and marched outside to the gardens before she did something Tokh wouldn't like.

Zheníhda was just Zheníhda. Her mouth ran from a separate brain, and half the time – just half – she wound up apologizing for her rants and made little peace offerings – a special dessert, a bouquet of flowers, a beautiful glass music box. Umara did appreciate them, but Zheníhda's words never found a way out of her heart.

Tokh was at his office in Keranihn that day. Kesseh had returned from school – female school was two hours shorter than male school – and she sought out Mímihn, who was dusting the furniture in Tokh's room.

"*Ama*'s in the bath and she fell asleep and I can't get her to wake up," Kesseh said.

Mímihn took it in stride. Umara's pills could make her sleepy, especially if she was nipping at *lunahl* as well. It wasn't the first time Umara had fallen asleep in the bath or at the table. Mímihn held out her hand. "She must be playing a game with you. Take me there, and we'll play it with her."

"Umara, where are you?" she crooned as Kesseh led her into Umara's bath. She put a hand out until she felt the edge of the tub, then felt around the rim until she came to Umara's elbow. Umara was sprawled forward over the edge, arms dangling.

Her skin was ice cold.

A whiff of vomit came up from the floor. Mímihn's heart stopped.

"Sleepy Umara! Kesseh, go get Zheníhda-*ama* and we'll all count together and yell 'wake up!', okay?" She stroked Umara's damp hair.

Kesseh returned. "Zheníhda-*ama* won't come. She says to let *ama* sleep."

A fire welled up in Mímihn. Usually she kept it well in check, too aware of her place and the need to be humble; this time she didn't. Her pretty mouth pressed into a hard line, and her face darkened. "I'll go get her. Kesseh, go into my room downstairs, look through my clothes, and find me the prettiest thing I have to wear. Try them on if you want; but make sure it's the very prettiest thing. I'll let your *ama* borrow it to make your *bo* happy when he comes home."

Kesseh left. Mímihn eased out of the room, Umara's ornate glass vase for flowers in her hand. She dropped it over the edge of the upstairs balcony and heard it explode on the floor below. She yelled over the balcony, "Zheníhda, get your *lihx* up here now or so help me I will discipline you myself! Now! Don't make me have to find you!"

Zheníhda belched flaming venom from below. "How dare you speak to me that way, *trixahg*!"

"Umara needs your help this very second! I need eyes! Hurry! Hurry! I don't think it's good!"

The panic in Mímihn's voice got through. Zheníhda rushed up the stairs. "In her bath," Mímihn urged, one finger trailing the wall to keep count of the doors.

Zheníhda gasped. "Umara!" Umara's eyes were half-open, her lips and nose and under her eyes were dark brown, almost black.

"Is she dead?" Mímihn cried.

"She looks it," Zheníhda said with fright. She pulled out her pocket com, found the blood-drop icon, the Kerasím-wide symbol for medical assistance, and pressed it.

Her next call was to Tokh. "Tokh, you need to come home. Now."

"I can't leave. I have work to do."

"No, Tokh. You must leave now. It's Umara. Medical is on its way, but I don't think it's going to be good news. You're her husband and you need to be here this minute. Tokh, I'm very frightened for her."

Zheníhda wasn't one to panic. "Alright. I'm leaving now."

She ended the call and turned on Mímihn. Zheníhda's hand slapped her face, then grabbed her by the wrist and shook her in her darkness. "I don't care what the emergency! Don't you ever, ever

211

threaten me in my own home! I am wife and you are property and I have the right to beat you! And I should for your words!"

Mímihn would not be intimidated. She couldn't slap Zheníhda, but if all were equal, she would have. She yanked her arm free. "Then you should have come when I first asked Kesseh to get you! Maybe if your chin wasn't so high in the air you could see when people need your help! How else can I get your attention if you don't listen?" She stroked Umara's cold arm, petted her hair, then leaned her head against the tub. "Oh Umara! You poor thing! You're too young to die! What do we tell Kesseh?"

Zheníhda's fire went out. A paper was on the floor. She picked it up and turned it over; it was a photo of Umara's first husband. She patted Umara's other arm. "They're Tokh's children; we'll let him tell them. Either way, I don't think there's anything we could have done."

Umara was indeed dead, and had been for at least an hour. The cause was an overdose of narcotics, ruled suicide by the voice notice she left Tokh on his mail.

> *My dear husband,*
>
> *You have been most kind to me. I thank you for marrying me, even if it wasn't your first wish. It made me feel special and wanted. I'm so happy to have been able to give you a son and daughter to be proud of. You're most noble and deserve better than I'm able to give. I have no strength left, Tokh. I can't take the needling day after day when I feel too weak to respond. I hate myself for my weakness, which makes me weaker, which makes me hate myself more. I just want the awful pain to stop. Tell Mímihn I'm thankful for her friendship. I do love you, Tokh, but I need to be with Bujan, where my heart belongs. Please remember me with kindness.*

It was a somber funeral. Umara had been a quiet person; it was hard to summon up cheer for a celebration of life, especially with two young children in tears. Tokh stood like a statue, a pale green mourning sash over his brown dress uniform. He coached his son on acting like a man, looking off into the horizon with dry eyes and a stone face, but eight year old Joralan's mother was dead and he was failing at pleasing his father. Zheníhda took the forefront, dressed veil to shoes in green; Mímihn stood with the servants, despite her desperate desire to comfort Kesseh. Tokh opened the house to the neighbors so they could pay their respects. Wives showed up by the dozen to support Zheníhda and learn any gossip. The husbands came to pay respects, but moreso to see the inside of the house and compare it to theirs.

Tokh tried, but couldn't avoid Gilmaneg the entire afternoon.

"Tokh! Tokh!" He clapped a hand on Tokh's shoulder and roughed it up. "I can't say how sorry I am for you. She was a delight, Tokh, an utter delight. I'd have married her if you'd been willing to give her up. I'm sorry you've lost her like this. If you need to borrow one of mine, you may take your choice, any time. Is that your consort over there?"

Tokh's eye found Mímihn sitting in a chair against the kitchen wall, out of the way of the guests. "That's my daughter. She stays with us when her husband is away. She's off-limits." He whispered to Kesseh to lead Mímihn to her bedroom and have her lock the door. No one would question a child holding hands and pulling on someone.

Tokh ended the hospitality by ordering Shanohr to clear away the food. The day weighed him down like an extra decade, twisting his heart in at least three directions. He didn't *push* anyone that night, but slept alone beside his memory of Umara.

"You're my wife," Tokh reminded Zheníhda. "These are my children. They're now your responsibility, since I know you'll object if I assign them otherwise."

Zheníhda sighed. "I already expected as much. They're like wild animals. It's time they had proper supervision and manners."

Umara had never been a driving force in the house, hidden away reading poetry or going about her tasks, but it still seemed much emptier without her. Zheníhda had no one to yell at but Mímihn, and Mímihn had lost the closest female to a friend that she had. There were other consorts in the neighborhood but she was the only blinded one, and therefore drew scorn. Shanohr wasn't hostile but she was old, and though consort was considered a servant, they were property; housemaid was the employment of a free person, and the distinction wasn't lost on either of them. Little by little the irritation that drove Zheníhda to pick at Umara turned itself on Mímihn.

"You think you're so high and mighty playing in the Lord's pants right now," Zheníhda stabbed at her. "Just you wait! I'm the One Wife now, and if he dies this estate and all its property goes to me! You're part of that property. You'll never see his funeral because I'll have you sold before they finish signing off on his death! And I will make sure you're properly beaten beforehand."

Mímihn's inner spitfire took over. "Why wait that long? Why not just kill me outright like you did Umara? Stab and jab me with unkind words until my heart dies and then tell me to take the coward's way out! I heard you! I heard you tell her that not days before her death! You killed her, Nihda! As sure as you stuffed the pills down her throat! Did you tell that little bit to Tokh? You can't stand the least bit of competition, because you can't compete anymore!"

"Don't you call me by my name, *trixahg*!" Zheníhda lunged at Mímihn and grabbed her around the throat. Mímihn heard the motion and felt the rush of air but couldn't escape it. She shrieked and slapped at Zheníhda's head, pulled at her hair until it came loose from its pins and rolled down her back. Zheníhda's veil fell down with it. Tokh came out of his office at the commotion.

"Stop! That's a direct order! Stop!" Tokh grabbed Mímihn around her waist and lifted her up and away.

"Tell him!" Mímihn spat between tears. "Tell him how you pecked her to death! Who's the coward now!"

Zheníhda shook with tears as well. "I am your wife, Tokh! This is how you let your property speak to me? You let her walk around here as if she's my equal and you never discipline her! Either discipline her or I'll file a grievance with the Female Concerns office and everyone will know how the great and mighty Tokh dishonors his wife and can't keep so much as a consort in line! I shouldn't have to put up with this!"

Tokh gave a heavy sigh. Zheníhda spoke truth. His voice wasn't as harsh as it should have been. "Mímihn, you're out of bounds and laid hands on my wife. That's unacceptable. Bend on the table."

Mímihn sobbed, but she complied. Tokh removed his incentive rod, extended it, and gave Mímihn three firm strokes on her backside, each accompanied by a jerk and a shriek that tore through his heart like a knife.

214

"Apologize to Zheníhda."

Mímihn bowed low. "I beg forgiveness, Firstwife. I beg forgiveness, Lord Tokh."

"Go." Mímihn fled.

Tokh did not forgive. He showed up in Zheníhda's room that night without a stitch of clothing.

Zheníhda took one look at him and turned away in disgust. "Has your gut gotten bigger or your *hihvat* gotten smaller?"

There was no humor in his voice. "You can measure by how far I shove it down your throat."

"Leave me alone, Tokh. You have a consort for that. Go bother her."

"She spoke truth today. You know it, but you didn't know I already knew. You took away Umara's heart, and now, right or wrong, you made me injure Mímihn. That means you take her duty."

"*Gah!* You should be pounding her twice as hard, then, and slapping her bottom every other *push*. Make sure she doesn't forget."

He knew she despised it more than anything, he knew, and she knew that's why he was insisting on it, to punish her. She beat and slapped at him but he forced her to her knees before him until she accepted him in her mouth. "Don't get bold! If I feel teeth, I'll tear off your jaw."

"You're choking me!" she mumbled, and punched him in his flank, but he wouldn't let up, not seeking pleasure but ramming against her lips as if he could reach her *lihx* from the other direction. When he spent himself, he held her head to him.

"Swallow it." Zheníhda gave a grunt of protest. "Swallow! Or I won't let you breathe until you do." She complied and he withdrew, leaving her gagging and spitting on the floor.

"I hate you!" she snarled, and spat on his feet.

He pulled her up and dropped her on the bed. Zheníhda screeched and beat on him with her fists as he threw himself on top of her and gave her a ruthless *pushing*.

He went back to his room and called Mímihn upstairs. Angry welts crossed her shapely buttocks, raised and brown and weepy. He dabbed a healing cream on them for her as gently as he could. "I'm sorry, *falahndi*, but she was right. I treat you too much like a wife and not enough like a consort." He held her to him, warm and naked

215

and nymph-like, wrapping his fingers with her black curls, and he kissed her forehead. "It's time I kept a long-overdue promise. Tomorrow, wear your nicest clothes, and you'll accompany me to Keranihn."

* * 30 * *

In Keranihn, Tokh met his neuroanatomist memory engineer Kassán, currently assigned to the palace, who contacted an eye specialist he knew. By lunch, Mímihn was being examined by the specialist, Kassán by Tokh's side as advisor.

"I agree," the specialist said. "If it was done chemically, there's nothing that can be done. Since she was put out for the procedure, it's likely they were severed. I won't know until I see them, but if it was done cleanly, we have a good chance of regaining some sight. It'll probably take several surgeries, it will never be perfect, but it should be functional. Once we get maximum results, we can correct the vision further through lenses."

Mímihn squeezed Tokh's hand, her stomach in such a knot it seemed as if all her innards had been caught up, and she could barely breathe around it. "It's too much to hope."

"When can you begin?" Tokh asked.

The specialist looked up at Kassán. One didn't put off the Emperor's chosen neuroanatomist. His patient may have been a consort, but she was a well connected one.

"I can do the first procedure tomorrow morning."

Mímihn was too wracked with nerves to think of eating that night. Kesseh found her weeping out under the trellis and told Zheníhda, who went out to see why before Tokh could accuse her of causing it and punish her again.

"There's no need to fear it. They'll make sure you don't feel pain."

Mímihn wiped at her eyes. "I don't fear that. I trust the doctor, and I trust Tokh's advisor. I remember him from Tokh's mission. Tokh says he's a very learned man and he believes him over all others. Did you ever want something so bad you feared your heart would burst if it didn't happen?"

Zheníhda thought a moment. Her cool manner softened for a change, and a shred of compassion slipped out. "Yes."

She sat down next to Mímihn. "It was two years before I was pregnant with Zenak. Tokh would be home only a short time, then sent away again. After a year I was afraid I would never have a child and that Tokh might divorce me. I was already nineteen. His mother would yell at me for failing him. I felt sick every time I saw someone with an infant. I went to a Temple and made offerings to the Gods of Fertility. I made offerings to the Mother Goddess. I made offerings to the Gods of Fortune. Then, when it was nearing our two-year mark, I realized I was pregnant. And when they said it would be a boy, I knew the Fortunes had heard my prayers."

Mímihn sniffed. "I went through that with Maghentor, but he beat me black and brown and set his friends on me when nothing worked. I don't care that I'm only a consort. I don't care that I'll never bear a child. I just want to see again. Even just a little. And I'm so very scared that it won't work. A little bit of hope is a terrible thing."

"Sometimes it is." Zheníhda took Mímihn's hand. "Come. We'll have a drink to your surgery. If you'd like, tomorrow while you're in Keranihn, I'll have Thrit bring me to the temple in the center of town, and I'll make an offering to Fortune for you."

Mímihn paused. "You'd do that for me, Firstwife? You wouldn't curse me instead?"

"No. Not for something that important. I'll do it in Umara's name. She would like that. I know she would."

Mímihn nodded. "Yes, she would."

Mímihn came out of surgery with her eyes bandaged. Tokh stayed with her overnight. For the consort of only a *dihnarwharl*, they were kept on the top floor in the VIP section – Kassán's name had quite an influence. The next day the doctor removed the bandages.

"Don't expect anything," he warned. "It was very promising, but it's much too early to tell if there will be any results. Close your eyes until I tell you."

Mímihn tried, but when the bandage was removed, she sat up and screamed. Her eyes flew open, runny and shining with ointments and dark bruises on her eyelids. "There's brightness! There's brightness! I saw it with my eyes closed! I can see a white! Most with this eye, but there's a brightness! Tokh! I have a brightness!"

218

She tried to leap from the bed to chase the brightness to the window. Tokh stopped her.

"*Shu, shu, falahndi.* You must listen."

She put her hands out toward him. "Tokh? Is that you? You're a darkness against the brightness! I can see that! You have a shape!"

The doctor made her lie down again. "That's most excellent for the day after surgery. The eyes must rest, however. The nerves must heal, and that will take time. We'll keep checking, but don't expect much change for several weeks. And as I said, it'll take several surgeries before we might restore useful vision, but this is a very good sign."

Mímihn came home with a verbal list of do's and don'ts on her hand unit, and a half-dozen medications. She was supposed to keep to dim light and wear dark shades outside so as not to overpower her healing eyes, but she couldn't help peeking at everything and bright light helped. Darkness had ruled her life for the last three years or so; she hadn't realized just how miserable she'd been until the light returned. She now avoided the dim upstairs corridor, and spent as much time as she could outdoors or by a window. Mímihn's left eye was fairly good at differentiating shadows and shapes; the right lagged far behind, able to see only scattered spots of light without form. She gained confidence in moving around, slipping outside to the trellis on her own, stuffing her face into the red flowers. If her nose was no more than a finger's length away, she could see foggy red blobs in the brightness, and the redness filled her heart with delight. She wished to bring Tokh every joy he desired, but by doctor's order she wasn't to share his bed for at least two weeks, for sudden motion or so much as shaking her head too hard could hurt the nerves.

Mímihn's second surgery followed four months after the first. She wasn't sure what to expect, perhaps a matching brightness to her other eye. As soon as the bandages were removed, she turned toward the window and gave a startled jump.

"Tokh?" She started to shake as if having a seizure, then cry. He bent down, and she grabbed his head and pulled it close, squinting desperately with her better eye.

"What, *falahndi*? Is it better?"

219

"*I see you!*" She blinked hard several times to rid her eye of tears. "I see you!" Her hands caressed his face with confidence, touched his eyes, his cheeks that were starting to sag, stroked his chin hank, tied up with a brown cord to match his uniform. He was thirty-five years older than she was; in Kerasi lives, old enough to be her wisefather. His face was foggy and distorted, his features no more than blobs, but she could find them. "You're the most beautiful creature I've ever seen!"

Mímihn's second surgery was a glaring success. With lens correction, she had almost thirty percent vision in her left eye, and five percent in her right. If she held things very close, she could see them fairly well on her left, while the right had larger spots of vision and more shadows. She couldn't stop trying to see Tokh, and when they resumed activities would insist he remain face to face. She examined the children as if she were a microscope, memorizing every curve of their faces with a beaming smile.

Mímihn had never been on good enough terms to touch Zheníhda's face, so she had no idea what Zheníhda looked like, beyond tall and thin. Her first impression was a surprise, and the wrong words slipped out. Zheníhda wore a purple satin blouse with elbow sleeves, and a black skirt. Her black hair was done up into tight rolls on her head, with the back ends sticking up like feathers, held together by a bright silver hair-clasp. A short veil of dark purple hung down her head, only long enough to cover her neck. She had high cheeks and sharp dark eyes and her single eyebrow had been plucked and shaped until it looked like a bird flying high across her face. She was a fair woman for her mid-fifties and still turned eyes if she walked the town without her veil. But the only words to slip from Mímihn's mouth were, "My Lord! You have the nose of a *hyrak*!"

It took all of Zheníhda's strength not to slap the eyes from Mímihn's head, too aware of her bird-beak. "YOU! You... hideous, ungrateful, mean-hearted *aaka*-licking *trixahg* of a *trixahg*! I'll stab your eyes from you with a fork while you sleep!" Zheníhda ran outside before she made it happen.

Mímihn tried apologizing. "I'm very sorry, Lady Zheníhda. You never let me touch your face, so I had no idea what you might look like. I made up a face for you in my head, but you don't look like I imagined. I was just surprised, that's all. Please forgive my rudeness.

I think you have beautiful cheeks and lovely clothes and I wish you would teach me to do my hair like yours."

Zheníhda held back bitter tears. "*Gah!* The only difference between me and your imagination is I have only one head."

Tokh brought Mímihn back to Keranihn several weeks later for another check of her eyes. The doctor gave her a book of patterns to look at several times a day, to strengthen the way her eyes saw things. When they were done, Tokh took her shopping. Mímihn loved being in the city, the people, the flashing bright store signs, the smells of fresh food and the expensive perfumes of *bhísroti* walking by, the melodies of the street musicians. The variety of life refueled her energy. Tokh led her into a store and told her, "You may choose a new outfit. Something you love."

Stores in Keranihn were used to dealing with the upper castes; their clothing was much trendier than anything back in sleepy Imahlva. Mímihn was excited by very bright colors, and tried to avoid vague patterns which confused her vision. She settled on a one-piece dress in brilliant orange with yellow cuffs to the short sleeves, a yellow veil to match and a new white and turquoise bead-and-feather bag in which to carry her com unit. Tokh chose a wide gold plastron necklace to match the dress. Mímihn had several beautiful items Tokh had given her, some of them textured beads or chains she'd been able to feel rather than see. This, from what she could see and feel, was the most extravagant yet, covering her upper chest like a small piece of fancy armor. He insisted she wear the outfit from the store.

"We have somewhere to go and I want you to look nice. I've made plans secret from both you and Zheníhda. You'll like them, but she probably won't." The letters over the door they entered were too high up for Mímihn to make out.

"What building is this?" Mímihn asked, but he didn't reply.

He presented the man at the counter with several folded papers. The man read them over, examined Tokh's official ID, scanned and tapped information into a computer, and handed him a new paper to sign. He made Tokh swear an oath.

"Tokh! You're not selling me, are you? Tokh, please tell me you aren't selling me!"

"In a way, yes; in a way, no," he said, though it was a cruel thing to do.

221

The man at the counter spoke to her. "Do you promise to serve your husband as a proper wife, protect his property, care for his offspring, and tend to all his needs, in health and sickness, obeying his every command, until one of you joins his ancestors?"

Mímihn's face wrinkled in confusion and she managed a gasp of air. "What does he mean, wife?"

Tokh held her hand and smiled. He bent close so she could see his face. "I'm doing what I should have done months ago, what I wish I could have done years ago. This is the marriage office. Answer the question, make your mark, and you'll be my second-wife."

Mímihn's hands covered her mouth and she screamed right there in the registry office. They were used to screams at marriages, but almost never from joy. She bent in half and screamed again, lost her balance, and fell backwards on her bottom in her brilliant orange dress. Tokh helped her up and she hung from his neck, attacking his throat with her lips. "YES! YES I WILL! I'll do anything! Tokh! My gracious Lord! For real? A wife? No more consort?"

"A wife, as real as Zheníhda."

Tears were blinding Mímihn's faint vision. "Where? Where do I mark?" She grabbed the pen and squinted hard, her nose almost touching the paper. "Put me on the line."

Tokh expected halting spidery letters like Zheníhda, memorized with great care, and was amazed when she wrote very prettily, if somewhat skewed,

mímihn rasas invihral, daras-giláhn

Tokh had never thought to ask her family name; she was only a consort, with no claim to family, nor did he ever tell her how to spell his. He didn't even need anyone to sign a paper saying she was being given away in marriage; she was his property to dispose of as he wished, short of unsanctioned murder. In this case, the husband was marrying his own property, so Tokh was in the position of both signing away the bride and marrying the same one. Freeing Mímihn was a financial blow; she was a very profitable asset it had cost him nothing to attain, but in the long run he would make it up on the taxes he would no longer pay on her. It shamed him, never asking her name. Being blind when she met him, he had no idea she was a better reader than Umara; she was smart on her feet, but he had never assumed blind Mímihn had been educated.

222

Tokh had always treated the Emperor's plan to place a female on the throne of Kerasím as a sort of parlor trick: *here is my smalldaughter, she is of my loins. I have educated and trained her as only an Emperor can, and she will sit on my throne and play Empress while the people frolic and her son holds the power.* Even after battling wits with the Human Union emissary he created in his basement on Kye, seeing her intelligence, how she thought, how she learned, how she could be reasoned with, Tokh had never taken her seriously, though his men sent back incredible videos of her wielding power on her own, pulling strings as if the Emperor himself was instructing her when she wasn't yet of marrying age within the Union. Masákh had sent him recordings of her speeches, arguing with authorities who didn't beat her for it but listened to her words. The Emperor couldn't sing her praises hard enough, and her continued success was a buoy under Tokh's career; he knew this, and made sure his men kept the lines of contact as thick as possible. He had escaped Union grasp and his head carried a high price; he dared not get close even to the border between their territories.

But it wasn't until that moment, seeing Mímihn sign her name with ease and delight, that Tokh realized how undervalued Kerasi females were. How much were Kerasi females capable of learning? Zheníhda's sharp tongue would have no problem commanding a squadron, if not men certainly of females. She could do it this very day, until she had to read or write something. He thought of Kesseh, just beginning the minimal education she would receive, and how in just a few years Joralan would be ready for the military academy, a place his sister could never attend. Tokh thought of the emissary Aila Perrin, who claimed nine years education when he sequestered her at the age of thirteen. Certainly his own daughter was no less intelligent than a Union child. Kerasím must have looked awful indeed, when a ten year old child in the Union had more education than even the Emperor's wives.

He didn't yet know what to do or how to do it, but Tokh vowed to himself right there in the marriage office that Kesseh would be educated to Union levels, even if he had to slip her behind Union lines to do it.

* * 31 * *

They flew home, though Tokh wasn't sure Mímihn needed the craft. She alternated between hugging him violently and squealing and running in place while she sat.

She held up a hand. "I know, I know, Tokh. I must now act like a proper wife. But give me a few more minutes to be so excited!"

Tokh's joy was watching her. She stepped out of the craft with confidence, back straight, shoulders square, enrobed in the dignity of her new position, and he remembered she'd already been a firstwife once, if a very young one. She followed him into the house at a proper distance and stood waiting, as if she were new. It was a new beginning, and she would play the role as she was due. This wasn't the time to ruffle feathers; enough were about to fly.

Zheníhda came to greet him. She looked down her nose at Mímihn. "Well, I'll never have trouble locating you in that. That's a very nice necklace, Tokh. You spent too much on it. She's consort; she should shine, but have no value."

"Please find Thrit and have him move all of Mímihn's things to the bedroom in the front corner. It has the most light."

Zheníhda's face soured. "We've been over this before, Tokh. A Lord does not place his servants at the level of his family."

"And you remain correct. Please greet Mímihn daras-Giláhn, my second-wife."

Zheníhda's jaw hung open. Her dreams of future wealth and glory, of laughing with glee as she sold Mímihn into bondage elsewhere, faded into the air. "Welcome to the house of dar-Giláhn, Second-Wife," she said with a minimal bow, but ended with, "I'm sure you'll have no trouble finding your way to your Lordship's bed."

Tokh patted Mímihn on her rump. "Go. Explore the room I chose for you."

At the absolute opposite end of the house from Zheníhda.

Mímihn kissed him under his jaw, then climbed the stairs to find the room she'd never set foot in.

224

Steam rose off Zheníhda's head. "TOKH! What did you do! Did you do that on purpose to insult me? What about her worth? She's young – she's an easy fifty thousand *dakra*! You just lost us a fortune!"

Tokh's eyes widened and his bottom lip pulled upward into a frightening line. "Are you questioning my ability to handle my estate? Do you know all of my accounts; do you know this for fact?"

Zheníhda knew she was out of line. There was nothing nearby to throw, so she kicked the row of chairs at the side of the table in a loud clatter. She kept the tears from her eyes, but she couldn't keep them from her voice. "Anything to degrade me! Have I not served you faithfully as first-wife for thirty-five years? Did I not bear you two strong sons, the glory of your name? Please tell me what I've done to deserve this! I'll be the pointed finger wherever I go! There goes Zheníhda; her husband took a consort for a second-wife! Do you ever stop just *once* to think of me?" She fought hard against it, a female weakness she in no way wanted to show him, but the tears won out.

Tokh stared at her for almost a full minute, his face blank as a cloudy sky. He moved behind and wrapped his arms around her; Zheníhda wrestled, she squawked, but he wouldn't let go, and at last she stopped fighting. He rested his cheek against hers, chin hank tapping her shoulder. "Have I ever said you've failed me, even once? Even when I was angry enough to block the air from your throat? In thirty-five years, I can count the times I've corrected you on one hand. You're the centerpoint in my compass; I can work freely anywhere I'm sent, because I know you'll always be there to point me home. I married her because I *wanted* to. For the first time in my life, I married someone because I *wanted* to. Before some higher-up realized I had only one wife and chose someone for me I couldn't refuse, and I'd be back to two wives *and* a consort. Do you understand that? I have two wives that I care deeply for, and I don't want any other."

Zheníhda was a tall stick of tension in his arms, but she bowed her head in agreement. Better the evil she knew than some new night-witch to share title with.

"I registered her at the Keranihn marriage office. We had a nice lunch, but that was the extent of her wedding party. No music, no family, no friends, no flower petals in the air or sword salutes, no celebration games, no wedding travels. She spoke her oath, signed her name, and that was it. Is that the kind of inspirational wedding you would have chosen for yourself, deserving or not?"

"No."

"And have I ever bought something for one of my wives, and not for the other? So that if you were to make a celebration dinner tonight, that there wouldn't be a gift for you waiting in your room?"

They were pleasant words, but Zheníhda wouldn't let herself be swayed. She gave a partial truce. "I can make a pleasant dinner."

"I haven't told her yet, but as she's taking Umara's place, I'll give her Umara's children to raise as well. You'll no longer have to burden yourself with them."

Zheníhda's words fought both to be said and not said, and thus came out a bit too abrupt. "I don't mind them terribly much. She's too young for such a burden."

Tokh brayed laughter in her ear. "You were a younger mother than that, and they're old enough to answer her call. You're no longer that young; she'll have energy for them when you wish to rest."

"There's too much air in her head for her to care for children."

Tokh turned Zheníhda around to face him, stern but not threatening. "Mími is not Umara. There's more to her than you know. Don't think she won't fight for her rights, and I warn you now, I will not get involved. If you fight, she will fight back. You'll find a way to make it work this time. Is that understood?"

"Yes, Tokh."

"What?"

"Yes, my Lord Tokh."

"Sometimes you forget that."

A sweet voice called from the stairs. Mímihn sat on the top step, out of Zheníhda's reach. She couldn't see anything from that distance, but she could hear the voices.

"Firstwife Zheníhda? Your decoration of my room is most beautiful. I'm honored to have it as my own."

Zheníhda shook loose of Tokh. It was a traditional deference to power in the home, not unexpected. "You're a wife of Lord Tokh; it's only fitting." She began to search for something to make for a celebration dinner.

For all the tension, it was a very pleasant meal. Tokh praised Zheníhda's efforts, the food, the setting of the table with ribbons and flower petals, the choice of the more expensive vintage of *lunahl* from his cabinets to accompany it, the fact she had dressed the children in their finer clothing and combed Jora's hair until it obeyed. Zheníhda kept quiet, face neutral, as invisible as she could be. Mímihn dined with everyone for the first time, face radiant, manners impeccable, playing the role of a brand-new secondwife to perfection. She served the meal to Tokh, then served Zheníhda, another symbol of respect for an incoming secondwife.

Mímihn cleared the table with Shanohr, as she did every night. She waited until Tokh was in the lavatory, and as she passed Zheníhda she said just loud enough for her to hear, *"And the man in charge said, 'No Sale,'"* punctuating it with two swings of her hips. Zheníhda gave a warning growl, but she kept her mouth shut.

Zheníhda took to her room after making sure the housemaid had properly cleaned the kitchen, and she'd put the children to bed. Sure enough, a flat box waited on her bed. She untied the ribbons that held it shut. Inside lay a necklace of graduated pink stones, each stone bead covered in a hand-made filigree of hair-thin melted gold lines and rich lampworked accents. Living in Imahlva among the upper castes, Zheníhda kept a very close eye on what was considered upscale and *haut couture*; she knew damned well the beads were considered the height of fashion at the moment, and what each bead cost. An entire necklace of them – Zheníhda's head spun to think of the expense. Far more than the beaten gold love-bird plastron he'd bought his *trixahg*. She would be the envy of the neighborhood, if not accused of dressing above her caste. Zheníhda left it in the box for spite. It would take more than a necklace to placate such a massive insult.

Not five *fasim* more, she opened the box and looked at it again, fingers stroking the amazing glasswork on the stones, but she shut the box and left it on her clothes-chest. Ten *fasim* later, so angry with herself she could have pinched herself all over, she put it on and sighed at the beauty of it.

She'd changed to a comfortable loose gown and was brushing out her long hair when Tokh entered.

"You're in the wrong room," she said, her words so dry dust rose with them.

"Did you like your gift?"

227

Zheníhda cursed herself again; the beads still circled her throat. "They're exquisite, but it'll take more than an empty pocket to buy my approval. I have no say in the fact I'm married to a fool."

"Don't insult the giver. What can be given can also be taken away. I wished to thank you for the dinner. Whether it was to please me or not, your details moved my spirit, and I know they meant even more to Mímihn."

"*Gah.* Your heart's like a stone; anything can move it with enough force. And I care more for the motion of my bowels than what your other female thinks." His hands went to her shoulders; she shrugged him off and turned away. "You're in the wrong room, Tokh. It's your wedding night; go to your wife."

"I'm with my wife. You are my firstwife, and I'll always come to you first." He nuzzled under her ear, trying to nudge her jaw upwards to give him access to her throat.

His relations with Zheníhda had been icy for the longest time. Sweet words no longer passed between them; she resented every finger he touched her with so he refrained from it, silently having his way while she lay there waiting for him to stop, and they parted without a sound. Tonight he took his time, ignoring her protests, caressing her as if it were her wedding night instead, breaking through her resistance until he knew she was enjoying it even if she pretended otherwise. He took her from the front, face to face, taking his time until she found the joy he hadn't given her in a very long while, the precious beads still looped around her throat.

He stayed above her longer than he needed, her arms around his neck in an exhaustion of passion, and she didn't complain or throw him off. He kissed her chin before rolling aside. "*First* wife."

He went to Mimihn's room, where she waited for him in one of her short nothings of nightwear no thicker than a veil, wondering where he was. He smelled of Zheníhda, but her arms slid around his neck to pull him to her. She knew what pleased him, and it took hardly a giggle and a shake of her bottom to bring him to a salute. He took her twice in succession, thought about leaving then, but when he stood up she knelt on the bed, shook her bottom with a giggle and slapped her own backside, he couldn't ignore the burst of fire in his loins. He attacked her to her screams of glee, lying on his back as she rode on top of him, watching the tips of her breasts bounce in rhythm.

228

He broke away to his room after that, then called both wives before him as he sat naked at the end of the wide bed, stern and threatening.

Zheníhda backed away. "No, Tokh! I'm too old for that nonsense. I won't do it no matter how you beat me. Please come to your senses."

Mímihn stood nervously, squinting and blinking in the dim light. "What does my Lord wish?"

"Undress."

Zheníhda huffed. "Tokh!"

Mímihn blushed and gave a quick bow before pulling off the short nothing. "It's okay, Zheníhda-Firstwife. Don't feel shame. I can't see that far in this light." Zheníhda stayed out of his reach, but she did drop her robe.

He sat, staring at them without speaking, Zheníhda tall and bony, her belly flat but the skin starting to slide downward, her breasts angled in the same arc as her nose, Mímihn thirty-something years younger, her belly just as flat but her hips and shoulders deliciously soft, the nipples of her golden breasts pointing at him like two teasing tongues.

He pursed his lips. Tokh wasn't making the same mistake twice. This would end before it began. "Who do you serve?"

"You, my Lord," they both answered.

"Two wives, serving one Lord. Don't forget that. That's your purpose, not to fight with each other. If it does nothing to further my pleasure or my glory, you shouldn't be doing or saying it, and that's my final word. If one of you falls short from oversight or illness, I expect the other to cover for her without fail, without word. That's my expectation and my law. Is that clear?"

"Yes, my Lord."

"You will both oil me."

He lay back on the bed while they each took a side, coating their hands with perfumed oil and working it into every inch of his body and hair, massaging deep into his muscles until Tokh sank into the bed, relaxed and content. They rubbed him, side by side, bare shoulders and elbows and hips bumping, leaning over him, skin to skin, until the oil absorbed and all three of them smelled richly of *flendohl* and *kardenahn* spices, and the warm masculine odor of *nenagah*.

229

"Zheníhda, lie behind me; Mími, to my front." He pulled Zheníhda's arm over him until she was tight against his back, naked and warm. He pulled Mímihn against his chest, and she curled into a ball against him.

"There. The firstwife is where she has always been, covering my back. The secondwife is before me, making me look to the future. Each of you have your place in service to me, different but equal. This is the way it is, and the way it will be; three of us as one, and there will be no complaints."

He held Zheníhda's hand, rested his chin on Mímihn's head, and went to sleep.

* * 32 * *

Zheníhda could no longer pick at Mímihn for being a consort, but she still wheedled her for being one in the past, with such caring phrases as *trixahg*-wife, or half-blind half-wife. She'd remind Mímihn she was nothing but a decorative toy, as she couldn't produce offspring and therefore couldn't honor her husband. Zheníhda informed her the only reason Tokh had made her second-wife was so that no one could assign him another wife; she was a stop-gap, and she'd see the truth when she got a little older and Tokh brought home another consort. Mímihn let the insults slide at first, knowing Zheníhda's insecure tongue. Not once did she mention Zheníhda's age or the fact she, too, could no longer produce sons, or that perhaps Tokh had grown tired of her. Eventually, even Mímihn couldn't take it anymore, and began to answer back.

"Peck peck peck peck. That's all you do." Mímihn said the words as if she were speaking to herself, but as loud as if she spoke to Zheníhda directly. "Peck peck peck peck. Squaaawk! Squaaawk! You're like a *hyrak*, peck peck pecking all day long. Perhaps it's because of your *hyrak*-beak. Maybe you can't help it. Peck peck peck peck squawk! *Hyrak*! Screech! *Hy! Hy! Hyrak*!"

Zheníhda's face turned dark brown. "You insolent little *trixahg*! How dare you!"

Mímihn tapped her own nose. "Peck peck peck peck! Here we go again! Maybe I should lead her outside and she can peck the bugs off the flowers. Are you just hungry, Nihda-Firstwife? Wasn't there enough food on the farm?"

The slap came hard from Mímihn's bad side. Mímihn guessed the distance by the blurry images and slapped Zheníhda back; it connected perfectly. Zheníhda slapped Mímihn harder; Mímihn grabbed Zheníhda by her hair and yanked her head downward. Zheníhda screeched and dug her sharp nails into Mimihn's ribs.

Shanohr the housemaid excused herself from the room.

By the time they were done, Mímihn's cheek had been raked open by Zheníhda's nails, and Zheníhda's shins were sorely bruised

231

by Mímihn's feet, with a thousand threats and insults thrown into the air.

"You wait!" Zheníhda spat. "You wait until Tokh comes home! I am Firstwife and you will respect me or you will be disciplined! I'll make sure there's no skin left to your bottom and I will salt your healing creams!"

Mímihn didn't care. She had found Zheníhda's weak spot, found the insult that hurt as bad as *trixahg*, and she wasn't going to let it go. "Peckpeckpeckpeckpeck! Screeeech! *Hyrak*-wife! Wait until I tell Tokh how you scratched me looking for your lunch! Stop being so jealous, *hyrak*!"

Mímihn fled outside; Zheníhda fled to her room; neither set eye on each other the rest of the day, but both lurked in wait to be the first to jump on Tokh the second he returned. Mímihn made it to him first, bowing, hugging him, and covering his neck with kisses as Zheníhda stalked up to them on aching shins.

Tokh traced the gouges on her cheek, evenly spaced a finger's width apart. "What happened to your face?"

Mímihn touched the wounds. She giggled, ever sweet. "That's what happens when a silly little half-blind wife doesn't see where she's going and walks into the trellis with her face. I was lucky not to fall into the pool! I have to remember bright light can overpower my eyes and make things disappear just as much as not enough light. Sometimes I'm just too excited to see at all. Come, my love-lord. Tell me about your day." She took his hand, but Zheníhda blocked the way.

Zheníhda's foul glare softened. To mention the fight now would seem petty, make her have to admit she was the one who scratched Mimihn's face and thus call Mímihn a liar. Mímihn had outplayed her. She gave Tokh a token bow and a small kiss to his jaw. "Welcome home, my husband. Let me make you comfortable while you wait for your dinner to be served."

Tokh had been right. Mímihn wasn't Umara, not at all. Umara absorbed anything bad thrown at her and cried about it when no one could see her pain. Mímihn listened for the whistle of anything coming at her and tried to knock it aside before it could hit. Once she found Zheníhda's weak spot, there was no more inequality. One insult from Zheníhda's lips, just one, and Mímihn would bow with arms spread, "Of course, oh mighty *hyrak*!" She never used it to pick a fight, not once, but she shut down Zheníhda's pecking machine.

Whether because she couldn't see well, or fear of failing her husband, Mímihn was an overattentive mother to Umara's children, keeping track of where they were at all times. She fretted when Tokh presented Joralan with a short but lethal sword on his ninth naming-day, pleading to let her keep it unless he asked to use it so Kesseh wouldn't be wounded, but Tokh refused. He expected his son to obey his lessons about weaponry, and the one time he discovered the boy's sword lying around unattended, he beat such terror into Joralan's bottom the boy stood for meals for several days, afraid to remove his sword belt for so much as bathing.

Perhaps because Mímihn's eyes were in such rough shape, she became a stickler for Kesseh learning to read. Kesseh would come home from female school, aching to run and play, and Mímihn would sit her down for the two hours until Joralan returned and make her read to her, anything and everything, from Joralan's story books to recipes with words instead of the common color-coded photos.

Illiterate Zheníhda stuck her chin in the air. "Why must you waste her time? Let her play! Reading won't help her get a husband."

Tokh held up a hand. "No. I will hear her read. Someone must be the best in every class. There's no reason it shouldn't be my daughter." If someday he managed to get her into a school of real education, she would be ahead of all the rest.

Mímihn's third eye surgery came a year after her second. With correction, she had fifty percent vision in her left eye. Colors blossomed bright and beautiful. She could identify large shapes like trees and buildings and vehicles from a hundred feet away. If she held her lap pad close to her face, she could watch ComNet programs or make out printed words. Tokh installed software that would magnify things for her; if she needed to see something – a wound or splinter on one of the children – she could aim the camera of the lap pad at it and see the image magnified as large as needed. Distant things were still fuzzy and indistinct, but no longer was Mímihn a stumbling, blind fool. Her right eye lagged far behind – nothing but bright light with grainy spots of shadows, interspersed with specks of blackness where the nerve connections were missing.

She could make out bright colors, knew if a shadow passed over her, could make out large, sharp patterns such as the black and white squares in her pattern-book, but reading or any sort of cohesive image was out of the question on her right side. The nerves had been more damaged, and they weren't healing. The doctor was confident they could improve it more, but for now he recommended rest. Mímihn's head was always angled a little to the right, keeping her good eye centered in her body, but now she could spot Zheníhda coming at her across a room.

It was Kitras's face that appeared on Tokh's viewscreen. Kitras had recently made Captain One. A promotion could do many things for an officer. If a commander liked him and wanted to retain him, an officer might move up to new duties within his unit. If he had special skills or another commander wanted him, he might be traded to a different unit. If the officer was very skilled or very connected, he would be cherry-picked by the top brass and assigned to positions that guaranteed great things in the future. The only thing that was certain in a promotion was duties would change.

"Hey, *Bobo!*" Kitras said on the screen. "How goes life with two wives?"

"Twice the pain," Tokh said, and they both laughed. "Did they change your assignment?"

Kitras scratched behind his chinhank. "Yeah, that's what I wanted to talk to you about. I was picked up by General Rhigandir.

"Most excellent!" Tokh said with delight. "I know him well. He has an excellent record and won't steer you wrong. He's got troops in several locations, lots of special forces. You're not going covert, are you? Elite corps, but very dangerous. You have a family to consider."

"I think that's the long-term goal," Kitras admitted. "I've beat everyone they put me against in marksmanship, and he liked my answers on the interview – said my thinking was remarkably like my *Bo*. Problem is, my new deployment starts in two weeks and is expected to last possibly a year. All the *pushing* way out in west Yomebor."

"The civil conflicts in Kanok Sohr?"

"Yeah. I don't know what's up, but there's a big drive to get that region quieted down at any cost, so they're sending in a lot of troops. I was wondering – you've got that big house and all – can I leave

Dalo with you and *Ama* while I'm gone? She just had the baby, and I'm sure she could use an extra hand. She worries about me too much when she's alone." Dalo had given him a third child and second son just six months before.

"You have my permission," Tokh said. "I know your *ama* would love to see the children. It will also give your brother and sister playmates to occupy them. Dalo and Mími seem to get along."

"Yeah, they sistered up pretty well. Good. I'll bring everybody out in about five days, then. Thanks, *Bo.*"

Zheníhda seized baby Niboh immediately and didn't put him down for hours. She'd spent a month with Dalo when Niboh was born, but hadn't seen him since. Niboh had thick arms and legs and a full head of downy black hair, and he was starting to sit up on his own. He looked up at Zheníhda's cooing face and gave her a happy rolling laugh. As much as Mímihn was dying to cuddle the baby, she knew Niboh would pretty much be off limits unless Zheníhda wasn't around. Lanag was now eight and a perfect match for his Uncle Joralan, while Kitras's daughter Faelihn was just five months younger than her Aunt Kesseh, already the closest of friends. The children disappeared in a flash.

Mímihn squinted at Dalo as she greeted her. "I love your hair! You changed it!"

"Yeah. I thought, you know, *some* people like purple, so I thought I'd be nice." Dalo changed the colors of her hair almost by the month. Mímihn had seen it both green and blue, and dark red with gold tips for the Emperor's Birthday holiday, but now it was styled downward in a smooth shoulder-length bob that had been dyed dark evening purple with lavender highlights. She wore purple eyeshadow and white liner around her eyes, making her look like an exotic animal, and although she technically wore a black veil, it was tied around her head in a big bow. Her shirt clung to her curves, and the hem of her layered skirt was pulled up and tucked into her waistband at the side, making it look ruffled and leaving one leg bare as she walked. Zheníhda reached out and flicked the tuck free so the skirt fell down.

"*Not* in front of my husband."

Since the family was Zheníhda's, Mímihn slept in Tokh's bed so Zheníhda could rest. The beauty of such a huge house was no one could hear Dalo and Kitras's vigorous caterwauling unless standing in the hallway. They slept late, got up for lunch, went back to bed, made themselves presentable for dinner, and went at each other again most of the night. By the second day, Dalo was having trouble sitting.

"Don't you think you're overdoing it a little?" Tokh said to Kitras in the privacy of his study. "You won't have energy left for combat."

Kitras smiled to himself. "It's not the first time I've gone more-than-a-hand twice in the same day, *Bo*. I don't know when I'll get the chance again, so I want it to be memorable. And it's not all my idea, if you know what I mean."

Tokh gave him a stern glare. "Be sure you're not leaving a fourth one behind."

"Three is it," Kitras assured him.

By the third day even Mímihn was rolling her eyes. Dalo sat on Kitras's lap and hand-fed him his breakfast while Zheníhda fed Niboh. Kitras wore his uniform; his gear sat packed by the door. He would fly into Keranihn with Tokh and leave for duty from the base there. Dalo looked sad but she didn't cry. She hugged him around his neck, bit him hard enough to leave one last mark among the bouquet of blotches he wore, and stepped back. She gave him an energetic salute that he returned and he boarded his father's private craft, waving to the children from the window. Dalo turned and hugged Mímihn, but when she lifted her head, her eyes were brave.

Even though Kesseh now had Faelihn to play with after school, Mímihn didn't let up on her extra lessons.

"Enough with that nonsense!" Zheníhda said. "She has someone to play with – let them go be friends."

"After she practices reading," Mímihn insisted. "Tokh approved it and she's his child, so I'll follow his orders."

To Mímihn's surprise, Dalo told Faelihn to join her. "If it's good enough for Kitras's sister, it should be good enough for his daughter, no? I think he'll be happy about it when he comes back. Maybe she'll be a better reader than me." Dalo was an excellent reader, reading aloud to Mímihn from some of Umara's poem books.

"Hmph." Zheníhda's sneer boiled upward. "Wives have gotten by just fine for thousands of years without that nonsense. You're

236

wasting their youth. They only get so many years to play before they must learn to run households."

"Don't you ever want to make sense of something?" Dalo said. "Write your husband a love note, read your son's school report, make sure a store clerk isn't cheating you?"

"I'm married thirty-five years," Zheníhda sniffed. "Why would I need to write Tokh a love note? If a store clerk cheats me, Tokh will find out and demand punishment."

Dalo rolled her eyes and sighed. "Don't be so old-fashioned, Zheníhda-*ama*. I can teach you, if you want. If a five year old can do it, so can you. Surprise Lord Tokh with an erotic note. I'll teach you to write the words. I send them to Kitras all the time. It brings him smiles while he's away."

Zheníhda's thin nostrils flared and she stood up from the table with a jolt. "I'm too old to learn such things." She left the room, but she did approach Dalo in private about improving her skills without Mímihn knowing – and without the erotic words.

"Am I really that old, Tokh?" she asked him in bed that night. "Is reading and writing that important for females nowadays?"

"I don't know," he admitted. "You've been very sheltered, always living near the bases or out here in the countryside. In Keranihn, most of the females dress like Dalo. It's a crazy time in the big cities." He played with her unbound hair, pulling it from behind her and spreading it over her breasts in a peek-a-boo curtain. "When I go in tomorrow, I'll buy you something more modern."

Zheníhda huffed herself up like an aggravated *hyrak*. "I won't dress like she does, inviting attention from every passerby. She thinks safety is a joke. Someday her luck will run out, and then she'll be sorry."

"You'll wear what I buy you, even if it's only around the house."

Tokh did buy her a new outfit: high-waisted black and white striped bloomer pants, a turquoise blouse with a wide neckline that showed her collarbones but not her cleavage, a black veil with subtle black sequins, and a silver and black pendant.

"Very nice," Tokh said with admiration.

"That color is lovely on you, Nihda-Firstwife," Mímihn said.

"*Now* you're in the right century," Dalo said with authority.

"I feel like a painted bird." Zheníhda wrung her hands and straightened the fabric obsessively. But when she dared to wear it to visit with the uppity neighbor ladies and they not only approved but started wearing similar things, Zheníhda began to strut.

* * 33 * *

Kitras called home every other week, easing Dalo's fears. He couldn't speak about his assignment, but Tokh knew there had been several bloody battles that hadn't made the global news. Tokh kept the information to himself, but he checked the military reports every night.

Without warning, Tokh arrived home early from Keranihn at the start of the week and rushed straight to his office room. It was three hours before he appeared, the children ravenous and half-asleep by the time he appeared for dinner.

"Something important, Tokh?" Zheníhda said as she sat. "They aren't planning on shipping you out again, are they? It's not something to do with what Kitras is tied up in? You've been local for so long."

"No, no, I hope not," he said with distraction. His mouth consumed his food, but his mind was elsewhere. "There are big happenings in Keranihn. Remember years ago, the big project I was chosen for, the one that won us this house? It's paid off at last. For the first time ever, the Emperor of Kerasím is going to meet with a delegation from the Planetary Union, here on Kerasi soil. They are sending twenty or so delegates, and if my sources are correct, my emissary is going to be one of them. I spent the last two hours in communication with Masákh, out in the Union. Security will be extremely tight. I'm hoping I can slither my way into one of the discussions. I would very much like to congratulate her, thank her, see what she thinks of Kerasím itself. We dared not bring her anywhere near our space before."

Mímihn thought hard. "The girl I met when I was with you? She was very young. Ai-lah. Wasn't that her name? Ai-lah?"

"Yes. That was her name."

Zheníhda's eyes narrowed. "She's not a consort, is she?"

Tokh shot her a cold look. "She's Union. She was under the Emperor's protection then, and probably will be again. I haven't been informed as to her current status."

"Union?" Dalo exclaimed. "You've actually met Union citizens? Which ones? What color were they? Did they have hair?"

Mímihn bounced on her chair. "Tokh! If you get to meet her, may I come with you? I'd like to greet her again as well. I'd like to see what she looks like. Maybe we can speak to each other better now."

"Masákh continues to improve her language skills; I have no doubt she could speak to you. I can show you videos. Masákh sends me all her public speeches." He sat back with a frown. "I fear I won't be allowed near the delegations. I remain the Union's most sought-for Kerasi, charged in a variety of Union crimes regarding the Emissary. Even if I don't use my name, my face could be known. The Emperor won't jeopardize his truce. It may be possible, however, for Masákh to arrange a videocall. It will depend on how close she is kept under guard. I don't know the planned itinerary. That information would be highest secrecy."

Mímihn looked crestfallen. "I understand. I don't want you to anger the Emperor, my Lord."

"It makes me realize a shortcoming, however. All this time, I should have been making sure Joralan had lessons in Union standard. Fluency at a young age will put him far above all other candidates for promotion and placement. He could all but walk into an *aghát* placement, possibly work at the palace itself. I'll have him shadow them for a month before he goes to the Academy."

Kesseh and Faelihn exchanged huge grins of excitement over mention of the palace, but Joralan seemed less thrilled. "Can't I learn it at the Academy? I don't want more lessons."

"No. You won't waste another day. I speak it, your brother Kitras knows a little, all my *aghát* are fluent, a few officers, even Khaním can pick at conversation. I'll start you first thing in the morning."

"Can I learn it too, *Bo*?" Kesseh asked. "I could speak to your Union Lady."

Tokh was about to toss her comment away, but he stared at her instead. If he could teach Kerasi to a female Union child to form a bridge of peace, why shouldn't his female Kerasi child learn Union? It might not help her in her life, but it wouldn't hurt her. Especially if the Emperor won his treaties. His daughter would be a shining star before anyone else, able to speak with Union females without concern from either side. At worst, she could be a servant to female Union diplomats. "Yes. I insist on it."

"Can Lanag and I learn, too?" Dalo asked. "We could practice with Kitras."

"And me!" said Faelihn. "I want to talk to the Union Lady, too."

"Of course. It seems I'll have a full school room."

"*Gah*. Waste of time," Zheníhda said. "Teach her something useful, like tying her shoes."

"I remember the words you taught me," Mímihn said. "*Ah-lo.* That is the greeting they use. When you greet a Union person, you squeeze their hand and tell them, '*ah-lo.*' And *khome*. It means walk with me."

"*Ah-lo,*" Kesseh repeated. "*Ah-lo,* Great Lady. *Ah-lo,* Union Lord."

Faelihn giggled. "*Ah-lo,* Kesseh. *Ah-lo, Dihnama.*"

Zheníhda snorted. "You sound like you're sneezing."

Tokh sat forward again and resumed eating. "I'll keep close watch on the Emissary."

Tokh worked later and later as the days passed leading up to the Accord. He came home, ate a little, fell into bed without a single *push* on anyone, and was up early to head back to Keranihn, if he came home at all. Guards were being interrogated to make sure they were appropriate to work with the Union. *Aghát* were also being scanned, including one of Tokh's own men. He wasn't allowed to be present at that scanning; Tokh hadn't had such a case of nerves since he himself was held and interrogated following his Emissary's escape. The officer, Ráhnif, was new, a member of his team just four months, unproven on hard missions. Tokh's relief when Ráhnif passed the test was so great he returned from a four-drink lunch too tipsy for duty, something he'd never done in his entire career.

The delegates would be arriving at an undisclosed time, kept at the palace, sent under guard for a structured tour of city and country, and returned to the palace for the official addresses, festivities, and signing of accords. The ceremonies would be broadcast live across the planet and out into the colonies; the rest of the visit would be filmed, edited, and aired as special programming each evening. Emperor Nághtas declared the entire planet on shut-down; anyone not on active duty – medical personnel, military personnel – would be sent home from work to watch the historic proceedings. Schools would be closed, and mobile viewing screens the size of walls would be trucked into *ghinadin* villages so the poorest citizens of Kerasím could watch as well. If the Union had their way, the Accord would start to pull the *ghinadin* out of poverty; it was in their best interest to know every word said.

Tokh didn't get his invite to the palace – he hadn't yet managed one, ever – but three of his *aghát* were directly involved with the delegates, and three more were stationed among the palace staff, in place if needed. That alone was an honor. General Trannor himself forwarded apologies from the palace: if there wasn't the price on Tokh's head, he would have been assigned to assist with the Union guests. Instead, Tokh was sent home, banned from Keranihn itself until the delegation left. Tokh's second-in-command, Khaním, would remain on duty at the Intelligence office.

To Mímihn's dismay, no calls would be forthcoming from the delegation. The higher-ups wanted no unofficial communications between Kerasi citizens and the Union. Everything was scripted and nothing left to chance. This was a historical first, and Nághtas wanted no surprises. Everything had to be flawless and accounted for.

Kerasi-wide ComNet began broadcasting live coverage of the affair three hours beforehand. Historical facts between the Union and Kerasím were discussed, and the direction the Emperor planned to take. Biographies and photos of each of the Union delegates were shown and discussed as to the importance of each player. Longer discussion ensued about the delegate Aila Perrin, a member of the Union Council on Kerasi Affairs and the youthful star of Kerasi-Union relations.

Mímihn sat curled on a sofa in the great room, studying her lap pad. "That's her! That's the one, isn't it, Tokh? She's so important now! I can't believe they have females on their government councils. Maybe she speaks for all the females. There's another one!" Kesseh leaned over her elbow, even though the same coverage was playing on the wallscreen, too far away for Mímihn's eyes.

Tokh paced around the great room, unable to sit. He wanted to be at the Accord in the worst way. There was so much he wanted to see, so much he wanted to ask the Union delegates, so many things he wanted to know, and he was stuck in Imahlva under gag order.

"The Union doesn't separate the sexes; all are counted as equal, all speak for each other."

"That's silly," Mímihn said. "How can a female know what it's like to be male? How can a male know what it's like to bear a child? That can't work."

"It does in the Union," Tokh insisted. "Masákh, Haghíde, and Mátokhan have been among them four years now. They see it daily. They work alongside the females as if they were males."

The Accord began in the middle of the afternoon. Tokh forced himself to sit, a wife on either side of him. Dalo curled in a comfortable chair to the side, bare feet tucked underneath her, Niboh asleep on her lap. Kesseh squeezed between Tokh and Zheníhda, while Joralan, Lanag, and Faelíhn lay on the floor at his feet. Given the historical significance and the part he played in it, Tokh invited Shanohr and Thrit to watch with them, on small chairs at the side of the room.

A parade of officials climbed the palace steps to cheers: *bhísroti* Ministers, *fáhganid* arch-generals and industrial magnates, *dahneg* senators, and many more. Cameras zoomed in, displaying faces with titles captioned underneath. Inside the palace, cameras caught the Emperor's wives and eldest smalldaughter taking seats to the side of the great senate hall. Females were never present at political functions, but Nághtas wanted to make a good impression, show the Union he was trying his best to meet their demands. His wives were dressed in Union-style clothing, but their hair and make-up were traditional *thósikh* overkill. In the main hall, cameras caught glimpses of the Union delegates, captions struggling to identify faces before they moved out of frame.

"That one!" Zheníhda pointed. "That's one of your men, isn't it, Tokh?"

Tokh beamed. "Haghíde. Right in the middle of things. Good. Stay on them, Haghíde. Stay with your orders."

The camera cut away to a Kerasi news crew on the steps of the palace, interviewing one of the Union delegates in Kerasi. She was young and human, with brown hair done up in a Kerasi wedding-weave, a dress with a voluminous skirt that screamed the height of crazy Keranihn fashion. And right at her elbow was his Number Two *aghát*.

Tokh sat up sharply and jammed the volume louder. "That's her! That's the Perrin female, with Masákh!"

Kesseh gasped. "*Bo*'s Union Lady! She's beautiful, *Bo*!"

"*Am-am*, look at her dress!" Faelihn squealed.

"*Shu! Shu!*"

They listened as she answered fluff questions about her experiences. The Emissary answered on her own in Kerasi, with Masákh prompting her with correct words now and then, even if her accent wasn't the best. She spoke for all of five *fasím* before cutting the interview short.

"Oh Tokh!" Mímihn said. "Did you hear how well she speaks now? She almost doesn't need Masákh." Her voice took on a teasing tone. "Did you see her looking at him? She looks at him with her heart, but he's not paying attention. Stupid male! Open your eyes!"

"They must give them huge amounts to spend, or she's from a high-caste family," Zheníhda said. "That dress is fit for *bhísroti*."

Mímihn squinted at her screen. "She's beyond beautiful in it. She's like a sunset, all the colors from one end of the sky to the other."

Dalo wrinkled her nose. "Too much. It's like she climbed out of bed and is pulling all the sheets with her. We would never have carried such a thing at my *bo*'s shop."

Tokh frowned. "What's she doing? Masákh! Pull her in!" On the screen, the Perrin girl skipped down the palace steps, her billowing wide dress rippling out behind her in a short train. She greeted the mass of women waiting at the sides, speaking to them, smiling, touching their hands, down one side of the gathered crowd and back up the other, greeting all castes with equal fervor. When she returned to the palace steps, the crowd went wild, jumping and screaming and waving at her.

"That was a suicide move, Masákh," Tokh mumbled. "You should never have let her risk herself. Control her."

"She touched them," Zheníhda said. "Why would she do that? She defiles herself, touching *whátaral* like that. You can't just go about touching anyone you meet."

Tokh shrugged. "The Union touches each other in greeting. My men have had difficulty adjusting to that. When I was stationed on Kye, the locals all touched each other. Perhaps she wished to demonstrate that fact."

The formal proceedings began. Emperor Nághtas headed his senate council in the grand chamber, an impressive, gilded room that held a thousand people. Anyone who was anyone, or knew anyone,

244

threw their weight to be invited to the Accord. Nághtas stood, rotund as a sun in his shining gold suit and his ceremonial crownlet, and opened the conference. The Union delegates were announced one by one as they walked to their seats at the Emperor's left side.

Kesseh pointed. "There goes *Bo*'s Union Lady!" Aila marched to her seat and waited for permission to sit, unlike some of her associates. Masákh stood behind her against the wall with the security officers.

"Look at all his medals, *Bo*!" Joralan said. "I've never seen a blue dress uniform before. Everyone else has browns and reds. I only see four of them."

"My *bo* has lots of medals, too," Lanag said. "He can shoot a spoon right out of someone's hand."

"My *bo* can cut someone's head off with his eyes closed."

"*Shu!* Of course they're decorated; those are my men," Tokh said. "Blue is for the *aghát*. You've met them, but not in dress. There are no less than sixty *aghát* in the city at the moment, including all of my team. See if you can spot them in the crowd." Every time the camera panned out, the boys raced to count as many blue uniforms as they could find.

The Emperor's speech included an unexpected bombshell: as of that moment, civilian capital punishment was illegal. Anyone demanding retribution would have to be heard in a formal court, and capital punishment would have to be approved by a *bhísroti* official

"That's crazy," Zheníhda scoffed. Her hands held a cup of *raffin* she sipped at. "No one's going to wait for a criminal to be punished. Justice should be swift. That'll make us weak in the eyes of the Union."

Tokh frowned. "It's illegal to take someone's head for any reason in the Union. I don't know how it will play out. He specifically exempted the military, however. We'll still have discipline in the ranks."

Heir Nadigh also rose to speak. His words were briefer, comparing his daughters to Union females. Tokh couldn't help but wonder in the back of his head if Nadigh's daughters had already been educated beyond other Kerasi women. Had he tried and succeeded, and that was what drove the Grand Plan, or was he waiting for his father's plans to take place and then take advantage of them? General Trannor had Nadigh's ear. Perhaps after the

Accord, Tokh would ask Trannor if he could inquire for him, for his own daughter's sake.

The head of the Union delegation spoke next, bland but peaceful, his speech translated several seconds later by a male voiceover. When he was done, a Union female, an older one of Noorish origin, greeted the room in Emperor's Tongue before beginning her speech in Union Standard. She'd been chosen to take on negotiations between the worlds until a permanent diplomat could be chosen.

The camera view cut to a long shot, showing the speaker, the Emperor, and many of the top advisors of both worlds. The woman continued to speak, when to her right a great green flash of light crossed the room. The camera follow it. The Emperor jerked backward in his seat, then slumped forward. His heirs and those next to him jumped up. The camera zoomed in to see what was going on, focusing on a huge charred area in the middle of Naghtas's chest. It panicked and zoomed out again as the room seemed to stand and inhale as one, then scream and try to run. People dove across the stage and ran toward the camera, which shook and blurred as people banged into it. A second beam shot from overhead and the Union speaker gave a jump and fell to the ground. The camera view was blocked by a herd of people pressing toward it. The picture cut to black, and after several seconds a generic "Patience for Technical Difficulties" title appeared.

Dalo's face was blank. "Holy Mother of Fortune. Did that actually happen?"

Mímihn looked up from her lap pad. "I don't understand."

Tokh jumped to his feet so fast he knocked Joralan in the head with his boot as he ran for his office. Mímihn sprang after him and Zheníhda followed so as not to be left out, the children at their heels. Dalo gathered the children and waited just under the stairs, near but out of the way. Tokh's door was shut but his words came through.

"Do not! Repeat, do not approach the palace. There will be panic and disorder. Find a safe location nearby and wait for instruction. I need you in place as rescue. Keep communication to minimum. Tokh out."

"What happened?" Kesseh asked in the hallway. "Why did the ComNet stop?"

Mímihn's words failed her. Zheníhda's composure crumbled as she answered. "They killed him. They killed our mighty Emperor.

He brought them here with all the goodness of his heart and they shot him before his council like an animal in a pen. Cowards! They'll declare war and your *bo* will be shipped away again. This is what happens when only one side tries to make peace."

Kesseh's eyes filled with tears. "Why would they want to kill our wonderful Emperor?"

Joralan's hand rested on the hilt of his sword. "Let them make war! I'll defend our Emperor! I'd be at military school right now if *Bo* would just let me go! Maybe he'll send me now, so I can be an officer like my brothers."

Zheníhda cuffed him in the head. "That's the talk of a fool! A living soldier never looks for war. If there's war it won't end quickly and you'll see battle far too young. I won't have my sons die at the hands of the Union."

Mímihn found her tongue. She yanked Joralan's arm. "You wish your *bo* to die? He's a high general with Union experience! If there's war, he'll be sent to command the battle lines! You should be begging the Fortunes for peace! Your *bo* could be in there receiving his next orders, and today could be the last time you see him alive! You could lose your brothers, too, leave Lanag and Khourbas and Zivas with no *bo* as well!"

Faelihn gasped and clung to Dalo. Kesseh cried harder. "You're mean, Jora! How could you want *Bo* to die like the Emperor?"

"I didn't say I wanted him to die, you stupid female!" Joralan's fire had burned out, and he looked about to cry himself.

Zheníhda lost her patience and shooed them out of the hall. "Go, children! Go sit in your rooms and think about our beloved Emperor until dinner, the wonderful Emperor that gave us this very house." Dalo took them upstairs.

"I, Tokh dar-Giláhn, General Four of the Great Army, do pledge my head and heart and will to the Emperor of All Kerasím, to be at his command for all needs, to protect and serve Kerasím and all its glory without regard to self, to give my life to the Emperor should he request it, and to forsake the rule of all others but the one true crown. In the name of Nadigh, Emperor of All Kerasím, I pledge my loyalty, duty, and honor to the Emperor."

Zheníhda covered her mouth with a trembling hand. "He's repeating his oath. That can only be bad news. They'll take him from us."

There was no friendship between Mímihn and Zheníhda, just a grudging acknowledgement that they had to cooperate if they wanted to keep their backs unstriped. Still, Mímihn reached out and put her arms around Zheníhda and hugged her; Zheníhda hugged her back. They stayed that way a full *fasim*, united in their fear.

Mímihn pulled away, hurried to the kitchen, and returned with a cup of hot *raffin* and a cold-meat sandwich on a plate. She knew not to disturb Tokh in a crisis, but serving him food was within her bounds.

She knocked softly and entered, placing the refreshments on a corner of his desk. Zheníhda stood in the doorway. He gave a brief bow of his head in thanks. Her caring hand slipped across his shoulders in support. "Please keep us informed," she whispered.

He gestured toward the blank communication screen. "I'm waiting for information. As you probably guessed, the Emperor was just assassinated on live broadcast. There's terrible panic at the palace. Everyone was trapped inside the senate chamber by two explosions that followed. Security collapsed and is trying to regroup, but it will be some time before it's known who's dead, who's missing, and who survived. Nadigh escaped; it's assumed he's in a saferoom somewhere in the palace. I have sent in my allegiance to Nadigh; it would be required whenever he took office, but I'm hoping that by volunteering my loyalty immediately and offering my men, it will help him build up the team he'll need to find his father's assassin. There are two balconies in the back of the Senate room; judging by the angle of fire, the assassin was in the top one, reserved on this occasion for the wives of the senate dignitaries, but no female could have fired such a weapon."

Anxiety and dread left Zheníhda with faint sobs. "Are we at war? Will they send you away? The Union is far bigger than the Coalition, even with the colonies. What if they try to invade us?"

"It's too soon to know. There are many Union casualties as well. Until the assassin is identified, no one knows why or where he came from, or how in a black hole someone got a weapon of that type into a high-security area. Something's not right. The Union delegation's been under observation the entire time they've been here. There's not one instance where any of them hasn't been accounted for by one security staff or another. Transmissions have been monitored. There's no possible way it could have been accomplished by anyone within the Union. None. Of that I'm certain."

"What about your emissary, Ai-lah?" Mímihn's voice had a mournful tone. "What about your men? Have you heard from them?"

Tokh gave an unhappy grunt. "Mátokhan is aiding security detail, Ráhnif assisting the delegation. Nothing yet on the others. I have men stationed outside the palace grounds, ready to grab them at the first word."

The comm system gave an incoming chirp, and all three of them jumped. A text appeared. Tokh gave a whoop of delight.

"They're safe! 'General's Two and Three secure in city with cargo intact. Await instructions.'"

"Ai-lah is alive?"

"Yes. Masákh got her out safely." Mímihn shouted with joy. Tokh elbowed her out of the way to reply, *G5 on standby. Recovery on signal. Cargo to be flown in.*

"What will happen?" Zheníhda said. "If the palace is under siege, where will they go? Back to the Union ships?"

"I'm bringing her here," Tokh said. "We're under emergency procedures. All troops are being mobilized for peacekeeping purposes; all reserves are now active, which does include Zenak. All spaceflight is grounded. Non-military aircraft are now grounded, but I have authority. I've already sent a craft to Palinet to meet them. She'll be safe here until she can return to the Union. We'll wait together for further orders."

"Here?! Oh Tokh!" Mímihn seized him around his neck and kissed him. "I can meet her again! I'll make up the guest room next to mine! When? When will they be here?"

"One to three hours, depending on how fast they get to Palinet." Mímihn squealed and shot out of the room.

"I'll see that the other rooms are ready for your officers. I'll send Thrit to see if a market is open; no doubt there will be a panic on food," Zheníhda said. "What do Union people eat? If she is *dahneg*, we can't risk offending her. What does she drink? How does she sleep? We've never hosted non-Kerasi."

"She'll eat anything you serve, as long as it doesn't have a head or eyes." Tokh switched channels on his equipment to send new orders. "They're much like us. Do as you would for your mother, and you won't offend."

"I'll be ready," she assured him.

* * 34 * *

The aircraft hovered over the landing pad, then touched down. Tokh jogged toward it, followed by Mímihn and his children.

Masákh was the first to descend, disheveled, dusty, and shaken. Tokh clapped him on the shoulder with a wide grin. "Masákh! You made it out safely! We feared the worst, until Haghíde's message. Haghíde!" He clapped Haghíde's shoulders with just as much enthusiasm. "So very glad you made it out in one piece."

Haghíde bowed. "Thank you, General."

Tokh ran his eyes over his Emissary Aila, watching for a recognition, a reaction. She was dressed like Kerasi royalty, taller, powerful, and most definitely more adult. She stared back, harsh and distrustful.

He bowed low before her. "Our experiment gone right. Welcome to my home, Aila Perrin. You do me and my household great honor. Whatever is mine is now yours. May you rest well here."

"Tokh dar-Giláhn," she said coldly, chin high. "Please tell me Kassán isn't in your basement, or I'll jump from your cliff."

Tokh paused to think her words through, then threw back his head and laughed. "No, no. He is at the palace, working for the Emperor. Do you remember my wife, Mímihn? She will see to you while you are here. She remembers you with great liking." Mímihn couldn't follow the Union conversation, but she peered around from behind Tokh at the mention of her name.

"She was your consort," Perrin remembered.

"My wife Umara died of a medical issue. I made Mími my wife the following year. She is now mother to Umara's children, Joralan and Kesseh."

"How noble of you."

Mímihn walked forward and bowed. *"Ah-lo, Ai-lah! Hahppy see!"* she said in standard.

The Emissary's face softened. She embraced Mímihn and replied in Kerasi. *"I am honored to meet you again, Mímihn."*

Mímihn squinted and broke out in a huge grin. Her fingers poked and prodded Aila's cheek and smoothed the brown hair falling from its hair-pins, fingered her necklace, touched the fabric of her dress, the voluminous long skirt torn off at the knees, and she sighed with longing. *"You're beautiful! Like a bhísroti!"*

"You can see?!"

Tokh explained. "A year ago I kept my promise to restore Mímihn's sight. After three surgeries, she has partial vision in both eyes," he said. "But come, friends. You've been in a most tragic battle. Wash, eat, rest, then we will attend to business. You'll be safe here. I'm under the Emperor's protection and have already submitted my oath of loyalty to Emperor Nadigh."

Aila bowed her head this time. "You are most honorable, Lord Tokh."

Tokh brayed with laughter again. "The *dahneg* is calling me Lord!"

Mímihn danced with excitement. "Khome! Khome!"

Aila entered the house with reservation, shrewd eyes glancing about, checking for dangers. She stepped aside so Tokh would be in front of her. She didn't give off the warmth of an honored guest but the impression of a trapped animal looking for a way out.

Tokh pointed to the crowd waiting inside. "My men you all know; may I present Aila Perrin, Union Council on Kerasi Affairs, an associate of mine from my greatest mission."

Aila choked so hard and long it sounded as if she were snoring. "Associate. Like it was voluntary. On my world, it's called prisoner."

Tokh tipped his head to her. "Refusing my honor is your choice. My firstwife, Zheníhda. Her sons are grown, off in the military." Zheníhda bowed low but said nothing. She had never seen a human before, let alone met one, and had no idea what to do.

He pointed to Dalo and her family. She bowed to Aila, keeping the baby upright. "This is my son Kitras's wife, Dalo, mother of his children here. He has been on a difficult assignment for several months, so we brought her here. Zenak and his wife are at Nar Rhede; we don't see them often. These here are Umara's children, now Mímihn's. *Go. You've seen the Human, now get out and let us speak.*" He waved everyone away.

"Khome! Khome!" Mímihn pulled on her arm.

251

Tokh watched Aila look to Masákh for permission – how little things had changed in four years – and he sent her off with a nod. She followed Mímihn to the upper floor.

Zheníhda and Shanohr made a dinner fit for a dignitary. Tokh kept a news program playing on the viewscreen on the back wall, sound minimized and captions on, replaying the catastrophe over and over. The conversation stayed locked on politics.

The Perrin girl remained full of fire, arguing right along. "I don't believe a word of it. Secretary Kel is opinionated, yes, but why would he kill top cabinet members? We're here to *make* peace, not destroy it. No. This is entirely on your people."

"And the Secretary Kel's stance on opening relations?" Tokh asked.

"Unfavorable," Aila said with defeat. "I fought with him more than once."

Tokh smiled, showing the points of his teeth. "Your fire never ceases to impress." He glanced up at the news program.

Aila followed the glance. "Hey! That's my face."

All heads turned to the screen. Tokh blasted the volume to life. Masákh translated it for her as the newsman spoke. Footage from her hand-shaking escapade rolled across the screen.

"The question of the moment is 'Where is Aila Perrin?' The Member of the Union Council for Kerasi Affairs is not among the dead, and hasn't been found among the living, nor has her Kerasi bodyguard. Was she part of the plot to destroy the house of Nághtas, and made a getaway with her fellow plotters? The question is who will find her first – those that want to save her, or those that want her to pay?"

The room turned to stare at her

"I'm next," Aila mumbled.

"You're safe for the time being," Tokh insisted. "Have no fear."

Mímihn stayed with the Emissary all night, keeping her "safe." Tokh spent time going over protocols and orders with his officers in the morning, then put them through target practice. Four years in Union territory hadn't dimmed their skills, to his satisfaction. His Emissary watched them practice, then insisted on learning weaponry alongside them; Tokh allowed it as she was a high-ranking guest, but her utter failure with a sword sent her storming back to the house, where she locked herself in her room and wouldn't come out, even to Mímihn's pleadings.

Disappointment sat sour on Tokh's stomach. He had expected better. He knew she had spine; she had argued to his face, dared escape him against orders. The indulgence with weapons was for his benefit, a silent judgment on skill, of which, apparently, she had none at all. Kesseh could best her with a blade. No Kyan locals had carried weapons, he remembered now. How easy it would have been to overtake them, had he wished it. Tokh had shown Zheníhda the basics of knives as a matter of her own protection; if she dared handle one, she would be less likely to hurt herself. Mímihn... Mímihn was a strange bird. She didn't ask him to teach her weapons, yet every time she'd been in a dangerous situation she somehow had a weapon on her, carried with such confidence it made Tokh uneasy. He'd never asked her where she'd learned to use a dagger – or any other weapon. Maybe it was time he did.

On the other hand, he wasn't sure he wanted to know.

By mid-afternoon Tokh tired of the Emissary's tantrum and disengaged the lock on the door. He stood in the doorway, stern and cold.

"You will accompany me or I will lead you by your hair."

Aila complied in silence. He led her outside to the grounds, wandering the walkways between the sections of lawn and gardens surrounding the swimming pool, as private and secure as they could get.

"Strong females are a novelty to us. We aren't used to their attempts at male activities. For a first effort, your aim with a pistol was admirable. I would suggest practicing as much as you can while you are here. A fool who overestimates his abilities is a dead fool."

"I can see that," Aila said. "Some women in our history never did more than raise children and make homes. Others began that way, but when their men fell in battle, they took their husband's place, either at war or at running their business. Others never wanted to be tied to home, and learned to fly or fight or play sport every bit as well as a male."

Tokh paused. "How? How are females educated? Are there special academies, or are they taught at home? When do they start; when do they stop? What type of programs are they taught? Are there special female teachers? And how are they taught?"

Aila laughed to herself. "You still don't get it. Union females are taught in the same classrooms as male children. The teachers are male or female; it doesn't matter. They learn the exact same subjects, whether it's math or music or rocket science or army combat. Yes, we have female generals. They all start by four or five and they must continue until seventeen or eighteen, but most study at least four to six years more. Doctors and surgeons and specialists, maybe ten years more. Whatever the boys do, the girls do too."

Tokh frowned. "That is not possible on Kerasím."

"Of course it is. You just have to do it. You did it to me; why are Kerasi females any different? I was a female student with male teachers, and I wasn't harmed, I was taught. Someone somewhere knew I could learn, and they told you to teach me. I never planned to become a diplomat; I filled the position you created me for. I never wanted to fire a weapon, but now your news says your people want my head. I must learn to defend myself or I'll die. It's very simple, really."

Tokh nodded. "That may be truth, one you will need in the coming days. Nadigh is sorting out his forces. Once he has amassed enough troops he trusts, Nadigh will take control and all will be settled."

"I want to make a statement to him, that I recognize him to be the one true leader of Kerasím, and pledge my loyalty to him and no other pretenders."

"No. Don't be seen on camera, anywhere. I will relay your message."

"But..."

Tokh stopped walking. They were by the wall at the far end of the property, overlooking the hillside where the land tumbled down into the sea. A breeze blew upward, shook the twisted red-leafed trees clinging to the hillside and whipped at their hair, flapping Tokh's unclipped chin hank. "I forbid it. I didn't want to distress you further with too much information. One hundred sixty five people died yesterday in the attack at Derahl Nohr, between weaponry and panic. Nineteen Union officials survived the attack, and four of their security guards. Three died later of injuries, leaving sixteen officials. You are the only one unaccounted for, and that has created speculation and multiple bounties, men looking for favor from the new Emperor. The problems begin in that they will hunt you down

254

allegedly for the bounty, but in reality to dispose of you. You are at extreme risk, and you must maintain absolute secrecy."

The Emissary lifted her head in alarm. "If they're hunting for me, every second I'm here I put your home at risk. I have to go back."

"I am working on that," Tokh said. "Most likely I will send you out to Yomebor, where one of my sons will meet you and keep you secure. It's a risky distance, but Yomebor is far from the capital. You should be safer."

Aila bowed her head. "I thank you most deeply."

The gravity of the situation ate at Tokh. He wanted to be down in Keranihn, at his office, helping rip open the minds of the men being detained. That was his job, that was where he belonged, that was the information he himself wanted to know, but he was ordered to stay put and guard the Emissary at all costs. There was a small chance they were all in danger, but no one knew where she was beyond the Emperor, so unless the line was bugged at either end, they were safe. Tokh knew his equipment was clean, and the fact that Emperor Nadigh was probably still in a saferoom on independent equipment meant he, too, was safe; it was the relays between them that couldn't be trusted. Tokh remained on his own night watch, just in case, keeping his finger on every latest development and allowing both *aghát* to rest. He roused the household before sun-up.

Mímihn bumped into everything in a nervous frenzy. She shoved a tote bag at Aila with changes of clothes. Then she stuffed food into it. Minutes later it was a tiny bottle of *flehdan* spirits and a box of herbed wafers. Halfway through breakfast she ran up the stairs and returned with a bottle of perfume and tucked it into a corner of the bag.

"Useless female!" Tokh snapped. "What in the Emperor's name does she need perfume for? She's going into hiding, not consort training!"

Mímihn was near tears. "In case she needs it!"

Zheníhda smirked over her breakfast. "Not everyone beds their way up the castes, *trixihn*."

Mímihn's cheeks turned a deep shade of bronze. She flapped her arms and made screechy percolating sounds like a *hyrak*.

Zheníhda flew from her chair, but Tokh cracked the flat of his sword on the table, silencing the room. He was too tired for nonsense. "The next sound will receive the next blow," he said, cold and powerful. Zheníhda returned to her seat. Aila put her arms around Mímihn, who began to weep.

"It's time," Tokh said.

The sky glowed with the coming of the suns. Mímihn couldn't see in the dim light, and kept a hand on Aila as they left the house. To cloud their trail, Haghíde and Masákh would accompany Aila to a fishing boat that would take them to their transport, three villages up the coast.

The Emissary bid goodbye to the children, thanked Zheníhda for her hospitality, and was crushed by a hug from Mímihn.

Aila stood before Tokh and bowed. "You confuse me, General Tokh. Last time, you reveled in my pain and fear. Now, you show me every hospitality of an old friend. I'm most grateful to you, but I fear I'll never understand your people."

Tokh clapped his hand on her shoulder as if she were one of his officers, and in many ways she was. His house, his rank, his very success was the result of what she had been able to achieve for him, no different than his *aghát*. She honored him; the least he could do was honor her. "What I did wasn't against you, the person. I acted as I felt the situation needed. You broke orders, I enforced them. No malice was intended. Not much, perhaps. You would be a brave warrior even if you weren't female. My house is always open to you."

Aila bowed again. "I thank you most graciously, Lord. You are a most honorable host."

It was too early for traffic noises, or for others in the neighborhood to be up and about. The higher the caste, the later they rose. Tokh's ears caught a faint sound above the background noises of the land, the distant hiss of waves, the chirps and squeals of wildlife, the rustle of leaves in the breeze. A high-pitched whine, growing louder. He tipped his head, listening, and his eyes scanned the brightening sky. He moved the Emissary aside and stepped forward. The *aghát* looked up and studied the sky as well.

"What?" Mímihn pleaded at the silence. "What is it? I can't see."

256

Inside the house, an alarm began to whoop from the perimeter sensors.

Dark dots appeared against the pale mint sky. Tokh pointed. "There! Inside! Everyone inside!"

No one moved. Three dots were growing rapidly larger, bearing straight at them.

"Vorex-class Daggers!" Tokh shouted. He shoved the Emissary toward the house. "Get under cover!" The females ran.

The first shots hit the far edge of the property. Plasma strafes pounded the grounds, blasting holes in the shadowy gardens, the paved walks and patios, the pergola drenched in the red-flowered *whenir* vines. Shots landed in the pool, vaporizing clouds of water that hung foggy and gray in the thin light. They raked across the courtyard where everyone had been standing just moments before. As the craft flew off, one last blast struck Tokh's landing pad. His precious aircraft exploded in a fireball.

Tokh stood like a statue in the destruction of his front yard, watching the craft depart as chunks of ash and aircraft rained down around him. "No markings at all, and no deviation from course. It's a warning, meant to frighten me." He raised his sword to the sky and bellowed, "I declared my loyalty! Long live Emperor Nadigh!"

He turned to the travelers by the house, coughing on the cloud of smoke from the burning 'craft. "The neighbors will be here any second to see what happened! Don't waste a distraction! Go!"

* * 35 * *

Dalo refused to go outside, keeping Faelihn and Niboh next to her and jumping at every loud noise, but Tokh and his family wandered outside after the last of the neighbors left, surveying the damage. The aircraft blaze had been put out by the fire service; it was a complete loss. Thrit was already at work, counting paving stones that would need replacing, pulling down the burnt timbers of the arbor and crispy *whenir* vines. The pool seemed to have escaped damage, though it needed to be refilled. Soot and debris from the arbor bobbed on the surface, and it would need scouring. Tokh ordered the boys to help Thrit. He looked down at Kesseh holding tight to Mimihn's hand, thought about the implications, and said, "Kesseh, go help them."

Zheníhda ruffled in an instant. "Tokh! What do you mean? She is a female child of a *dihnarwharl*. She doesn't do yard work. Nor should she be working alongside a male servant. What if the neighbors see her?"

Tokh glared at her. "Do you not wander outside and stick flowers in the dirt? You, wife of a high-*dihnarwharl* general of Imahlva? Do you not stand by servants and order them?"

"Well, yes, but ..."

"Then why can't my daughter, who is closer to the dirt, stick a flower back in the ground? I didn't order her to cart stones or haul my aircraft, just help as she is able. She can turn a tap on and off to fill the pool. Let her scoop the debris from it with the net. That will leave Thrit free to do the heavier tasks."

"It's not proper!"

"I don't care what's 'proper' anymore!" Tokh shouted. "I've worked on the Emperor's goal for female progress for almost fifteen years! And what's good for the Emperor is good enough for me! Why should a Union child be more educated and more capable than a Kerasi one? Their females pilot the stars! I have three sons and one daughter, and I know that my daughter is no less capable than my sons. I'll raise her with the same education and the same goals, and she'll surpass all other females. When Nadigh's reforms come to pass, *my* daughter will already be in position to take power, where all other females will need years to catch up. My daughter will help rule this world, just like my emissary helps rule hers, just like the Emperor's daughter will rule his. If you don't like it, then go inside and twist your hands. That is my word, and that will be my law! What Joralan does, so will Kesseh."

"She'll never have a husband that way!" Zheníhda hissed. "She'll be lonely and hate you all her days!"

"On the contrary," Tokh said. He pulled a piece of smoking trellis down and rolled it out with his boot. "Those of high position will be the first to beg for her, because she'll have power. You'll see."

Mímihn served Tokh his lunch at the table. At the other end, Zheníhda was coaxing food into one-year old Niboh. From back in the office came a chiming beep.

Tokh lifted his head and looked at the time. "Too early. They have not arrived yet."

Mímihn rubbed his shoulders. "Then ignore it. You can take a break from your war games long enough to take some food. A general is mortal, too."

Zheníhda rolled her eyes toward them. "Not if you listen to him."

The chime repeated, a higher, insistent pitch painful to the ear. Tokh slid his chair back. "I must take it." Mímihn gave an annoyed sigh and sat by her plate to wait for his return. His voice carried loud from the other room, and she rose to stand by his doorway instead.

"What do you mean, went down?" he barked.

"Asabar 6195 was shot down over Bhon," Kitras said on the screen. "Scan picked up a human on board. They followed every procedure to the letter. Someone knew. Tracking showed the craft stationary on the ground for several minutes before it was blown up."

Tokh's copper face paled to a sickly mustard. "What! Survivors?"

"At least two," Kitras confirmed. "Someone hit the emergency beacon after the crash. We've picked up locator pings from Masákh and Tótoghar, moving in different directions."

"He wouldn't have left her," Tokh said. "Heading?"

"One toward Bhon, one circling northward."

Tokh split his screen, opened a map of the area, pulled it in tighter. "A decoy. She's still alive, or they wouldn't have bothered. Are you still in Bihndorahl?"

"Yes."

"Where is General's One?"

"With General Rhigandir at the moment."

"I'll speak with Rhigandir. Get to Bhon immediately, find out what's going on. Infiltrate anything suspicious. Have General's One set up shop there; scan all levels, leave nothing unmonitored. Get them off the street at all costs. Make Masákh the priority. There's a military hangar twenty minutes north; land there. I'll arrange transport from there."

Kitras gave a sharp nod. "It will be done, General. With flight, we should be there in two hours."

"Like a rocket, Kitras. The Emperor wants her alive."

Tokh cut the call and paged General Rhigandir. Rhigandir had his trust. Enough to trust him with his son, though perhaps not quite enough to trust him with too much information. Trust on Kerasím was a very dangerous thing. "Rhigandir! What's going on? Why are my men being shot from the skies on your watch? This isn't a good time to be making enemies."

Rhigandir was a good ten years older than Tokh, and every day of it showed. He bowed his head and raised his hands in supplication. "Forgive me, Tokh. We don't know why. It wasn't my men. The order came from a *fáhganid*, that's all we know. No one will question a *fáhganid*, not even you or me."

"Bihndorahl is Perdihlon Vor's territory. He doesn't care what goes through his air, as long as his supply of *dhurwah* isn't interrupted."

"Perdihlon's at Derahl Nohr, with the rest of the *fáhganid*," Rhigandir said. "That's the problem; all the governors and magistrates went to the palace for the celebration. There's a complete void of power out in the regions. No one's realized it, or there would be riots. Perdihlon will pass interrogation; he knows nothing and his loyalty follows his liquor. I don't see any such order coming from him."

Ideas swirled through Tokh's head. "Where there's weakness, there's opportunity. I'm sure with the right amount of *dhurwah* he'll be happy to tell someone what he knows. Is there a master list of who went to the palace? Who has returned? Anyone still there we have connection to? Perhaps they'll exchange information for a speedy release."

"I'll work on it," Rhigandir swore. "Anyone who's returned is sitting silent, pretending they aren't home. At least five *fáhganid* were executed. Some are screaming at the *bhísroti* to do something, others are dumping files and bank accounts to make themselves clean. The *bhísroti* aren't about to help them; they're in the same danger. They're all trying to distance themselves from each other, in case they ever raised a glass with someone who's drawn Nadigh's ire."

Tokh nodded. He had access to the databases listing all *fáhganid*; that was a privilege of a general. The list of those executed would be available on news waves. He'd put out his feelers and see who had escaped the immediate purges. He'd find out who downed his craft, but it had to be fast. It would be a sleepless night.

"Get my men to Bhon as fast as physically possible," Tokh told Rhigandir, "and I'll share my information with you before midnight. Tokh out."

Tokh sat at his desk and thought long and hard. He could rationalize the scare-bombing of his yard as a random warning, but a *fáhganid* giving orders to bring down a ship meant someone was after him, or after his Emissary. There weren't many officers Tokh counted as enemies; disgruntled ones perhaps, miffed at his rapid rise in rank, his success, his house, or his weak ties to the Emperor, but he was unaware of anyone who might wish him actual harm. Were his communications being monitored, or were someone else's? He needed to know if his family was in danger or just his emissary. Tokh had personal contacts with four *fáhganid*s, one or two of whom he somewhat trusted. He called up an old security code, set it to scramble, and sent to an old access number.

Tokh's supervisor, *fáhganid* General Trannor, came on screen after almost a full minute. "Tokh dar-Giláhn, why are you using an outdated security line?"

"I don't trust anything current, and I know this line was exceptionally secure at the time. General, we've worked many years together and neither of us has turned the other wrong. I need information and I'm trusting you to trust me with it. My house was rake-bombed this morning, by three unmarked Vorex Daggers; my

261

wives, children, and smallchildren all home with me. Now I learn my craft has been shot down on *fáhganid* order over Bohn, one carrying the Emperor's cargo. I need answers, Trannor, and I'm not in a mood to play games to get them. What's going on? Do I need to move my family somewhere safer? And what do I tell the Emperor, when he has trusted me so? Who's behind this?"

Trannor's face froze. In one second, he gave away more information than he had over the course of the last year. In that one second, Tokh knew his superior had been caught unaware, and had no idea what was happening. In that one second, Tokh was relieved to know Trannor wasn't behind it, and still deserved his trust.

"What are we coming to? Tokh, you're my greatest success. You've done me highest honors, many times over. Please know I speak truth when I say, I have no knowledge of this. You know for certain it was on *fáhganid* order?"

"The downing of the cargo, yes, I'm certain. I know nothing about who bombed my home."

"Was your cargo damaged?"

"I don't know. It's believed to have been retrieved, secured, and rerouted at this time."

"And your home?"

"Nothing I can't fix, though my personal craft is destroyed. I can't address the situation rapidly without it."

Trannor sat back. Tokh couldn't be sure if he was trying to solve the issue or edit information. "The government is staggering, Tokh. Nadigh reigns, but there's a scramble for power; those that can shake loose competition are doing so, alliances are trading, there have been many high-level murders during the chaos. Don't see it as weakness; there's a window where Nadigh will discover who his enemies are and who he can trust. He's cut the power of the upper castes – declared both *bhísroti* and *fáhganid* castes null and void. They fall back to *dahneg*, as they were a thousand years ago. Even I am now nothing more than a *dahneg*. I needn't say that has caused tremendous outcry – but it will help sift out the dangers he's searching for. After they've slaughtered each other and he knows who's who, he'll take his throne."

It was Tokh's turn to stop breathing. "That's unprecedented. The backlash will want his head."

"It's a change in title, nothing more; the rest is simply prejudice. We're caste-heavy, and it's hurting us. In time, he'll consolidate more castes, pull us back to a handful, ease the restrictions that limit good workers, make the *bhísroti* actually work for their privilege. Merge the *ghinadín* back with *soláhrin*, which will prove his efforts to the Union. Give it time."

Trannor sighed. "Bohn falls in Perdilon's territory, but he remains at the palace. He's been cleared of wrongdoing. He may be *fáhganid* – may *have* been *fáhganid*," he corrected himself, "but he has no spine. He wouldn't attack my men even on someone else's order. I would assume it's someone who knows of your involvement with the cargo. That's a wide net, but not impossible to untangle. I'll work on that. What's your goal for the cargo?"

"Secure and wait for the decision on where it should be restored."

"Be careful, Tokh. Keep only to what you trust most. Consider all communication compromised. I'll keep you informed on a channel I trust."

Tokh bowed his head to the screen. "Thank you, General."

Tokh slept very little. He *pushed* neither of his wives, didn't sleep in his bed but dozed in the chair in his office, one ear on his monitors. Zheníhda and Mímihn brought him food and kept the children outside to give him quiet.

"Come eat with us at the table," Zheníhda insisted at dinner. "There's nothing more you can do right now. Sitting here won't make things happen any faster, it just makes you sick. You need to walk around, get your blood flowing."

"It will be dark soon in Bohn." He tapped over to a screen that told him the current time and weather in Imahlva and the time and weather in Bohn. "The last known signal was two hours ago. I have men on the way but they won't be in position until after dark. Masákh knows how to go underground, but there's no way of knowing who is trustworthy at the moment. If he goes silent, we won't have a chance until sun-up. That's a long time when you don't know who is after you. *KHRRR!*" he growled in frustration.

He did appear for a few *fasim* to gulp down his dinner with the family before running back to the monitors. The boys watched him from the doorway, silent as dust, until he invited them in and showed them what he was doing. He spent a second sleepless night before the silent monitors. After dawn he got word the first half of his team had been recovered unharmed; one less worry, but it wasn't until just before lunch that another message came in on short-scramble.

G2 retrieved with cargo intact; no damages. Will hold pending further instruction.

His yell brought most of the household running.

"Did you find your Great Lady, *Bo*?" Kesseh asked.

"Are they okay?" Mímihn held her breath, afraid of the answer.

Tokh slumped back in his chair, face to the ceiling, exhausted to his bones. "Mátokhan has retrieved them. They're uninjured. He'll keep them there at Rhigandir's safehouse until we're given instruction. They're fine."

Mímihn squeezed her hands together. "Praise the Emperor! Give my thanks to General Rhigandir as well."

Tokh nodded wearily. No general anywhere gave two farts what another general's wife thought.

"Good," Zheníhda said, entering the office. She waved a hand toward the wall of switches. "The crisis is over. They're safe, they're sheltered, and you can rest with a clear conscience. Turn all of this off and take yourself to bed for a few hours. You'll need to be rested for the next crisis."

Tokh closed his eyes and nodded. "I think I will."

Tokh did exactly that. Zheníhda "forgot" to wake him until seven hours had gone by. Tokh checked his messages but there were few, and none important. He spent the rest of the afternoon conferencing, making arrangements and sending orders.

"We'll bring her back," he told the household. "It's safer than anywhere else. In a worst-case scenario, with a single call I can have an air squadron here in half an hour or less."

"All the same, I'll sleep down here on a sofa," Zheníhda said. "If the house blows up, I want to be able to run outside before it collapses on me."

Tokh waved everyone away. "Gah. Everyone sleeps in their own bed. We'll be fine. They'll be driving back, and it'll take them an entire day. They won't arrive until tomorrow evening, so everyone can sleep well tonight."

Sleep he did. Tokh *pushed* Mímihn just once, then slept like the dead. It was a quiet day, and he crept out of his office for a half-hour at a time. Emperor Nadigh had taken his throne, a handful of officers and ministers beside him. Many were those of his father or from his family: two uncles, his brother Moragh, and in her first official appearance, his daughter Rimas, standing stern beside him, now publicly named as the Heir Apparent, sparking outrage around the globe and making lawmakers rumble. Rimas was a powerful figure, as tall as Zheníhda but with shoulders that would have done a male proud. For a sturdy female of almost forty years, she wasn't harsh to look at. Her brown hair had pink stripes, yes, but it was pulled tight from her face, controlled and sleek. A weapon belt circled her hips; she wore *Emperor's Revenge*, the sword of the Heir, its ancient hilt covered in chasing and jewels. Her husband stood by, pale and weak-looking, a former-*bhísroti* investor, but Tokh didn't know yet if he was an inner council member or just an escort for his wife. Tokh hadn't expected to see real reform in his lifetime; now, in a matter of days, the order of Kerasím had spun from its foundation, the power of the elite had been cut, high castes eliminated, and a female put in line for the throne – changes that should have collapsed the regime, but still the sun rose and set, and regular citizens went about their business as if nothing had happened. Even General Trannor didn't seem phased by his demotion to *dahneg*.

Tokh felt old and out of touch. The world was changing faster than he could keep up, in ways he hadn't anticipated. He doubled his resolve; if there was to be a female Emperor, she would no doubt want female advisors as well, and Kesseh would be ready and waiting, whether Zheníhda approved or not.

265

* * 36 * *

After the children were in bed, or at least sent up stairs for the night, Tokh settled in by his monitors. He flicked on a surveillance channel, and just inside range a small orange dot appeared. His satellite tracking had a reach of sixty or seventy *nalis* from the house. The blip was Masákh's vehicle; it moved steadily closer, perhaps an hour out. In the kitchen, he could hear his females putting together a late meal for the guests.

He put the monitor on a small corner screen and sent messages to his supervisors. An emergency alarm shrieked under his hands, startling him. His eye glanced at the surveillance monitor; the vehicle was still thirty or forty *fasim* out, but the signal was coming from Masákh.

Tokh slammed the receiver on, only to hear incoherent shrieking. "This is Tokh! Report!"

His calmest, most reserved and proper *aghát* could barely form words. "Gone! They took her! We've got to get her! No time! We've got to get her! I'll kill them! I'll kill them straight up to the Emperor!"

"Took who? When? Where? Soldier! At attention! Report!"

"I have to get her!"

"SOLDIER! REPORT!"

Masákh's voice shook with emotion. "Roadblock. They hit us with a magnetic dart. Four men, minimum. Gurih got off a shot but they hit us with control sticks. They shoved her into a transport and took off. They'll kill her!"

Tokh's breath left him, and his chest squeezed so tight that it hurt. *No no no no. Not now. Not so close to safety.* "What kind? Markings? Anything, Masákh?"

"Big, a – a room on wheels. It's dark. We're losing time! General, we've got to move now! I've got to follow them. Gurih's with the vehicle. I'm following on foot; I'll get a head start."

"Stay with Gurih!" Tokh ordered. There was no reply. "Major, stay with the vehicle! That's an order!" The link clicked off. Tokh tried three times to re-establish contact, but Masákh wouldn't answer. Tokh shrieked a growl and hit several buttons. "I need air and ground support, emergency speed, accompanying coordinates. Authorization encryption attached. Speed is critical; repeat, speed is critical. Receive further instructions at intercept."

"Confirmed, General Tokh. Intercept scrambling now," said the voice at the other end.

Tokh closed that line and paged Gurih, the driver assigned to transporting Masákh and the Emissary. "Gurih, report! What happened?"

Gurih repeated the same story, calmer and with more small details.

"Where's Masákh?"

"He took off," Gurih said. "He said he was pursuing and ran after the truck. Even if it were daylight, there's no way he could catch up – they had a full five-*fasím* jump on us."

Tokh swore something fierce. "Stay with the vehicle. When the rescue arrives, pick up Masákh, put him under detention, relieve him of his weapons, and get back here immediately. Instruct air support to scan the area, look for large trucks, warehouses, factories, depots, anywhere a large truck might not be noticed. Make note, inform me at once. Tokh out." He took a deep breath, steadied himself, and hit the button to make a call to General Trannor, emergency priority. If only he'd had enough time to grab a glass of something strengthening first.

An hour passed before running lights turned into his yard. Two security officers emerged from the front of the vehicle; Masákh and Gurih from the back. Tokh met them in the courtyard. Masákh dropped to his knees before Tokh, head bent. If it were possible for a Kerasi soldier to sob, Masákh was making a strong attempt. His voice was that of a broken man.

"I respectfully submit myself for disciplinary action. I allowed my personal feelings to interfere with my duty which is unacceptable behavior for an officer. I disobeyed a direct order and abandoned a fellow officer. I have surrendered my weapons and submit that I be relieved of duty due to overwhelming emotional conflict at this time."

Tokh stared down at Masákh's head. Disregard for his order felt like a betrayal from a trusted friend, direct contempt when Tokh

267

needed help the most. He understood Masákh's emotional involvement, but it didn't excuse his behavior. Masákh was a Kerasi officer, first and foremost. The world was crumbling around them and Tokh needed every one of his officers in top form. He fought the urge to kick Masákh in the face.

"Remove your uniform," he growled. Masákh shrugged out of his jacket and folded it on his knees. Tokh walked behind him with a disgusted swagger, and in one swift move removed his incentive rod, telescoped it open and delivered five strokes across Masákh's shoulders, not sparing his strength. Masákh grunted with each but didn't shrink away. Blood seeped through his shirt.

"Rise, and get inside," Tokh spat. "You're an officer of the Kerasi army, sworn to the Emperor himself. You will control yourself as such. Your world is in crisis and needs every loyal officer; you will not be relieved of duty on my watch."

Zheníhda and Mímihn had food and drink laid out. Tokh motioned the officers to the table. He put his arm out to stop Masákh. "You may eat in the kitchen with the servants." Masákh bowed wordlessly and turned.

Zheníhda gasped. "Major, you're bleeding! Come! Come in here and I'll see to you."

"I'm fine," Masákh insisted.

"I won't have blood on my furniture, so unless you plan to sleep outside, you'll be attended to."

She and Mímihn helped him out of his shirt as he sat. "Mímihn will get some healing cream, while I get some water."

When she gathered all the materials, Zheníhda realized she couldn't help him. To touch the bare skin of another male was unacceptable, and Tokh was obviously mad at him and wouldn't help, either.

"I'll do it," Mímihn said. "I can do it without making contact." She picked up the wiping cloth and wrung it out.

Zheníhda grabbed her hand. "You are wife, not consort. You will not."

Mímihn bowed and put the cloth back into the water. "You're correct, Firstwife."

"Call Thrit." Thrit hurried in as fast as he could, wiped down the officer's wounds, and dressed them with antiseptic.

"Do you have another shirt, Major?" Zheníhda asked, but he shook his head. "I'll see what I can find for you." Mímihn brought him a plate of food and a glass of *flehdan* on ice. He bowed his head in thanks.

Tokh chewed Masákh out before releasing him to bed, but in private. He knew Masákh's feelings for the girl ran deep. He'd promised her to him years ago, but the Union had retrieved her before Masákh could take possession. Masákh had been playing things the Union way for the last four years, keeping her at his fingertips, turning her heart toward him, waiting for her to come of legal age in the Union. He'd come so very close to having her, his heart now as committed as his loins, only for her to be stolen by his own people. The Union didn't execute prisoners, but Kerasi wouldn't think twice.

Masákh kept his head bent and wouldn't look Tokh in the eye. "With all due respect, General, I would prefer to remain on duty and wait for information. I won't sleep."

"Then lie there and think of who would have a stake in her kidnapping," Tokh said. "Those above are following paths I can't. This isn't just a Kerasi issue, Masákh. Someone has been killing the remaining Union delegates right under the Emperor's thumb. Three have died, one has been kidnapped, now two, and the Emperor is livid. He insists it didn't come from our people, that the Union is killing their own, but he hasn't been able to prove it. He looks guilty, refusing to turn over the dignitaries while they die, but it would look worse if he made unsubstantiated claims that the Union was behind it. There must be teamwork here, to the highest levels, with much funding supporting them. You work behind the scenes in Union space. You know many of their officials. Open your mind to suspicions. Aila's well-known both here and in the Union, creating the perfect target. We'll find her, but I know it won't be tonight. Go. Rest. You'll need to be at your best in the morning."

"General, I don't mean to question your integrity, but what if we can't trust your superiors?"

Tokh sighed painfully. "Do you not think that hasn't crossed my mind? We never know the role we play until the game is finished. I have known Trannor almost fifteen years; he's always supported me. My successes are his as well, and he knows it. I must have faith in him, Masákh. He's very close to Nadigh. If he proves false, then

269

Nadigh's rule is already forfeit and we'll wind up in an interstellar conflict and lose three thousand years of culture and progress, because we can't win that war. Faith, Masákh. It's all we can feed off, some days. Rest. Implore the Fortunes if you choose. I'll take any advantage I can get right now."

Tokh spent the night in his office once more, but got more sleep than he'd hoped. There was little chatter on the comm. Of higher priority was the disappearance of the Union's top representative, the Secretary Kel, right out of his palace room. Two palace guards escorted him from his room and left the grounds without anyone questioning them. No one recognized the guards. Arch-General Six, The Most Revered General Ruligh Var, Director of Securities and Information, had no fewer than ten units of men working on the issue; Tokh's own son Kitras was one of the operatives on the trail of both missing dignitaries; he was the only one with his skill set who spoke Union. It confirmed Tokh's belief that learning Union was crucial for his younger children.

The morning brought no better news. Gurih and the two security officers returned to their posts. Tokh's *aghát* Haghíde and Tótoghar arrived at the house. Surveillance gave them aerial views of everything within sixty *nalis* of the kidnap site; the number of possibilities was in the thousands. Tokh tasked Masákh with eliminating the least likely buildings, and sending ground crews to check some of the more likely candidates. There was nothing, not even gossip on the unsecured lines or on coded channels Tokh knew how to decrypt. Trannor was just as stumped but had narrowed the field of likely candidates. There were only so many *fáhganid*. Once he weeded out those who were loyal, those that were hiding to avoid notice, and those who protested loudly against the Emperor but whose hot breath disappeared when shadows loomed, he had trimmed his list to eight possibilities. Four of those still hovered at the palace. Two were entrenched in their homes under tight security. One had been away from home on a vacation, and one was unaccounted for. Trannor focused his remarkable reach on those two. Even if unaccounted for, communications and bank transactions would paint a reliable picture. Everything came down to waiting.

Deep into the night, Tokh's communication station chirped for him. He roused from a heavy doze and hit the switch. The message was on a privately encrypted signal, for Tokh only.

Kitras's voice whispered to him from the darkness. "General! Your Emissary is here!"

Tokh's heart raced, and he awoke to full alert in a single second. "Where? You're certain? Alive?"

"I've infiltrated the officers guarding the Secretary Kel. We tracked him here, but they're holding your Emissary as well. I've seen her. She's in a separate cell, bound and under heavy guard. It's right in the open; there's no sneaking her out. She's well, but the gossip is that it's not for long. The *fáhganid* in charge is General Banukh. He plans to make an example of her. I don't know how or what or when, but I think it's soon, and I don't think she's meant to survive it."

Banukh kal fier Sanehl, the missing suspect who'd fallen off the planet. Tokh hit switches, pinpointing locators and recording information. Kitras's position was just thirty *nalis* away. "Keep her safe as best you can, above all else. She's a brave one; she'll help you if you can get word to her. I need twelve hours to get a rescue in place. Get me that time. General, out." He sent a wake-up call to his men with one hand and woke up General Trannor with the other.

Tokh and his men met with General Trannor, General Angh, and a mere handful of other trusted leaders at a military facility an hour north of Imahlva. Just six hours remained of Tokh's timeline, and Kitras was increasingly nervous at each update. Speed was imperative, but a botched rescue was worse than no rescue at all.

The suns rose while they pored over maps. Between what brief bits Kitras sent, and the information Trannor had access to, they had not only the layout of the neighborhood but a plan of the inside of the vacant factory building as well.

"This is the corridor where Kitras says she's being held," Tokh pointed. "This room, but sometimes this one, which has visual access to the rest of the floor. If Banukh sees you, he could kill her."

"I can drop a team onto the roof, no problem," Tótoghar said. "It's a clear shot, nothing surrounding it. If I have a Whysperlyte, I can hover right overhead and they won't hear me. They'll still see me coming, so someone's going to have to take out sensors."

"Jamming is easy," Tokh mumbled, his thoughts elsewhere.

271

"I will lead the rescue," Masákh said. Anger had taken over his despair, and his clear-headed thinking had returned.

"No."

Masákh's eyes blazed with a golden light. 'General, I can do this. I'll lead the rescue."

Tokh stared back, solid and immovable as a cliff face. "You're a diplomat, Masákh. I need someone who can direct action, not sit around a table and discuss the problem."

"I've led your *aghát* team for five years, with and without direct supervision. I've faced unknown enemies, battles – I have more tactical and weapons decorations than any other team member. What more do I have to prove?"'

Tokh pursed his lips. Masákh was correct, but he hadn't commanded a true battle in ten years, perhaps. He was long out of practice. And he was under reprimand for insubordination. On the other hand, the Emissary would fight her way to him if necessary. "We'll divide the rescue into two units. Unit one will see to securing the building and taking down the troops within. Angh, that will be your men. Unit two will consist of six personnel who will be responsible for securing three targets: the Perrin female, the Union Secretary Kel, and General Banukh, whom you'll detain for questioning on order of Emperor Nadigh himself. You may lead that party."

"I'll second him," Haghíde said. "We were trained together, we know how to move together. Aila trusts both of us. We both know the parties involved and can speak Union."

"The Secretary Kel is to be taken alive," General Trannor decreed. "Nadigh wants him for interrogation. He'll release all other Union delegates once he has Kel in custody."

Tokh gave a nod of agreement. "It will be done. Kitras will lead you in once you arrive. Trannor's officers have more specialized training; they'll cover you. You get in, get the girl, get the Secretary, get out. If you can isolate and restrain Banukh, General Trannor will be waiting to move in and take him for questioning after the building is secured. Your orders come from General Five Trannor, *fáhganid-dahneg*, *Tansohr Keralihn*, by order of the Emperor, and that supersedes Banukh's rights. Don't fall for him pulling caste on you. Understood?"

"Girl, Secretary, secure general if possible," Masákh confirmed, and Haghíde repeated it.

"We'll be monitoring from a mobile comm station, half a *nali* out," General Angh said. "Grab your gear; we rendezvous two *nalis* from target with the rest of the team. We'll go over the final approach there."

Sitting back was the hardest thing for Tokh to do. He was a man of action, always had been. He was used to being in the thick of things, but Generals didn't get dirty; they sent other men to do the dirty work. He wanted to be the dirty one again, especially on this mission. He had trust in his men. He'd trained them himself, knew they wouldn't fail, but he had no idea what they were up against. Right or wrong, his best men were on the line. It was their lives, it was the life of his emissary, the life of a Union official, and worse yet, the life of his son, long before the needs of the Emperor came into play. If his team was the one to rescue all of them... the Emperor would likely be quite grateful, perhaps even supply a new aircraft. All Tokh could do was sit back with the other commanders inside the cramped surveillance vehicle and wait.

Time ticked. The lead officer in Angh's assault division was wired; they heard the okays, the countdown, and the opening attack, catching the people in the building by surprise. Shouts and orders were given on both sides, panicked yells and weaponfire, but in a way it made things worse. The officer had a camera wire, but the view was foggy from smoke bombs and it wasn't the action Tokh wanted to follow. One by one the assault division called secure to their sector as those still alive surrendered and were bound on the ground. Of Tokh's men, Haghíde was wired, but his visual stopped working early on. The shouts and conversations coming through made no sense. Shots were fired, and glass broke. Tokh could pick out the higher voice of his emissary shrieking in the background, and once or twice caught the sound of Kitras's voice. There were too many sounds of weaponfire, of yelling, and the deep thumps of sturdy objects being banged or broken. Tokh sweated on the edge of his seat, desperate for information.

When the noises stopped, he pointed at the comm. "Update."

"Report on hostage situation," General Angh said to his man.

"Unknown," said Angh's officer. "There's a lot of smoke. I can't tell from here. Hold on." There was movement, some mumbling between officers, then another voice came on the mic.

273

"Hohnar reporting, sir. I can't get close. They're in an office that took a lot of fire. I think there's an officer down. They've got medical working on him right now."

"Is the female alive?" Angh said at Tokh's prompt.

"From what I can see, yes. One of the officers is holding her. They're going to airlift the wounded in a few."

"Keep us posted," Angh said.

Fifteen agonizing *fasim* passed before Haghíde buzzed the com. "Report!" Tokh spat the word out so fast he bit his tongue.

It was difficult to hear; by the background noise they were in a rotored aircraft. The weepy moans of a female in distress were loud in the com's pickup, overpowering the audio, while other voices carried on in the background. Haghíde had to shout to be heard. "Mission accomplished, General. Aila Perrin is secured. Colonel Kassán was also prisoner and is also secured. Arch-General Banukh is dead by the hand of Secretary Kel. Secretary Kel is dead by the hand of the Emissary. Emissary Perrin has minor wounds and will be routed to the closest female hospital for treatment. Masákh is wounded. Colonel Kassán says the injuries are serious but not life-threatening. Closest hospital is three *fasim*."

Tokh absorbed the news with a strange detachment. "And Kitras? What about Kitras?"

"He's aboard, unharmed, and will accompany Masákh to treatment."

Tokh's sigh of relief took every molecule of air from his lungs. He bent over and rested his head on the communication console, drained of energy. "Keep me informed when situation stabilizes. Tokh out."

It was well after dark by the time Tokh finished inspecting the facility, met with Trannor, congratulated his men, checked in on Masákh and Kitras, and ended his day retrieving Haghíde and the Perrin girl from the Hospital for Female Concerns. He burst into the room, only to be taken aback. Haghíde sat on the hospital bed, the Perrin girl before him, the strongest, smartest female Tokh had ever met. Haghíde's arms were around her, a forbidden physical contact. The girl was covered with small cuts, her wrists dark with bruises, her face marked from a blow at some point. She shook as if caught in a groundquake, making breathy sobbing noises with each shiver.

274

Tokh's eyebrow peaked with inquiry; Haghíde shook his head. He tried to release her, but she shrieked and clawed at him until he resumed holding her.

Tokh had no idea what to do or say. What was appropriate to a Kerasi female might not be appropriate to a Union one. He didn't know how to judge the subtle behaviors of a Human. He stuck to what he knew best.

Tokh bent forward and clapped his hand on her shoulder. "You are the bravest of brave, my female warrior. I've been told your aim is to be feared after all. I came to bring you to safety. Mimi is most excited for your return. My craft is waiting. Come."

The Perrin girl never focused on him, never looked in his direction, but she reached out and put her arms around his middle, a most improper contact. Haghíde released her. Tokh stiffened, certain she meant something in a Union way, not a Kerasi one, though he didn't understand. He smiled with embarrassment, prompted her to let go, but she didn't move. After a moment with no improvement, he bowed his head, lifted her in his arms, and carried her from the building without a word.

37

Mímihn ran outside at the first sounds of incoming aircraft, darting spotlight to spotlight. Dalo followed only a few yards behind, desperation swelling her heart. Zheníhda brought up the rear, less anxious about the arrivals but needing to know how many men might be staying the night. Mímihn bounced on her toes, hair whipping about her face as Trannor's borrowed craft came to rest on the landing pad and the engines died back. The door opened and the steps deployed, spilling light into a circle. Tokh was the first down them, no worse for wear, then several of his officers. The women bowed, but only in brief greeting.

"Kitras?" Dalo said with an agony of hope.

Tokh pushed her hair from her kohled eyes and chucked her under her chin. "Uninjured. He's with Masákh. He sends you his heart, and a promise that he'll call you tonight as soon as things settle."

"Where's Ai-lah?" Mímihn asked, then recoiled as Haghíde appeared. He walked backwards down the steps, holding both of Aila's hands, coaxing her to move her feet. Aila made it to the ground, then sank to her knees and pulled her arms over her head. Every so often she'd gasp Masákh's name in a soft hiccup. Mímihn knelt by her, ran a hand over Aila's hair, then glanced at Tokh in horror.

"Tokh, where's Masákh?"

"Injured. He was out of surgery when I saw him. His injuries aren't serious," Tokh said.

"What did they do to her?!"

"I'm still getting reports on that. I'll give you information when I know it. Haghíde, carry her upstairs."

Mímihn skipped and hopped around him as Haghíde lifted Aila and brought her inside. "Put her in my room. I'll watch over her. I'll stay with her." She bounded up the stairs ahead of the crowd and pulled down the satin covers to her bed. The Emissary felt the bed touch her and let loose a terrified scream. She clawed and slapped at

Haghíde until he let go. Aila ran until she hit the wall, then sank down to the floor.

Mímihn was on her a second later. "Aila! Aila! *Shu!* It's Mimi! Just Mimi! You're with friends. You're safe now. You're safe. It's over. *Shu!* Hold me! I've got you. Haghíde, how do I say that in her language? How do I tell her she's safe?"

"*You are safe. You are unharmed.*"

Mímihn repeated it several times. *"Yuar sehf, Aila. Yuar sehf. Yuar un hahrmt."* She held Aila tight, rubbing her arms, kissing her hair, crooning to her. Aila's sobs softened.

"What did they do to her!" Mímihn's hand caressed the bruised cheeks, touched the little cuts on Aila's hands. Her eyes filled with tears when she saw the bruises from restraint cuffs circling the wrists. "Oh, Tokh! How badly was she assaulted?"

A look of pain flashed over Tokh's face. "According to Kitras, she remained untouched, but they planned to turn her loose with five men at once. She was aware of the plan. Kitras said they got to her with only five *fasim* to spare."

Mímihn gave a moan of pain and squeezed Aila tighter. Dalo picked up Aila's hand and rubbed it. "I can fix this. Dalo, bring me strong spirits. Zeníhda, fill a hot bath." Dalo sprinted out the door.

"What would you know of nursing?" Zeníhda sneered. "She needs rest, not a bath."

Sparks seemed to fly from Mímihn's lips even as tears fell from her eyes. She shook almost as much as Aila. "I know this, *Hyrak*! I know this too well! I spent eight weeks in consort training. Older females understood, but sometimes they'd bring in little girls, just legal. They were so young, with grand dreams of *bhísroti* finery and romance, no idea at all. The first day of breaking, they'd be put with eight or ten men. They'd return like this. The strong ones could be talked back. Some of them never recovered. Every week at least one would kill themselves. Knives were counted after meals, so one night this tiny little girl slit her throat during dinner. I'd been a wife three years; I knew what they faced. I couldn't bear to see their pain. I saved those I could, raised their spirits, taught them to be strong. Aila isn't one who gives up. I'll pull her through this. This I can do without my eyes. Now do as I say, Old Wife! The bath is for her spirit, to wash away the bad things. When the bad is gone, she'll rest with peace."

Zheníhda's mouth pinched up, but she entered Mímihn's bathroom without a word. Dalo returned, running so fast she couldn't hold the corner and smashed her shoulder into the doorframe. She knelt by Mímihn, two bottles and a glass in her hands.

"*Varvet.* Good. Pour me a little."

Dalo poured a splash and held out the glass; Mímihn tried to get Aila to drink, but when she failed, she dipped her finger in the liquid and rubbed it over Aila's gums seven or eight times.

"There. We'll let that sink in for a *fasim.* That should help enough to get her to drink."

Tokh gave her a nod. "Do your best, Mimi. I trust your care. Dalo can help you. Come, men."

"Tokh, leave me Haghíde," Mímihn called after him. "If she speaks, I must know what she says."

Tokh turned to him. "I'll stay," Haghíde said quickly. "I remain on duty as her guard."

"Ha *Ghíde*," Aila hiccupped.

Mímihn squeezed her hard. "Yes, Aila! Haghíde is here. You know he will protect you. *Yuar sehf. Khome, khome!* Dalo and I will help you into the bath. You'll feel so much better after." With her prodding and Dalo's help, Aila rose to her feet and moved with tiny steps to the other room.

All of Tokh's officers were accounted for. Masákh was improving. Reports were coming in from everywhere, including recorded video footage from Banukh's hideout, and it wasn't pretty. It was perhaps the first time Tokh had felt embarrassment at being Kerasi, and he didn't like it at all. The humiliation that Banukh put the Union emissary through, the closeness she came to a catastrophic assault, weighed heavily on him. The news wouldn't sit well with the Union, ruining the last twenty years' work and destroying the fragile peace. For the first time he saw the action not as a Kerasi male for whom females were pets with benefits, but from the victim's perspective, thought about his daughter being in such a position, or his wives, and rage rose thick and boiling through his middle. For just a second he thought about what Mímihn might have gone through in consort training, not as a divorced wife and shamed female serving a purpose but a person who was forced into such a condition against her will, hour after hour, day after day, and he

278

turned his mind away immediately. He couldn't bear to think about such things, just to realize Mímihn, and even Zheníhda, were far, far stronger than he ever gave them credit for. He thought of sweet, dreamy Umara, who never had their strength. She could endure a second marriage to a total stranger, but a single sharing was more than she could bear, and he blamed himself for not seeing it.

His Emissary wasn't faring well, though he wasn't sure why. Kitras insisted she hadn't been assaulted, but the Union girl remained silent and shaking. Tokh sought advice from Kassán, who had excellent knowledge of human body systems.

"Treat it as combat sickness," Kassán said. "I'll check my files, call you with an order for medication she can handle. It will make her sleep. Let her mind work it out on her own. I spoke to her not long before the rescue and she was quite sharp, so it's probably nothing beyond the release of stress."

True to Kassán's word, the medication helped ease the Emissary's terrors, though it was two more days before she was able to hold a rational conversation. Mímihn called him upstairs when Aila awoke; Haghíde followed.

The Emissary sat on the foot of a lounge, but didn't stand when he entered the room. She'd stopped shaking, but showed no emotion at all.

Tokh sat on the opposite lounge. "You are up from bed. That is a good sign."

"Thank you," Aila mumbled. "Thank you for rescuing me."

"You remember. That is excellent. I didn't provide much more than transportation. Haghíde brought you out."

"*Soyavoh.* Thank you."

"I would not have left you," Haghíde swore. Tokh had promised the girl to Masákh, and Mímihn swore with no uncertainty that he had the girl's heart wrapped up like a package, but Tokh wasn't blind to Haghíde's actions, either. Haghíde's heart was also drawn to her, but he lacked the confidence to say so, or perhaps he knew Masákh had claim to her. Tokh hoped it would remain just a longing. It was nice to know that if something happened to Masákh, Haghíde could probably turn her affection to him without much difficulty, but he didn't want his officers in a blood-feud over a female.

The conversation paused. A sob caught in Aila's throat, and she gave a hard shudder.

"You have combat sickness," Tokh told her. "You are strong, but even the strongest can suffer it when the battle is too intense. In ten years I have never heard a word of praise cross Kassán's teeth, yet he had choice words to say about you. That is most impressive." She sat on his lounge chair, a huddled empty mass of female human frailty, but he saw no weakness.

Aila forced herself to murmur, "All I did was plead for my life. I kept hoping, and hoping... Anything to buy time." Another sob seized her.

"I sent word to the current officials in charge to inform your parents you are safe and recovering. They would like to send people here to speak with you, check on your condition. Do you wish to speak with them?"

The Perrin girl's face scrunched up as if she were in pain. "For a short time. Tomorrow, though. Not today."

"Understandable." He stood up. "I'll leave you in Mimi's care."

The next morning the Emissary dressed on her own and came down the stairs for the first time since returning, but Tokh found her mid-morning in his sitting room, crying like an infant onto Haghíde's lap. Again he couldn't decide if it was an acceptable Union behavior, or something that might cause conflict between his men. Haghíde nudged her until she sat up and wiped her face on her hands. Haghíde stood up at Tokh's presence, but the Emissary didn't even try. Tokh let it slide.

"I apologize for the tears," she managed.

Tokh sat before her, motioned Haghíde to sit. This was a day he wasn't looking forward to. "Apology is not needed. You are still very much ill, but I'm afraid your day has become most difficult. I had several calls this morning I'm not happy with. You are scheduled to meet with your Union representatives this afternoon. However, the government of Kerasím wishes to meet with you before then, to take your statement as to what happened and question you as necessary. I informed them your condition is most delicate. They insist they'll speak with you first or the Union must wait until they do. I will do whatever I can to support you, but I cannot refuse them. I don't like this; there's no one to give you legal counsel, and I don't know what they are looking for. There is a faint but real chance that because you are not a Kerasi citizen, you could be charged with treason. You were in the presence of one believed to be

280

implicated in the death of the Emperor, and the murder of a *fáhganid*. I believe I can block that; I'm waiting for guidance. I expect an investigator here within the hour. If it is who I'm hoping, you should fare well."

Trannor was formerly *fáhganid*, a high-level investigator, *and* currently the Director of Union-Kerasi relations. It made the most sense.

Aila drew a trembling breath. "That's only fair, I guess."

Tokh returned to his office at the signaling of his comm. He'd gone back and forth between various personnel, trying to find out information, playing with various scenarios, trying to pry any information from Trannor's office he could use to his advantage, but Trannor wouldn't take his calls. By law, a non-Kerasi female had no more legal rights than a chair. She was the property of the male in charge of her, but being Union, no male had charge of her. She was a legal orphan, and that wasn't a good thing to be on Kerasím. Aila was at the mercy of the Emperor. Tokh knew how the game was played. He was the pawn between them, calming the victim, keeping her safe, pretending to understand while the powers above plotted their means to use and control her to their advantage. Tokh didn't put his life on the line for the Emissary for nothing five years ago. He didn't rescue her twice for his own entertainment. He'd grown to respect her, despite her gender, despite her race, despite her youth. She was the hope for his daughter. He couldn't feed her to the system.

One by one, his choices for aiding her were shot down by Trannor's legal aid. He had one recourse left that might or might not save her, but did he dare? It was unprecedented, therefore it left a hole in the law that had never been addressed. Would the Emissary object? Would it create an interstellar incident, even if he didn't pursue it further? It had the potential to ruin him; it also had the potential to raise him up and make him a force to be reckoned with. It all depended on the prosecution, what the Emperor was after, who was doing the interrogating, and whether or not the Emperor would execute him for overstepping his bounds and interfering in interstellar politics. Tokh couldn't decide, and the uncertainty ate at his stomach.

Aircraft circled overhead, more than should have. One touched down on the landing pad. One landed in the front courtyard. Another landed on the side grassway, crushing a border of flowers to avoid landing in the pool. Tokh and his crew watched them all from the front door. Brown *bhántim* guards came running up from the side yard, formed a perimeter, and stood at attention. From the landing pad, officers in gold uniforms marched forward, identically matched in the cut of their chin hanks, the angle of their belts, the shine of their boots stepping together so precisely it was hard to tell where one left off and the other started. They stopped at the third craft and waited at attention.

Tokh's hair prickled up. This was not a normal investigation crew. Only Imperial officers wore gold. They could seize the girl and remove her from his property and he wouldn't be allowed to utter a word about it, not even plead to Trannor. There was nowhere to hide her, and no time to do it.

The door to the final craft lowered. Two imperial *fáhganid* – now *dahneg* – servants marched forward, one to each side of the door. Tokh assumed they were the officials sent to take statements, but no.

"All kneel before her Royal Excellency, Rimas, daughter of Emperor Nadigh, Heir to the throne of Kerasím!" shouted one of the officers.

Lihx-ring of a trixahg! Tokh fell to his knees as if he'd been shoved. All around him, people dropped like flies.

"All rise," came the command in a calm but definitely female voice.

In person, Rimas was tall and broad as Tokh himself, and her father's power emanated from her as she walked. She wore smooth black pants, ones that admitted the wearer had thighs and knees under them, and a bright blue shirt that left no doubt she was female. Black boots rose to her knees, low heels clicking against the stones. The front of her long brown hair was braided back from her face in a half-dozen small pink braids, while the rest ran wild over her shoulders. She wore no veil at all, not even a ribbon. Never had Kerasi men bent knee to a female. No wonder the *bhísroti* didn't want her near the throne.

She strode forward with confidence, not leaving a spare second to doubt her authority. "General, show me where we will meet."

The dining table in the great room had been polished to a gleaming luster. "With your permission, my wife Zheníhda will attend table," Tokh said. He froze in a deep bow, eyes to the floor. He hadn't been this intimidated in years, and never, ever, had he been this intimidated by a female. He had no idea what to do, how to speak, what to expect. The words *Heir Apparent* scared him far more than her gender; gender didn't seem to factor in at all. The thought of refusing to accept her authority over him never entered his head. Not a single thought of bedding her, or even her attributes, crossed his mind. Was this how his *aghát* felt near Union females? His only instinct was to turn and flee, and that he could not do.

"As long as she doesn't speak. This is a private interview," Rimas said. She took the center seat on one side; her officers filled in on either side of her, while guards stood both inside and outside the front door, allowing no passage in any direction. Guards could be seen through the back windows, patrolling the grounds. A camera was set on the table before her Highness to record the interview.

"The interviewed may sit. Her counsel and translator may sit with her."

Aila bowed and took the seat across from the camera. Tokh sat next to her.

"You wish to speak for the interviewed, Lord Tokh?"

Tokh made up his mind, do or die. Let the *ghanakti* dice fall where they would. "Your Majesty, I was given care and supervision of the subject since she was of the age of thirteen. I have educated her, sheltered her, and treated her as family. She is as a daughter to me. She was given protection by Emperor Nághtas; I would grant her also the acknowledgement and protection of the line of dar-Giláhn."

Rimas sat back. Her face didn't change, but it was obvious she hadn't expected that. "You're prepared to accept responsibility for her actions on Kerasím, good or bad, to discipline her as required, to care and shelter her as long as she remains unmarried, as it reflects upon you, even though she is a human?"

"I am."

"You vouch for her loyalty to the Emperor of Kerasím, above all others?"

"Not above all but equal to, as the facts of the previous weeks will show."

The Perrin girl stared at Tokh, but had the sense not to speak or argue as he feared.

Rimas rapped her knuckles on the table twice. "Let it be known from now forward Union representative Aila Perrin is acknowledged by General Four Tokh dar-Giláhn, is covered by the protection of his name and is as one with his line and all property therein. She may use the name Aila Perrin daras-Giláhn for all purposes Kerasi and more."

Aila bent her head. "Thank you, Lord Tokh," she said, though it was certain she didn't understand what was happening.

"Now," Rimas said. "You left the palace after the assassination. Please explain what happened after that, in every detail possible, so we will know what you know without needing harsher methods."

* * 38 * *

Rimas's interrogation lasted the rest of the morning, prying out details with more patience than Tokh himself would have given. Afterward he escorted Rimas to her aircraft.

"I hope you know what you're doing, Lord Tokh," she said. "My father speaks highly of you, but accepting responsibility for the actions of one who is technically still an enemy of the Empire is a dangerous line. She's born of the Union, she serves the Union. Don't let personal feelings interfere with common sense."

"I don't, your Most Revered Lady Heir." He made up the honorific as he spoke; she was the first female *Thosikh* in line for the throne. There were no titles for her yet. Three hours, and still he trembled in her presence like a frightened child, terrified of making a mistake and insulting her without intent. He hadn't been this fearful on his first command. He hadn't been this fearful of her father. "She has fought hard for the late Emperor for four years. I don't anticipate her loyalties to change. If my instincts serve me, I foresee her ties to the Empire becoming only stronger, with or without the permission of her government. If I may humbly make a request, what will be the outcome of this inquiry? What should I prepare for?"

Rimas gave him a small smile and tipped her head. "My inquiry is complete, General, and that will be my report to the Emperor. Based on information I received from various sources, I didn't suspect her involvement in the death of my wisefather, and her answers have done nothing to change my opinion. Rest easy, General. You're cleared. I wish you luck with her."

Haghíde carried the Emissary to her room, where she fell into an exhausted sleep. Tokh poked her awake with the collapsed thickness of his incentive stick two hours later. No matter what their relationship, past or present, legal or illegal, he wouldn't touch a sleeping Union female. Aila sat up.

"I know you require rest, but the Union delegation will be here soon."

She rubbed her face. "What did you mean before, what you told Rimas? I am one with your line? What is that? I didn't want to question you in front of everyone."

"That was the correct action." He held his hands behind him and paced aimlessly. "As a foreign female, you have no legal rights on Kerasím. I didn't believe Nadigh would use you to some end, but I don't know the will of the Emperor. I used a maneuver that would grant you legal protection, should such an incident occur."

"You adopted me?" Tokh stopped pacing, unfamiliar with the word. "You made me one of your own children."

Tokh resumed pacing. "If a female claims her child is mine and I deny it, she has the right to demand genetic testing. If she claims a child is mine and I don't deny it, truth or not, the issue ends; there is no claim to prove. Although it is impossible for you to be my offspring, by claiming you as mine, there is no law that says I must prove it. Rimas couldn't deny me."

"You used a hole in the law that never existed before."

Tokh pointed his finger at her. "Precisely. I claimed you as my own offspring, accepting responsibility for all your actions and granting you full protection of my lineage. Kerasi law does not extend into Union space, but while you are on Kerasím, your actions and behavior are now tied to me. Do not abuse my name and reputation; bring shame to my house on either world and you will not like the punishment."

The Emissary slid off the bed to kneel before him. "You give me too much honor, General. May I never disappoint you, and may my actions serve to glorify your honor."

Tokh stopped before her, and a thoughtful smile broke out. Her words rang with honesty, not the bootlicking she used to give him. How far their relationship had come in little more than a week. "They already have, for many years."

Aila Perrin sat on the patio outside the kitchen by the time the Union representatives arrived. Tokh was somewhat surprised she didn't run for the aircraft, begging to be removed immediately. He knew she was still upset, but couldn't tell if the fatigue was genuine or a ploy to gain sympathy from one or both sides. He and Haghíde met the dignitaries alone.

He bowed from the waist to the first male off the aircraft, and used his best Union speech. "Greetings. I am General Tokh. On

286

behalf of the Emperor and all Kerasím, welcome to my home. May I share my unhappiness over the tragedies of the last week."

The male before him bowed in return. He was an inch taller than Tokh but no smaller across the middle. He had no goatee, but a large mustache in a blinding shade of white that matched his hair. "We thank you, General Tokh. We are greatly saddened over the tragedies you have endured as well. I'm the acting Secretary General for the Planetary Union, Bindai Hhani. We've heard you have taken excellent care of our councilmember, and we're most grateful."

Tokh bowed again. "It has been my honor. This is one of my *aghát* officers, who teaches inside the Union."

Hhani didn't offer a hand, just returned the bow. Someone knew their job well. "Of course. Captain Haghíde. It's good to see you again, Captain."

Haghíde bowed. "Thank you, Secretary Hhani. I am pleased to see you as well. Welcome to Imahlva."

Hhani motioned to the people behind him. "You may know Ross Halian, our official diplomat to Kerasím. He's been working here for several years now."

"I have heard many good words of you," Tokh said.

"It's an honor, Captain Halian." Haghíde bowed, and Halian returned the greeting.

"This is Doctor Ellia Baisch, and Councilwoman Vanora Aikerman," Hhani finished.

Haghíde smiled and bowed his head. "Lady Aikerman. I am pleased that you escaped the palace without injury. Councilwoman Perrin was most anxious about your situation. She will be happy to know you are well."

Aikerman was similar to Zheníhda in build but much older, as far as Tokh could tell, her silver hair as short as an initiated cadet, most unfemale. He was feeling at a distinct disadvantage: his *aghát* knew almost everyone the Union government sent, and Tokh had only heard of the two males, never met either of them. He hadn't realized Haghíde was that well connected inside the Union.

Aikerman smiled and tipped her head to Haghíde. "That was very kind of her to worry about me, with all the troubles she was up against. She is here, isn't she?"

Tokh straightened up. "Of course. She is resting outside. Come." He led them around the house to the patio, with its stone table and padded resting chairs, while Haghíde went inside to keep an ear on communications.

Emissary Perrin rose to greet them, hugging each in turn, male and female, without regard, and they returned the touches. She saved the older woman for last, touching longer. Someone that familiar to the Emissary should be familiar to Tokh, too. He would research the woman after she left.

"I'm so, so happy to see you, Vanora! I didn't see your name on any of the casualty lists, but I worried anyway." Aila sank back onto her chair. "I can't imagine what you went through."

Aikerman tossed the thought away as she sat. "Bah! If anything, I let you down. I'm retired intelligence, child. It was my job to know where you were at all times, and your protectors slipped you from my grasp the split-second I stopped to help poor Hawet. They know their stuff, I'll give them that."

"I had a feeling. I know my parents."

Tokh sat to Aila's right. Zheníhda scurried in and out, bringing refreshments from the kitchen and disappearing just as quickly. The conversation dwindled to an uncomfortable silence.

Tokh picked up the cue. "Do you wish to speak with your people in private? I will return to the house until you call."

"Ka," Aila said, quick and sharp. She had the audacity to grab his arm, holding him to the chair, most inappropriate. Tokh sat back.

"There's nothing I would say to them I wouldn't have you hear. I've gone over my ordeal in every detail with your government; there's nothing I can add to that. You have every right to be here."

"Are you sure about that, my dear?" Aikerman asked. "We don't want to take up too much of the general's time."

There was a leading edge to her voice, but Tokh hadn't been around enough Human females to know if it meant anything significant or not. Judging by the fact the Emissary had replied in Kerasi, and touched him, it was no doubt a silent message. Perhaps the Emissary knew something was wrong but couldn't say it; his heart said the Emissary wouldn't double-cross him, though his head urged caution. This was his first major foray into Union politics, with no guidance from above. He didn't know the players or the politics involved. Secretary-General, Tokh knew, reported directly to the President, only a few steps down in rank. Certainly the palace must think highly of him, to host such an important guest without Imperial guard. Captain Halian had met extensively with Emperor

Nághtas and was working out scientific exchanges of information over the time-travel experiments. This Tokh also knew. Aikerman had just claimed to be retired from intelligence; no doubt she was there to spy and report back. That much attention was a great honor indeed. On the other hand, he had two powerful Union males sitting at his table, and his head remained a wanted prize inside the Union. Tokh's level of caution jumped several levels, and his thumb slid aside the strap that secured his weapon in its holster.

Aila lifted her face to the green-blue sky. She smiled with contentment. "If you wish me to speak, the general stays."

They spoke for more than an hour, Aila recounting as much of her ordeal as she could, and asking a number of questions of Halian and Hhani. She passed Baisch's simple physical exam, to Tokh's relief.

Baisch patted her arm. "You're a lucky lady. Outside of some stress and exhaustion, you're in pretty good shape. A little rest and you'll be on the lecture circuit in no time. The tranquilizers you're taking aren't my first choice, but they're not harmful at that dose."

"If you're able to travel, we're ready to take you out of here," Halian said. "Your parents are in orbit. They're very anxious to get you back up there."

Tokh's insides clenched. He expected her to leave when her people returned to the Union, but he hadn't considered the idea she might leave this very second. Mímihn would be heartbroken.

To his great relief, she shook her head. "No. I know my parents will try to create a diplomatic incident out of it, but I need to rest first. I feel very safe here. I'd like to wait a few days, maybe even a week, get some energy back, if that's possible."

Ah. Tokh nodded to himself. He knew perfectly well what would happen in a few days, or even a week. Mímihn was right. Her heart was tied up like a gift.

"We're still working closely with the Emperor," Hhani said, "so we're not leaving orbit too soon. Doctor?"

"As long as she's not under any undue influence, I'm okay with that," Baisch said. "Perhaps Ross can check in on her. Is that all right with her host?"

Tokh kept his head high; it was strange, yes, but in truth, right now he was an unofficial direct agent of the Emperor, making unsupervised decisions about foreign dignitaries and policies like a member of the Inner Circle, and that was a powerful feeling. All his long years of preparation, his effort and sacrifice, had led to this very moment. At this exact moment, he was in charge of the future of Kerasi-Union relations, General Four Tokh dar-Giláhn himself, when by years of service he should have been only a Colonel Two. The future of galactic peace hung in his own courtyard.

"I offer her my home as I would my own offspring. She may stay until she desires to leave, with full protection of my unit. Forgive me; I have not met many Humans, and never have I hosted another Human female. I may ask a question?"

Hhani waved a hand. "By all means, General. Anything."

"Are all Earth females as strong as this one? Do they think tactically by nature? They all speak other tongues? Do you train only select ones in military style, or is that part of all education? We understand you feel your females are equal at tasks to your males, but never did we imagine this would be so true."

The Union team looked around the table and gave a collective nod.

"Aila's certainly something special," Ross Halian said with a grin. "I'm sure you've realized by now she doesn't like to sit back and let others do all the work."

"Oh, I'd say at least half of us are go-getters like that," the Lady Aikerman said. "I spent twenty years working in the space fleet, then went on to surveillance. In my younger days, I would have given you a good run for your money. Which is why it makes me sad to have to do this."

She stood up and took a step back from the table. She reached inside the waistband of her trousers and withdrew a hand weapon, a Kerasi weapon, trained on Aila and Tokh. The other Union guests gasped and shoved their chairs back.

And there it was. Tokh's hand was on his pistol before his next heartbeat, waiting for an opening. He hadn't expected treachery from a diplomatic party, not one that had been cleared by the palace. The faces of the other dignitaries suggested they were not expecting it, either, and the danger was real. *A rogue? Or another of the Union's half of the assassination party?* The Emissary stared like a frightened statue, giving him no clues.

"Vanora, what the hell are you doing? Put that down!" Halian said.

"Don't move, General Tokh. Keep your hands where I can see them. Ross – don't try it. I've got twice the experience you have. You see, Aila, you weren't supposed to survive that hopeful little conference the Emperor planned. I was there to make sure of that. You've been so nice to her, General, it's a shame to make you take the blame for the massacre of four Union officials here on your property, but then, you're still wanted for crimes inside Union space, so it's not a surprise at all. Oh, don't look so shocked. I know exactly who you are. I'm sorry, but there's now ample evidence the Kerasi are just too barbaric and violent a people to have open ties with."

Tokh didn't twitch a muscle. His hands remained slightly raised and in view, but he knew he had the advantage. A good assassin shot fast and disappeared. A bad one talked about it for an hour before hand, allowing anyone with half a nerve to shoot them first. Tokh just had to keep her talking until the right moment. *Gah!* Proof females were useless for military positions.

"You will never leave my property alive. Females make poor assassins. You have neither the strength nor the stomach for it."

Aikerman smiled. "You have no idea what I can do." She raised the weapon.

A shadow passed Tokh's eyes as he snatched his weapon free. As his hand raised, something exploded on the table. Bits of shrapnel pounded against his shirt and cheek, followed by a wave of liquid. As the shrapnel fell, his weapon fired in a blinding flash. Aikerman stumbled backwards and fell flat on the stones of the patio, a perfect gory shot deep into her chest, her blaster resting in her open palm. The Union doctor gave a shriek of fright. Tokh stood up and holstered his weapon.

He bowed to the Secretary Hhani, cringing backward in his seat. "My apologies for the death of your delegate, but no one threatens me or my guests and does not accept the consequences."

Hhani eased back into his chair. His head kept turning between the general and Aikerman's body, his face as white as his mustache. "My apologies, Sir, for a danger I had no idea existed. You have my sincerest thanks, and those of everyone at the table."

"That's the fastest draw I think I've ever seen," Halian said with admiration.

Baisch dashed over to Aikerman, but it was obvious that if she wasn't already dead, she would be momentarily. "What the hell happened? What exploded?"

"I don't know." Tokh poked at shards of glass on the table and came away with a larger piece that had the remnants of a gold *lunahl* label clinging to it. He glanced at the empty sky overhead. The kitchen doors were closed, and no one in the house could possibly have flung a bottle at that angle and made it land like that.

As they stared, the doors flew open and Mímihn ran onto the patio in a frenzy. Haghíde followed her on the run, weapon drawn, Zheníhda and Dalo not far behind. Mímihn threw herself to her knees before him, pleading and wailing, while Haghíde checked the fallen delegate.

"Stand up, female!" Tokh barked. "Speak! I don't have time for nonsense!"

"Forgiveness, my great husband! I beg forgiveness! Please don't be too harsh! I did what I thought I must. I hid on my balcony, listening to conversations when I shouldn't. I know this, but I wanted to see the Union ladies and hear their speech. I don't know what you spoke of, but when the old lady holds a weapon to my Tokh, to my dear friend Aila, I must do something. If Aila can be so brave to stand up to *fáhganid*s, then I can be brave, too. I closed my bad eye and tried to hit her with a bottle of *lunahl*. I missed and hit the table instead. I'm most sorry for not minding my own business. Please, my dear husband, don't be harsh with me! I only meant to help!"

The words sank in. Tokh's head tipped back and he let loose a braying laugh. He lifted Mímihn off the ground and kissed her throat. "My life saved by a half-blind wife!"

The Emissary laughed off her panic as she listened to the sequence of events; Ross Halian explained it to the doctor and Mr. Hhani. Aila rose and gave Secretary Hhani a hard hug. "Please explain to my mother why I'll be recovering here instead of with her. I feel far safer here than with my own people at the moment."

The last thing Tokh wanted was another lengthy inquiry and investigation teams crawling through his home yet again. Imperial ships landed across his yard and down the street; the neighbors wouldn't dare get in the way but swarmed Justice Wahtegahn's house just above Tokh's, peering down over the walls and trees and trying to guess what had happened at the Tokh estate yet again, until hours later when the officials left and they could swarm Tokh proper. The Perrin girl snuck upstairs and took one of her tranquilizers; she crashed asleep on his sofa, rousing with the greatest difficulty, unable to answer more than the simplest of questions.

The palace sent First Royal Advisor Moragh to investigate, brother to the Emperor, someone far more experienced than Rimas, along with General Trannor. They brought three independent translators from the palace, ones with no ties to Tokh and whose translation wouldn't be suspect.

"No!" the Secretary Hhani insisted to them. "I want assurance no charges will be brought against General Tokh. The Union isn't angry about this. We are most grateful. General Tokh has the highest praise from the Union, and we thank him endlessly. The Union will not be holding General Tokh responsible. Do you understand? No charges! No charges! We give him only thanks!"

The Union official clapped both hands on Tokh's shoulders. Tokh couldn't help but turn his head and stare. They weren't friends or teammates or relations, yet the official was touching him as one. He would have to ask Haghíde if that was a good sign or bad one.

Again Tokh felt the world had spun out of control, but this time it looked a little more hopeful, with so many witnesses on his side. Nothing had gone right ever since they tried to make contact with the Union, and Tokh began to feel great sympathy for the new Emperor.

Haghíde was another thorn under his belt, apologizing every hour. "General, I submit myself for disciplinary action. It was my failure that a weapon was brought onto your property. I should have searched all visitors for weapons; I did not. I relied on my familiarity with three of the guests and didn't question. I hesitated to question a Union official of high standing without your request. I placed your wives and children at risk. My error almost cost several lives. I apologize most deeply, Lord General. It will never happen again."

Tokh raised a hand, but didn't hit him – yet. "Haghíde, if you bow before me one more time, I'll beat you until your eyes bleed."

Haghíde started to bow in reply, but caught himself. "Yes, Lord General. Thank you, Lord General."

* * 39 * *

On the following morning, despite the ongoing investigation, Tokh gave the household good news for a change: Kitras was granted leave and would be returning to the estate. Dalo ran herself in circles, counting down the minutes.

The aircraft skirted overland before lunch, a plain brown transport with no special markings. It crouched like an insect on the landing pad.

The door opened and a short set of steps unfolded. Kitras jumped down and put his hand out, but the second passenger refused the help. The passenger's leg wore a plastic splint, he leaned on a walking stick and a stripe of his hair was missing where a head wound had been repaired, but Masákh worked his way down the steps on his own, to the cheers of several in the yard. Dalo ran to Kitras, children following on invisible strings to mob their father.

Tokh clapped his officer on the shoulder. "Masákh! It's good to see you up and about. You look fit for duty. I'm assured from many sources the tales of your courage are not exaggerated."

Masákh dipped his head in gratitude. "Thank you, Lord General. I did no more than duty required."

"From what I heard and saw on the recordings, it was a battle for the history books."

"It was very brief." Masákh's eyes searched the courtyard until they located the Perrin girl, half-hidden in the back of the group. His face gave away nothing.

The Emissary ran up to him, but she knew better than to touch. Her arms flapped helplessly before collapsing to her knees in front of him, forehead in the dirt, and putting a hand on his boot.

Masákh twitched with embarrassment, but she didn't move until Mímihn darted forward and pulled her away.

It was all Tokh could do not to laugh. His officer tried so hard to remain cool and indifferent it was painful to watch. Whatever

Masákh had done to pull her attentions to him, it had worked. The Emissary followed him like a newborn *bagresh*. No personal assistant was more attentive as she served his meal. She said barely a word, more wife-like than Tokh's own wives, jumping to meet his needs before he could think of them. He called Masákh into conference after lunch.

"I know medical released you from duty for several weeks, but I want you to use the time to clear your mind. The situation between you and our emissary is becoming laughable. You must either go upstairs and take her properly as is long due you or be strict with her about leaving you alone and consider the pursuit ended. The choice is yours, but it must be addressed before you return to duty. I won't let this carry on longer."

Masákh hung his head. "It's not that simple, General. She's Union. If I bed her against her will, it will create an interstellar incident. It can't be done."

"Make sure she's pleased and she'll forgive any indiscretion on your part."

"It doesn't work that way inside the Union. Her parents would bring legal action against me and I would lose my position and influence and be returned to Kerasím with dishonor. There are days when it's extremely difficult not to seize her and take what is mine. Almost. I almost bent her with her permission, but she cited the need for duty before pleasure, and I realized she spoke truth. To have entered such a relationship before the mission would have been to jeopardize it. It would have tainted the concerns of both parties and called into question anything either of us said or did, left us weak for extortion."

"The mission's over. If she allowed you to touch her then, you have every right to go and demand she allow you now."

Masákh nodded. "You're correct, General. I'll approach her tomorrow and remind her of her own words."

"Masákh," Tokh said with disapproval. "You don't advance by waiting until tomorrow. You must seize opportunities as they come. I tell you, you won't fail."

Masákh looked away. "I regret to admit my leg pains me, General. I've stood more today than I have since the battle. I'd prefer to seize such pleasure when I can enjoy it. To fail such an endeavor because I couldn't stand or kneel would be most embarrassing."

Tokh patted him on the shoulder. "Yes, that wouldn't be recommended. Perhaps first thing in the morning, before you walk much. I won't hold breakfast for you. Go, then. Rest your leg. But heed my words. I'll work on the issue from the other side." He waited until Masákh was upstairs, and called Mímihn to him.

She slipped into his office again late, as Tokh was shutting down and logging off for the night. Mímihn pressed him back in his chair, hiked her ruffled skirt, and sat straddling his lap. She leaned forward and nipped him in the side of his neck, sucked the pain away with her lips, and proceeded to unbutton his shirt.

Tokh raised his eyebrow in amusement. "What brings this on? I would have been upstairs in five *fasim*."

Mímihn ran her hands across his chest, untucking his shirt. The ends of his belt fell aside next. The pointed tips of her nails scratched at the front of his trousers, tickling him before she reached in and freed his privates. She slid down between his knees, her kisses moving lower until her tongue blazed a trail down his *hihvat*.

"I made a promise to keep you busy so you wouldn't page your officers tonight and interrupt their rest. So I'm keeping my promise."

"I told Ma… Masákh… I would… Would let him rest." Tokh's grunts of pleasure deepened in tone. He pulled Mimihn's head down so she would take him into her mouth but she fell backwards out of his reach. She rolled to her feet, flipped her skirt up and wiggled her golden bare backside at him. "If you want it, come and get it, but you have to catch me first. First one up the stairs chooses position." She opened the door and took off.

"MIMI!" Tokh throbbed in unfinished agony. He rose from the chair with difficulty, held his pants up with one hand and tried to cover himself with the ends of his shirt as he stumbled for the stairs.

Zheníhda had breakfast ready, but only the children seemed to be on time. Everyone else stumbled down an hour later. Dalo and Kitras remained absorbed by each other; Tokh wasn't sure they even knew other people were at the table. They sat so close their chairs touched, and Kitras would poke her in the ear, in the nose, in the cheek. Each time Dalo would giggle and blush a deep bronze, and elbow him in return.

Mímihn darted around Tokh like a summerfly, serving him food and drink, changing his dishes. Each time she passed she would tickle the back of his head with her nail tips, kiss his ear, or hug him and nip at his neck. Tokh chuckled at his memories of the night, and it was a night worthy of memory.

Zheníhda's glare burned with poison. "Would you like us to clear space on the table?"

Tokh wrestled the arms from his neck. "Only if you're offering to please me here and now."

Zheníhda shut up.

His eyes rolled to watch his officers. Masákh and Haghíde made light conversation, nothing out of the ordinary, but Masákh was trying too hard to ignore the Perrin girl. He didn't address her, didn't converse with her, didn't so much as look at her. The Perrin girl's head bent, eyes focused on every bite of her meal. Every so often her eyes would sneak to Masákh, then snap down again, her face a distinct pink color. She, too, was trying too hard to pretend he didn't exist. Masákh must have laid her flat. If she was angry, she would never look. She wore a blouse with a collar that covered her neck, hiding her skin. Either way, they seemed to have made their peace.

He called Masákh aside after breakfast. "Is there something you need to tell me, Major?"

For a brief second Masákh look shocked, as if a terrible secret had been leaked. He tipped his head downward, unwilling to look Tokh in the eye. "Probably, General, although I'm not sure how to phrase it or how you'll react. Because of the uniqueness of the situation, I'm not sure of the legalities involved. I... admit to bedding your daughter last night. Your new daughter," he corrected himself in a panic. "Not the young one."

Tokh had forgotten he'd claimed the Emissary as his offspring. It made for a good joke, but he could understand Masákh's hesitation. Of course, if Masákh was serious about that relationship, he should never have dared touch the Emissary. "Ah! I see. You took liberties with my offspring under my own roof, when I treated you as guest. You know what I could do to you for this?" He kept his face stern but amusement sparkled in his eye.

Masákh squirmed. "General Tokh, I'll take whatever punishment you see fit to give. No disrespect intended, General, but your harshest won't come close to the punishment I'll endure once her mother learns I've bedded her. It's an obsessive fear of hers. I

297

don't, however, believe she can bring charges against me, as the Emissary is of legal age."

Tokh chuckled. "There are times when a female's wrath can be worse than a male's. Did she object? Tell me, Masákh. I don't care how much you force you used, but I must be prepared for repercussions."

Masákh relaxed as no punishment appeared to be forthcoming. "No, Lord General. She didn't. She approached me of her own will, but due to Union custom doesn't wish the fact public."

Tokh dropped the authority role. His fist tapped Masákh's shoulder. "Good. It's out of your systems. You both needed that, before the smell got any worse." He grinned at his officer. "Was it worth the wait? I've never sampled Human. Kyan, Centauri, Churmadesh, even a monstrous wet lipping from a Geminid captive once, but never Human. They say we're compatible, but sterile, of course. Did you go the full hand?"

Masákh gha Lil, decorated major in the Kerasi army, hung his head and blushed. "It was… an experience worth waiting for. It was late and I'm still weary with recovery, so I stopped after four. I would recommend the experience should you get the chance, General."

Tokh gave a soft snort of amusement. "Go. Get out of here. Enjoy her while you can."

* * 40 * *

The notice arrived by courier late in the morning, an official dispatch from Derahl Nor, the palace itself. Tokh opened it immediately, read it, and fell back in his chair, heart pounding. He reread it, making sure he understood every line and anything that might be hiding between. Here was the edict he'd been wanting for so many years, and the seal was most definitely authentic. He held the paper as if it were glass and walked to the bottom of the stairs.

"Wives, attend!" he called out. Zheníhda drifted down the stairs; Mímihn slipped inside from the patio.

"I just received a notification from the office of the Emperor. I'll read it to you." Zheníhda listened patiently, but Mímihn leaned over his arm and squinted at the official seal and print.

"What does it mean?" Zheníhda asked when he finished.

"It means we are invited to the palace for an award ceremony. Me, my team, my wives, the entire house."

Zheníhda's hands clutched her heart. *"Wives? To the palace? The Palace of Derahl Nor, the Emperor's Palace, the one in Keranihn?"*

"Wives," he confirmed.

Mímihn exploded. Her hands covered her mouth, and she began to shriek and scream. Her feet ran in place, she spun in a circle, and she screamed again.

"Stop that!" Tokh ordered. "What are you screaming for, you fool! Do you want to bring the neighbors down on us, wondering what's going on? Haven't we given them enough cause for gossip, for the next hundred years? Stop your nonsense!"

Haghíde and Kitras burst into the house from the front, followed by Dalo, then the Perrin girl helping Masákh to hobble faster than he should have. "General? We heard screams."

Tokh glared at Mímihn. "I have a five-year-old wife."

"We're going to the palace!" Mímihn shrieked. She yanked the paper from Tokh's hand. "There! Right there! That's the word wife!

Even Nihda can read that much! Read to them what it says! I want to hear it again!"

"Please, Tokh," Zheníhda begged. "I want to hear it, too."

Tokh yanked the printout back. "It's an invitation to the palace, two days from now. 'Be it known General Four Tokh dar-Giláhn, his wives, son Kitras dar-Giláhn and wives, recognized daughter Aila Perrin daras-Giláhn; *Aghát* officers, Command Officers, will make themselves present to the Emperor for a private honors ceremony and reception, overnight accommodations, and so forth. Transportation will be provided."

Murmurs rebounded around the room. "Did you hear that?" Mímihn gushed, her arms flapping. "Wives! I'm a wife, and I'll go to the palace and see the Emperor! Me! Me! And now I can see him!" She squealed and spun in a circle until her skirts flared outward. The glow on Zheníhda's face said she wanted to do that, too, but couldn't break free of her dignity act. Her hands wrestled themselves instead.

Aila folded her arms. "I don't exactly trust the palace."

"Security will be most tight," Tokh assured her. "It will be in private chambers and is limited to fifty honorees, families, and select Union dignitaries who have been cleared. No weapons are permitted and all attendees will be searched. Nadigh won't be fooled."

"We'll need clothing," Zheníhda realized. "Not one of us owns a thing worthy of wearing to the palace. We don't have much time. Tokh, find someone to accompany us to the city."

"You'll all go, and leave me to my work," Tokh said. "I have to get my men back here immediately."

Tokh's men trickled in all the next day: Tótoghar, Ghírandar, Mátokhan, Tokh's second in command Colonel Khaním, Colonel Dahven, Major Kaghán, Captains Trihn, Sohrel, and Fless, and four Chiefs in green, creating an impromptu party of old friends that started mid-morning and ran until the drunken singing had been going on for at least an hour. Ráhnif and Kassán were already at the palace; they would join them there. Zheníhda had catered food brought in for the crowd; she and Mímihn would never keep up with the demands of fifteen rowdy Kerasi officers. The Emissary filled and cleared dishes alongside the wives, enduring the hands pinching her backside and the rude questions asked of Tokh.

"What did the notice mean, recognized daughter, General?" said Major Khagán. "Did you get caught dipping where you shouldn't have? I should think a general would know better. What did your battle-wife have to say about that one?" The room gave a rowdy howl and stomped their feet. Zhenihda overheard the comment; Khagán's next plate of *vortag* legs seared with such spice he blistered his tongue on the first piece.

Tokh pulled Aila onto his lap as he would a child. "I've looked after her long enough to claim her as my own. It's by my order she was educated to the position she holds in the Union. She brings me honor and glory. I don't have to prove it; I say she is, and I'll protect her as such. Therefore I'd better not see a single one of you trying to corner her somewhere! Your hands are not to touch her." The finger that pointed to his men was two cups of *dhurwah* past its steady aim.

He eyed her with suspicion when she kissed his temple and said, "*Soyavoh, Triskaris-Bo.*"

General-father. He gave a snort of amusement. What changes four years could make.

Captain Trihn was sprawled in a chair, so numb with *gohr* he could no longer hold his glass. "It's not my hands that want to touch her." The room brayed again. Shoulders were slammed, and drinks sloshed onto the carpeting.

"Does that include Masákh?" Haghíde slurred.

"Masákh knows how to follow orders."

And Masákh did. He just had different orders. At Tokh's suggestion, Masákh offered his room to Colonel Khaním on the pretense of sharing a room with the other *aghát*, but instead he joined the Emissary. Tokh assigned Lanag and Joralan night watch: they were to camp in the dining room and make sure no one wandered out of bed. No matter how serious they took it, both were sound asleep two hours later when he checked on them.

With family and officers they numbered twenty-six, plus luggage, a morning trial that tested patience and plumbing. The private Imperial shuttle was so large it couldn't fit on Tokh's landing pad. It settled itself in the main courtyard before the house, cracking paving stones with its weight, but everyone had a seat.

Even Mímihn could make out the palace as they approached, the glowing white building larger and grander than anything else in sight. While the females and children squealed and sighed over the sight, Tokh tried his best to look indifferent, craning his neck to see out the glass on the far side of the craft while his insides quivered with awe. The Emissary rattled off points of interest to Mímihn like a tour guide, things Mímihn might not have been able to see; Tokh filed the information in his own head. It was wrong that a Union dignitary should know more about the Great Palace than a General Four born to Kerasím. At least Kesseh was learning it, too.

Twelve armed security officers met them on the roof-top landing pad, along with a colonel in charge of welcoming them. Tokh disembarked first, acknowledged the officer, relayed his orders, and turned around. His unit disembarked behind him and waited in formation.

"Ghit!" he barked, and they snapped to attention, his command officers in front, then his *aghát*, then his greens. Kitras stood at the end of the *aghát*, a captain not of Tokh's command, but higher ranking than his Greens. With the area ceremonially "cleared," Tokh held out a hand and Zheníhda descended, veil down, her hand sliding into Tokh's. Mímihn followed. Aila followed her, her own veil down, then Joralan and Kesseh, and finally Dalo and her children, the children long threatened by promises of horrific punishments if they didn't honor their father and wisefather with their best behavior. Being at the Palace, Dalo did succumb to wearing a veil – bright blue spidery netting that came no lower than the bridge of her nose. The colonel led them through security doors to a holding room, where each of them was scanned, frisked, photographed, imprinted, and relieved of any weapons, right down to Dalo's toddler, Niboh. Nadigh wasn't playing.

It was only with great reluctance Tokh turned over his sword. "What if I promise to leave it in my quarters, scan me if I leave the room?"

"I'm sorry, General," the colonel explained. *"Tansohr Keralihn.* It's the order of the Emperor, and it's expressly written to include every last person, no matter what the weapon, no matter what the rank or caste, save the Heir herself. Your weapons will be safe and waiting for you any time you wish to leave the palace."

They were shown to a guest suite on the fourth floor, dominated by a common area with a glass wall overlooking the gardens and a balcony for fresh air. Six bedrooms were attached, men in the rooms

302

on one side of the center and women in rooms on the other. The Greens were sent to dormitories at the end of the hall.

Tokh and his family tiptoed across the carpets as if walking on glass; they had thought the house in Imahlva was unimaginable luxury, and this guestroom made their spectacular home look like a *tapatíhn* cabin. Mímihn opened the door to one of the bedrooms and began to cry. Sunlight streamed in from the windows, making the room bright enough for her to see the layers of carved woods coated in gold, the bed with a ten-foot high canopy and brocaded draperies layered over it, the voluptuous statues in the corners and the artwork on the walls. The walls were a pale green to match the sky, the high ceiling painted with clouds to extend the illusion. The pulls on drawers and doors, the lamps, the finials on the tops of the chair stiles, were all of some form of crystal, catching the sun's rays and scattering rainbows everywhere. Mímihn wandered wall to wall, afraid to touch or sit on anything.

Zheníhda didn't make it that far. She sank to her knees on the thick carpet of the sitting room and bent her forehead to the floor, mumbling to the Fortunes. Dalo looked about with her mouth open, oblivious to Niboh fussing to get down. She broke the trance of the room by announcing, "Holy Mother of Fortune!" The Emissary and most of the *aghát* simply chose rooms and placed their travel bags in them.

Tokh stood in the middle of the room for several minutes, taking it all in. This was just a guest room, an area assigned to them to prepare for the ceremonies, and sleep off the aftereffects. He couldn't imagine what the rest of the palace looked like. He helped Zheníhda to her feet. She walked to the great glass doors of the balcony and opened them, gazing out in wonder at the lawns and gardens and forest as far as her eye could see. Tokh hadn't heard her so silent in… Perhaps ever.

And, in a petty way, it annoyed him. For fifteen years he'd imagined setting foot in the palace, dreamed of an invitation. He'd hoped that chance would have come after completing the Emissary Project, but the peace was so fragile and he was a wanted head in the Union so the Emperor steered clear of anything linking him to Tokh. When the Accord was about to happen, Tokh wanted so very much to be in the audience, to see what he'd worked so hard for, risked his life for, even if it was from the very worst seat in the senate, but the Union hadn't forgotten his name and Nághtas didn't want him anywhere near the city while the Union was nearby. Tokh understood, but it hurt just the same. An invite at any other time wouldn't have been so difficult, would it? He'd met Nadigh a few times, spoken to him when he was still Heir. Tokh knew he hadn't forgotten his name, even if Tokh was just a lowly *dihnarwharl*. And yet, here in the palace, the mightiest residence on Kerasím, home of the almighty 152nd Emperor Nádigh Ramán gol Suhr Zaghíl, Tokh's *aghát* and his emissary moved about with ease, as if they'd lived here as a matter of course. There was nothing disrespectful in their actions, but… They didn't seem to be appreciating it as much as they should. *The Palace of Derahl Nor, for Fortune's sake!*

Tokh was considering making everyone remove their shoes when the door chimed before he could put the words to air. He answered it. Ráhnif, the youngest and newest member of his *aghát* team, bowed before him and entered. Ráhnif had been stationed at the palace throughout the Accord crisis, acting as one of the assigned intermediaries for the Union delegation. Tokh expected him to be familiar with the palace.

"Bright day, General. Welcome to Derahl Nor. Are these quarters adequate for everyone?"

Tokh looked about. He still hadn't seen into the bedrooms, but to sleep even on the floor of the palace was the honor of a lifetime. "Absolutely. I think this is bigger than my home."

"It's average for a guest suite. Some are a bigger, some are smaller. Did they bring you refreshments?" Ráhnif realized there was nothing yet on the table, and reached for his pocket com. As he tapped the first command, the door chimed again, and he let in two servants steering carts loaded with various delicacies and bottles of chilled *muhr* and *lunahl*, of a bottler and vintage Tokh had never seen. In moments, they had spread the table with a feast of exotic and breathtaking treats.

"Eat, everyone," Ráhnif urged. "The escorts will be calling for you in three hours. Don't be late. The doors will be locked and no one will be able to leave or enter once the ceremony begins. Dinner will follow. In the morning, I've arranged for a tour before you leave." The children were the first to the table, oohing over the fancy presentations. The adults followed, still afraid to touch.

"Where will the ceremony be held?" Masákh asked. "In the banquet hall, or the throne room?"

304

"Both were severely damaged in the attack; reconstruction is only in the measuring stage," Ráhnif said. "*Where* is the secret of the day. No one knows but security, not even the kitchen staff yet. Nadigh's being very, very careful with what he does. We probably won't know until they come for us."

The door chimed again. Ráhnif opened the door to admit Kassán, wearing a new dress uniform. It was clean and pressed, and of a correct size. His remaining hair was trimmed and lay against his head like a snowbank, and his chin hank was groomed and pinched tight by a black band with a silver medical emblem in the center. It wasn't like Kassán to look... respectable. Amazing, the things the palace did to people.

Thirty minutes before the ceremony, two guards appeared at their door, escorting a matronly female. "My name is Trillihg, and I'll be the caretaker for the children of your suite. They may accompany me to the nursery now."

Tokh glanced back to the room. No one mentioned the children wouldn't be staying with them. Dalo was delighted she wouldn't have Niboh on her lap all evening, but Tokh didn't like the idea of his children being out of his sight, in a strange location, even if this was the palace. "Very well, but I'll accompany them there to observe the room. I won't have my children hidden from me."

"By all means, General." The woman bowed. She accepted Niboh and Dalo's bag of baby needs. Kesseh held Faelihn's hand and held onto Tokh with her other. The boys followed.

Ráhnif followed him out. "It's standard, General. There's always allowance made for children. The nursery has a play room where all the children from the various guests will be gathered. There will be at least one caretaker for each suite. It's not meant to be a cause for concern."

Tokh nodded. "I'm certain, but I'd be derelict in my duty if I didn't know where my children would be staying."

The nursery was on the same floor, one hall away, the corridor so long Tokh couldn't have seen it if he'd stood outside his rooms. The playroom was a child's dream, an outdoor play area moved inside, with a dining area and resting area with child-sized cots and sofas if desired. The girls squealed with joy and took off. Tokh held Joralan back.

"You listen, you do as instructed, you show your very best at the palace, but you will remain alert and in charge of your family, do you understand? Know where they are at all times, know who they are playing with, ask names and remember them. Don't let them leave the room with anyone, for any reason. If there's a major concern, you have my permission to have me paged. I'll come and retrieve everyone when the celebration ends. That is my direct order. Is that understood?"

Joralan's face was quite serious for a ten year old. He saluted his father. "Yes sir, my Lord General."

Tokh smiled and patted his head. "Go and enjoy yourself, then."

* * 41 * *

The ceremony would be held in a private ballroom on the fifth floor, a fact Tokh didn't learn until they left their suite escorted by palace guards. Another bodyscan took place in the hall, and Tokh's entourage was announced to a fanfare.

Tokh walked slowly, unsure what to expect, what the room was, who was there, what the protocol would be. A platform at one end raised the royalty. In Nághtas's day, draperies would have lined the wall behind the dais; in Nadigh's reign, loose draperies could hide the unexpected, and the expensive fabrics were stretched directly onto the wall and framed in gilded trim. Chairs were set up in rows with a wide aisle between sections – males on the larger side, the sprinkling of attending females on the other, with a thick fringed rope keeping the distinction, but no caste sectioning. To the side of the dais were chairs for fifteen Union delegates, those who still dared to come planet-side. One or two appeared to wear some type of military uniform, not dissimilar to Kerasi, but in white or blue. To the other side sat several highest-level Kerasi advisors, General Trannor among them. A guard directed Tokh forward.

Nadigh's throne had been rescued from the Senate chamber and brought to the room. It still bore his father's bloodstains, something Nadigh refused to remove. He sat at attention, back straight, chin high, no longer Nadigh the Heir but Nadigh the Emperor, dazzling in his gold suit of office. Moragh and Rimas stood flanking him, no less official. Both wore gold cloth, but it didn't sparkle with metal filaments like Nadigh's. Rimas's skirt was narrow and came only to her knees, with a military-cut jacket above it, declaring her both female and powerful at the same time. Her pink and brown hair was pulled back tight and rolled up to a knob on her head, without a hint of veil. To prove Nadigh's commitment, all six of his wives were in the front row of the female section; not one of them was harsh to look at.

The thrill of the room, the thrill of the location, the presence of the Emperor and all his private cabinet made Tokh's insides flutter and cramp. This was it, the very beating heart of Kerasím, and he was here inside it. From this assembly of people rolled every law, every grace, every mercy, every decision that built or broke an entire planet, more hallowed than the Imperial Senate. Beads of sweat slid down into Tokh's eyebrow; he hoped the Emperor wouldn't notice. He took a steadying breath and marched forward, a level-four general in the Emperor's Army. He dropped to his knees before Nadigh; his entourage followed in such perfect formation he couldn't have planned it. When they were given permission to rise, Tokh stood to the side at his most formal, medals and ribbons and awards hanging off him like armor, and presented each of his party to the Emperor before they were shown to their seating sections. Zheníhda and Mímihn gripped hands like two overwhelmed schoolgirls. Aila Perrin, known to the Emperor as a Union dignitary and now the claimed daughter of a Kerasi general, knelt, then walked over to the section reserved for females, to sit with her "family." That she didn't choose to sit with the assembled Union guests surprised and honored Tokh.

Two more teams entered and paid respects, General Rhigandir's unit and General Angh's, then Nadigh tapped his ceremonial staff on the floor. All doors were locked. No person, no signals, no information would enter or leave the room, as invisible and non-existent and anonymous as it could be. Nadigh stood, tall, fierce, commanding, and read a statement thanking everyone for their support and loyalty to him and to Kerasím through a most difficult time, explaining how it showed even more that increased openness and cooperation both at home and toward other worlds was imperative to their own society continuing to grow.

"As an example, I declare this room caste-free for the night: all shall sit together, eat together, share the food and tables; if necessary, touch each other, all as one. Male may still separate from female, but female shall be present, without threat or harm. This is my word; this is my law," Nadigh ordered. "If anyone objects, you may leave the room now without reprisal. Should a difficulty arise later, it will be taken as an offense to me and dealt with harshly. This was to be my father's law had he lived; in time it will become my law, and we will perfect it tonight, so that we here may be the example for all others to follow. You are the ground-breakers." A low murmur broke out in the room. Nadigh waited, but not one person moved to leave.

He continued. "The future of Kerasím begins this very moment. I want every person here to help me make that future. You here, male and female: you are my chosen to make that future happen. You will be my leaders of tomorrow. You will shape the futures of the generations to come. You have proven yourself through difficult times. You were loyal to my father, and you have chosen to extend that loyalty to me. For that, I am grateful. You are truly the best and bravest Kerasím has to offer. The past weeks have been trying ones not only for my family, but for all of Kerasím. Those of you here tonight have been elemental in keeping order, in working together, in solving crises of interstellar proportions in the best interests of our people. It's only right that I honor such loyalty."

Nadigh called men up unit by unit, calling each officer out and briefly recounting his part during the crisis. Medals and ribbons went out for bravery, heroism, loyalty, injuries; three officers were granted caste privilege. Through it all, Tokh tried to ignore the sweat dripping down his forehead until it started to make its way through to his eyes, and he was forced to take off his glove and wipe it away. Of the fifty honorees, eighteen were his men, a large percentage, and a great prestige. His chest swelled with pride when Rhigandir's unit was called and Kitras received three ribbons, for heroism, loyalty, and service.

Tokh's unit was called last, dragging out his nerves. This wasn't just answering to General Trannor, this was the mother-loving *Emperor of Kerasím*, for Fortune's sakes! Thank the Fortunes his stomach was empty.

Tokh heard his name called; he rose and proceeded to the front with military drill, dropping to a knee and bending his head. Nadigh went into detail on the length of his service, how he was the first to declare loyalty after the assassination, how he had worked tirelessly toward Nághtas's goals of opening relations, right down to opening his home and his lineage to Union citizens. Nadigh presented him with new citations for loyalty, service, foreign relations, and for his stopping the assassination of four Union delegates: another for heroism. Tokh's heart shivered with the praise, but the last honor shocked him.

"General Tokh dar-Giláhn: *dihnarwharl* is a caste that is supposed to be honorable above all the rest. You have repeatedly proven yourself honorable beyond that of mere *dihnarwharl*. For

309

that, I grant you the status of *dihnarwharl* with *dahneg* privilege, to you and your offspring, from now until your line ends." Nadigh drew his sword and tapped Tokh on the back of his neck three times. "Rise, General Tokh, *dahneg by privilege*."

He stood to a thundering of leg-slapping and foot stomping. *Kerasi males do not cry*, Tokh reminded himself, but he felt his eyes burning, and he had nowhere to look but at the Emperor. Not since his run-in with combat sickness had Tokh felt so lost and disoriented. He couldn't see Zheníhda in the crowd; he hoped she hadn't collapsed at the news. Nor did he hear screams from Mímihn, a sign she hadn't heard the words or perhaps had fainted. He saluted the Emperor and stood to the side as his men were honored in turn, while he pulled himself together.

Tokh's greens received two honors. His *aghát* all received one for loyalty to the Empire and one for special service. Masákh, Haghíde, and Tótoghar received another for bravery, and Masákh for his injury in battle. What neither Masákh nor Tokh expected was Masákh being granted an Order of the Inner Circle, placing him with perhaps only twenty others – Mátokhan being one of them – who could be trusted to work directly on order from the Emperor, with no middle-man. It was a most prestigious award, and one Tokh was certain had political reasons behind it. Like Mátokhan, Masákh worked behind the lines and had made ties with those in places of power within the Union – besides sleeping with one of their dignitaries. The Emperor could request information or actions without anyone else knowing his moves. It was another honor to Tokh; not one other general could claim two officers inside the Inner Circle.

Tokh's officers were sent back to their seats. Nadigh wasn't done, however.

"There is no precedent for this, not with my father, or his father, or his father before him. My last award is to a female. Not only a female, but a Human female, who has shown unending loyalty to the throne of Kerasím. Even when threatened by death, she would not withdraw her faith in me. She protected Kerasi citizens at the expense of her own kind, risked her life to rescue others. Her courage and spirit are an example for Kerasi females. Her honor was such that she was accepted into the line of dar-Giláhn as one of its own. I spoke with her when I was but Heir and she made great impression on me. In just a few short weeks, she has amazed me. I

310

have fifteen daughters; she is much like my own daughter Rimas: strong, proud, intelligent, and certain of her mind. She is an inspiration to all of Kerasím, both for what females are capable of, and for our females to aspire to. My father, Emperor Nághtas, knew this, and awarded her a medal for bravery at a very young age. I never expected to give this honor so early in my reign, and never to a female. Aila Perrin daras-Giláhn, Council member of the Planetary Union, for unwavering loyalty to the Empire of Kerasím, I award you the Star of the Empire, our highest honor."

The room broke out in confused knee-slapping, except for Tokh's crew, where it pounded above all the rest, and the Union assembly, which clapped hands just as hard. Tokh glanced over to the women's section. His emissary had gone white in her face, as stunned as if she'd been hit with a control stick. Mímihn nearly pulled her head off with a sharp hug. The Perrin girl came forward to kneel before the Emperor, head to the floor.

She rose on command and allowed him to place the gold ribbon and silver star around her neck. Nadigh placed his hands on her head, and they spoke back and forth.

Rimas took her hands next and congratulated her. Aila turned to the room as the slapping began again, but her eyes were riveted on Masákh, her smile so wide it made Tokh's face hurt. Masákh kept his face *aghát* blank, but the pride in his eyes made Tokh shake his head in amusement.

* * 42 * *

The banquet following took place in an adjoining room. Tokh kept his eye on his emissary. Her people were present. She went to them, showing off her decoration. She touched them and they touched her, as Union people did, male and female. Two she touched more than the others, including one of the uniformed males. The female bore a resemblance, and he guessed they were her parents, but it didn't make sense. Why would the great and powerful Admiral Perrin risk coming to Kerasím? Tokh would make inquiries as to the roster of Union personnel present. His pride swelled, however, when the Perrin girl left the Union group and returned to his table for the meal.

"You choose to dine with us instead of your own kind? I'm honored," he told her.

"This is the last meal I'll share with Mímihn. I couldn't deny her that," she explained.

"You are most kind to think of her."

The banquet was one of the most pleasant formalities Tokh could remember attending. The Emperor's hospitality included an unending supply of highest quality spirits, and Tokh sampled his fair share. He gathered with several of the generals, praising the Emperor's hospitality. The Emperor himself left his table and mingled with the people present. *The Emperor of Kerasím.* Was this what Emperors did behind closed doors of the palace? Yes, Nadigh wore gloves, but he laid his royal hand on Tokh's shoulder and spoke to him, apologizing – apologizing! – for having kept him at a distance from the palace for so long.

"With the change in relations, Tokh, I think it's time you considered a seat on the senate," Nadigh said. "I'm still arranging titles and positions, but with your interstellar experience and your ties to the human female, I think we need your expertise. I'll see you're notified when the arrangements are finalized, another week or so."

Tokh felt as if the stars themselves had come down and settled on his shoulders, twinkling their light through his skull. "I await your command for whatever you see fit, your Majesty. You honor me too well."

Nadigh made a point to speak with Zheníhda and Mímihn, thanking them for their bravery and loneliness while Tokh was away. He reached out and took Zheníhda's gloved hand in his, and in a flash Tokh realized he'd allowed himself to become star-blinded. No matter what the Emperor preached about a casteless society, he was still the Emperor and could demand rights from any female at any time, any where. It would be an honor and a privilege, but Tokh couldn't help wanting to jump in front of his wives and block the contact, send them home. His guts twisted up into a painful knot.

Zheníhda bowed and murmured nonsense about it being her honor. Mímihn burst into tears.

"I apologize, your Imperial majesty," she gasped. "I am awed by your presence."

Nadigh wiped her tears with his gloved fingers, then brought them to his lips. "Tears of joy are the most honest of gifts. Our world needs more of them. Do not apologize, beautiful Lady."

When the Emperor moved on, Tokh collapsed in his seat and ordered Dalo to bring him another *dhurwah*. He'd barely steadied his nerves when the Perrin girl rushed up to him, shoving an unwilling female before her. Aila stopped in front of him and bowed; Masákh and an older uniformed male followed her.

"My apologies for the interruption, Lord General. I wish you to meet my parents, Leila Perrin and Fleet Admiral Ramden Perrin, Undersecretary for the Union Defense Council. Mom, Dad, this is General Tokh, who has taken me in as a member of his family, sheltered me under his roof, cared for me when I couldn't, and gone through great expense and difficulty to keep me alive, both now and five years ago. If you want to thank anyone for my standing here beside you tonight, you thank *him*. I'm tired of you vilifying people you've never even met."

Tokh stood up, eyes blazing with delight. It *was* true! After all this time, the legendary Admiral himself, tall, trim, with silver hair and a white uniform bearing a colorful array of decorations, not unlike Tokh's own. This was the meeting Tokh had coveted for years. Was there no end to the wonders of this night?

"Ah! The great Admiral Perrin of the Union Fleet! I am most honored to meet you, Admiral! Your power and strength caused us much grief. It is good that we may meet and come to understandings before trouble occurs." He held out his hand, the way of Union greeting.

Ramden Perrin grasped his hand cautiously. "I'm at a loss, sir. I don't understand how I've brought you grief when we've never met."

"For a year I listened to stories about the great Admiral Perrin and how he would blow my base from the planet, how massive his fleet was, and how he would exact revenge should his daughter be harmed. We spent many man-hours searching for your fleet, monitoring for what move you would make, and what to do when you arrived. When my *aghát* made it behind lines, they met you and saw you were indeed a man of power. It has been a great asset for us to have your assistance instead of your hostility."

Perrin accepted the information with a raise of a silver eyebrow. "I see. Well, I wouldn't dispute the claim of harm, but I'm not sure how much assistance I've given. You're the General Tokh Aila speaks of, the one that held her hostage all those years ago? The one who damaged her speech and dumped her in the time stream? We spent many man-hours searching long and hard to capture you, Sir, but you slipped by us. You're still wanted for questioning. It puts me in a difficult place just talking to you."

"Then question me, here and now. I followed my orders and did my duty, no more, no less. If your daughter had stayed submissive like a proper female, there would never have been a need for force. As you are aware, she is difficult to restrain. The fact I am misrepresented in the Union is the reason we must meet here."

"You above all people should know about duty, Daddy," Aila said. "Sit! Sit here with the general. He can tell you all about how he has helped me, right down to stopping Vanora just as she was about to kill me." She pushed him into a chair and dragged her mother to the female end of the table.

It was the meeting Tokh had dreamt of. He had no fear of the Admiral here; they were on Kerasím, in the Emperor's palace. There was nothing the Union could do except withdraw from the evening. The Admiral started out with caution, then fired up. Old anger overtook him and his questions became hostile, questions about his

314

daughter's captivity. Tokh let him rage, then walked him through the answers step by step, as much as allowed without breaking into matters of security. Once again Tokh shivered with the thrill of knowing he was changing the course of Kerasi politics, of Kerasi history, just by having a conversation. Perrin's fire eased as his questions were answered. If anything, Tokh was amazed at the amount of misinformation the Admiral had. Surely their intelligence was better than this? No wonder it had been so difficult to start negotiations.

"She did not explain these things to you?"

"Well, yes, she tried," the Admiral stammered, "but we didn't believe her. It went against everything we thought we knew, and we didn't know how much her mind had been tampered with."

"It pains me, that your information is so poor. What you believe is only a partial truth, with more importance assigned it than it deserves. It proves the strong need for more open information, as my Emperors have worked so hard to achieve. Have given their lives for," Tokh admitted.

"I'm deeply sorry about that," Perrin said. "I assure you, Secretary Kel acted on his own, with no knowledge or support from the government. We believed we were sending delegates in peace. If I had any hint of such a plot, I would never have let my daughter be on that mission, if I had to hold her back in chains."

"I believe you. I have a daughter as well, and I would do no differently."

Aila Perrin reappeared beside her father and rubbed a hand down his back. "Find things to talk about?"

Ramden Perrin nodded. "Yes. I think we've cleared the air somewhat. We don't see exactly eye to eye, but it's a start."

"Mother says we're boarding soon."

"I suppose I'd better see to her." He stood up and bowed to the general.

Tokh stood as well. "We will see you to your ship, make sure you get there safely. Come," he said to Aila. "I will return you to your people."

He walked her over to Secretary Hhani, no longer a strange name on a list. "I return her to the Union as promised. I trust you have removed any dangers to her. I have put her under the protection of my name; should your people try to harm her, it will create an incident between our worlds."

315

"Aila's a very valued member of our staff," Bindai Hhani said. "We regret the incident that took place at your home. We were unaware of the deals going on, a great mistake on our part. I assure you, we are cleaning through our staff, and it won't be repeated. The Union thanks you, General Tokh, for all you have done for us. We would encourage you to make a formal visit, be our guest, let us show you the best we have to offer, instead of some of the worst."

Tokh chuckled, the points of his teeth showing. "It is a gracious offer, Secretary Hhani, but I don't travel where there is a price on my head."

Hhani's face colored up, a trait that didn't seem limited to females of the species. "I will personally see that you're cleared of any charges against you. I think you've earned that right."

"I've only been pleading that for the last four years," Aila said wryly. "They never should have been there to start with."

Tokh gave a nod. "You do that, and my sources confirm it, I would be willing to make the journey. My wife has become fond of Aila, and would very much wish to visit her."

Hhani smiled. "Very good. Contact Aila with possible dates, she'll contact me, and we'll see what can be arranged."

"I will wish to tour your military schools, compare them to ours, as well as your educational programs for females. I wish to see how you develop students like Aila. My daughter will be among the first to benefit from the Emperor's extended female programs; I wish her to learn to be as quick and tough as your females."

"None of that's classified; you may tour as many as you'd like."

Tokh gave a short bow. "Most excellent. Thank you."

Tokh and the majority of his contingent, plus eight palace guards and their three translating liaisons followed the Union delegates to the roof. The rest of the Union party boarded the shuttle while the Emissary bid everyone goodbye.

Aila approached Tokh last. The engines on the shuttle began to rev up, making her raise her voice. "General, despite my fears and mistrusts, you've been far too kind. I'm deeply in your debt. I hope I can repay you some day."

"There is no debt, just repayment for wrongs earlier in the course of my duty. It took longer than expected, but everything did go by plan, just not the way we believed it would."

"I'd like to come back and visit, if I may."

Tokh held his head high, and his eyes narrowed just a little. "You are dar-Giláhn. I will be insulted if you don't. I will expect you for the New Year's celebrations. I will recall Masákh, and you will either follow him or be without."

"That's not going to happen," she said with a grin. "I'll stay in communication, but don't trust the line. This is still all too new, with no working treaties yet."

"New to you, not to me," he said with a bow. "You will learn." He stepped forward and clapped a hand on her shoulder, the most he dared do.

Aila waited until he was done, then shook his hand in both of hers. "Thank you again, General." She had one foot on the shuttle step when she turned around and shouted, *"Hasak sim toh Haverowakh!"*

A pain in the ass to everyone. Tokh tipped his head to be sure he heard right, then let loose with a hard, braying laugh. He raised a fist high. "Yes! Yes you are!"

Having left the celebration rooms, they couldn't return. Guards escorted Tokh's party back to the fourth floor. He stopped with Dalo to retrieve the children. Only the boys were still awake.

"Report," he said to Joralan.

Joralan saluted. "We had fun, Sir. Lanag beat me on the flight simulator, but I beat him on the combat one."

Tokh tapped the boy's shoulder with his fist and chuckled. "Good for you. Come."

With the Perrin girl, Mátokhan, Masákh, and Haghíde gone back to Union territory, there was an empty bedroom, which Tokh claimed for himself. He called Zheníhda in while Mímihn put the children to bed. He wasted no time grabbing her off the ground, kissing her, and falling onto the bed with her locked in his arms.

"What are you doing! Tokh!"

He attacked her neck with glee. "We're at the Palace, Nihda! The palace of all the Emperors of Kerasím! We just dined with the Emperor! I've never in my life thrown a *push* into a *dahneg* female, and by all the stars in the universe, I'm going to do so while I'm sleeping at Derahl Nor. And you'll be the first *dahneg* female I will *push*!"

317

Zheníhda squealed like one of the children and kicked her feet. "Oh Tokh! It's too much to think about! Today is like a dream. It can't be real. It just can't. I almost fell down when he spoke to me. I don't know how I didn't. And it's only *dahneg* by privilege."

"He did away with *bhísroti* and *fáhganid*, Nihda. *Dahneg* is the top caste. The top, just below Thósikh! Whether it's no step or half a step, we are now 99% equal to anyone in our neighborhood! I have the right of refusal now! He wants me in the Senate! I can die happy. I've done it all. Not that I want to die tomorrow," he corrected. "That would be a waste of my experience."

Nihda pulled her legs up and locked them around his back. "*Push* me, Tokh, *push* me like the Emperor himself."

He *pushed* her like royalty, her best jewelry around her neck, her long hair spread around her on satin pillows that shimmered like a store display, until even Mímihn raised her head at the noises leaking from the walls. He called for Mímihn and gave her the same, then collapsed into heavy sleep, every joy he'd ever dreamed come true at last.

* * 43 * *

The palace was just a building and they'd only attended an awards ceremony, something that occurred almost every day at one base or another, but the spirit of the house changed. The Emperor's attentiveness to his subjects, at least in Tokh's household, had transformed them. Perhaps it was the fact the Emperor showed appreciation for their work in a very personal way. Perhaps it was having wives and whole families attend that made it different. Perhaps it was as if the Emperor having asked females to be present – only twenty-one had attended, six of them the Emperor's wives and four of them were Tokh's – made it seem as if the wives had been initiated into a secret society, working alongside the men, and they were eager to help. No one was sure, but at Tokh's house, the bickering disappeared, his wives united in the cause. Zheníhda now laid into Tokh about female education as much as Mímihn.

She badgered him about Faelihn. "She's your smalldaughter, the same flying age as your daughter. You'd educate one and not the other? They'll finish school within the next year. I'm sure if you asked Kitras, he'd agree his daughter should not be ignored."

Tokh whirled on her with impatience. "What would you have me do? Hire a teacher from my own pocket and start a school just for them? Dalo should live here forever? Kitras is a captain; he shouldn't still be living on his parents' property. He has *dahneg* privilege now; he can live anywhere he chooses."

"Perhaps he could get an apartment on the other side of the cliff. Then they wouldn't be so far away."

"I'll see what I can do."

And he did. It took several months, but Tokh found an affordable apartment on the far side of the city with no ocean view, one with three small bedrooms, and Kitras moved his family base there. When her official schooling ended on Kesseh's eighth naming day, Tokh hired a retired *rhibáni* schoolmaster and set up a classroom in the servant's quarters over the vehicle hangar, insisting on the same curriculum male students would follow at that age.

Within a week, Kesseh and Faelihn had four more young females as classmates, girls whose parents also wanted to be on the right path before anyone else. Tokh was pleased; he charged the parents an equal portion of the cost, and eased the drain on his accounts. The other mothers or nannies also took turns chaperoning, freeing up Zheníhda and Mímihn from the daily duty.

Tokh lay with Mímihn in his bed, talking between the *pushing*. She cuddled close, head on his arm, face buried against his chest while he rubbed the warm skin on her back. "If I could give you anything to make you happy, what would it be?"

Mímihn smiled and played with his chin hank, twirling it on her finger. "I have everything I could ever want, my Lord. I have the kindest husband of any wife. I have an envious house, beautiful clothing, shining jewelry, and children to love. I've been to the palace, I've been blessed by the Emperor, and I have enough eyesight to see the world with. There can't be a happier wife on Kerasím. Every day I'm living my cloud-dreams." She kissed his chin.

He kissed her forehead and held it for several seconds. "What if I gave you a child of your own?"

Mímihn laughed, but there were tears hiding under the amusement. "You know I can't do that, Tokh. That's the whole reason I was given up to be consort; I'm sterile. No matter what my heart wishes, I can't. I've been *pushed* on thousands of times by two husbands, an owner, and uncounted guests. It doesn't happen, and the problem is mine."

"But do you want to bear one?"

"I would turn my insides out, bearing children for my Lord if he wishes it. But it's a fool's dream."

"I have the name of the physician who treats the Emperor's wives. I'll get you an appointment if you wish. We'll find out why you can't conceive. If they know why, maybe they can fix it."

Mímihn's face lost its glow, and she shrank from him. "I don't know, Tokh. Things like that bring hope. I used my luck with my eyes. I can't be so lucky twice, and I don't know if I can bear the pain if the hope dies. They may be doctors to the Emperor, but they weren't able to give him a son."

He pulled her back to him. "He produced five sons; every one died of a genetic issue. That's not a fault of the doctors. Then don't hope until we know. Go in just wanting to know why, and if the doctor says he can fix it, then we'll hope."

Mímihn had no enthusiasm, so very unlike her bubbly self. "If you wish me to go, I will, but I can't hope."

Tokh stood witness while Mímihn underwent extensive examination and scanning, without a single whimper or complaint. The light had gone out of her, as if her soul had gone elsewhere and left her body behind. Again he marveled at her bravery.

The doctor looked over the results. "Did you ever have an infection, a sickness in your parts? Something that smelled bad, or created a fluid of odd colors or smells? Did you think you were pregnant once, but the baby never grew?"

Mímihn shook her head too fast. Tokh could tell she was holding back. He rubbed her shoulder. "You won't anger me, I promise. You must tell him. It could be the answer."

Mímihn squirmed, and her voice started off faint. "When – When I was first married to General Maghentor, a few months after, I got a pain in my belly, all through my parts. It seemed to swell a little, but not with a baby. Pressure hurt, and yes, I had strange fluids that leaked from me. It hurt very much when Maghentor *pushed* me. I couldn't help crying after a while, it hurt so bad. It made him mad, but I couldn't help it. I was very young and I didn't know anything was wrong. Eventually the housekeeper grew tired of my cries and brought me to a doctor, who said I had gotten germs from Maghentor *pushing* me. He gave me medicine to place inside, and it would clean up Maghentor, too. After a few days, I started to get better. I was a very little girl. I didn't know what was wrong or right." Mímihn wiped at her eyes.

"That infection is probably what made you sterile." The doctor called up images on his monitor for Tokh. "These are the tubes that carry the female cells to where the male's fluid waits for them. The cell travels to the womb, mixes with the fluid, the cell is fertilized, and a baby is made. In your case, Lady Tokh, your tubes are scarred from that infection. They're thick and gnarled, like dried meat. The cell can't pass through to your husband's fluid. The easiest way to fix that is to collect some of your cells, mix them with your husband's fluid in a dish, and then put it back inside you as if it occurred naturally. The cell settles into its home, and a baby will grow."

"It's that simple?"

The doctor nodded. "It's that simple."

She gripped Tokh's hand and squeezed it tight. "Tokh! You brought this hope on me. Don't you let it die! Don't you dare!"

Mímihn was quiet on the flight back to Imahlva. She didn't hang on him, lost in her own thoughts. "Tokh, before we try such a thing, can we make one more try at my bad eye? I need eyes to chase small children. I won't have time afterward for the luxury of rest."

"We'll schedule that as well."

Tokh went to his office while Zheníhda and Mímihn prepared dinner. Mímihn was cutting meat into small pieces when the cuts became harder and the knife began to bang onto the cutting table. She whacked at the meat, beating it, punishing it, then began to stab it, more and more violently. The tears began with the banging and progressed with her rage. The knife wedged into the wood and she yanked and pulled at it, crying and shrieking.

"Mímihn!" Zheníhda snapped. "Cube the meat, not shred it!" She backed up as Mímihn's rage increased. "What's the matter with you?"

The knife stuck fast. Mímihn tore at it furiously, then stepped back, hands to her face. Her face was the darkest, foulest color Zheníhda had ever seen on it. Mímihn could be flighty, she could be feisty and disrespectful with her words, but she never took on murderous rage. Not life-is-wonderful Mímihn.

"I hate him! I hate him! Fortunes help me, I hate him! I tried! I tried to be a good wife, no matter what. I tried! Even when he wronged me, I never spoke bad words about him! But I hate him! Oh Nihda! Everything! Everything bad in my life, every bit of pain I have ever had since the day I became fourteen has been his fault! Every single pain! I swear, I will go to his grave and dig him up and I'll kick him until there are not two bones left together, and I'll sweep them into a pile and I will shit rivers onto them! I swear I will!" She collapsed onto the floor in a heap, crying so hard she couldn't breathe.

Zheníhda knelt beside her, confused. Zheníhda had her life, Mímihn had hers, and they never shared them. She lay a hand on Mímihn's heaving shoulder. "Who?"

"My first husband, Maghentor. Fourteen and a day, I was! He was sixty eight! He didn't have love for me, he just wanted a son. When my belly hurt, he still *pushed* me until I cried. When I didn't have a child, he beat me and yelled at me. Then he brought his friends to me, hoping he could pretend one of theirs was his. I must've bedded fifteen of his officers, and no baby. So he divorced me and sold me as a consort. And I endured all the humiliation that brings, tied up, beaten, *pushed* on eight or ten hours a day and made to do horrible things until I prayed to die. But I lived. And I was bought. And I tried so hard to be a good consort. I smiled when he beat me. I hid food when he would feed his wives but not me. I didn't cry when his actions brought me pain. I went to his friends willingly when ordered, even when I wanted to die instead. Then because I was so pleasant, he blinded me. And still I tried to be kind and pleasant. And still I smiled when he called me names and beat me until I couldn't walk. And then Tokh rescued me and I've had the best years of my entire life. I'd do anything for him. And today I find out that the reason I endured such pain and humiliation for four straight years was because that *trixhor* Maghentor gave me a filthy disease that fused my tubes so the fluid couldn't go where it needed. When I married him, I had every ability to give him children. He took that from me. HE did! HE made me sterile! And then he beat me for becoming sick from his diseased old *hihvat*! I'd have children, I'd have eyes that work, I would never have been so crushed by all that pain. I HATE HIM! Fortunes help me, Nihda, I hate him!"

Zheníhda's icy heart went out to Mímihn. She sat her up and hugged her like a child. "I'm so sorry, Mími. Tokh has done his fair share of wrong to me and I'll never forgive him, but I forget sometimes how terrible life can be for others. I think that's part of why Umara annoyed me so much: she had every happiness I had. Why wasn't my life good enough for her? And then Tokh brings you along like an insult, like two wives aren't enough to make him happy, and you're so happy and obedient it makes me mad in a different way. It was like giving a *ghinadín* too much charity; you had no right to such happiness, using my luxury. And now I apologize. I was too upset and angry to think of why you might be so happy, or what happened to you before you came here. You were consort to a *dahneg*, yes?"

Mímihn gasped and nodded.

"So you knew greater luxury than I. I'm sorry, Mímihn. I'm sorry Maghentor was a beast to you. They should never have married you so young to such an old man. You were lucky he didn't die on top of you." Mímihn nodded.

"Come." Zheníhda pulled Mímihn up to sit at the table. "Shanohr, please finish making the dinner." The housemaid scurried over.

Zheníhda wasn't allowed to touch the pepper rum. It wasn't even kept with the spirits, but she found the most expensive bottle of *dhurwah* and brought it to the table. "We'll drink to the death of your pain. It's the past and you have a good life now, one that would insult your previous husband, Shit-on-His-Bones."

Mímihn gave a faint laugh. "I hate Maghentor, but I hate that *hihven khatorahkt dahneg* a hundred times more. I won't foul my mouth speaking his name. I can't speak of the things he made me do."

"Then don't. There's no shame in something when you have no other choice but death." Zheníhda poured them both a spot of the spirits. "What is it with *dahneg*s? Are they all sick when it comes to *pushing*? Tokh was forced to lend me once to a demanding *dahneg*. He broke my teeth, my face, and bloodied me so bad Tokh won harsh justice against him. It was that *trixohr dahneg* across the road that drove Umara to her death. I don't know for certain what he did, but it never left her thoughts and she felt shamed by it."

Mímihn drew a sharp breath. "I didn't know, Zheníhda. That's terrible! He hurt you like that for amusement?"

"No. There are things I will do for another's pleasure and things I won't. Most of the time Tokh accepts that. The *dahneg* didn't. I have no regrets. I'm sure the *dahneg* does, however. He had to explain to his wife how he lost a *khata*. I'm sure he never gave the truth."

Mímihn gave a soft laugh. She reached out and squeezed Zheníhda's hand. "I'm so sorry you were hurt like that."

Zheníhda squeezed the hand back. "Everyone carries regret, Mímihn. There's no shame in that."

When Tokh came to dinner, his wives, never on kind terms, were clearly drunk and laughing together. It was never a good sign when two enemies joined forces.

"Is there something I should know?"

"Comparing war stories," Zheníhda giggled. "We've come to the conclusion that honor aside, this household will remain *dihnarwharl*, those with honor. We've realized *dahneg* males have no honor, and therefore allowing you to see yourself as *dahneg* would be a dangerous thing to both of us. If you wish to wave your *dahneg* status about, you'll do it out of the house. Here, you're still just a *dihnarwharl*, and you'll be held to their honor."

Tokh eyed them with suspicion. "I won't argue with drunken females. Hope that we don't have sudden guests, with yourselves like that."

Zheníhda batted her eyes at him and laid a hand across her chest. "Why, yes, we are!" she said, and across the table Mímihn burst into high-pitched laughter.

"This can't be good," he mumbled.

But it was. Zheníhda began treating Mímihn as a daughter instead of a rival, and Mímihn, who had always been subservient to Zheníhda, seemed to shoulder more responsibility and act like a wife and not a child. Tokh wasn't sure what had happened, but he wasn't about to curse it by demanding answers.

He questioned Kassán about Mímihn's sight, seeking the neurologist for answers before the ophthalmologist. If the nerves weren't there, there was no point in going further.

Kassán frowned at the imaging. "I've read the surgical notes and I've seen the scans. I witnessed the first two surgeries. I'm not sure, Tokh. Granted, fifteen percent is so low it's worth trying."

"Only the bad eye. She's not willing to risk what she has in the good one."

"Improving the bad will improve the good one on its own. Having to work in tandem will strengthen it. Right now it's doing the work of two. Any additional input will ease the strain. I'd like to be surgeon on this one, with the ophthalmologist standing by as consult. I'd observe the nerves directly, make the finest of connections. It'll be a longer surgery, but you may have better results."

"Then we'll try it."

Mímihn wasn't nervous about the surgery at all, once Kassán assured her he wouldn't touch her good eye. She came out of surgery moaning in pain, with both eyes bandaged.

"My eyes, Tokh! Why are both covered? He insisted only one!"

Tokh's voice came through her darkness. "*Shu, shu, falahndi.* If you can see out of one, it will move the other, and they need it to rest. Kassán assures me, he operated only on the one."

She found his hand and squeezed it. "I don't like the darkness, Tokh. It scares me. I'm scared I'm blind again. I can't go back to being blind. I can't bear it!"

"*Shu, shu.* I promise you won't be, or I'll see to it Kassán's eyes are implanted into you."

"Why does it hurt so much? It's never hurt like this before. My head feels like an airship has crushed it."

"*Shu.* I'll make them get you something for the pain."

With her other surgeries, Mímihn was home the next day, breaking the rules and overusing her new vision. This time, she spent three days in a drugged haze, her eyes bandaged, still in so much pain she couldn't put that side of her head against a pillow. It wasn't until the third day that Tokh was present while Kassán examined her. He removed the wrappings and Mímihn was thrilled to see everyone with her good eye, until she heard Tokh give a gasp.

"*Kassán!*"

Kassán squinted and poked at her bad eye. "That's to be expected. It looks quite good, actually. Close your left eye, and tell me what you see with the other."

Tokh's hands closed around Kassán's throat, holding but not squeezing, yet. His voice dropped, chilling and slow. *"What did you do to her?"*

"Tokh?" Mímihn's fingers touched her face. It was grotesquely swollen, the eye almost shut by edema. It hurt with even the slightest pressure, all the way up to the top of her head. She couldn't see the brown-black bruising that covered the side of her face, or the line of sutures that ran clear across the top of her head behind her hairline, supporting the skin-sealer.

Kassán held still, but only amusement crossed his face. "If you want me to explain what you see, you'll remove your hands."

"If you've done anything sinister, I'll have you quartered before your head is removed." Tokh's hands came down, but one rested on the hilt of his sword.

Kassán clucked. "After all these years, General. Kassán, fix this! Kassán, come here! Kassán, take care of this! And yet you doubt and threaten me at the first ignorance. I expect a substantial apology."

326

He pulled the swollen skin wider around Mímihn's eye. "Can you see my finger?" He held it a few inches from her face.

Mímihn squinted in the dim light. "Yes, I can." She closed her good eye. "There's one. Now two. Now one again. The image in the center is much clearer. I can tell it's a finger. The edges are still spotty, but I can see much more in the center."

"Excellent." He let the swollen lids close again. "The swelling will subside in a week, as will the bruising. The previous surgeries involved removing the eye and operating behind it. That limits the reach of the surgeon. Instead, I left the eye in place, where it wants to be, and removed a section of bone next to the eye." He traced a light path over the swollen orbit by her temple. "This allowed me to access the nerves as they sit, pulling up nerves that were too short to reach before. I attached as many nerve bundles as I could find, and more importantly rerouted capillaries to feed them. Then I cemented the bone back in place. It will heal as strong as it was before. Now, because she is female, and because she has far too pretty a face, I hid the incision inside her hairline and peeled her scalp down to expose the area I needed. When I was done I simply rolled the skin back up over her face, and when it heals, there will be no visible scars unless she decides to shave her head.

"Of course," he said with a more characteristic sneer, "if you would have preferred, I could have slashed open her face, did my work, and then stitched it all up for a nice fat brown scar. Give her something to talk about, certainly. Would have saved me a lot of time. The pain comes from the healing bone. I can do nothing but give her medication for it until it has healed. Patience. In three weeks you won't know she has had surgery."

A look of horror crossed Mímihn's face as she heard the news. Her fingers explored the incision across her head. "Holy Mother of Fortune!"

Tokh hung his head and made note to send Kassán a very expensive bottle of Pepper Rum. "I'm most sorry to have doubted you, my friend. Understand I'm extremely protective of my wives, and I didn't expect to see such injuries."

"*Gah.* I wouldn't disappoint you, Tokh. I enjoyed the difficulty of it. The important thing is that the eye is working. Tomorrow we'll add more light, and if all is improving, she may return home then."

Mímihn was thrilled. As the week progressed, then the next, the eye grew stronger. Her field of vision was still small, a misshapen stripe in the center and some spots of lights around it, but she could make out shapes well enough to read up close. Her eyes coordinated again and she had some depth perception, and her clumsiness eased. With correction she had almost forty percent vision in the useable section of bad eye, and sixty percent in the good one. She was still dreadfully nearsighted, but her eyes were functional again.

"No more," she declared. "I'm content. I won't risk losing any just to gain a little more. I can live with this."

The next day, Tokh brought her to the fertility specialist in Keranihn.

"What if it doesn't work?" Mímihn fretted.

"Then we do it again," the specialist said. "We can try every month. Almost everyone experiences a pregnancy within three tries. Most of it depends on the reason for the infertility. Yours isn't a problem with the cells, so I have every belief it should take on the first try. We do this, wait two weeks, and see if it took. If it didn't, we do it again two weeks later."

Mímihn looked mournful instead of happy. "I can't let myself hope yet. If it doesn't happen, my heart will shatter."

The physician patted her arm. "Trust me, it will work. Did you want to pick the sex?"

Mímihn turned to Tokh. "You wish a son, don't you?"

"I have three sons and a daughter. I'll leave the choice up to you," Tokh said.

"I don't know! I wish to bear you a son, but it would be nice if Kesseh had a sister, no? I can't decide. Surprise me," she told the doctor. "No! Wait! That *trixohr* Maghentor wanted a son from me and I couldn't give him one. I'm glad I never did, because he didn't deserve one. I want a son. I want to bear a son for a man who deserves one, no matter how many others he has. I want – no, I *demand* to give a son to a righteous man. And if it wasn't so far away, I'd travel to Maghentor's grave and dump the baby's diaper on it."

The doctor eyed her strangely. "Very well. We'll screen for male cells before we implant. That's common enough."

"Okay then," Mímihn said with confidence. "Let's do it."

They were the longest two weeks Mímihn could remember living. She wouldn't let Tokh touch her, lest he somehow drown it in his fluids or bump it loose. She stayed in bed or lying flat as much as possible.

"Time to get up, Umara," Zheníhda jabbed. "There is no reason for you to be in bed at lunch time."

"I don't want to risk it falling out," Mímihn said.

"If it's truly a baby in the making, it won't fall out. It's too early for you to feel sick from it, so get up and go wash your children's laundry. The world doesn't stop because you're pregnant. If you think you're going to be lying down for the next eight months, you're sorely mistaken."

Mímihn rolled to sit up, so she didn't strain her belly. "Fine. Then come with me, Nihda. Get Thrit and come with me to Temple. We'll pray to the Fortunes that I'm indeed pregnant."

"Okay," Zheníhda said at last. "We'll go. Only because I don't want to be around if you aren't."

Mímihn's nerves returning to the specialist were worse than undergoing the procedure. She couldn't eat breakfast, and wore a veil over her face so Tokh wouldn't see her crying all the way there. Hope was the very worst pain there was.

"I warned you, your problem was mechanical, not biological," the specialist said. He bowed at Tokh. "Congratulations. It's a baby. I'll give you the name of one of our neonatologists to go over things to expect, and how to have the healthiest baby."

"Truly? Just like that? You're certain? I'm pregnant? After ten years?" Mímihn stared at her belly. She began to shake and cry again, then jumped to put her arms around Tokh's neck. "Oh Tokh! Thank you! Thank you! My Lord, you're truly the greatest husband on this planet!"

* * 44 * *

Mímihn tiptoed around the house. She didn't feel pregnant, though she wasn't sure how pregnant was supposed to feel. She avoided Tokh when Zheníhda's week ended and hers began.

She tried squirming out of his arms. "You can't, Tokh. I won't risk hurting the baby."

He held her tight, his breath warm on her ear. "I have *pushed* my way through five pregnancies. *Pushing* does not harm the baby. Your doctor told you that, and all those downloads you have tell you the same. It's so small right now it doesn't even have a head. Don't make yourself crazy." Mímihn let him do what he wanted, but she couldn't relax enough to find pleasure in it.

Mímihn had made it to five months, her flat little belly just starting to round out, when Tokh got the news. He came home from Keranihn four hours early, shoulders bent under an unspoken burden.

Zheníhda knew the look. "You're traveling again, aren't you. A baby on the way, and they send you off. You're too old for that nonsense."

"Yes, they want me to train a crew, but not yet. I received news from my brothers. My father has died."

Zheníhda put her arms around him. "I'm most sorry, my Lord. He lived a long life."

Tokh had never brought Mímihn to meet his family. She rubbed his arm. "All my sorrows, my husband."

Tokh sat heavily at the table. "Ninety-two years, yes. Longer than most. He outlived his firstwife, Galisse, by three years. I have to fly back to Nar Rhede for a few weeks, settle his estate with my brothers. There's a bigger issue, however."

Zheníhda's head snapped up. "No! Tokh, no! Please say it won't be so!" Mímihn frowned, not understanding.

"What am I to do? Suntahr and Kaloh are Galisse's sons. They have no claim to my mother. She's eighty-one. I'm her eldest son. It's not like I can claim we don't have room."

"Tokh!" Zheníhda glanced at Mímihn. "You can't do that to Mímihn. It's not fair."

"What's not fair?" Mímihn said cautiously.

"His mother Filuhr." Zheníhda spat the name as if it poisoned her tongue. "She's a vulgar snoop into private things and private places. She's a midwife of a past age and has no shame. She'll shove her nose up your *lihx* faster than a new husband and then criticize you on it. If she knows you're pregnant, you're doomed. She'll be on you like an *aaka*-fly and never let go."

"Oh." Mímihn rubbed her belly as if protecting it.

"Tokh, you can't bring her here."

"I have no choice, Nihda!" Tokh's voice raised, but in frustration. "With luck it'll only be for a little while, until I find a good care facility."

"Do *not* let her near Kesseh! She was bad enough with the boys!"

Tokh's face said he hadn't thought of that. "It's not my choice. I'm the oldest son. It's my duty."

He was gone just over two weeks. Mímihn and Zheníhda rearranged the downstairs spare room and made it pretty with bedding from one of the guest rooms, as Filuhr couldn't climb the stairs so many times a day. It wasn't as grand a room as the upstairs, and it looked out onto the retaining wall behind the house, but it was bright and welcoming and right next to the downstairs bath.

The walk from the landing pad to the house had never seemed so long. Tokh's exasperation carried across the yard, mincing his steps and shuffling behind his mother, who leaned on a walking stick. Filuhr wasn't even as tall as Mímihn and perhaps only the weight of Kesseh, her fuzzy white hair pulled up onto her head in a miniature knot.

She walked up to Mímihn first, waiting by the door to greet her. Filuhr squinted upward. "You're Tokh's daughter?"

"No, Lady Talekh, I'm Mímihn, Tokh's secondwife," she bowed. "I'm most pleased to meet you. It's an honor to welcome you to our home."

She gave Mímihn a sharp eye. "You're awfully young to be his wife. I told him not to marry them so young. Babies get stuck when

331

the hips are too young, rips the mothers apart and kills them both." She tapped Mímihn's flank with her walking stick. Mímihn paled and stepped backwards without another word.

She caught sight of Zheníhda standing tall on the other side of the door, and her face dropped. "YOU! You're still alive? Oh no no! Tokh! I won't live with that vile destroyer! Tokh! Take me away from here!" She turned and tried to head back to the craft.

Zheníhda smiled an icicle, chilling the warmth of even an Imahlva day. In all their fights and disagreements, Mímihn had never seen Zheníhda's face so frightening. Her voice carried an odd tone of triumph. "Welcome, *Ama* Filuhr. It's been many years. How nice to see you again. Come, I've prepared a *special* room for you."

"Oh no you don't! You already tried to kill me! You think I've forgotten? The most ungrateful wretch I ever met! No, Tokh! I can't be under the same roof with her. She'll be the death of me!"

"*Ama*, you have no choice right now," Tokh said, and he took her by the arm.

"What? I said no!"

"Just come and have lunch!" he said, louder.

"Okay," Filuhr said, and she allowed Tokh to lead her into the house. "But that one's not allowed to touch my food! Let the baby one do it. I warned you, Tokh, not to marry the little ones. Where's the fat one?"

"Umara died, *Ama*. Three years ago, now."

She stared up at Tokh with a foul expression. "Did that one kill her?"

"No, *Ama*. Let me show you where you can leave your things."

"I'm not staying here, Tokh. I can't run like I used to."

Tokh raised his voice in exasperation. "Then let me show you a safe place to escape her!" He led Filuhr to the back room.

Zheníhda turned to Mímihn with a raised eyebrow.

"Holy Blood of the Emperor!" Mímihn whispered. "What are we going to do? She's crazy as a land fish. She thinks you tried to kill her."

"I never tried to *kill* her," Zheníhda said. "I just sort of... chased her with Tokh's sword. I never touched her."

Mímihn's jaw fell open. "You *what*?"

Zheníhda laughed and related the story. "And when she went all righteous *dihnarwharl* on me, I went and got one of Tokh's swords. She never forgave me for not bowing to her will. She's the most pompous, inflated female I have ever met. Do *not* tell her you were a consort."

Mímihn squeezed her hand as Tokh came out of the back hall. "Oh Nihda! You must tell me more of your stories like that."

Zheníhda had prepared one of Filuhr's favorite dishes for lunch but let Mímihn do the serving, as it wasn't right for Tokh to do such things. "You'll like it here, *Ama*," he said with as much cheer as he could muster. "It's warm and sunny most days, and the sea air is good for the body. You can sit outside, walk among the flowers, or soak in the pool if you like. Thrit will take you down to the shore, if you ask him."

"I want to go home, Tokh. Please take me home. It's so terribly hot here. I want my balcony."

"*Bo*'s gone, *Ama*. They reclaimed the apartment. You have no choice."

"Take me to your sister's. Nihrin won't let me live like this."

"You can visit her for a bit, *Ama*, but you can't stay there permanently.

"Then take me to your brother Hamiran."

"It's not Hamiran's duty, *Ama*. I'll find you a place you'll like, but I can't do it by tomorrow. You must be patient."

The room fell silent for a moment as everyone managed to eat a few bites.

"So, Tokh, do you bed them together? It can be very helpful to a man your age, one stroking you while you *push* on the other. Does the little one find you enticing, or do you have to force her?"

Mímihn spit a wave of *tanit* juice across the table. She jumped up to clean it. "I'm so sorry, Tokh. Forgive me." Zheníhda bowed her head to hide a smile.

Tokh slammed a fist on the table, rattling the plates. "*Ama*! Listen to me very carefully: my children will be here at dinner, and there will be no discussion of body parts, of *pushing*, of reproduction, or anything to do with any of it! Do you understand me?"

"You're awfully touchy. Are you having trouble achieving stiffness in your ring? It's very common in males of your age you know, and makes you all meaner than a swarm of starving bloodbugs. It's nothing to be ashamed of. Your father started with trouble sometime in his sixties. There are things that will help both

333

of you. Maybe the Murderous Bag of Bones doesn't excite you, but I'll bet that little one there can still twist your *khatas* into a knot." Filuhr cackled. Mímihn's cheeks burned a dark brown, and she stared into her plate.

Tokh threw his fork down. "I'm not yet sixty, *Ama*. If you can't stop such talk at the table, you'll eat alone. Wives, come." He stood up and walked outside. His wives followed without a word.

He crossed the courtyard to the cliff wall and leaned on it, letting the breeze and water view soothe him. Zheníhda's hand slid over his shoulders.

"What are we going to do, Tokh?"

He sighed hopelessly. "She's old. She doesn't know where she is half the time. Tomorrow she'll wake up and not know why she's here or that my father's gone. She's done that for the past two weeks. I don't know what to do. She doesn't mean to annoy people, she just says what comes to her head."

"No, that's one thing I'm sure of," Zheníhda said. "She has every intent of angering us."

"I'll hire a companion for her, someone who can be at her beck and call most of the day. And I'll find a good care home for females. I have *dahneg* pull now. I'll ask in Keranihn. There must be nice places the upper castes send their crazy old people."

"You weren't exaggerating." Mímihn leaned in to whisper, as if the old woman could hear them outside. "Has she always been like that?"

"Yes," Zheníhda said.

Tokh shot her an unhappy glare, but he said, "She was a respected midwife, delivered a thousand babies. She's used to helping people have healthy, happy beddings and babies. She educates both males and females on bedding practices. It may bother everyone else in the world, but not her. She'll discuss anything with anyone who holds still. She means well, but I don't want Jora and Kesseh near her alone. If Jora were a little older, I'd let her discuss anything he wanted with her, but I think eleven is still too young for those details. And Kesseh has plenty of time before she needs to hear such ideas."

"I agree," Mímihn said.

Tokh turned around and stared at the house. "I'll go to the job office and see what I can find for a companion. She'll behave for Nihda, but go easy on her until I get back."

He returned with a sixty-something *nhásarwharl* woman with arms the size of tree trunks, someone who would have no trouble helping his mother in and out of the bath or carrying her, if needed. He gave her strict instructions that his mother could speak about anything she wanted in her bedroom or to the companion, but was not to speak a word of anything sexual around the children. The helper moved in to Mímihn's old bed in the servant's quarters.

Tokh lay in bed next to Zheníhda that night, naked and powerless. "I can't, Nihda. At least, not tonight. The rocks in my stomach are too big. A little old female with only half her wits, and she has me terrified to touch my wives. She'll hear some kind of creak in the flooring and tell me I'm doing something wrong. How can someone who only means to help people cause so much guilt?"

Zheníhda lay with her head on his chest, happy he didn't want to do anything else. "Because we're too close to her. We don't see her as a professional giving wanted advice, we see her as your *Ama*, forcing information on us that we don't wish to hear. She never understood that separation."

"She's my *Ama*, yes, and that's why I feel so bad not wanting her in my home. Is that wrong of me, Nihda? We have the space. Wouldn't you be upset if Zenak and Kitras didn't want you in their home when you're old?"

"We've never had a good relation with your *Ama*, Tokh," she reminded him. "You haven't spoken to her in five years. I think we have a much better relationship with our children. We visit Zenak once a year, and he comes here for two weeks. We had Kitras's family living with us for almost a year, and moved them here so the children could be closer to each other. That's far different than any relationship we had with Filuhr. We're closer to your brothers than to your *ama*, and they're much older and of a different *ama*. Mímihn's the one I worry about; Joralan remembers his real mother well enough. If he hasn't bonded well with Mímihn, he could refuse to care for her. Her only hope is if her child is male."

"It is," Tokh admitted. "She hasn't announced it yet, but it is. She was allowed to pick the sex. She wanted a sister for Kesseh, but decided having a male heir would be a fitting insult to her first husband."

Zheníhda smiled. "Good for her."

335

The companion eased much of the strain of the house, while Tokh tried to find a place for his mother. He was the eldest son; care for his aged mother was supposed to fall on him and his wives, but Zhenída and Mímihn had buried their differences and he wouldn't allow anything, especially his mother, to ruin that harmony. Most homes for elderly females were filled with those who never married or never bore sons, and therefore had no one to house them or speak for them. Most were horrible places where old females were given a bed and little else, beaten on by caretakers or other residents, dirty and diseased in the most awful of conditions, with nothing to do but stare out a window all day. Many died within a year. Tokh didn't wish that fate on his mother; he wanted her to live happily, just somewhere other than his house. He thought about the rooms over the vehicle shed, but she'd have too much difficulty with the stairs.

The companion had a two-hour break in the evenings, to take her meal in peace. Filuhr sat on the sofa watching a program on the wall screen. Mímihn tried to be nice.

"Is there anything I can get for you, *Ama* Filuhr? Perhaps a cup of *raffin*?"

Filuhr stared at the wallscreen, her thin lips chewing something invisible. "No. I want to go home. Tokh has no right to keep me prisoner here."

"I'm sorry you feel that way. It must be very hard to leave your home after so many years. I don't ever want to leave this house."

Joralan and Kesseh ran through the room, chasing each other with play swords. They stopped to battle not far from the sofa, Jora parrying every swing Kesseh made, until she swung from underneath and touched his side.

"Tagged you! I win! Ah-ah! I beat you! You're going to fail at military school, stabbed by a female!"

"And I'll take your head off in your sleep!" he countered, and swung at her neck from out of reach.

"Ah! Ah!" Filuhr croaked. "What is she doing with that! Take it! Take it from her! A female has no business swinging a sword."

"They're just playing," Mímihn said. "Go, children. Your wisemother's watching a program. Play outside, but not near the walls."

"Tokh! The child has a sword! Come take it from her."

"It's okay, *Ama*. Tokh knows. He gives Kesseh lessons to use one appropriately."

Filuhr gave her a crazed look, as if Mímihn had lost her mind. "A female has no right to a sword."

"There's nothing wrong with learning to defend yourself. Tokh wishes Kesseh to be strong and brave, and not be afraid of assault."

"They'll kill her if she fights back. It's illegal to strike a male. It's best to allow them their business easily, and then leave without injury."

Mímihn looked as if she'd swallowed something sour. "The world is changing, *Ama*. The Emperor has changed the laws. It's not always legal to assault females anymore, and by the time Kesseh is grown, it will be her right to say no. She's Tokh's daughter; she'll be powerful."

Filuhr continued to stare. "Blasphemy! She'll never have a husband. She'll be a stone around his neck and the neck of her brother forever."

"I think she'll have the best husband that way, one who won't be afraid to leave her alone."

They fell silent, but the next time Mímihn looked over, Filuhr had tears on her face, and she was shaking.

Mímihn put her hand on Filuhr's arm. "*Ama*, what's wrong?"

Filuhr's chin was pulled up tight, wrinkling her face further. "I'm not a fool! I've seen how the world works. He's setting my smalldaughter up for a life of sadness. Tokh has always disappointed me. First with the Bag of Bones and her disrespect, always lying to me, and now raising his children to be wild undisciplined things. It's a horrible thing to witness."

"*Ama*!" Mímihn took offense. "No one has lied to you! You underestimate and dishonor your own son. He's the most wonderful husband and father anyone could ask for."

Filuhr glared at her, wrinkles folded in as the skin of a fallen *trobe* fruit. "As you sit there and lie to my face? You think I can't tell you're pregnant? No, you're not showing under that dress, but I spent seventy years with pregnant females. I can tell by looking at your face. I'm old but I'm not useless, Little Thing. He hides joyous news like that from me, for what? The one thing that can make me happy, give me something to look forward to, and he keeps that joy from me. I don't want to be in such a house as this, where everyone is mean to me."

Mímihn saw the truth in her words. "No one is trying to be mean to you, *Ama* Filuhr. That's not something I run up to people and shout at them. I had great difficulty getting pregnant and I won't tempt the Fortunes by bragging about it. If you wanted to know, you should have asked. I'm five months, and it will be a male. If that makes you happy, then I'm glad for you."

"So he is having difficulties in the bed."

Mímihn's words grew sharp. "If you weren't Tokh's mother, I would slap you! That kind of nasty speculation is exactly why Tokh doesn't tell you things. It's none of your business at all, but I'll tell you anyway. I suggest you try very hard to remember it. No, Tokh has no problems bedding me like a man half his age. The issue was mine. My previous husband gave me a disease that made it hard to conceive. Now he's dead and Tokh has given me revenge in this precious little boy. I'm thankful for your concern over my baby, but I won't be driven to craziness by unsolicited advice. If I have a question, I'll be sure to come to you first and ask, but don't tell me what to do."

Filuhr sucked her chin up again and turned away. "I want to go home."

But Mímihn won her over by making a point to ask her a question three times a day, and one day, when Mímihn felt fluttering in the middle of lunch, got Filuhr to smile by letting her feel her belly.

It took Tokh two weeks to find Filuhr a permanent place, in a spotless *dahneg* home only fifteen *fasim* from his sister Nihrin's house. It was a welcoming place, run by compassionate females who were paid good wages and supervised by a *dahneg* who cared about the reputation of the facility. And Nihrin could visit frequently.

"I feel bad," Mímihn said in the quiet following Filuhr's departure. "I'll make it a point for Tokh to make a visit once the baby is born, to make her happy."

Zheníhda gave a snort. "With luck, she'll be dead before then."

"No. I mean it. I want her to see her new smallson. I want to see some sort of joy on her face. I don't want to be that joyless and miserable when I'm old. Then she can die."

Filuhr had barely been placed when duty called.

Mímihn clung to him. "You can't go. I need you, Tokh. Don't they realize you're having a baby?"

"They'll remind me you are the one having the baby and that my part is over, and then they'll laugh at me." He freed himself and kissed the top of her head. "If I'm not back sooner, I'll make sure I'm here before the birth."

He gave Zheníhda a last embrace, sucking on her earlobe. "Help her," he whispered in the ear. "Don't play any of your games. I don't want her so overcome with nerves it hurts the baby."

"I'll behave," Zheníhda swore. He entered the waiting craft without looking back. It lifted off in a gust of exhaust. Mímihn couldn't help waving her arms at it, in case he was looking out the glass.

"Don't be so mournful," Zheníhda said. "It's not like he's off-world. He'll call us by the end of the week."

"It's not the same," Mímihn said with an empty heart, and walked out to sit under the new trellis by the pool.

Mímihn braved the last months of her pregnancy alone, speaking to Tokh only over the ComNet, dropping her skirt to show him her ever-expanding belly. To her she seemed as large as a spacecraft, but Zheníhda marveled at the fact she'd managed to grow a perfectly round little ball of baby, without gaining a bit anywhere else. Zheníhda kept a wall of politeness between them, not interfering but being supportive when asked.

"An end-of-the-year baby," Zheníhda mused. "Too bad he wasn't a little later; he could have been born on New Year's Day. That's a lucky thing."

"No," Mímihn said. "Tokh wants all his officers here to celebrate, and Ai-lah has promised to come back. I don't want to ruin his plans by having the baby in the middle of it. It must be born on time, so Tokh will be here."

Mímihn kept her appointments with the doctors. She rubbed her ball, talked to it, and watched the days tick by. Kesseh had made ten years' worth of plans for the baby, more anxious and impatient than Mímihn.

She sat at the table, head in her hand. Zheníhda noticed her grimace. "Eat something. You'll feel better."

Mímihn shook her head. "No. I don't feel like it. My stomach hurts too much. I really just want to go back to bed and lie down."

Zheníhda paused. Mímihn was two weeks from delivery. Tokh would return in three days. "How does your stomach hurt? All the time, or now and then?"

"It goes away, but it keeps coming. *Gah!* I'll go rest."

"No, sit. Let me know when it stops and starts."

Zheníhda sat with her and watched the timer on her personal com. Mímihn curled over and gave a faint groan with the last one. Zheníhda put her hand on Mímihn's belly and felt it, hard as stone.

She cuffed Mímihn on her shoulder – she knew better than to hit her in her head and put her vision at risk. "You foolish rock! The baby's coming! Your pains are four *fasím* apart! If you'd waited any longer he'd be born right here at the table. Shanohr! Grab Mímihn's things and call for Thrit. I'll call for transport."

"Forget that!" Mímihn shouted. "Call Tokh! He promised me!" She yanked her comm from her pocket and tapped the icon for his emergency connection.

"Now, Tokh! I need you now! It's coming!" she shouted into the pickup. "You promised me you'd be here! Hurry!" and she closed the line before he could say a word.

Tokh secured a private craft – the privilege of a level-four *dahneg* general – and flew for Imahlva at the fastest possible speed, a trip that still took three hours. He usurped his privilege again and called for clearance to land directly at the Female Concerns hospital. No matter where he stepped, someone seemed to be trying to stop him, behavior he wasn't used to. Two people were ahead of him in the line to find out which floor she was on, then the floor attendants didn't want to tell him what room she was in, then they wouldn't let him in the room.

"General! Fathers aren't allowed in birthing rooms!" the attendant said, blocking the door. He saw the *dahneg*-privilege badge on Tokh's black casual uniform and didn't attempt to touch him.

Tokh, however, didn't care. He could hear Mímihn's yelling through the door, and shoved the attendant out of the way.

The doctor glanced over. "Please wait outside. Fathers aren't allowed in here."

The room frightened Tokh, though he would never admit it. Half looked like a treatment room and half like an operating room.

340

Mímihn lay on a bed, writhing in pain while a male attendant held her down and a midwife wiped her face with a cloth.

She reached out to him with a huge smile. "Tokh!" He shoved his way to her and kissed her sweaty head. "You're here! I was trying to hold him in. I wanted you so badly. I can't see what they're doing."

"I'm here. I said I would be here, and I am." He glanced up at the doctor. "You will give her something to ease the pain. Now."

"You need to leave," the doctor repeated. "She's ready to deliver and you can't be here."

"She's my wife and it's my direct right to bear witness to any procedure she undergoes. I will not move."

The door opened and two armed guards entered, both of *dahneg* status – probably demoted *fáhganid*. They took one look at Tokh and stopped.

"Get him out," the doctor said.

The guards bowed in Tokh's direction. "That's General Tokh," said one. "He's a senator."

The doctor gave a growl of irritation and waved them out. He gave Mímihn something to ease her pains. "Stay back out of the way, then, and let us work."

Tokh hadn't been allowed in with his other wives, nor had he wanted to be there. Birthing was female business. He hadn't seen his children until they were presentable. This time, he held Mímihn's hand, both curious and horrified to watch his son come into the world not even ten *fasim* later. It was most definitely male, and the first cries from his lungs were miraculous to Tokh's ears.

The midwife wrapped the baby and placed him on Mímihn's chest. Tears of joy covered Mímihn's face. "No more. No more am I a worthless consort. I'm a wife and a mother, and this is my own child. I gave birth to a son." She touched the little head covered in soft black fuzz, the rounded bump of nose, the fine faint shadow of his future eyebrow. She kissed his forehead as if kissing the very universe and handed him to Tokh.

"Here is your son. I bore him for you. Thank you, Tokh, for giving me my dreams. He's not very big, but he's more than the Emperor has."

Tokh took the baby out of politeness – he wasn't a fan of infants who did no more than shit and scream, but the comment about the Emperor hit home. This was his fourth living son – fourth – and the

Emperor had none. Not one. Six wives, fifteen daughters, and six dead sons. The Emperors had reshaped a planet, reshaped the destiny of a people, all because there was no living male heir from the eldest son. And Tokh had four. In that way, he was richer than the Emperor himself. He looked down at Mímihn's sweaty, tear-streaked face, beaming with adoration, and his breath caught. A single tear made it out of his eye but it was on the far side, and with Mímihn's poor sight she wouldn't see it.

He smiled at the baby, then handed it back to Mímihn. "No. He is perfection, and he's my gift to you, the greatest jewel I could find." Mímihn held him to her face and cried harder as Tokh leaned down and kissed her head.

"Thoren dar-Giláhn," Mímihn told Zheníhda, bursting with pride. She held the baby out as if showing off a trophy.

Zheníhda took him with a girlish smile. "Oh Mímihn! He's truly beautiful! I can't tell you the last time I saw such a beautiful baby. I like the name, too. You did well."

Mímihn glowed as if the sun hovered over her. "Thank you, Nihda. Thank you for your help. It meant a great deal to me. I was so afraid without Tokh."

Zheníhda gave a soft snort. "The last thing we needed was a sickly baby about."

Mímihn took Thoren and went to let the children hold him.

Zheníhda raised her eyebrow at Tokh. "Fifty-eight years old and you're the father of a newborn. Your smallchildren are more than ten years older than that."

"The Emperor himself has an infant brother. Do you want one? They said they can use the same procedure for you as well."

Zheníhda's laugh implied that he was crazy. Tokh put his arms around her from behind and nuzzled her ear. "Thank you. Thank you for caring for her while I was away. I know that's the second time you were stuck with that, and you probably wanted nothing to do with her, but I apologize for things beyond my control."

"She wasn't that bad. She didn't whine or sulk, like Umara. I would hate her for her unending happiness – I *should* hate her for her unending happiness; only a fool is always happy like that; but how do you hate a happy person?"

"You know it's you and me for the next six weeks," he purred, swaying with her. "I brought Mimi a small gift, and one for the baby, but if you unpack my luggage, you'll find there are several very nice gifts with your name on them."

Zheníhda snorted, but it was with amusement. "Really? I thought males thought the greatest gift lay in their pants."

"*Gah.* I'll unwrap that one for you later." He ran his tongue behind her ear.

Zheníhda pulled away. "At least tell me you brought your gear inside."

Mímihn made Tokh keep her promise. Although he was loathe to do it, he flew out with Mímihn overnight when Thoren was just two weeks old, to visit his mother and sister.

"*You,*" his mother greeted him. "You're not taking me back to your house, Tokh. I like it here. There are no Bags of Bones here."

Looking around at the frail aged females, he wanted to disagree. "No, *Ama.* Mímihn promised to visit you, and she brought you a special surprise." He held out his hand and Mímihn entered the room. She placed Thoren in his wisemother's arms.

Filuhr's face cracked a huge smile. She still had most of her teeth, thought the points were worn flat. "Oh, Tokh! He's yours?"

"Yes. His name is Thoren."

"Ohhh!" She kissed Thoren's gold-blushed cheek. "You precious thing! Tell me all about your delivery, Little One. Are you making enough milk?" She called out to all the other elderly females, and they limped and hobbled over. "Come! Come see my newest smallson!"

Mímihn looked up at Tokh, and she winked.

An unemployed servant.

A daughter whose individuality chases away suitors.

A teen expelled for disciplinary reasons.

A family secret that could tear apart a friendship.

A battle only twelve men will survive.

A bright nine year old seized by the army.

A desperate plan to hold onto power.

A doctor whose ambition knows no rules.

A woman whose reproductive capacity is more important than she is.

So many people played a part in Emperor Nadigh's Emissary Project. You know their names, but you don't know their history. Collected here are twenty short stories, of Tótoghar, Mátokhan, Kitras, Dalo, Tokh, Rimas, as well as the origins of the Kerasi caste system. Experience the joys, the shames, the horrors, the glories. Join them on an unforgettable journey into the essence of Kerasi life.

Kerasi:

Foundations

Short Stories of Kerasim

Available December 2018

Nineteen year old Aila swore to her mother she wouldn't marry Masákh until she turns twenty-one, and she meant it. She also swore when she left Kerasím last year she would return to visit her friend Mímihn for the New Year celebration, and no matter what her mother says, Aila means to do it. She believes whole-heartedly in the Kerasi, and in Emperor Nághtas's plan to put his daughter Rimas on the throne after him.

But Mímihn insists that if Aila is truly her friend, she and Masákh will get married now so Mímihn can witness it, and Aila fears the pressures could tear apart the fragile peace treaties between their worlds if she says no. But before Aila can return to the Union, Mímihn's past threatens to harm her, if fear doesn't kill her first. Then Masákh is pulled away for a troubling task that he can't discuss. Aila must either wait on Kerasím or leave without him – if she's ever granted permission. Idealistic Aila is pulled into the web of deceit and treachery undermining Kerasím, and only through disaster does she realize just what it means to be female on Kerasím, and how big the struggle is for Kerasím to ever change. Only one person can possibly calm Aila's anger and prevent a possible war, but will even Rimas dare to cross the Emperor?

CHANGING WORLDS

Power doesn't like to lose

Book 4 of Prisoner of the Mind

2019

Susan Olesen began publishing her own magazine at the age of fifteen and hasn't stopped writing since. When away from the computer she has raised four children, three foster children, various unofficial adopted kids, and a geranium that won't die. If it's hungry or homeless, it will find her. Follow her on Facebook at Susan Olesen Author Page, or at cheshirelibraryblog.com.